'We predict big things for Emma Kavanagh . . . addictive.' *Good Housekeeping*

Also available by Emma Kavanagh

Falling
Hidden

Emma Kavanagh

THE MISSING HOURS

arrow books

1 3 5 7 9 10 8 6 4 2

Arrow Books
20 Vauxhall Bridge Road
London SW1V 2SA

Arrow Books is part of the Penguin Random House
group of companies whose addresses can be found at
global.penguinrandomhouse.com

 Penguin
Random House
UK

First published by Century in 2016
First published in paperback by Arrow Books in 2016

www.penguin.co,uk

A CIP catalogue record for this book
is available from the British Library.

ISBN 9781784752644

Typeset in Sabon LT Std by Palimpsest Book Production Ltd, Falkirk, Stirlingshire
Printed and bound in Great Britain by Clays Ltd, St Ives Plc

 Penguin Random House is committed to a sustainable
future for our business, our readers and our planet.
This book is made from Forest Stewardship Council®
certified paper.

For Ma and Auntie Debs
Your courage in dark times has shown us all the light

Acknowledgements

I want to first of all thank my mum and dad for instilling a sense of independence and honesty in all of us from an early age and for raising us in a place where imagination and creativity was central to our upbringing. I thank my brothers and their wives for being supportive, smart and inspirational, my good friends Dave, Pete, Simon and Michael for their insight and the laughs and to my wider family for reading and advising on early drafts of this novel, giving helpful advice and, on occasion, not so helpful advice. And I would especially like to thank my wife for she is my compassion, intelligence and fortitude multiplied by a thousand. She has to be given the frequent late nights drafting this manuscript and the subsequent snoring. Mine, I'd like to point out, not hers.

I'd like to thank my agent Marilia Savvides at Peters Fraser and Dunlop for her enthusiasm and hard work in getting this novel all the way from rough draft to finished product and for jumping on board so quickly and with lots of passion. I'd also like to thank the other people who support me at PFD, Laura, Kim, Alexandra,

Jonathan, Zoe and Rebecca for their hard work behind the scenes negotiating contracts and looking into tax affairs that I'd run a mile from!

On the editing and publishing side my sincere gratitude goes to everyone at Simon & Schuster UK in getting this manuscript from digital to ink, especially my editor Anne Perry who is always quick with a superb suggestion to a dilemma. A job in crisis resolution awaits if she ever decides to take it. My thanks also go to Kay and her excellent copy-editing, which identified a number of things that had slipped through the net, Justine and Rhiannon for their creative wizardry and Jo for bringing the book through to publication.

I'll have probably left someone out in this and for that I apologise. This mistake and any other mistakes I might have made in the factual aspects of the novel are my fault and mine alone so let's hope I have hidden them well. Or got lucky.

I'm not sure how to end this so I'll just say: Thanks again, everyone!

The disappearance of Selena Cole

It was the silence that frightened Heather. It seemed to come from nowhere, a creeping, drowning vacuum racing across the playground, down the muddy bank towards where she sat, both feet planted firmly in the rocky brook. One moment the air had sparkled with her younger sister's laughter, the aching creak of the swing, then nothing.

There was a thrumming in Heather's chest, like a small bird had flown in there and was trapped, its wings beating against her ribcage, only Heather couldn't tell if it was the anger that bubbled up inside her seemingly all the time now, or if she was afraid.

It was anger. She screwed her face up, scowled at the water's surface. Thought for a moment that the water reared back in terror.

Anger was easier, she had learned.

She looked down at her feet, where her red patent shoes shimmered beneath the bubbling water. Mummy would be so cross with her. She had told her not to wear the shoes, that they were for school, that they weren't to play in. But Heather had screwed up her face, made her eyes all small

1

and stern, had said she was going to wear them anyway. Had waited for the thunder, her mother's face sliding into that flat expression, the one that said she was up for the fight, waited for her arms to cross across her narrow waist, the look that said, 'Fine, I can stand here all day.' Heather would have given in then. Honest she would. She would have puffed and rolled her eyes until they ached, but she'd have pulled the red patent shoes off, slipping her feet instead into the warm embrace of her wellie boots.

But that hadn't happened.

Instead Mummy's eyes had got full, the way they did when she was thinking about Daddy, and she had turned away, shrugging her shoulders. And Heather had stood in the hallway, staring at the red shoes, thinking how pretty they looked against the twisty tiles, and wishing she had just put her wellies on anyway.

Heather Cole sat on the bank, the tree stump hard against the small of her back, and listened, as hard as she possibly could. She cocked her head to one side, as if that way she could make the laughter come back. She glanced behind her, up towards the top of the embankment. Maybe Mummy was coming to find her. Maybe she'd taken Tara out of the swing and they were on their way to get her, only she couldn't hear their steps because of the water.

That could be it.

'I don't know, Orl. Heather is just so angry. All the time. It's like . . . ever since we lost Ed . . . she . . . it's like she hates me.'

Heather had stood in the silent hallway, hadn't moved or breathed, just pushed her ear against the living-room door. Could hear the tears in her mother's voice. Heard Auntie Orla sigh.

'She doesn't hate you, Selena. Really she doesn't. She's just . . . she's seven. She's grieving and she doesn't know how to handle it. Of course she's taking it out on you. You're all she has left.'

'I know. But she was such a daddy's girl. Sometimes I wish . . .'

'What?'

Then her mother had sighed like a giant gust of wind. 'Nothing. It doesn't matter.'

Maybe they had left her. Had Mummy taken Tara and simply gone home? She had said that Heather was angry all the time. Heather knew what that meant. She was naughty. Daddy used to call her his little spitfire. Heather preferred that word. It sounded better. Maybe Mummy had left because she just couldn't deal with Heather any more.

Heather scratched at the dirt beside her, watching her white nail turn slowly black. No. Mummy wouldn't do that. Would she? But then nothing in Heather's world worked the way it used to work, and so now she simply didn't know.

The bird's wings beat faster now.

Heather pulled her feet free from the water, the rushing cold making her shiver. She began to clamber up the bank, steeper than it had been when she climbed down it, arching hand over hand. It will happen now. Now. Now. She strained. Was that it? Was that Mummy's voice? Wasn't it? No. It was just the wind. As the ground flattened out beneath her fingers, she raised her head to see the cloud-soaked sky, the dew-slicked slide, the swing hanging slack.

She stood looking around the empty playground. She wondered if she was dead. It seemed that her breath had stopped. Was this how it had been for her father? That he had simply . . . stopped? That everything had fallen silent and then he was just gone? But no. She had heard the whispers, the word that Mummy and Auntie Orla were so careful never to say when they thought she was listening. Bomb. She was seven, only seven. But she knew what a bomb was. In her mind there was noise, more noise than seemed possible. Heat. Fire. And then nothing. So perhaps it did all come back to silence in the end.

Heather Cole pulled herself up, stood on the crest of the bank. She tried to breathe, the way she had seen her mother do it when she was trying to stay calm, when fear was only inches away. She sucked in a breath through her nose, held it, then exhaled, the sound whistling into the silence.

They were gone – Tara, Mummy. She was alone.

She felt tears prick at her. Felt her lip shake.

It was the shoes. It was the stupid red shoes. If she had just put the wellies on like she'd wanted to really, they would still be here. Heather looked down at her sopping wet feet, hating them now.

Then there was a sound, a wail that punctured the silence.

Heather swivelled her head, left to right, trying to locate the source of the sound. Then she saw it. Tara sitting in the slack swing. She was still there. Tara was still there. Heather pushed the awful shoes into the long grass, took off at a run across the playground, ran like her life depended on it, past the slide, the empty roundabout, to the limp-hanging swing and her three-year-old sister.

'Tara! Tara! It's okay! I'm coming!' She slip-slid on the gravel, her voice coming out small, and even to her own ears she sounded younger than her seven years.

Tara's head snapped towards her and she stared at Heather with those huge blue eyes, their mother's eyes, so everyone said. Her face had pinked up, the way it always did when she cried, her lower lip jutting forward, shuddering.

'Mama, Heafer. Mama's gone.'

Investigating a vanishing

DC Leah Mackay: Tuesday, 9.46 a.m.

'She was here? When the girls saw her last?'

I sense rather than see the PC nod, because I'm not looking at her. My gaze has been trapped, caught on the empty swing. It has begun to rain, soft drops, more like a mist than anything with any guts to it, and the water is pooling on the red plastic of the seat, transforming the rusting chain into a Christmas garland. Dr Selena Cole would have stood here, just where I am standing. Would have reached out her hands, wrapping them tightly around the metal chains, her three-year-old daughter sitting beneath them. Maybe they were laughing, the little one thrilled and a little scared as her mother pushed her, backwards, forwards.

I take a breath, feel the emptiness chase me, diving in, down my throat, nestling in my lungs. The vacuum where Selena Cole once stood. I look at the mountains that tower around us, dwarfing the tiny hamlet of Endleby. Hereford feels so far away from here, and yet it must be, what, five miles at most?

'The little one, Tara, was on the swing.' The PC, Sophie

I think her name is, tucks her chin inside her jacket, voice disappearing into the fabric. 'Mother was pushing her. Heather, the seven-year-old, had gone down to the stream.' She indicates a shallow rise, an infant summit climbing to an oak tree, then dropping away out of sight. 'There's a little brook there, over that hill. When the girl came back, her mother was gone, sister was alone.'

'Heather didn't hear anything?' I look down towards the road, my eye following its gentle curve. Twenty metres, thirty maybe, and then the house, stone-built, double-fronted, screaming of age and money, immediately abutting the playground. Selena Cole has vanished so close to her home.

'Nothing. The neighbour – Vida Charles – found the girls, must have only been a short time later, sobbing their hearts out.'

I nod, and as I nod, I try to find the line, the one that delineates my life, separating the mother from the detective. Her girls, Selena Cole's. Not my girls. Mine are fine. Mine are safe. I shake myself, pull myself up taller, like the extra inch will make a difference. It's baby brain. I'll blame baby brain. Can you do that when your babies are nearly two years old? I guess if it's twins then you get an extension.

'The girls okay?' I ask.

Her girls, Selena Cole's girls, aged three and seven.

Sophie shrugs. 'As okay as they can be, I guess.' She sighs, nods towards the house. 'The neighbour is in there with them. I've got a call in to their aunt and she's on her way.'

'The father?' I ask. My gaze moves from the swings across the gravel, the grass, down towards the road. Where did Selena Cole go? What happened? Did something just snap in her? The demands of parenthood or marriage or just life suddenly overloading her, so that in the end she couldn't remember exactly who she was, couldn't push through the noise and the responsibilities and the chaos. Did she stand here, one daughter on the swing, the other playing, and then just turn, walk away? The road is right there. Did she get into a car, drive off, leaving her children behind?

'The father is dead.'

I look at Sophie. 'He's dead?'

'Do you remember that terrorist attack in Brazil last year? He was there – Ed Cole. Apparently they ran some kind of consultancy business together, he and Selena. Pretty successful by all accounts. They were at a conference when it was hit. She survived. He didn't.'

'God!'

'I know. Those poor kids.' Sophie says it abstractly, like it is a story she has read.

I study her for a second. Decide that she doesn't have kids.

I look back at the house. Think of the weight resting on Selena, the grief. Was that it? She was her girls' world, their security, their sanctuary. But a support beam can only hold so much weight. Did Selena collapse in on herself, her knees buckling from the pressure of it all?

I glance at Sophie. 'We need to get the word out. We may be looking for a body.'

She nods slowly. 'Suicide?'

I stand where Selena stood, reach out my fingers, touch the chain of the swing that she touched, imagine that I can hear the belly laugh of a little girl, the flip-flopping footsteps of another.

Selena. What have you done?

I pull my coat tighter around me. The rain has finally decided to put some effort in, large drops softly plunking against the swing in an easy rhythm. Even though it is early in the day, the sky is the colour of battleships. 'I need to speak to Heather and Tara.'

The lights are on in the house. All of them, it seems. The wide-eyed bay windows gaze outwards, spilling an orange glow into the small walled garden. I can see the children inside, bundled together, still wearing their coats and buried so deep inside the cushions on the sofa that it is hard to distinguish them from it. The elder holds the younger within her arms, her long biscuit-blonde hair spilling over her like a shawl. Her lips are moving and I study her, trying to make out what it is she says. Then her face is transposed with that of my Georgia and suddenly I realise that she is singing, her mouth shaping the words to 'Let It Go'. Tears prick at my eyes. I think of Georgia, spinning around the kitchen, a clumsy pirouette, singing the *Frozen* song loudly and keylessly. But it's not Georgia. I shake my head, a sharp, hard movement that makes Sophie look at me, curious. It is not Georgia, but Heather Cole, seven years old, cradling her sister, Tara Cole, three years old. And their mother has vanished.

'Shall we?' Sophie gestures to the door.

I nod.

The house is warm, uncomfortably so after the chill of the outside. The hallway wide, autumnal Victorian floor tiles giving way to hard-wood trim, the walls a deep luscious red. I cannot help but feel that this is what it must be like to stand inside the ventricle of a heart. There is a strip of pictures in heavy iron frames. Heather and Tara, two slender blonde girls, their heads together, smiles all but identical. Heather and Tara again, but this time they hang off a woman – late thirties, her hair dark, cut into a chin-length bob so that it swings, trailing across her lips. I stand, transfixed by the image of Selena Cole. I wouldn't call her beautiful, rather striking, with her large eyes, her full lips, her slightly uneven features. I stare at her, wondering where it is that she has gone.

There is another picture, a third to complete the triptych. Heather and Tara and Selena with a man. Ed Cole, I presume. I breathe in, inhaling the loss this family has had to bear. He is handsome in an offhand kind of way, broad and rugged, a nose that looks like it has been broken once, or even twice, his head shaved, lower face swathed in a beard, light veering to red. There is a sparkle to him, so much life that it seems impossible he could be dead.

I find myself thinking of Alex. We have a photo on our mantelpiece, the four of us knotted together, Georgia on my lap, Tess on Alex's, taken when the girls were eighteen months old, everyone laughing even as Tess tries to squirm away, her eye caught by a nearby cat. It was a good day. A bright day. Before I came back to work, when I could still legitimately claim to be a mother, a detective. After all, it was a career break. A break. That means you are returning, that you will come back exactly as you left, not as some impoverished facsimile, there in body but not in spirit.

I hear Sophie enter the living room ahead of me, realise that I have taken too long.

The girls are still huddled together on the sofa, an elderly woman perched beside them, her back straight, fingers plucking at her thick wool trousers. She looks up as I enter, expression serious. The neighbour, I guess. The one who found the children.

'Mrs Charles? I'm Detective Constable Leah Mackay.'

She nods her head once, firmly. 'Vida Charles. I live a couple of doors down. Their neighbour,' she adds, redundantly. 'Mind, my house isn't like this. Only a little one, mine. My husband was a postman. Retired now, of course. So, you know, we couldn't afford a big house. Not like this one . . .' She trails off as if she has forgotten how the thought ends.

I nod, smile. But I'm not thinking about her. I'm thinking about the children. The little one, Tara, isn't looking at me. She is holding her sister's hand, her gaze far off, as if the enormity of what has happened is simply too much for her little mind to process. But Heather is looking at me; her gaze has not left my face.

I sink down, sitting on the sofa beside her.

'Heather? I'm Leah.'

She studies me appraisingly. 'Are you a policeman . . .' she catches herself, 'lady?'

I nod. I keep the smile, as if it will somehow ease her pain.

'You're going to find my mum.' It isn't a question. It is a statement. She says it as a mantra, one hand stroking her little sister's hair. 'She'll come back then.'

She is Tess, asking another police officer where I have gone. She is Georgia, instructing another police officer to find me, to return me to her.

I nod again. Try to forget that I want to cry.

A Start in Kidnap and Ransom

Dr Selena Cole

(Originally published in *London Us* magazine)

It began with a kidnapping. A woman, thirty-five-year-old Astrid, readies herself for work one fine London day. She kisses her husband, Jan, and her four-year-old son, Gabriel, goodbye, and then hurries to catch her train. By the time she returns, a little over eight hours later, both her husband and her son are gone. Vanished into thin air.

Astrid is my sister.

You do not go looking for kidnap and ransom. It comes looking for you.

I was on the train when she called me, watching the sun sink on a satisfying spring day. It had been a day like any other, my world replete with the walking wounded, returning servicemen fresh from war, trying to make sense of the world they had returned to, how much of themselves they had left behind. It is about finding a new normal, I would tell them. Learning to live in the world as it is now, in the body you have now.

The words are easy. Empty. You do not understand the weight of them until your normal also disappears.

'Selena . . . my baby. He's gone.'

The police tracked them as far as Poland. Have there been any problems? they asked my sister. In your marriage? Your lives together?

I thought we were happy. I thought we were all Jan wanted.

Is parental kidnapping still a kidnapping?

Looking at my sister, her world ripped from beneath her, I would have to say yes.

I have never been known for my patience. I began to examine my brother-in-law, to look at his life in a way I never had before. Did you know about the other women? About the drugs? But Astrid was too far gone by that point, sunk so far into herself that my words failed to reach her. What did she have to live for now? Her whole world had vanished.

You reach out when you are in darkness. You grasp at any hand you can find. In reaching, I found Ed's hand. I took it and never let go. That, however, is another story.

I know people, Ed said. Let me make some calls.

Two weeks after the vanishing of my brother-in-law and my nephew, Ed and I boarded a flight to Krakow. They are staying in a house in Katowice, Ed told me, a couple of blocks from Jan's parents. There is a woman with them, young, attractive. I'm putting money on it being a girlfriend. How about we pop over for a visit? Have a little chat with your brother-in-law?

I didn't tell my sister I was going. Now that I have children of my own, I wonder at that, at the temerity of it. But then it made sense to me. I had to keep this clean, clinical, unassailed by the emotional baggage that my sister would inevitably bring.

We can simply take Gabriel, you know, said Ed. Rent a car, scoop him up, make a run for the border. If it comes to it, we can get him out.

I looked out of the aeroplane window at the rolling greenness below. No. It's too dangerous. If it were to go wrong . . .

So, asked Ed, what's the plan?

I shrugged. I'm going to talk to Jan.

It would be my first ever negotiation.

I think I knew, as soon as Jan opened the door, what the outcome would be. In retrospect I would see it written plain across him: the exhaustion, the fear, the sense of one who has gone too far, walking too heavy on a ledge that will not hold much longer. Ed calls it my gift. My ability to sense the pressure points, to see where my opponent will give, where they will stand firm. But I still think it all came from that day, from the desperate need to make this right. It had to work. There was simply no other choice.

We talked for hours, Jan and I, as my nephew lay sleeping in the next room, Ed sitting watchful and waiting. Until, in the end, an accord.

He had only meant to leave. He had a girlfriend. He wanted to be with her. He hadn't meant to take Gabriel, that had never been the plan. But when push came to shove . . .

You know how it goes.

But my nephew had cried for his mother every day for two weeks. Had dug his heels in, becoming recalcitrant, intractable, as only a four-year-old can.

He needs to go home, Jan had said finally. I made a mistake.

We left early the following morning. Jan drove us to the airport. Kissed his son goodbye.

In the years that followed, I have often questioned what I was thinking when I went there. How far was I prepared to go? Would I have kidnapped Gabriel in return?

Yes.

I would have done that and more.

And yet I learned a powerful lesson. That persuasion can work better than force. That words can ease the road to freedom, can allow the kidnapper to believe that a release is for their own greater good. That not all manipulations are bad.

And when I doubt myself, I think of Astrid, her suddenly small figure curled on the sofa, barely glancing at us as the door opened and we walked in, and then something, some mother's instinct, telling her to look up, to see me carrying her son's sleeping form, and that change – relief, ecstasy, wholeness – flooding through her. When I fear that I will fail, I think of my sister. And then I know that I will not.

The body

You don't forget the smell of death. Not ever. It has a familiar quality; even if you've never smelled it before, there's a sense that you've known all along what it will be like.

I study the body, a corpse in name only. Because from here, on the narrow road on the mountain, all I can see is grey fabric, a flash of skin, shockingly white against green grass.

It has been dumped, there is no other word for the end of this human. The road is narrow, used only rarely and then with care. On one side, steepness, leading higher and higher until the rocky crags vanish into a net of cloud. On the other, a narrow shelf of grass and shrubs and then the fall. The body lies on the shelf. Like someone has driven by, opened a car door, shoved it out and then left.

That irritates me, more than the rain, the mist, the frigid cold. The laissez-faire of it all. That whoever did it, ended this life, was too busy, in too much of a hurry, to hide the body. I look to the curve of the road, where a car would have traced the lines of it, slowing, stopping, a door opening, and the deceased – whoever they were – pushed, lifeless, to the roadside. Death should be about more than that.

I walk slowly along the tarmac, feet squelching with each step. The rain has started, moving straight into high gear. It bounces off the surface, plopping on my suit sleeves. A heavy mist is rolling in across the valley with the inevitability of the tide, pressing down on top of me, everything beyond the next few feet a blur. I balance my steps, a boy walking along kerbstones, my overshined shoes keeping tight to the black line of the road, and it feels like a game, that if I lean a little too far to the left then I will be gone, tumbling into that bowl of greenness.

There are no houses here.

If you follow the arc of the road, tracing it down the hillside that is about to be swallowed in cloud, the eye struggles to pick out anything, just layer upon layer of green. No towns. No villages.

Nothing.

What the hell were you doing up here?

I glance back to the body, the mysterious dead, my gaze snagging on Willa as she moves about it, white forensic suit stark against the grey of the day.

'Nearly done?' I yell. My words slip away, fighting with the rain.

She stops, looks up at me, and I hear her voice, distant, reedy, straining against the wind. 'Patience is a virtue, Sergeant. You should try it some time.'

Sergeant.

Eighty-two days. I have been a detective sergeant for eighty-two days.

I'm working very hard to pretend I know what I'm doing.

I nod, although I'm pretty sure she can't see it. 'Okay. Carry on.'

I hear the flutter of a laugh, so out of place in the wind and the rain and the smell of death.

What were you doing up here? How did you, whoever you are, manage to get yourself killed on a mountain in the middle of God's green nowhere?

'Hey, Willa?'

'Sweet God! What?' She is looking up at me, her hands on her hips.

She's fine. That's her 'I'm listening' pose.

'You seen any cars pass by since you arrived?'

I can just about make out a heavy sigh. Or it could be the wind.

'No, Finley. I haven't noticed. I've been too busy chatting to you.'

I grin, wave. 'Right. Sorry. Carry on.'

Eighty-two days. I shiver, rain seeping beneath my collar. It's my first murder as a detective sergeant. That's no surprise. We don't get that many murders here, buried on the border of England and Wales, surrounded by mountains and countryside and sheep. It's hardly Mogadishu. But the call came into the office: a dead body on the mountain road, a little way outside Hereford.

We all sat up a little straighter – you do when you're CID in a small force and someone says the word 'murder'. I looked for Leah, my eyebrows raised in silent communication, but she had already gone, on her way to the missing person case.

And the pieces slid into place for me. The missing person, found.

I blink the raindrops away. Think that I need to call my

sister, give her a heads-up that her missing person may not be missing any more. She laughed when I handed it to her. A nice easy one, she said. Grown woman pops to shops without telling anyone, will saunter back in an hour or two wondering what the hell CID is doing in her living room.

I look at the body. I don't think anyone is going to be sauntering anywhere any time soon.

'Sarge?' The uniformed officer hurries closer, ducking under his hat, like that will make a damned bit of difference to the rain, and I glance over my shoulder, looking for the sergeant. The person in charge. Then I realise. It's me.

The patrol car is parked at an uneven angle, blocking the road, its blue light swirling. The back door is slightly ajar. I can see the foot, wet from the rain, twitching, a tan work boot tapping against the door.

'Sarge?' says the uniformed officer. 'The witness, he wants to know if he can go.'

I look from him to the car and the tapping foot. You and me both, mate.

'I'll come and talk to him.'

The witness is chewing his nails, has brought them down to the quick. He is broad and rugged, I'd guess maybe fifty, fifty-five. He looks up at me, down, his eyes darting back through the windscreen to where the body lies.

'Darren Crane?'

He nods, and I can see the muscles in his jaw, pulled so tight that you'd swear it was lockjaw.

'I was only going to work,' he says, not waiting for me to ask. He isn't looking at me, is staring through the wind-screen, his eyes clamped on Willa, on the body. 'I drive this way every day. You never see anything on this road. Quiet road it is. And I'm driving along slow, like because of the weather, and I see this, well, pile of clothes, so I thought.' His words come too fast, each chasing the tail of the one that came before it, his breath quick, unsteady.

Is he about to have a heart attack?

'I don't know why I pulled over. Not really. There was just, there was something about it. Something not right, you know?'

He looks up at me, eyes seeking reassurance. I shuffle through responses in my head. I'm not really the reassuring type. But he's looking at me and he's waiting, and so I arrange my face into what I hope resembles a smile, and wonder if he believes me.

'So, I pulled in.' He gestures, to the grass verge, the body, his words coming easier now. 'I thought it was clothes, see. I thought . . . we have problems with fly-tippers sometimes. They come up here, dump stuff, and I thought that was what it was. Then, it was weird, it was like the whole thing shifted, and then I could see . . . well, it was a body, like.'

He stops, coughs, and I suddenly realise it is to cover a sob.

Jesus.

I wish my sister was here. She's the people person. I'm more the doer.

'You, ah, you okay?' I ask.

He coughs again, wiping his face with a hand. 'Aye, well, shock, see. You don't expect it, do you? To find a body, I mean.'

I should call Leah, warn her. That her missing woman isn't going to be coming home. There were kids, too. Two of them. Two girls. Just like Leah's twins.

Dammit.

'Poor bastard, though. I mean,' Darren Crane looks at me, expression searching, 'what do you think he did? You know, to end up here?'

'Well, I . . .' Then I hear what it is that he has said. He.

My thoughts sputter, and now I feel like I've been walking down a staircase and the bottom step wasn't where I was expecting it to be. I take a long breath, sucking in the smell of death.

'Finn?' calls Willa. 'Detective Sergeant! Any chance?'

'Stay here, please,' I mutter.

I head back to the car, pull on the white Tyvek suit, the cold wind wrapping its way along the mountain road, tugging at it. Place a mask over my face.

Willa studies the scene at her feet, her head circling as she scans it for any details she may have missed, her lips moving in private calculation. I step closer, feeling the tension race up my back, across my shoulders. Knowing that at any moment she is going to turn and walk back towards me and tell me what she has found, and then, just like that, it will become my problem. Well, not my problem. The problem of about forty of Hereford's finest. But it will feel like my problem.

I guess that's the trouble with having been a sergeant for eighty-two days. Everything feels like your problem. There has been no time for the shifting ground to settle beneath my feet, no time to settle in, to establish myself in this new role amongst the people who were my friends eighty-three days ago. They look at me differently now, like dug-up World War II ordnance. It may be harmless, inert, just a lump of old metal. On the other hand, it may blow up and take your leg off. Who knows?

Willa waits, looking at home here, in amongst the death and the odours. An attractive girl, dark and, appropriately, willowy. You wouldn't look at her and think that she spends her days surrounded by dead people and bodily fluids.

I cough, awkward suddenly. 'You all done?'

'For now.' Her voice is muffled by the forensic mask. 'You want to see?' She doesn't wait for me to answer, just moves aside, pointing towards the inert form.

The body is lying on its side, and for a moment, you could fool yourself that he was asleep, curled in on himself as he is. I see dark hair, cut neatly, a steel-grey suit, skin so white that it seems to glow. Oozing darkness, blood that has seeped from a wound in the neck, settling around his collar.

'Can you believe it?' asks Willa.

'No. Well, yes.' I feel like I have walked in halfway through a conversation. 'What?'

'Well, I mean, I don't know him well, but still . . .'

I move, with careful footsteps, closer to the dead body and the edge, closer to the drop down below. His eyes are closed, his face is slack. He looks different to the way he looked when I saw him last. More dead, mostly.

'Shit,' I say.

'Yup.'

Auntie Orla

I close the front door softly behind me, ease it on to its catch. I cannot bear to let it slam, to have the Cole girls be startled by the sound. They have enough to be afraid of. It's stopped raining now, but the memory of it still hangs in the damp air. I stand there on the doorstep and breathe in the chill autumn air. Look to the mountains, their peaks lost in cloud. I feel like I am waiting for her, that if I just stand here long enough, the low metal gate will swing open and Selena Cole will come walking through it. That there will be a reason, something that explains and absolves this vanishing.

Selena Cole has been missing for two hours. Two hours away from her little girls. She doesn't know where they are. She doesn't know that they are safe, that they aren't just sitting in the playground, on the rain-sodden grass, waiting for her to return. She has to return. She has to come back so that she can find them, usher them into the warm.

But it's been two hours and she hasn't come back. Which makes me think that she cannot. Which makes me think that something is very badly wrong here.

Heather sat, her sister curled into her so close that there was no daylight between them, watched me like I had the answers, her face creased into a frown far too old for her years.

'She was wearing jeans. She had a white jumper on.' She handed the information to me, a precious parcel, and you could see her thinking that this stuff was critical, it was what would bring her mother back to her. 'Her hair was down.'

I sat alongside them, tried not to notice when the younger girl shuffled away from me, still closer to her sister, even though I wouldn't have believed that was possible. 'How was Mummy when you saw her last? Was she happy or sad?'

The elder girl thought, her gaze resting on her little sister's fingers, wrapped inside her own. 'She was sad.'

'Is Mummy sad a lot?'

A stricken look flitted across her face, and I wanted to kick myself, wanted to take it back, to make it okay, but I could do none of those things. The little girl stared past me, at the red patent shoes on her feet, and tears filled her eyes, spilling down her cheeks.

I stand on the doorstep. Simply breathing. In. Out.

Where are you, Selena?

Did you walk or were you dragged?

I went through the house, an intruder, rummaging through drawers, opening cupboards, looking for something that might hold a secret. I stood in Selena's bedroom, longer than I needed to, gazing out of the low windows, the framed view of the hills beyond. This would be her sanctuary, a space of her own. The bed had been made, the cover pulled straight and tight, pillows stacked at its head. Did she do that this morning, in amongst the noise and life of two young children? Or was the bed not slept in at all?

Two bedside cabinets, painted in a distressed white. On one, the detritus of life: a book, a glass of water that had begun to accumulate dust, hand cream, the top not quite screwed on. On the other, a shrine to death: a family picture, the four of them preserved in a gilt frame, a hardback book, its angle so perfectly square that it must have been lined up that way. The husband's side, I presumed.

I stood, watching the dust motes dance in the light, taking a moment to breathe. Then I pulled open the drawer. Looking for a diary. A letter. Something. Anything.

What happened to you, Selena? Was it the grief? Or did that monster get you? The one that chases mothers, the one that screams that you will never be enough, that you are failing, that your children will lose simply because their mother is you. Did it overwhelm you finally, forcing you to stumble, fall?

I thought about last night. Sitting on the floor of my laundry room as the washer whirred, the dryer shook, my head aching with all I had to do. Wanting to cry and knowing that I couldn't, because Tess and Georgia still needed their bath, still needed their story and for Mummy to do the voices they loved. Still needed so much. And that fleeting, traitorous thought of how easy life used to be, in the before.

I searched through the drawer. Jewellery boxes, perfume, a photo album. And a small bottle. I pulled it free, squinting at the faded writing in the low light. Cipramil.

Selena was taking antidepressants.

I tucked the pills into an evidence bag, just in case. There was a name on the bottle, the prescribing physician,

Dr Gianni Minieri. I made a quick note in my notebook, wondering what Dr Minieri would have to say.

I stand on the doorstep, look at the tumbling hills, and think. Selena was grieving. Selena was depressed.

I look to the garage door.

It is closed.

I stand there, staring, my feet seemingly unwilling to move. It is Schrödinger's cat. If I do not open the door, then Selena Cole is both in there and not in there, both alive and dead. If I do not open that door, then we can stay balanced on this knife edge, and I will not have to tell her children that their last remaining parent is gone.

But the problem with balancing is that sooner or later you always fall.

I walk slowly across the drive. The rain has soaked the crisp autumn leaves, slippery beneath my feet. The ground feels treacherous, the wisdom of my senses no longer to be trusted. I reach out for the handle, a pre-emptive catch for a fall that has not yet happened.

I grasp the handle, turn, push.

The garage door slides upwards, revealing darkness. My brain screams, rushing through the new experiences. Is that death? That smell, the one that never leaves you, is that it? Or is it my brain filling in the blanks, handing me what I expect to find? The formless shapes in the gloom, is that her, her body hanging from a makeshift rope attached to the rafters?

I blink, feel the darkness diminish.

No.

There is the car – a red Range Rover Evoque. Nice. Expensive. There are shelves, neatly stacked with tools, seed boxes.

There is no body. No Selena.

I breathe, allow my heartbeat to settle.

Move into the gloom.

The smell that I first thought was death is simply oil. It hangs here, stale, musty. The shape that I thought was a body is just some drop cloths, flecked with blue, hanging from a shelving unit.

Nothing to see here.

I feel the bonnet of the car. Cold. Look inside. A coffee cup has been abandoned on the centre console, a pair of sunglasses on the passenger seat. In the back, a booster seat and a child's seat. No Selena Cole.

Thank God.

And yet . . . she is not here, and her car is. Where did she go? How did she get there?

There are answers somewhere. People do not simply vanish.

I look around the gloom, waiting, as if it will change, as if the answers will spring out at me from the balsa-wood shelves, the box of tools that sits open. But all that happens is that the cold garage gets colder still, and a shiver runs through me.

I slip under the garage door, ducking my head. Where is she? Her babies are waiting for her.

The road is quiet still, little traffic passing. The world seems empty after the sound of the rain. Waiting. Then I hear the scream of a car engine, see a Mini Cooper swing around the bend and come to a sudden halt outside the Coles' house. The driver flings the door open, long copper plait swinging violently. She sees me, stops.

'You're the detective?'

I cross the drive, meeting her at the small metal gate.

27

Smell cigarette smoke carried on the wind that whips at her skirt, the navy fabric snapping against her thick wool tights. 'DC Leah Mackay. You are?'

'Orla. Orla Britten.' Her accent is pure north, her voice loud, jarring to me after the quiet. 'Selena, she's my sister-in-law. Did you find her?'

I shake my head. 'Not yet.'

She stares at me, and then says, 'Is she dead?'

The word catches me, the hard accent making it harder still. I feel my guard climbing.

'Why? Why would you think she was dead?'

She looks from me to the still open garage, to the house, and back. Sighs heavily. 'I'm sorry.' This comes out quieter, her head dipping down until it almost touches her chest. 'It's . . . it's been so hard lately, there's been so much. So when we got the call . . .'

'We?'

'Me and my husband. Seth. Only it wasn't we. He's on his way back from New York. Was working there. It was me. I was on my own.' She has drifted off, seems to have lost the thread of the thought.

'You were saying?'

She shifts, giving herself a visible shake. 'It's been a bad year. Or two years. My brother, Ed . . . he died. And it just . . . we don't seem to have been able to pick ourselves up from that. You know?'

I cross slowly to a bench that sits beneath a stunted wooden overhang, press my hand flat against it. Dry enough. I glance at the woman, pat the bench beside me. 'You want to sit?'

She looks at me for a long moment, then moves closer, carefully tucks her skirt underneath her. There's a hole in her tights, small and round, just above the knee. She plucks at it with her fingernail, worrying at the loose wool thread.

'I'm so sorry for your loss,' I offer. 'Your brother, I mean.'

'It . . . it was a shock.'

'I'm sure.' I study an apple tree that stands in the corner of the front garden, its trunk scarred with age. Think how nice it would be to have an apple tree like that.

'What do you do, Orla?' I ask.

'I'm the financial director for the Cole Group.'

'Selena's company?'

Her gaze flicks upwards and there is something there, words that sit right on her lips, but then she looks down again and they vanish. 'Yes. Hers and my brother's.'

'So,' I say. 'What exactly is it you guys do?'

'We're a kidnap and ransom consultancy practice. It's only small, just Selena and Ed initially, but they gradually expanded, took more people on.'

'Kidnap and ransom?'

'Kidnap for ransom is big business in some parts of the world,' Orla says, voice distant. 'Most of the companies who operate there – say Mali, Nigeria, places like that – take out an insurance policy on their workers that covers them against kidnapping. The Cole Group trains companies on the best ways to protect themselves, helps them establish crisis management plans. But if things do go wrong and someone is kidnapped, we are dispatched to handle the situation. Selena's a psychologist, a doctor. With that and Ed's military background . . . it's a good company. We have a good reputation.'

'So . . .' I say. 'You negotiate with the kidnappers?'

Orla shrugs. 'Sometimes. Depends on where in the world we are.'

'And Selena runs the company?'

'Selena used to run it. But after Ed . . .' She glances at me. 'Things are different now. Selena's taken a back seat. My husband Seth and I, we run things day to day.'

I nod, let the silence sit for a little while. 'Orla, is it possible that your sister-in-law has simply left? Walked out?'

She looks at me, a flash of anger distorting her features. 'No. She would never do that. Never. She would never leave those girls.'

A gust of wind blows through the apple tree, its near to bare branches dancing. 'I need to ask you something else. Why was your first thought that Selena was dead?'

Orla purses her lips, like they are holding a cigarette, and I can see her fingers dancing, pulling at the hole in her tights. 'She's . . . like I said, it's been hard. For all of us. I've been helping out as much as I can, with Selena, the girls. But there's only so much you can do.' The hole is bigger now, the size of a fifty-pence piece. 'I've tried to get her to talk to me. She's private. Always has been. But I can tell sometimes that she's been crying, even though she'd never say. She'd rather die.' She catches herself, the word ending abruptly, and looks at me. 'I didn't mean it like that.'

'Is she suicidal?' I ask, my voice soft.

Orla shakes her head slowly. 'I don't know. I hope not.'

Case No. 8
Victim: William, Oscar and Genevieve Arthurs
Location: Dubai, United Arab Emirates
Company: Global Comm Tech
21 April 2005

Initial event

Lisbeth and Stephen Arthurs returned to their villa
in Dubai Silicon Oasis at approximately 11.15 p.m. on
the night of Thursday 21 April. Dr Stephen Arthurs
is a UK national and senior manager for Global Comm
Tech who has headed up their Dubai office for the
past two years. Mrs Lisbeth Arthurs, also a UK
national, works for Emirates Travel, a tour company
operating throughout Dubai.

Upon returning home, Mrs Arthurs went to look in
on their children, William, aged nine, Oscar, aged seven,
and Genevieve, aged four. She discovered that all three
of the children's bedrooms were empty. Further investigation established that the family's nanny, Nada Al
Marri, had also disappeared.

Mr Arthurs immediately notified the local authorities
of the disappearances. He then contacted a colleague
at Global Comm Tech, who subsequently placed a call
to GCT's insurance provider, Everguard. The Cole Group
was notified by Everguard shortly after.

Response

The response team in this case was made up of myself (Ed Cole), Selena Cole and Orla Cole. This was Orla Cole's first case for the Cole Group. The team arrived in Dubai within eighteen hours of the disappearance and immediately attended the Arthurs' home. Local authorities were already in attendance and had, shortly before our arrival, received initial contact from the kidnappers, demanding that a ransom of $1.6 million be paid for the return of the four hostages.

Immediate priority was establishing the circumstances of the kidnapping. CCTV footage was unavailable; it appeared that the monitors had been turned off at source. Discussions with Mr Arthurs established that the family had received a number of threats over the previous six months and had attempted to make security provisions to protect themselves. Those provisions had failed:

Questions were raised over the fourth hostage – the nanny, Nada Al Marri – in terms of whether she should in fact be considered a hostage or whether she was complicit in the kidnapping. The Arthurs family remained staunch in their support of Ms Al Marri, who had been with them for four years and who had a wide range of excellent references. Local authorities investigations into her background suggested no evidence of criminal wrongdoing and no ties with criminal gangs. She was thus officially designated the fourth hostage.

Both Mr and Mrs Arthurs were understandably deeply distressed, and Selena Cole became their primary point of contact, thereby allowing her to provide support and information to the family. We made strenuous efforts to encourage local authorities to begin a negotiation process in order to ensure the safety of the children. Both myself and Selena Cole were clear in our opinion that a negotiated settlement was by far the most realistic option and the one most likely to ensure the safe return of the hostages.

. However, we met with a significant degree of resistance on this point and were informed in no uncertain terms that paying the hostage-takers would not be permitted in this case.

At this point, Lisbeth Arthurs suffered a total collapse and was rushed to hospital.

It is fair to say that there was a high level of tension, as both Global Comm Tech and the Arthurs strongly advocated the payment of a ransom. The local authorities, however, with little regard for the concerns of the parents, began planning a tactical assault.

Following on from this, Orla Cole felt unable to continue with the case and returned to our accommodation.

I pressed local authorities to at the very least demand proof of life so that we could establish the well-being of the children. At this point, all three children were placed on the phone to their father, who was able to positively identify them. All three children showed signs of extreme emotional distress. We were, however, unable to obtain proof of life for Ms Al Marri. This raised many questions, primarily whether she had in fact been killed early in the kidnapping. The Arthurs family were clear on the level of affection felt by the nanny for the children, and were of the opinion that she would have put herself in harm's way in order to protect them.

The proof-of-life call had enabled us to establish that the children were being held in the same location as their kidnappers, and following investigations by the local authorities, a likely safe house was identified a little over twenty-four hours later. A trace on a subsequent call, purportedly to negotiate a ransom, confirmed the investigators' suspicions and an immediate tactical assault was called for.

I remained with Mr Arthurs while the raid was under way, whilst Selena Cole stayed with Mrs Arthurs.

What follows is a report received by local authorities.

A tactical entry was made into the safe house in which the hostages were believed to be held at 3.15 a.m., Sunday 24 April. Initial surveillance had indicated the presence of two male hostage-takers in the premises. Both of these were shot and killed upon entry. The tactical team progressed through the house and eventually located the hostages in a bedroom at the rear of the house, where they were being guarded by a third hostage-taker. This hostage-taker was also shot and killed. One of the hostages received a gunshot wound to the upper thigh. The other hostages were deemed to be in good physical health.

Note

William Arthurs was shot in the course of the tactical rescue whilst trying to shield his younger siblings from danger. The wound he received was life-threatening. He was immediately transported to hospital, and after some hours in surgery, doctors were able to save both his life and his leg. It has, however, been indicated by medical staff that he is highly likely to walk with a limp and to have some considerable pain for the rest of his life. Following three weeks in the hospital, he was eventually reunited with his parents and younger siblings, both of whom survived their ordeal without any sign of physical harm.

It wasn't until some hours following the tactical entry that a full and complete understanding of events was conveyed to both the Cole Group and the Arthurs family. The third hostage-taker shot in the assault was Ms Nada Al Marri. She was found in the bedroom with the children. Whilst reports from the scene are unclear, there has been suggestion that she was armed. Later conversation with the Arthurs children, however, indicates that she was in fact trying to protect them, and that she placed herself between them and the gunfire.

Further investigation revealed that one of the male kidnappers was in fact Ms Al Marri's cousin. Eyewitness reports indicate that Ms Al Marri was seen sitting in the passenger seat of the kidnap vehicle, thus suggesting that she had some role to play in the unfolding events. However, the children remain staunch in their defence of their former nanny. Their account is that she attempted to protect them throughout.

Whilst officially it has been recorded that Nada Al Marri died a criminal and a hostage-taker, it seems likely that the truth will never really be known.

The family as a whole has been deeply traumatised by their experiences. Following on from these events, the Arthurs returned home to the UK and are currently receiving counselling from Selena Cole in order to help them recover from the severe trauma they have suffered.

It is the opinion of the Cole Group that had a ransom been settled on, no physical harm would have come to the children in this case. The hostage-takers, whilst clearly operating within a criminal mindset, had nonetheless provided for the children's physical well-being whilst they were in captivity. They were well fed, clean and showed no signs of physical abuse. The final call between local authorities and the hostage-takers had reduced the purported ransom to $30,000. Everguard Insurance have indicated that this payment would in fact have been lower than the ultimate cost of the Arthurs' medical bills, generated as a result of the tactical rescue. This, coupled with the ongoing pain experienced by William Arthurs as a result of his injury, leaves me in no doubt as to the wisest course of action in this case.

A formal complaint has been filed with the UAE authorities. As to this time, no reply has been forthcoming.

Those left behind

'Did you know Dominic well?' Willa asks. The rain has stopped now, although the clouds still hang over us, around us, waiting to pounce. We stand beside my car, Willa turning so that her back is to the chill wind sweeping across the valley.

I settle my gaze on the body on the ground. Not a body now. A person. Dominic Newell, defence solicitor. They are just words. And yet they change everything, when you realise that the dead body is someone you have seen walking and talking and laughing. How do you compartmentalise that?

'I dealt with him a couple of times. Seemed like a nice guy. He had a good rep down at the station. Worked hard for his clients.' I look down. 'Leah knew him better than I did. She rated him.'

Willa nods, a silence descending. She has pulled her mask off, is wearing lipstick, a cherry red, stark against the gloom of the day, the scent of death. She gives me a look, seems to be looking right into me. Unnerving. And . . . something else.

I look at Dominic Newell again. I expect him to stand,

to push himself up, dust himself down, give one of his famous movie-star grins. But he won't. He's dead.

What the hell happened to you, Dominic?

I sigh.

'You okay?' Willa's voice is soft, supportive, jarring almost in its tenderness.

'I'm fine.' The words fly out, a kick when the knee is tapped. I'm always fine. It's a standing joke in my family. That the day I am less than fine, the sky will fall. I give Willa a quick smile. 'You know me.'

She studies me, appraising. 'This your first murder as a DS?'

'Yup.'

'Stressful.'

'Mm hmm.'

'But you're fine.'

I grin. 'Of course. Never better.'

She nods, pursing her lips, like she is thinking of pushing me. Am I a challenge to her, I wonder, a puzzle to be unravelled? Or is it something else? But I bat that thought away quickly enough.

My phone buzzes.

Willa watches me. 'Everything okay?'

'Dominic's next of kin.' I flash the screen at her, Christa's response to my earlier question highlighted in blue. 'Isaac Fletcher.' I scroll through the address. 'Looks like I'm driving to Cardiff.'

I shift the car keys in my hands. Only dimly aware of Willa's presence now, my mind already on its way, telling Dominic Newell's partner that his body has been found dumped by the side of a lonely mountain road. 'Right,' I say. 'Better get on with it.'

I set off steadily, my gaze searching the verges as I go. Do I expect to see Dominic's car simply parked up, waiting for me? The murderer standing beside the precipitous drop, hands out, waiting to be cuffed? That would be nice.

I look for houses, industrial units. Anything that might, by some obscure twist of fate, have CCTV, ANPR, something to provide me with some insight into the death of Dominic Newell. But all I see is the gathering clouds, the valley below.

What were you doing up here, Dominic? Or were you already dead when you arrived?

Traffic slows me as I hit Cardiff, a long line of cars snaking its way along North Road, brake lights adding some colour to the dreary day. I hit speed dial on my phone.

'Hey.'

'All right, sis?'

Leah's voice is quiet, echoing, and I hear a door closing. 'Yeah. Still nothing here. The kids . . . they're taking it pretty hard.'

The missing person.

'I bet,' I reply, because I can't think of anything else to say. I know my sister. With her, this case will be all about the children. Every case is now, since the twins. I guess it's a parent thing. I really wouldn't know. 'Um . . . Look, I have some news.'

'You're getting married?'

'Ha ha. Right.' The traffic has ground to a halt now, enmeshing me in a twisting mass of roadworks. I sigh, lean back against the headrest. 'No. The thing is . . . we found a body.'

There is a silence on the line, heavy enough that it dawns

on me what I have said. 'No, no. Not your body. I mean . . . not your body, not your missing person's body.'

'Finley . . .'

Dammit. She's full-naming me.

'Is the body a woman?'

'No.'

Leah sighs heavily. 'Christ, you scared me. Okay, so . . .'

'Lee, it's Dominic Newell.'

Another silence. Then, 'Dominic Newell the defence solicitor?'

'Yes.'

'You can't be serious?' The words are little more than a breath out.

'I just came from the scene now. Looks like he was stabbed in the neck and then dumped. Right there on the side of the road.'

'Oh my God! I . . . Poor Dominic. I just . . . I can't believe it.'

'You were friends, right?'

A silence, then a sigh. 'Not friends. Not really. We would chat when he came into the station. I mean, I liked him. He seemed . . . kind. But I didn't really know him.' Another sigh. 'Jesus, Finn.'

'Yeah.'

'Have you told . . .'

'I'm on my way there now.'

'Poor guy.'

'Yeah.' The lights turn to green, traffic beginning to creep forward, and I ease the handbrake down. 'I know. Lee, you better wrap it up there. The SIO is pulling everyone on to this. They're going to want you back at the station.'

I move into the contraflow, my gaze catching on the

workmen as they stand amidst orange cones, laughing. So it takes me a moment to realise that she hasn't replied.

'Lee?'

Then, 'Finn, I think something is wrong here. This woman, Selena Cole, I don't believe she just walked away. She has two little girls. She's a widow, so there's no father on the scene . . . I just don't buy it.'

A squeal of tyres, the car in front of me braking hard. I slam my foot down, skidding to a stop just inches from its rear bumper. My heart racing.

'Jesus . . .' I suck in a breath. 'Okay. Look, I get that. But this is going to be huge. You're going to be needed on this one.'

'But . . .'

'Lee, I know you don't want to think that she's left willingly. She's a mother. You're a mother. But she's not you.'

'I didn't say she was.'

The car in front of me stalls, the rut, rut, rut as its driver tries to turn the engine over. Typical. I consider my words, a skill at which I am woefully out of practice. Get back to the station. That's an order. But then I think of childhood fights, Leah with three years on me, a hellcat temper, carrying me bodily from her bedroom when I just would not leave. Yeah. Maybe not.

'Okay,' I say, attempting softly-softly. 'Look, I just think you need to be careful. Not get too emotionally involved. You know?'

The car in front has moved off, sputtering black smoke in its wake, and I follow, keeping a safe distance in case the thing explodes.

'Leah?'

'Yeah. No, I know. Look, I've got to go. I'll see you later.'

And she is gone. I suppress a sigh. So much for softly-softly.

I pull into the car park that skirts the modern high-rise that Dominic and his partner called home. Gulls dip and glide towards the grey waters of Cardiff Bay, its colour matching the sky, hard to split the two apart. Seems like it is closer to midnight than to noon. As I climb from the car, cross towards the apartment building, I listen to the birds caw, think that for the rest of my life, whenever I think about this murder, I'm going to think about those damn gulls.

I stand for longer than I should, staring at the rows of doorbells. One button up, one button down, and someone else's world is changed for ever. But not today.

I press the buzzer for Dominic and Isaac's apartment.

One beat. Two.

'Hello?'

'DS Finn Hale. I'm going to need to speak with you.'

Is this the moment? These words, are they enough for Isaac to know that his world will never be the same again? A long silence. An 'okay'. The buzz of the door unlocking itself.

I grasp the handle. Here we go.

As Isaac opens the door, I know that he knows. Maybe not the specifics, what particular catastrophe I have brought to him. But I can see the fear.

I say the words, quickly, like that will make it any easier, pulling off a plaster to minimise the pain.

It doesn't work, not with death.

Isaac sits with his head in his hands. His fingers dig into his dark hair like they are looking for a way to burrow through the scalp, tear out the news I brought him. He is crying, but it is a silent cry, marked with the tremor of shoulders, a sudden gasping intake of breath.

The apartment is large, immaculate, floor-to-ceiling windows that give out on to the grey of the bay. From somewhere, I hear a radio, music playing, a reminder of an easier time. And of course, those damn gulls.

I sit next to him on the long leather sofa.

'This can't be happening.'

'I'm sorry.'

'I just don't believe it.'

'I know.'

'We're going on holiday. In two weeks.' His accent has a twang to it that, in the context, is hard to define. 'We . . . It's booked.' He looks up at me, his pale eyes liquid, saying it like it will somehow make a difference, as if now that I know this, I will take back my words. Your boyfriend, Dominic, is dead.

I shake my head. 'I'm sorry,' I say again.

Isaac looks beyond me, empty eyes watching the seagulls wheel.

'Isaac, I need to ask you, when did you see Dominic last?'

'Yesterday. Before he left for work.' It is American, the accent, the edges of it rounded down so that it is flecked with Welsh. His voice sounds hollowed out, like he has gone already, left his body behind.

Is he picturing the rest of his life now, empty of the man he loved? Or is he seeing Dominic's body, slumped and useless?

I lean forward, trying to catch his eye, pull him back to me. 'He never came home last night?'

'No.'

I hang on that word. No. You always look to the spouse first. Because marriage, partnerships, they will strip you bare, sometimes leading to an anger that can slide out of control.

So I am told, anyway.

'Were you concerned?' I say the words carefully. Gently. Gently. 'Worried about him?'

He turns his gaze back towards me. 'I thought he was working. He works long hours.'

'But for him not to come home at all, was that unusual?'

'I guess.'

'You weren't worried, though?' I keep my voice easy, try to keep the accusation out of it.

'No.'

He didn't come home. Dominic didn't come home. And yet his boyfriend did nothing. Why?

'Are you sure?' Isaac asks.

'I'm sorry?'

'It might not be him. Are you sure it's him? Maybe it was somebody else.'

I think of the body, folded in on itself. 'We will, of course, ask you to come in and make a formal identification.' Isaac sits up, a look of hope flooding his features. 'But I must tell you, Isaac, I'm very confident that the body is Dominic's.'

I watch his face, look for the lie in the display of grief. But all I can see are the tears. His hands are over his mouth now, long, slender fingers stoppering it up.

'Can you think of anyone who would want to hurt Dominic?'

He gives a bleak laugh. 'He's a solicitor. He deals with scumbags every day.'

'So has he had problems?'

Isaac shrugs. 'They get angry when things don't go their way.'

'Do you have any names?'

'There was someone, a guy Dom's been representing for years. He's been causing trouble, got aggressive with Dom.'

'His name?'

'Um, Beck, I think? Beck Chambers.'

What the darkness takes

DC Leah Mackay: Tuesday, 11.02 a.m.

We walk into the house slowly, our footsteps a funeral dirge. I hear Orla draw in a breath as she stands in the open doorway, and I can tell that she is steeling herself, gathering her resolve for what is to come. She steps over the threshold, pulled forward on an invisible string towards the sound of voices that seeps beneath the closed kitchen door. Not voices. One voice. The neighbour. She is twittering, a flow of words that has become a monologue thrown at an unresponsive audience.

Orla pauses before the door, placing one hand flat on its wood panel. It is like a blessing. Or maybe a prayer.

I stand behind her, and ridiculously, I feel tears prick at the back of my eyes.

Please God, let me find Selena Cole. Let me bring her home.

Orla breathes again, then twists the handle, pushing it inwards. The kitchen is warm, the overhead lights battling against the dark, dreary day. The girls sit at the kitchen table, Tara's legs dangling uselessly above the floor. There are glasses of squash, dark enough that you know that one sip will make your teeth hurt. A plate of plain digestive biscuits. The girls, though, are simply sitting there, waiting.

I grit my teeth in anticipation of what will inevitably come.

Their heads snap around, drawn by the sound of the door, their faces a battle of expectation and fear. Then they see us. And, like an act that has been rehearsed, their heads sink.

Tara recovers first, pushing herself awkwardly from her chair, her small bare feet slapping against the cold kitchen floor as she runs to her aunt, her face crumpled. I watch Heather as Orla takes the younger girl in her arms, watch as she studies the knots in the wooden kitchen table, digging her thumbnail in so hard that I know it must hurt. I am expecting her to cry. But instead she simply sits there, stabbing at the table with her fingers.

'A'tie Ora? Did you bring Mummy home?' asks Tara, releasing her aunt from her grip so that she can peer behind her, face expectant.

'Not yet, sweetheart.' Orla sounds like she will cry, like there is a battle for control raging within her.

I carry on watching Heather. She is still wearing those red patent leather shoes. She is still wearing her coat. I feel the neighbour – Vida Charles, was it? – looking at me, glance up to see her shrug, shake her head. It occurs to me that she seems irritated that her kindness and maternal generosity have gone unappreciated.

'Heather?' says Orla. 'Are you okay?'

The little girl nods. She has dug a gouge now into the untreated table, and I sense Vida notice it, see her mouth open to object. I don't know why. It's not her table. An objection on general principles, I suppose. I catch her eye, shake my head once, and she subsides, her mouth moving like she couldn't quite catch the words in time and that even unbidden they have escaped her.

'Can I have a cuddle?' Orla opens her arms to her elder niece, waits.

Heather sits, staring down at the gouge, then pushes herself back from the table, her head down, footsteps those of a man facing his execution. Her aunt enfolds her in a hug, and I think that the little girl will relent, but her back is stiff, her arms pokers at her sides.

Then I hear Orla, her voice a secret that only Heather is meant to hear. 'She's coming home, Heather. Mummy is coming home.'

The little girl goes even more rigid, if such a thing is possible, looks like someone has sent a jolt of electricity right through her, and her expression breaks, the flat sea suddenly flaring up into a storm. She starts to cry, long, shaking sobs, her face buried in her aunt's shoulder.

I look away. God forgive me, I look away. I cannot see any more.

My eye catches Vida's and I indicate the door, an invitation and a summons, turning before I know that she has accepted, until I am in the quiet sanctum of the hallway. I can still hear Heather crying, but it is quieter now, and the jagged edges that rip into my heart are blunted.

I look to Vida. 'Let's go into the living room, shall we?'

It is quieter in here, dark. I move towards the window, look to the sky. The clouds are massing again, dense, a storm waiting to break upon us. It feels like a portent.

'Well,' says Vida, 'awful, isn't it? Just terrible for those poor children. Imagine losing your father like that, at their age too. And now their mother gone off who knows where.

It just breaks your heart. And they're such pretty little things too.' She stops, considers. 'Well, the younger one is. I could just take her home with me. Sullen, the older one. Spoilt, I dare say.'

I think of Heather, her narrow arms holding her little sister tight, singing to her, not letting herself cry, because she is the eldest and she must be the protector now, and I feel anger bubbling up inside me.

'She's under an awful lot of strain,' I say, my voice harder than I have heard it in a long time. 'I think she is holding it together admirably, given that she is only seven.'

Vida glances at me quickly, then nods. 'Oh yes. Terrible times. Like I said, poor things. So,' she said, 'do you think it's tax fraud?'

'What makes you say that?'

'Well, there's no shortage of money here, is there? Big old house, fancy car. That Range Rover of hers is brand new. I said to my Henry, there's something funny about her. No sign of her going out to work, car doesn't move from day to day. Where's the money coming from, eh?'

I nod, biting my tongue. I don't know why it bothers me. I don't know Selena Cole. What this neighbour is saying could be entirely true. But the truth is, it bugs me, this plucking at the missing woman, gets right under my skin.

'It's not tax fraud.' But a little voice whispers to me that I don't know this. I don't know anything, only that Selena Cole is missing. Tax fraud. I test the words, like prodding a filling with your tongue. And the thing is, you don't know anything until you actually know it. So it could be. It could be that there is something else here, something darker that I'm just not seeing yet.

I gesture to the sofa, take the wingback chair nearest the fireplace.

'So,' I say, 'do you know Selena well?'

'Well, no. Not well. She's . . . Mrs Cole and I are from different walks of life, you see. Me and my husband, we've been here, ooh, must be forty years now. Seen the area change, we have. Well, you do, don't you? Used to be a time when we knew everyone in the hamlet. Our children used to all play together out in the fields out back. But now . . . I mean, you know how it is. People die, people move on. It's all different now. Henry and me, we don't know anyone any more.'

'So you don't know Selena?' I snap the words off at their stems, thinking how Finn would laugh at me, how I chide him to be gentler, more patient, and here I am.

Vida leans towards me, tone low, conspiratorial. 'She always strikes me as very stuck-up. They've only been here a couple of years. There used to be a husband, you know. Handsome man. Dead now, of course. He was nice enough. And Mrs Cole used to be all right, if you like that sort of thing. But now, no, she never bothers.' She drops her voice to a whisper. 'Proper snob if you know what I mean. Would walk right by you on the street without so much as a hello.'

I see it as if I was there. Selena Cole, magically alone, alive, here. Walking. Just walking. Maybe her sister-in-law has taken the kids for an hour, told her to go out, get some air, grieve. Selena walking, and although her footsteps are falling on these pavements, not being here at all. Instead being in Brazil when a bomb has gone off and the air is dense with sirens and screams. Or perhaps at a graveside, one where she goes to place flowers, even though she knows her husband is not really there, because what killed him was a bomb – do you even get a body back after something like that? Do you get anything? And this stupid, silly woman marching into her grief, demanding to be noticed.

'No.' Vida leans back against the sofa. 'You mark my words, she's done a runner.'

I'm going to slap her. I swear to God.

'Why would she have done that?'

'You know how these women are. Careers, that's all they care about. Selfish, I call it. Like being a mother isn't the most important job in the world. It was different in my day. I stayed home, I raised my Theresa myself. I never had a day off. Never asked for one, either. You don't if you're a mother, do you? Not like that these days. All these women, their children coming second to whatever nonsense they're up to all day, shipping the little ones off to day care, grand-parents, whoever will have them, it seems to me. No.' She nods triumphantly, the expression of one who has solved an enigma. 'You mark my words, she's walked out. Dumped those little kiddies.'

I look out of the window, watch as the wind whips at the branches of the apple tree, and feel like I have taken a body blow. That this vicious, judgemental bat has reached inside me and taken hold of the worst of me, pulling it to the surface and then throwing it back into my face.

'Mind,' Vida's voice startles me, flicking its forked tongue against my consciousness, 'you know about the psychiatrist, don't you?'

'What?' I grip the arms of the chair tighter, partly to prevent me from launching myself at her.

'Selena was seeing some psychiatrist, up in London.'

I study her. 'You said she didn't speak to you. How would you know that?'

The elderly woman tosses her head, a light blush creeping across her features. 'There was a card, from a Dr . . . Mini-something, in the kitchen. Psychiatrist.' She looks up at me. 'Well, I couldn't help it. It was just lying there.'

'Maybe it's someone she works with,' I suggest. 'Selena is a psychologist.'

'No, she's definitely seeing him. There was an appointment on her calendar for next week.'

'Right. And where's her calendar?'

This time she at least has the decency to look shamefaced. 'The office.'

I feel the sinking begin to recede. This woman is not a credible source of judgement, for me, for Selena. I watch as her eyes dart around the living room, from the tasteful, expensive furniture to the family pictures taken in exotic destinations, and can see her lips tightening in disapproval. She is someone who is disappointed in life, loaded with bitterness. She is not someone who should be allowed to define success. Not mine. Not Selena's.

I stare at her, let the silence hang. 'You went into her office?'

'Well,' she says, blustering. 'I was just . . . checking.'

'Checking?'

'In case Mrs Cole was in there.'

She stares at me, bold, the faintest flush of red to her cheeks.

'Right,' I say.

Case No. 16
Victim: Victor Cannon
Location: Beirut, Lebanon
Company: Cannon-Kane Financial Services
3 September 2006

Initial event

Mr Victor Cannon, founding partner of Cannon-Kane Financial Services, failed to arrive home from work on 3 September. Mr Cannon is a UK national, but has operated his business out of Lebanon for the past ten years. At 7.15 p.m., Mrs Hala Cannon, Mr Cannon's Lebanese-born wife, became concerned for her husband and contacted his office. Concerns were further raised when it was ascertained that Mr Cannon had left his office at 4.45 p.m., indicating that he was returning directly home. According to Mrs Cannon, he should have arrived by 5.30 at the latest. All attempts to raise Mr Cannon on his mobile or to identify any locations in which he might have stopped were unsuccessful.

A search of the local area was conducted. Mr Cannon's car was found in the car park in which it was usually left, with no sign that he had in fact returned to it.

At midnight, Mr Cannon's business partner, Mr Sóad Kane, raised the alarm. An initial call was placed to

Cannon-Kane's insurers, Biltstrom, in which Mr Kane expressed fears that Mr Cannon had been kidnapped en route to his vehicle. This fear came on the back of a series of kidnap-for-ransom events experienced by employees of the Cannon-Kane company in previous years.

Response

The response team consisted of myself (Ed Cole) and Selena Cole. Having received the initial call at 2.16 a.m. on 4 September, we were on the ground in Beirut twenty-four hours later. The Cole Group was familiar with both Mr Cannon and the Cannon-Kane company, having provided consultancy services on all three previous kidnap-for-ransom events experienced by the company in its recent history.

Upon arrival at the scene, a command room was immediately put in place within the buildings of Cannon-Kane, and contact was made with all relevant parties. What then followed was highly unusual within the case history of the Cole Group.

We received no contact from the kidnappers.

Seventy-two hours passed, in which the emotional state of Mrs Cannon became increasingly fragile. No calls were made to either the Cannon home or the Cannon-Kane offices. No ransom demand was received.

At the end of this seventy-two-hour period, Selena Cole put forward the idea that there might be more to this kidnapping than first appeared. As a consequence, she spent some considerable time sitting down with Mrs Cannon, Mr Kane and the various employees and acquaintances who made up Mr Victor Cannon's daily life. Her goal was to obtain as full and complete an understanding of the hostage as possible.

Within a relatively short period of time, Dr Cole had reached the conclusion that Mr Cannon's state of mind prior to his disappearance was unstable enough to cause her no small degree of concern.

It became apparent that Cannon-Kane was in fact close to financial collapse, and that the most likely outcome for Mr Cannon would then be bankruptcy. Although reluctant to discuss such personal matters initially, following much prompting, Mrs Cannon revealed that she and her husband had recently discussed separating and that their marriage had been going through an extremely difficult time of late.

A search of Mr Cannon's office and questioning of his employees revealed that he had been drinking heavily and had made, on more than one occasion, references to the fact that the world would be improved should he be removed from it.

Another search of the local area was organised, this one concentrating on isolated spots, abandoned buildings, etc. Five days after the initial call was placed, Mr Cannon's body was eventually located in a disused warehouse approximately half a mile away from the Cannon-Kane offices. He had hanged himself.

Note

In the aftermath of this case, ongoing psychological support was set up for Mr Cannon's wife and colleagues by Selena Cole. Following our experiences in the Cannon-Kane case, the Cole Group expanded its portfolio of services to offer training in trauma risk management (TRIM) for each of its clients, as well as establishing a crisis line available 24/7 for those employees in a state of immediate crisis.

Eighty-two days

DS Finn Hale: Tuesday, 5.36 p.m.

I flop into my chair. The office is still busy, people coming, going, even though the light is beginning to fade. I look out of the window, my own reflection looking back at me, lines of traffic criss-crossing my face, people heading out after a long working day. It's different for us. We won't be going anywhere any time soon.

'Christa,' I call. 'You get anything back on Beck Chambers?'

She looks up at me, seems to take a moment to shift from what she's doing to what I'm asking her. 'Chambers . . . no. Not yet. He paid us a visit this weekend. Spent the night in one of our superior rooms after a night of heavy drinking. Was released Monday lunchtime and has, apparently, vanished into thin air. We've got a team trying to dig him out.' She glances at the clock, spares me a quick grin. 'They'll be racking up the overtime tonight.'

'Won't we all?' I mutter.

I glance to Leah's desk. Still empty. She should be back by now. I pick up the phone. Put it down again. Then stare at it. Like that will make a difference.

I called my neighbour, on my way back to the nick. A retired teacher, Stan, says he's getting fat, that the sedentary life style doesn't agree with him. He laughed when he heard my voice. Another late one, then? Ah, you youngsters. Yes, I'll get the dog, take him for a good run. I'll not be running, though. Just to clear that one up.

I look at the photo stuck to my computer. Strider. A long-haired German Shepherd. He was supposed to be a police dog. That, it had seemed, was his destiny. But his trainer said he was just too stupid. Lovely dog, affectionate as the day is long. Unfortunately dumb as a brush. It's been, what, four years now?

He's still stupid.

It didn't take Isaac too long to run out of tears. It took him less time still to run out of words. So in the end, we just sat there, me and him, sharing a stultifying silence.

'Is there someone I can call? Someone you would like to be with you?' I asked. It feels a lot like guilt, this awareness that you have changed a person's life simply by the act of arriving at their door. This man, this seemingly ordinary man, was living a perfectly normal existence, and then I show up, bearing my basket of bad news. You want someone else to come sweeping in, some overbearing mother, some calm and collected best friend, hell, some hobo that you picked up off the street. Anyone who can diffuse the impact.

Isaac made a sound. For a second I thought he was crying again; took me longer to figure out that it was a laugh.

It's funny what it does to you, the sound of laughter in the middle of a murder. An effect similar to footsteps in a dark alley.

I watched him closely.

He looked up at me, a rictus smile. 'There's no one.' Shook his head.

'Okay . . . Parents?' I floundered, grasping at straws, still trying to fit him into a category, because in grief he was the victim. Then he laughed again, and the walls of that category juddered.

'My parents are back in the US. Wouldn't matter much if they lived next door. They don't speak to me. They don't approve of . . .' He waved his hands, indicating himself, the room, the world. 'Well, they don't approve of me. I went home, after I met Dom. I wanted to tell them face to face. Be a man about it. Fess up to being gay.' He laughed again. 'My dad punched me. Broke my tooth. Told me they were done, that I had upset them enough.'

I nodded, shifting in the quicksand of the conversation. 'Okay. Friends?'

Isaac looked at me, shook his head. 'There is no one else,' he repeated. 'There was only Dom.' Then another smile, my hackles climbing further. 'It's ironic, isn't it? You worry so much that you will lose them, because you love them so much, that you cling and cling, and then you lose them anyway.'

I nodded, my thoughts elsewhere. 'Isaac, would you mind if I just took a quick look around? See if I can spot anything that may give us a clue what Dominic's plans were, how this happened to him?'

He agreed with a wave, head sinking back into his hands.

I moved through the apartment. Everything modern and shiny, all squared away. Thought how different it was to my little barn conversion, a slice of paradise in the middle of the countryside. A slice of paradise with a used cup on every surface, takeaway cartons ruling the kitchen counters, and the ubiquitous smell of dog. Yeah, I thought. I could wreck this apartment inside an hour.

I kept my expression flat, my eyes roaming the kitchen counter, the knife block. Five slots. Five knives. Across the floor, looking for signs of blood, an attempt at a clean-up. Into the bathroom, scanning the sink, the bathtub, looking for any indications that someone had got themselves covered in blood, washed it away. Pawing through the dirty laundry and thinking that life does not get much more glamorous than this.

I'm not sure what it was I expected to find. Whatever it was, it wasn't there.

I am getting the sense of being stared at. I turn away from the window, look back into the office with its banks of desks, long-outdated computers.

'All right, Finn?' Oliver asks.

We were friends once, me and Oliver. At least, I think we were. He is a mercurial guy. You never entirely know where you are with him. At one time I thought he was, well, kind of cool. Sharp-witted, smart. I liked him. But then you realise that those sharp wits are not as much fun when they are pointed right at you, that the smart is not so appealing when it is being used to undermine.

Oliver wanted the sergeant's post. My sergeant's post. He failed his boards. I didn't.

We're not friends any more.

'Yup,' I say, careful to shift my expression into neutral. I pull myself up straighter. Glance around. Looking for an inspector, a chief inspector . . . the chief constable. Anyone that means I am not the highest rank in the room. But no. Of course not.

I suppress a sigh.

'So, where are we up to now, guys?' I try to sound confident, but I can tell by Oliver's eyes, the way they narrow, the rise of his eyebrows, that he has seen straight through that ploy. He glances across at Christa at the desk next to him and I see the silent message he sends her. I know what it says. What a prick.

No. I'm pretty sure we are no longer friends.

'Well, Sarge.' Oliver drags the word out, resting heavily on it. 'Uniform found Dominic Newell's wallet. It had been tossed out on the road, a couple of miles from the body. No money in it, but credit cards, ID and such were all there. Still no sign of his keys, though.'

'And the car?'

He shrugged. 'Who knows. It's not at his apartment, it's not where he normally parks it at work, and there's no sign of it in the surrounding area.'

'Okay. Who's on that? We need that car.'

Oliver gives me a long look. 'You mean you haven't used your sergeant superpowers to find it yet?'

Yeah. And I'm the prick.

I flick on the computer, ignore Oliver until the urge to punch him recedes. Think of Isaac. You look to the spouse in a murder. It's pretty much the law. You look to the spouse first because they are the person closest to your victim and there is a thin line between love and hate. So your first consideration has to be: what makes it evident that this person is not the killer?

I think of Isaac's raw grief, the shock, then that laughter, so out of place. Is it possible that he is a murderer? I think of his hands, large, the kind of long fingers that my mother would describe as pianist's fingers (a comment that always prompted much hilarity when I was a teenager). I looked for cuts, scrapes, anything that would suggest that he had been wielding a knife lately, that it had slipped.

But there was nothing, no neon lights showing me the way.

Could he have done it?

Of course he could. In theory.

I think of the photos in the apartment, a gallery of couple shots, Dominic and Isaac pressed cheek to cheek. They looked happy. They looked like they were in love.

But it is impossible to judge any relationship from the outside. Like trying to reconstitute a cake when all you have remaining is crumbs. You take a picture, you smile for the camera, you set the scene for the way in which you want the world to perceive you and your love.

It's all a lie, when you come right down to it.

My sister knows my views on this. The Facebook generation. All dedicated to capturing their version of true love's dream. But none of it is real, I complain. That's not for you to determine, Leah says. Their relationships may not be exactly like those pictures or those statuses suggest, but perhaps there are moments of that. You have to have a little faith, Finn. Sometimes things, people, really are as good as they seem. My sister has way more faith in people than I do.

'Christa,' I say, 'did you know Dominic?'

She is concentrating on something, doesn't hear me right away. 'Huh?'

'Dominic. You knew him?'

'Well, yeah. I mean, I knew him well enough to chat to in the nick, or if we saw each other out and about.'

'What did you make of him?'

'Seemed a good guy.'

I think of Dominic Newell, living and breathing. He was, or at least he seemed to me, confident, sorted.

'He talked about his partner a lot,' she offers.

'Isaac? What did he say?'

'Oh, you know. This and that. Talked about the holidays they went on, how he was doing in school – he's a teacher, you knew that, right?'

I study her. 'What was your impression?'

'Of their relationship, you mean?' She shrugs. 'Good. Seemed solid. If you'd have asked me yesterday, I'd have said they had a happy relationship.'

'And today?'

She looks at me, grins. 'Always look to the partner first.'

I grunt.

'I still can't believe it, you know.' Christa has leaned back in her chair, her dark curls billowing out around her head like a pillow. 'I mean, Dominic dead. I was talking to him on his way into the station just yesterday morning.'

I push myself up in my seat. 'Wait, where was this?'

'Here.' She gives me a flat look. 'He was here for Beck Chambers.'

The Rescuer

Tobias Kender

(Originally published in *K&R Today*)

They were building a road, a swathe of asphalt that cut
through the blasted desert lands of northern Colombia. Night
had begun to creep closer, the searing blue sky staining
crimson as the sun began to set over the plains. They should
have finished by now. It was always a good idea to be out
of the way by the time evening came, to head back to the
bare-scrubbed hosteria with its paper-thin walls, preternat-
urally narrow beds. But on that day there had been a delay,
a problem with the materials. And so they were stuck there,
on the plains of La Guajira, as the sun began to set.

You have to wonder if they were twitchy. If they were
looking over their shoulders, waiting for the other shoe to
drop. Colombia's reputation as the kidnap capital of the
world is hard earned, with more than 3,500 recorded cases
in the year 2000. Things have settled down a little since
then, though, and with the peace accord between the govern-
ment and FARC, kidnappings dropped to a somewhat less
terrifying level of 299 in 2013.

Not that those statistics helped. Not on that day. As the
sun began to sink behind Sierra Nevada de Santa Marta,

the workers of Baeliss Construction noticed a dust storm approaching from the north. Only it wasn't a dust storm. It was a convoy. Three pick-ups. Innumerable men with guns. They tumbled out on to the dusty plain, waving their AK-47s in the air, shouts staccato and unintelligible to the foreign workers who only wanted to build a road.

They took five in the end. Five men, all but one UK nationals. Loaded them on to the pick-ups and took off into the setting sun.

There was a time when a Colombian kidnapping was a long-term arrangement. When a victim, often a well-targeted wealthy businessman, would be picked up going about his usual day, would be taken into some remote jungle setting and held, for weeks, months, sometimes years. The trend, however, has shifted. With the reduced role of FARC, the Colombians are seeing more and more kidnaps by organised criminal gangs. They want money and they want it quickly. *Secuestro exprés* is a thing now – express kidnappings that happen in a flash and are over just as quickly, leaving their victims a couple of million pesos worse off.

But this wasn't that. There was no quick trip to the bank for these five men, no hurried payment of their life savings for a speedy release. They were simply gone.

What came next was what comes next in many of these cases. A flush of barely organised chaos. A flurry of calls to the UK, insurance companies scrambling, negotiators hitting the ground with barely a second to figure out what country they are in.

If you ask anyone, they will tell you that there was a plan. That there was always a plan. If you're going to do business in one of the kidnapping hotspots of the world, you need a plan, right?

The first step involved a company called the Cole Group, a boutique kidnap and ransom consultancy firm with a powerhouse reputation. Its founders, Ed and Selena Cole, have built quite a name for themselves throughout the industry.

And so the call was made, and within thirty-six hours of the kidnapping, Selena Cole, a psychologist specialising in kidnap and negotiation psychology, was on the ground in La Guajira. She doesn't look like someone who belongs in the murky world of K&R. You could more see her teaching on a university campus, or tending to your tonsillitis in her GP surgery, than sitting in a windowless office in Baeliss Construction's Colombian HQ running a negotiation.

'It's always a tense time when you begin a negotiation with a kidnapper that you have never dealt with before. You don't know them. They don't know you. So in the beginning, it's all about putting them at ease, steadying their trigger finger so that no one gets hurt.' – Selena Cole

Based out of Riohacha, a wannabe city with desert one side, ocean the other, Selena was walking into a quagmire. You see, there are professionals in all walks of life, people who know how the game is played. And that brings with it a certain level of comfort, that everyone is playing from the same rule book, heading for the same destination. The same is true in the world of kidnap for ransom. The experienced players understand how these things work, that even kidnappers have a certain set of rules they must play by. It is an oddly comforting fact in a world that offers little in the way of comfort. But with the rise in criminal kidnappings throughout Colombia, the rules are changing. You get kidnappers now who simply do not know how much they can ask for, who begin by wanting the moon, who may get dangerous once they realise that they simply cannot have it.

This is where Selena Cole began, with an extreme figure, one that no insurance company would ever pay.

I cannot tell you what that figure is, mainly because I don't know. It's the rule in K&R. You don't talk about the numbers. You don't reveal how much you paid, in case the next guy asks for a little bit more, then the guy after that a little more still.

> 'Negotiation is about building a relationship, allowing the kidnapper to see that everyone is working towards the same goal – a successful resolution, a safe release for the hostage. It's just that some relationships are tougher to build than others.' – Selena Cole

Day after day, Selena Cole sat in a dark hole of an office and worked the phones, talking, charming, occasionally chastising, until, gradually, the ransom figure began to drift downwards.

It's a controversial business, the payment of ransoms to kidnappers. Recent legislation in the UK has made it illegal for insurance companies to knowingly pay money to a known terrorist organisation. And there is little doubt that the money used goes directly into funding criminal activities – drug dealing, terrorist operations. But those involved in the industry say that, at this time, there is no other way, that the payment of a minimal ransom is the safest and most effective way of ensuring the release of the hostage.

One Wednesday morning, the drop was made.

One Wednesday afternoon, five weary, frightened men were dumped on the outskirts of Riohacha. Exhausted but very much alive.

'In those five days, I thought I was going to die. In my head, I kept saying goodbye to my wife, my three children, over and over again. I thought I would never see them again. But I am alive. And now I get to go home to my family.' – Hostage, aged 42

'It is an area fraught with moral ambiguity. You know that part of what you do is funding criminality, and the thought of that, it's tough. And yet, ultimately, what we are doing is bringing families back together.' – Selena Cole

There are no right answers in a question as complex as this. And whilst kidnaps keep happening, undoubtedly there will be ransoms paid. We can criticise, stand on our soapboxes and deride those who contribute to criminal enterprises, but ultimately we are not the ones who will have to make the sacrifice if they do not. So perhaps we should wait – judge not, lest ye be judged – and ask ourselves, could I make the sacrifice if it was me?

Coming home

DC Leah Mackay: Tuesday, 10.48 p.m.

I stare into the night. The curtains are open, a gaping jaw framing the darkness beyond, the pinpricks of orange street lights in the distance. I should close them, should think about going to bed. But still I sit, my knees pulled up tight, laptop balanced on my lap.

I managed to finish on time today, there or thereabouts. Managed to get to the crèche early enough that the twins weren't the last children there. Tess flung herself at me like she hadn't seen me in a year, Georgia sparing a moment from the doll whose hair she was brushing to throw me a wave. It's always been like this with them. Twins identical in all but their reactions to the world. Georgia fearless and forthright. Tess cautious and clinging.

I finished on time. Leaving Selena Cole still missing.

I stare out at the street lights, watch them flicker. Is she walking beneath those street lights? Or is it in darkness that we will find her, her body curled in on itself like a foetus in the womb? Are you alive, Selena? Or is it already too late?

A creak of floorboards above my head makes me start,

and I look up, although I know there is nothing to see. It is nearly eleven. Alex will finish work soon, will pack up for the night. Will he come down? Ask me if I'm coming to bed? Or will he simply go, allowing me to fend for myself? My stomach flips at the thought, and I wonder distantly when it all became so damn complicated.

My mobile buzzes. My brother.

Having a nice relaxing evening? Jammy cow.

I know where Finn is, or at least I imagine I know where he is, because I know how these things go. He is sitting at a desk, shuffling papers in a bright artificial light. Or he is sitting in a darkened room, surrounded by screens, watching grainy CCTV footage. It is this way with a murder. The rest of the world stops, cases coming to a grinding halt, families vanishing into a chaos of background noise. You don't eat, you don't sleep, at least no more than a couple of hours a night. You work and you work and you work, until it is solved or until the overtime budget runs out or until something worse happens.

I type a reply, thumb moving quickly across the flat screen. *Yeah. Until tomorrow.*

My baby brother. People laugh, the two of us together on the same CID shift. We have been called Topsy and Tim more than once. And in truth, there seemed little hope that Finn would follow where I led. He had a good career of his own, serving his country. First Battalion, First Fusiliers, armoured infantry. A hero soldier. Then came love, a tumultuous relationship that would barely hang around long enough for him to get settled back into British life, and when the dust settled from a particularly stormy break-up, Finn had lost everything. His career. His girlfriend. His home.

I was a PC at the time, drowning in a never-ending series of night shifts, fighting the local drunks at three in the morning and growing increasingly frustrated with humanity. I had complained about it to my brother, thought I'd done a pretty good job of putting him off policing for ever.

Apparently not.

It was, as time would show, a perfect fit for him, a job that allowed him to pick up where the military left off, and fairly quickly, he leapfrogged right over my head, Finn chasing promotion whilst I was laid up, fat and pregnant.

Am I jealous? No. Yes. Mostly I'm just tired. And the jobs I have to do, they're enough for now.

I draw the line at calling him Sarge, though.

I continue to gaze at the street lights.

I got a message on my way home from the crèche, a heads-up from the DI. Wrap up your case, you're moving to the murder team tomorrow. The girls were sitting in the back of the car, identically tied in to their identical car seats, singing 'The Wheels on the Bus' loudly and out of key. My insides sank. I knew it was coming. You do, when you're CID and a murder comes in. You know that it's all hands to the pump. But I looked into the rear-view mirror at my two little girls and wanted to cry. I wouldn't be there to put them to bed tomorrow night. In all likelihood, the night after that and the night after that. I would vanish for them, just as certainly as Selena Cole has vanished for her girls.

I set the phone down, rest my head back against the sofa, old enough and used enough that it is beginning to sag. I think about tomorrow. I think about my juggling, all of the balls that I will be setting down. Motherhood. Cooking. Cleaning. Laundry. Selena Cole. Alex will pick the girls up from crèche. He'll bring them home, give them their dinner, put them to bed. They will be fine. But Selena Cole . . . she will simply remain as she is. Gone.

Where are you, Selena? What happened to you?

I stood in the Cole kitchen, kept my voice low.

'Your sister-in-law.' My head was close to Orla's, my gaze on the girls, sitting back at the kitchen table now. Orla had convinced them to eat, had made them toast, smeared thick with Nutella. Vida watched, forehead heavy in disapproval. 'She was seeing a psychiatrist?'

Orla pulled back, stared at me. 'She . . . It was after Ed . . . she needed a little help. That's all. It's nothing. Nothing at all.'

'And the antidepressants?'

Orla's mouth moved, an answer that came without words, and then, as always happens with children, Tara said something, pulling her attention away. I let it slide. Perhaps best that she doesn't spend too long thinking of the implications of that.

In my head, there is an image: Selena Cole, a woman who can take on the world, unstoppable, indomitable.

And then there is the other image: Selena Cole, drowning in grief, hanging from some rafter somewhere we have not yet thought to look.

Which one is true? Or are they both true? Can she be both one thing and the other?

I scroll down the Google search listings again. It was not a complicated search. My missing person was (or is) a woman of substance. Her name in the search bar, and articles pop up, one, two, ten. The Rescuer, they call her. Like she is some superhero. Perhaps she is. Perhaps her superpower is invisibility. I rub my eyes. I really should go to bed. What, I wonder, would I find if I typed my own name in instead? Very little, I suspect. I've never been to Colombia. I've never been to Poland to rescue my nephew. I spare a moment to think about Finn, what the hell that would be like, him having a son, let alone a kidnapped one.

There is another creak from above me, Alex's footsteps heavy and slow across his study, the groan of the door.

I stare at a picture of Selena that accompanies an article, her hair tied back, her frame swamped in a bulletproof jacket.

How long will she have to wait now before I can find her? It is cold, even for the time of year. So that should preserve the body, if indeed there is a body to preserve. It's not like in the summer heat, when the flesh begins to break down, flies rushing to the scene like, well, like flies to a carcass.

On an impulse, I pick up the phone, dial the number. It is answered on the first ring.

'Orla? It's Leah Mackay. I just wanted to see if you'd heard anything.'

She sounds exhausted, her accent heavier now than it was this morning. 'Nothing. The kids . . . they . . . they're really upset. I only just managed to get them to sleep. My husband'll be here soon. He's on his way down from London, so . . . things will be easier then.' She says it like she is trying to force herself to believe it, and I wonder what it is that she believes this husband will do to fix where we are.

'Orla, look, I've been doing some reading, looking into your sister-in-law's background, what she does . . . I understand she does work in Colombia, places like that?'

'Yes. Not so much lately, but before . . . yes.'

'I . . . Orla, I don't want to worry you any more than is necessary, but is there any way she could have been kidnapped herself? I mean, one of these Colombian gangs . . .'

She goes quiet for a moment. 'I just . . . I don't think so. I've never heard of them operating outside of Latin America. I mean, yes, the job can be dangerous. It involves going into high-risk areas. But that danger, it's contained, you know? It doesn't follow you home.'

'I see.' I stare at the photo. 'Okay. Look, call me if you hear anything. No matter what time it is.'

'I will,' says Orla. 'And thanks.'

I set the phone down, have not even let it go before it begins to ring again, its vibrations dancing an insistent beat against my leg.

'I thought you were working,' I say.

Finn snorts. 'Yeah, well, someone's got to.'

'Anything happening?' What I mean is, have you solved it yet? What I mean is, have you found the murderer of a good, decent man, so that I may return to my wild goose chase?

'Nah.' He sighs, and it catches at me. The closest my brother ever comes to sadness is that sigh.

'You okay?' Then I realise what I have said. 'Yeah, I know, I know. You're fine . . .'

He gives a bark of a laugh. 'Always. No, just got back from identifying the body with the boyfriend.'

'I'm sorry.'

'Well, it is what it is. Hey, I've got a question for you.'

'Yeah?'

'You know him?'

'Who? Isaac?' I shift a little, setting my laptop down on

the sofa beside me. 'Not really. I've met him a couple of times.'

'You think he could have done this?'

I think of Dominic, his voice bubbling with affection when he spoke Isaac's name. Another floorboard creaks above me, then another, on the stairs this time. 'I don't know, Finn. I would like to say no, but then I guess you never know what goes on inside another person's relationship.'

The living-room door opens, and Alex slips in, running his fingers through his dark hair so that it stands on end. He gives me a quick smile and I mouth the word 'Finn'. It occurs to me that my husband is handsome, with his dark hair that remains thick, bright blue eyes that, if you are lucky, seem to laugh. Strange, isn't it, to think that way about a man whose life you have shared for eight years. But then I suppose it goes that way sometimes, that life forces you to step outside of yourself, looking in at your marriage as a stranger rather than one who is buried within it.

'Yeah,' says my brother. 'I guess I'll have to defer to your judgement on that one. You know that briefing is at eight, right?'

'Mm hmm.'

'What?'

'What what? Nothing. I'll be there.'

'You squared away your missing person, right?'

'Well,' I say, 'she's still missing, so not really.'

A hefty silence, and I can tell that my brother is debating whether to put his foot in it or not.

'Lee, it's a murder.'

Foot in it it is.

'Yes, Finley. I'm aware of that.'

'No, I'm just saying . . .'

'Look, I have to go.' Alex is staring out of the window, his arms folded, trying to look like he isn't listening. 'I'll see you at eight.'

I hang up, watch Alex as he pulls the curtains tight shut. It feels wrong somehow, shutting the night out. Who will be watching for Selena now?

'Everything okay?' he asks.

I nod, close the laptop and lean my head back against the sofa. 'How was work?' He's an IT consultant, a wizard in a world of things I know nothing about.

He shrugs. 'You know . . .' He looks smaller now, younger. Opens his mouth, closes it again. 'I'm off to bed.'

I could just stay here. My hand rests on top of the closed laptop. I could stay up, keep digging, wait for him to fall asleep. I could do that.

'You coming?' He sounds hopeful. Fearful.

How the hell did we get here?

'I . . . yes. Yes. Okay.'

The reappearance of Selena Cole

DC Leah Mackay: Wednesday, 5.55 a.m.

When the phone starts to ring, it shakes me awake, making my heart thunder in my chest. I turn, wildly at first, trying to remember where I am, look to the clock. My hand reaches out, groping for the phone that vibrates hard against the bedside cabinet.

Alex groans, covers his ears with his arms.

'Sorry,' I say, picking up the phone. 'Hello?' My voice sounds slurred to me, like I have been drinking.

There is an intake of breath on the other end. 'Detective Mackay?'

'Yes?' I'm trying to place the voice, female, a hard edge.

'It's Orla Britten. Selena's sister-in-law?'

'Oh, hi.' A vague recollection of handing Orla my card, telling her to call at any time. 'Is everything okay?'

'Yes. We . . . we found her. We found Selena.'

When I hang up the phone, I sit, for an unsteadying moment sure that I have dreamt it.

'Who the hell was that?' Alex's voice is heavy, thick with sleep.

I push back the covers.

'Lee, where are you going?'

'My missing person. They found her.'

'Okay. So?'

I pull on my suit trousers, hastily buttoning my blouse. I don't look at him. Because he has a point. Missing person found. That's it. Job done. The case is over. What happens next is nothing to do with me. Yet still I carry on getting dressed.

'Jesus, Lee.' He has turned away from me and I can see the bulk of his arms over his head.

'Are you okay to get the girls to crèche?' I hover by the bed, hesitant now that it is time to leave.

Alex grunts, not looking at me.

I hurry along the long hospital corridor, my heels clacking loudly. It is quiet in A&E. Just one other cubicle is in use, the curtains tugged tight around it, the soft sounds of snoring oozing their way from inside. I have been here, time and time again, with prisoners in handcuffs, the complainant left with a bleeding head wound because 'she's a slag, i'n she?'. I have never seen it this quiet before. It feels right somehow that it should be like this for the reappearance of Selena Cole, that the world is holding its breath, waiting to fill in the blanks.

She is stretched out, a pale figure, skin almost translucent against the dark of her hair. People move around her, a man in a white coat, his hands dancing quickly across the surface of her. Orla stands to one side, her eyes red and lined.

I feel my step slow, almost like I am afraid to go any further, see what I will see next. But my low heel catches, thrown off by the change in my pace, and scrapes across the linoleum floor, the sound shockingly loud in the silence. They turn to look at me, the doctor, Orla.

And Selena Cole.

I stare at her. I know that I am doing it and yet still I cannot stop. She is alive. She is before me, but the image of her is fluttering – one minute her inert body is swinging from a home-made noose, the next she's alert, watching me. It seems that my brain cannot catch up, its expectations confounding the truth before it.

Selena is watching me with navy sinkhole eyes. She looks like I imagined and yet at the same time she does not. There is the dark hair, a shimmer of red, that falls to just above her shoulders. But it isn't sleek like it should be; instead, roughened wild strands snake their way across her face as she lies on the hospital bed. There are the same wide features that I saw in the photographs, uneven and looking like they shouldn't work, and yet somehow, when taken as a whole, coming together to make her look striking. But her lips are dry, chapped, her skin pale, like she has spent too long in the cold. Her cream sweater is blotched with mud, giving it a dappled effect. She has been crying.

The doctor spares me a quick look. We have met before. Medical staff, police, different sides of the same coin. We gravitate to the lame, the weary, the crazy. I can see him frowning, trying to place me, and I say quietly, 'Stabbing in Hereford. Twenty-six-year-old male.'

The frown deepens then vanishes and he gives a quick, brisk nod. 'That's right. Good to see you.'

'Everything okay?'

He knows what I'm asking. Like I said, different sides of the same coin.

'No serious injuries. Some bruising, bumps and scrapes. No sign of concussion. Which is, well . . .' He lets the words trail away.

I'm about to ask. I'm about to say, well, isn't that a good thing? But I don't get the chance, because then the doors fly open and a gurney hurries past us in a blur of metal and groaning and blood.

'Be right back.' He turns, his coat billowing behind him like a cape, and I spare a moment to consider the lie. It's what we all say – just a second. Even though we know that what lies in front of us is bigger than a second could possibly encompass.

Now there are only three of us left. Me, the sister-in-law, and the woman who vanished.

I smile. 'Hi, Selena. I'm DC Leah Mackay.' She nods. Her navy-blue eyes dart back and forth across my face, reading me. I can see now that there is mud in her hair, across her face, that her fingernails are stitched with it. She seems stunned, unsteady, is gripping the metal bars of the hospital bed like she is on the deck of a storm-tossed ship.

'Hi.' Her voice is throaty, the words fully rounded, singing of a decent school, a good family. 'You're the detective?'

I nod. Yes. I'm the detective. It is so clear then, so uncom-plicated. I'm the detective, responsible, capable, whole.

'We've been worried about you,' I say.

Selena Cole nods. Her eyes are swimming with tears, a dam that is one moderate rainfall from bursting.

'Are you okay?' I ask.

Selena looks at me. Takes a deep breath. And then it's like she changes in front of me, her expression tightening, eyes becoming calm, as if she has simply shrugged off her victimhood. 'Yes. My girls . . .'

Orla moves by me, takes her sister-in-law's hand. 'They're safe. They're asleep. Seth is with them.' She glances up at me. 'My husband. He arrived back from New York yesterday.'

'Selena,' I say softly, 'can you tell us what happened?'

She stares at me, her lips moving like she is struggling to form the words. 'I . . . I don't know.'

'You . . . what do you mean?'

'I don't know. I don't remember what happened.'

I had prepared myself for many answers. Yet I had not anticipated this one. I nod slowly, even though I have no idea what I am agreeing to. Now I'm thinking head injury. But the doctor, he said no concussion. I look around, trying to find him, even though I know that he vanished through the swinging trauma-room doors, that even now he will be up to his knees in blood.

'Okay.' I'm playing for time, trying to get my brain to catch up with events. 'What is the last thing you remember?'

Selena shifts her gaze, staring up at the ceiling tiles above her, the long, narrow gaudiness of the strip light. 'Heather. Heather wanted to go and play. She was . . . she had so much energy. You know how they wake like that sometimes? Like a fizzy drink and someone has shaken the can? I thought, well I'll take them. I mean, it was early, but we'd been up early because Tara couldn't sleep and she'd woken the house up. So I thought, what does it matter what time it is? I'll take them. Before the rain comes.' Her fingers pull on the bed sheet, plucking it from the mattress, releasing it, plucking it again. 'I remember putting their coats on. Heather, she wanted to wear her good shoes. They were supposed to be for school, but I . . . she was so determined. I remember closing the door behind us.'

'And then . . .'

She turns towards me, looks at me dead on, a single tear sliding down her cheek, splashing silently on to the linoleum floor. 'Then there's nothing.'

Orla gives a low cough. 'A taxi driver found her sitting on the bank of the River Wye at about 3 a.m. She had no coat, no handbag. He said she seemed confused. He brought her to the hospital.'

'I remember being beside the river.' Selena looks at her hands, at the mud that stains her fingernails. 'It was so cold. I don't know how I got there. I just . . . I didn't know where my girls were or what had happened. Then the taxi driver passed me and he stopped and . . .' She closes her eyes, covers them with her hands and lets out a sob. 'The girls. I left them alone.'

I hang there for a minute, floating between two worlds. Then Orla sweeps forward, clutching at Selena's hand, shushing her like you would a small child.

'It's okay, Mogs. It's okay. They're fine. Vida found them right away. She took care of them. They're fine.'

I think of the Cole girls, sitting together on the sofa, wondering how their world had shifted this time. 'Fine' is perhaps overstating it.

But I don't say that. What I say is 'Mogs?'

Orla looks up at me, her face flushed like she has been caught out. 'It's what my brother used to call Selena.'

Selena wipes her eyes and smiles a small smile. 'It was after Mog the cat. I told him on one of our first dates that they were my favourite books when I was a kid. It kind of stuck.' She shakes her head slowly. 'I'm sorry. I wish I could tell you what happened. But I can't.'

I don't know what it is, maybe a shift in the light, maybe

a small movement that Selena makes. But I am staring at her sweater, at what I took to be mud.

Selena sees me looking, sits up a little straighter. 'What?'

'Dr Cole,' I say. 'Is that blood?'

A good man

I hang on the pavement, Cardiff traffic roaring. The door to the offices of Hartley & Newell stands ajar. I am, I admit, steeling myself, bracing for what comes next.

People flow past me, some stopping to give me a look, the rock in their particular stream. That would have to be my Native American name.

But then perhaps they are looking at me like that because they aren't blind, because they can see that I look like a bag of boiled dog shit. As it were.

It was gone two when I got in last night. Even Strider was too tired to care, a brief glance, a quick wag of the tail, nothing more. I tumbled into bed, still fully clothed, lay there wishing I'd thought to put the heating on the timer, wishing that this old building had something even vaguely resembling insulation, and then, when I got really pathetic, wishing that I had someone who could have turned the heating on for me. I fell asleep at that point, insomnia a useless force against the need to escape introspection.

The pavement shimmies beneath my feet. An overweight

84

woman wearing a backpack scowls at me and I grin back. She speeds up. Seems reasonable.

I look up at Hartley & Newell, then sigh heavily, theatrically, push my way through the flowing bodies. Where the hell are they all going? That's what I want to know. Is there a party to which I've not been invited? I slowly climb the three broad steps.

It is the scene of a tragedy. You would know that even if you didn't know. There is an air here, a heavy mist of grief. From a back office, someone talks in soft tones. One voice, no corresponding reply, so a phone call I'm guessing.

I walk to the reception desk, offer the girl behind it my warrant card. 'Detective Sergeant Hale.'

The girl looks up at me. My God, she's thin – the kind of thin where the head is bigger than the body, like you are balancing a ball on a stick. I wonder when she ate last. Where her parents are. And realise that, yes, I am officially getting old.

'What?' She looks confused, like I have spoken a foreign language.

She isn't wearing make-up; she is agonisingly pale, pretty in a suffering kind of way. She looks like she is twelve years old. Okay. Maybe not twelve. Twenty-two? Twenty-three at a push.

'I'm CID. I'm here about . . .'

'Dominic,' she says quietly.

'Yes,' I agree.

She doesn't say anything for a moment, just looks down at her bitten nails. Then, a breath of air. 'He was such a good man.'

There is the click of a phone settling into a receiver, slow clacking footsteps. Bronwyn Hartley leans against her office door and offers me a thin smile. 'DC Hale.'

'It's DS now.' The words slip out and I curse myself. Like she cares.

Bronwyn nods, but I'm not sure she has actually heard. Her mascara has run, formed thick lines around her eyes. I know Bronwyn, in that ambiguous way that I know many people – the same way I knew Dominic. That is to say, not at all, not really. I know her to say hello to. I have sat across a table from her as she works to defend the indefensible.

'You all right, Fae?' Bronwyn looks at the thread of a girl at reception.

Fae is crying now, quietly, using her sleeve as a handkerchief. She makes a little noise. Whether it is a yes or a no, I have no clue.

Bronwyn takes it as a yes, looks back to me. 'You want to come on through?'

Bronwyn Hartley is attractive in an overly developed kind of way, with her thickly powdered cheeks, her densely crimson lips. I notice that the make-up looks clumsy and uneven. She must be . . . what? Fifty, maybe? But today she looks older, is walking like each step pains her. She pauses in the doorway, ushering me through, a nursery-school teacher shepherding her charge.

'Fae,' she says, over my shoulder. 'Go grab yourself a coffee, okay?'

She closes the door without waiting for a reply, sealing out the mourning. 'You should sit.' She does the same, sinking into a high-backed leather chair. The desk divides us, and she rests her hands on it, painted nails luminous against the polished wood. They're yellow. I find myself staring at them, wondering obliquely when this became a thing.

'So,' she says. 'Sergeant. Congratulations.'

I smile. Cannot think of any suitable words in response. I can still hear Fae, even through the closed door, quiet tears that have become sobs. It's a pungent reminder that, in truth, no one here gives a stuff about me.

'How are you doing?' I ask.

Bronwyn looks at me, surprised, and I wonder if I am that transparent. Or is it simply that in our superficial dealings, she has gained a better grasp of me than I have of her? That she has figured out that I don't really do sympathy, that empathy is a skill of which I am in short supply. I open my mouth. Want to tell her that I am trying something, that I am attempting to be more than I have been. Then I shut it again, remembering that it doesn't matter, not here, not today. Because all that matters is this death.

'I'm . . .' She shakes her head. 'I'm alive. That's pretty much all that can be said for me. I still can't believe it. It feels like I haven't taken it in. Not yet.'

'No.'

'Dominic . . . he was such a good man.'

It is the second time I've heard him described that way since I walked through the front door. I wonder if it is true. Or is it simply a case of death washing away all the sin, until all you are left with is the remembrance of the victim's best?

'Tell me about him,' I say.

Bronwyn smiles. 'He was a good man,' she says again. 'Very clever, educated. Kind. He always wanted to help. Wanted to give people a chance. To see the best in them.'

I think of my sister. Were someone to ask me, I would say exactly the same about her. I think about the rain that I poured on her parade last night and feel a flush of guilt.

'He didn't just want to represent our clients, he wanted to help them. Make their lives better. You know about his work with users, right?'

I shake my head.

Bronwyn smiles. 'Dom always did love a hard-luck case. We get a lot of drug users through here, as you can imagine. Petty crimes to support the habit, violent crimes when they're high.' She pulls a face. 'To be honest, I've not got much patience with it myself. But Dom, he was a big believer in fixing the root cause of the problem. Encouraging clients into rehab, trying to get them to make their lives better.' She sighs heavily. 'He was a far better person than I am.'

'Did it work?' I ask, curious.

'Sometimes. Mostly not. Of course, we always had Fae to hold up as an example of how a person can turn their life around.'

'Fae?'

Bronwyn flicks her acid-yellow nails towards the door. 'Lovely girl. Had a bad run of it a few years ago. Got into drugs. Brought low by some man, I think. But Dom took her under his wing, set her up with a counsellor, rehab.' She shrugs widely. 'I was sceptical, as you can imagine. But no, in fairness to the girl, she pulled herself together, got clean, got a degree.'

'And got a job,' I offer.

Bronwyn grimaces. 'I took some persuading. It was a good call, though. You won't find anyone more reliable or hard-working than our Fae. Just goes to show, I guess.'

I look to the closed door. 'I'd never have guessed.'

'Well why would you? This was years ago. People can change, you know, Finn.'

I look back at her. 'Tell me about Dominic and Isaac. What was their relationship like?'

Bronwyn plucks at an invisible thread on her sleeve. 'When he met Isaac . . . it was love at first sight. For Dom, at least. And for Isaac too, I think. They made such a good couple. I was happy for them.'

That last bit jars, sounds wrong after what came before. It is held up at me as a shield. What is it protecting her from? I raise an eyebrow.

She studies me, considering, and then sighs. 'Dom and I, we met a long time ago. Nearly twenty years. We were both new to the firm . . . a small operation, delusions of grandeur; it went bust years ago. But we clicked. I . . . God, I fell head over heels for him. We started dating – he hadn't come out then. We were together for a while. A year or thereabouts. And it was good, you know? But looking back, I knew it wasn't the same for him. You do, don't you? When you love someone more than they love you?'

I nod, like I have any idea about anything. Like I'm not a thirty-two-year-old man with the relationship history of a fifteen-year-old.

'He admitted it, in the end. Said that he was confused, that he thought perhaps he might be gay.'

'That must have been tough.'

She looks up, smiles grimly. 'I survived. We split, obviously. But we never stopped being friends. You can't. Not when you love someone that much.'

'And then he met Isaac?'

She shakes her head. 'There were others before Isaac. A

couple of serious ones, but nothing really stuck for him. Not until Isaac.'

'And that didn't bother you?'

'No. Well, I was married myself by then.' She pulls a face. 'That didn't stick either.' Then she considers. 'Although, to be perfectly honest, the women bothered me. There were a few of those for Dominic too, and even when I was married, I used to think, if you're going to be with a woman, why not me? Anyway. Then he met Isaac.'

'Tell me about Dominic and Isaac,' I say again.

Bronwyn gives me a long look. 'Isaac . . . he loved Dom. They were happy together. Dom and I, we talked about everything. He never told me about any fights, about any issues. They just . . . they loved one another. And I've never seen Dom so happy. It wasn't Isaac, Finn. It couldn't have been Isaac.'

I nod. Pretend that I believe her. When really what I am thinking is what Leah said – how can we ever know what goes on inside a relationship? Can we really say for sure whether the ice under it is glacial thick or paper thin?

'What about the last time you saw Dom?'

'I . . . It was a normal day. Just any other day. I was in court. I'm not sure what Dom had on, but you should check with Fae. She can pull his diary for you. I saw him when I got back to the office. Four, four thirty, maybe. We had a quick chat, nothing special – just, you know, chit-chat – and he left about six. I keep thinking, if only I had known that it was the last time. There are so many things I would have said to him. I wish I had known it was the last time.'

'Were you still in love with him?' I don't know why I ask this. I don't know why it matters. I just suddenly have an overwhelming urge to know.

But Bronwyn has looked away now, is brushing tears from her face, pretending that she hasn't heard me.

I don't push it. I let it slide.

After long moments, she turns back to me.

'When he left,' I say, 'did he say where he was going?'

'Home,' Bronwyn says. 'He was . . . No . . . that's not right. He said that he had to leave, that he would have to stop on the way home.'

'Where?'

'He said he needed to see Beck Chambers.'

Case No. 25
Victim: Alexa Elizondo
Location: Caracas, Venezuela
Company: Private case, unaffiliated with any insurance provider
19 June 2007

Initial event

At 2.45 p.m. on 19 June, Mrs Alexa Elizondo, a sixty-one-year-old widow, had gone to the local market in order to do a food shop for her employers. Mrs Elizondo had been employed as a housekeeper by the Rayer family, an American family with a string of businesses across the Americas, for ten years. Having finished the food shop, Mrs Elizondo was returning to the vehicle provided to her by the family for such purposes when she was the subject of a kidnapping. The family's driver attempted to intervene but was shot and killed in the process.

Following Mrs Elizondo's kidnapping, Mr Matthew Rayer immediately began taking steps to ensure her release. Whilst his own K&R insurance provision would not extend to cover Mrs Elizondo, the Rayer family's relationship with their housekeeper was such that they were willing to cover any costs incurred in ensuring the housekeeper's safe return.

A ransom demand of $10,000 was issued within twelve hours of her abduction.

Whilst Mr Rayer was happy to engage in no small measure of financial outlay to ensure the safe return of a member of staff who had become as close as family, the sizeable nature of this demand gave him pause.

Following some consideration, however, the decision was made by the Rayer family to pay the ransom, their financial position being one that could cover such a hefty demand without too much strain.

A drop was organised as per the kidnappers' instructions in a large park on the outskirts of Caracas. An employee of Mr Rayer took the cash to the stipulated site. Following the kidnappers' instructions to the letter, he left the ransom and then proceeded back to the Rayer family home to await confirmation of receipt and instructions for the collection of Mrs Elizondo.

A call was received an hour later thanking Mr Rayer for his 'down payment' and requesting a further payment of $500,000 in order to secure the release of Mrs Elizondo.

Mr Matthew Rayer contacted the Cole Group immediately following this call.

Response

The response team in this case consisted of myself (Ed Cole) and Selena Cole. We arrived in Caracas eighteen hours after initial consultation. Upon arrival, it became immediately apparent that the kidnappers had been reassured by the Rayer family's speedy capitulation to their demands and so felt comfortable pressing their advantage.

This left us in a somewhat compromised negotiation position, as the kidnappers were now aware of the ease with which Mr Rayer could access large amounts of money. An awareness that substantially added to the degree of danger presented to Mrs Elizondo.

Selena Cole led the negotiations, the early portions of which were dedicated to calming an extremely inflamed situation. A number of threats were made to the life of Mrs Elizondo. The severity of these threats was made clear by the sounds of the hostage being beaten and, we were later to discover, raped whilst Dr Cole was forced to listen, unable to intervene.

The weight of these events on both Selena Cole and myself cannot be overstated.

After an extremely tense period of negotiations that lasted for ten days, Dr Cole was finally able to persuade the kidnappers to agree to a second payment of $20,000. It was made clear to them that the family's resources were now at an end, and that their willingness to engage in financial outlay for a person who was, ultimately, merely an employee, had been exhausted.

These negotiation tactics were not shared with the Rayer family, all of whom were extremely distressed and were in fact prepared to invest whatever funds should be required in order to effect the release of Mrs Elizondo.

The exchange was undertaken by myself, with Dr Cole as back-up. This was deemed necessary due to the extreme level of trauma inflicted on Mrs Elizondo, and in fact proved wise.

Upon release, Mrs Elizondo suffered an immediate collapse.

We transported her to the nearest hospital, where she was deemed to be physically well, although severely traumatised. A rape exam confirmed that she had been sexually assaulted.

Mrs Elizondo remained in hospital for three days, throughout which she remained extremely confused, agitated and in a highly dissociative state. Her recollection of the events surrounding her kidnap was almost non-existent, and she was unable to describe what had happened after her departure from the Rayer family home. This amnesic state was identified by Selena Cole as being a function of the trauma to which she had been subjected.

An extensive programme was put into place by Dr Cole, designed to help Mrs Elizondo recover from her experiences.

Unfortunately, she never got the chance to implement it. On her third day of hospitalisation, Mrs Elizondo suffered a massive stroke. She died two days later.

Note

Following the events documented in this case, a memo detailing the consequences of handling kidnapping without the aid of professionals was sent to all clients of the Cole Group. It emphasised the increased dangers presented to the hostage when a ransom is paid without any effort to negotiate, and made clear that NO ransom should EVER be paid without the express instruction of a K&R consultant and/or under the guidance of the appropriate local authorities.

An impression of a victim

DS Finn Hale: Wednesday, 9.58 a.m.

When you are looking for a murderer, the best place to start is with the victim. Who were they? What did their life look like? Because in some way, that life has placed them alongside the person who ultimately killed them.

I let myself into Dominic's office and stand there for a moment in the dim grey daylight. There is a lingering waft of cologne. It fills up the small room with its closed windows, knotting itself up with the leather of the books. I try to identify it. But then, unless Dominic's choice of cologne was a Lynx spray, I'm unlikely to have too much success. I'm a philistine, I know.

The room awaits his return. There is a coffee mug on the desk, the remnants of his last cup dark at its base. You need to find the victim. Because when you find the victim, you will find their murderer.

I snap on the light.

The room is smaller than Bronwyn's, buried at the back of the town house that serves as Hartley & Newell's offices. An excuse for a window that looks out on to a yard beyond. I glance out, think that this room would always be dark, that sunlight would be gobbled up by the boxed-in square that represents the garden.

There are no walls.

Or rather, what walls there are are buried beneath banks of books. The modesty ends here. They line up, legions at attention, leather-bound, rosy red. They swamp the room, drowning it in now useless knowledge.

I walk the lines of them, a general inspecting the ranks. Can see dust accumulated over the mahogany shelves, the marks in it a Morse code that says: this book I have recently read.

Then the desk. It is neat. Squared away. I think of my own desk, the way the paperwork leans, threatening to tumble. But Dominic . . . he liked things to appear a certain way. He's dusted the desk. Or at least someone has. But if it were a cleaner, wouldn't they have dusted the bookshelves too? So, no cleaner. Him. He has dusted the desk, arranged it just so. So that when a client or a colleague sits across from him, they see his world as neat, orderly.

I look back to the shelves. You wouldn't notice the dust if you were sitting. Isn't that interesting? The cleanliness not for cleanliness' sake, rather to create an image. There is a framed photo sitting beside the computer. Dominic and Isaac, in ski gear, cheek to cheek. It is angled outwards, so that you would see it if you were a visitor.

I ease myself into the visitor's chair, study the picture. They are good-looking men, both of them. They look happy.

But then it's about what you want to portray, isn't it. No one takes a photo of an argument.

I study the men's wide smiles and wonder what came next for them. Did someone end up crying after they'd said cheese?

I stand up, move around the desk. This is the thing. I

need to know who Dominic was, not who he was showing himself to be. And if you want to know who someone is, you need to see what they hide.

I pull open the top drawer.

There is the usual detritus of office life. Pens, paperclips, Post-it notes. And sheaves of paper, slick beneath my fingers. I pull them free. A leaflet for a drug intervention charity. One for a rehabilitation centre. A list of numbers, drug hostels. I leaf through them. A good man indeed.

I hear footsteps, a knock on the door, soft enough that for a moment I wonder if I was mistaken. Then again, louder but only just.

'Come in?' My voice sounds guilty, like I have been caught rifling through women's underwear, and I cough, try it again. 'Come in.'

Fae is carrying a mug. She has stopped crying now, but still looks pale enough that I am waiting for her to faint. Her pixie-cut hair sticks up at odd angles, looks like she has slept on it. Then I think of the bags beneath my own eyes, my unshaven jaw. I'm really not one who should be judging. She offers me a quick smile. 'Bronwyn asked me to make you a coffee. I didn't know . . . sugar . . . I didn't know if you did, so I didn't because . . . well, you can't take it out. Can you?'

She is looking at me expectantly, and I suddenly realise it is an actual question.

'Oh. No. Thank you. No, I don't take it. Um . . .' I have no idea what we're talking about.

I see her eyes flick away from mine, think that I can't really blame her, see them land on the paperwork in my hands. Feel a flush begin to creep up my neck.

Fae nods towards the papers. 'Bronwyn told you?'

'Told me . . .?'

She sets the coffee down carefully on a coaster. Smiles a small smile. 'It's okay. I don't mind. I think it can be good for people to know that lots of us have things in our past we're ashamed of. That you can overcome them.'

I wave her to a chair, and she perches on the edge of it, knees clasped tight together, feet wide apart.

'Would you mind . . .?'

She shrugs. 'I was in uni. Law. I met a guy. He introduced me to some stuff.'

'Some stuff?'

'E's to begin with. Then we began to branch out. It was . . . I'd try anything. It was just dabbling. That was what I told myself. I was a student, away from home, having fun. Everyone did it. Then dabbling became . . .'

'Addiction?'

Fae nods. 'Addiction,' she agrees quietly. 'You don't see it coming, you know. The way it creeps up on you. One day it's fun, just a little something to take the edge off. The next . . .' She sighs heavily. 'The next you'd climb over your grandmother to get it.'

'And Dominic?' I ask. 'Where did he come in?'

'I'd dropped out of uni. Was living in a bedsit with my scumbag boyfriend. Neil. He got picked up on shoplifting charges and Dom ended up representing him. Neil, he, he had a temper. Could be difficult. Dom could see that and he kind of took pity on me. Encouraged me to get away from the drug scene. It didn't hurt that Neil ended up inside. I got clean, went back and finished my degree. Then Dom offered me a job here. I don't think Bronwyn was keen, not in the beginning, but she's okay. She came round.'

'She speaks very highly of you now.'

Another small smile. 'That's Bronwyn. Barks to your face, praises you behind your back.'

'You and Dominic, you must have been close.' I try and soften my voice. 'After what you had been through.'

Tears bubble up, overspilling, and she wipes at them with a sleeve. She nods, makes a noise of assent.

'Can I ask, when did you see him last?'

She scrubs at her nose with her sleeve.

'Monday. He left before I did. I worked late, me and Bronwyn. I went home, I don't know, eight, I guess.'

I remember what Bronwyn told me. Dominic needed to see Beck Chambers.

She sat at her desk, in her altogether grander office, watching me, allowing me time to align my thoughts, waiting for the inevitable.

'Tell me about Beck Chambers,' I said.

She nodded, slowly, gave an unconvincing smile. 'These things,' she said, 'they unfold with a certain inevitability, don't you find? The lover, the criminal. You always have to get them out of the way first.'

I gave her a flat look. 'You're not the first person to mention the name of Beck Chambers. According to Isaac, Dominic was having problems with him. Dominic was in the nick representing him on the day he died. Now you sit here and tell me that he was heading for Beck's the last time you saw him alive. Yes, there is definitely an inevitability to this.'

Bronwyn sighed. 'I know. It's just . . .' Shook herself, sat up straighter. 'It's nothing. Let's just get on with it. Beck Chambers. We have worked with Beck for years. He's had some problems, mostly alcohol-related. He's a useless drunk. Has never done anything too heinous. He's ex-military.

Served in Afghanistan. Musa Qala. Big military operation against the Taliban. Beck got shot a couple of months after that. They say he was incredibly brave, that he put himself in harm's way to save Afghan children in crossfire.'

I was getting warmer, could hear the sound of tread on gravel. Struggled to focus on Bronwyn.

'But he'd threatened Dominic?'

'Psh.' She waved her yellow nails and I watched them, mesmerised. 'They argued sometimes. They go way back. Have known each other for years now. They disagree. Beck would never hurt him. Dominic knew that. Look, I'm not saying Beck hasn't got a temper. He has. Keeps getting himself into trouble with it. He drinks. In short, the man is a fool. But this? No. No way would he have done this.'

A man with a temper, with a drinking problem. Dominic with a single stab wound to the neck. The way you might die if someone you were with simply lost control, lashed out before they realised what they were doing.

We needed to find Beck Chambers. Quickly.

I set the papers down on the cleared desk, sparing a moment to think what Dominic would have said.

'Fae,' I say. 'Do you know Beck Chambers?'

Fae looks at me, seems to be sorting through my words. 'Vaguely. He's back and forth here a lot.' Waves to the rehabilitation leaflets in front of me. 'You could call him one of Dom's projects.'

'What is your impression of him?'

She thinks for a moment. 'He's always been nice to me. Very polite. I know he's got issues, I know he gets himself into trouble a lot, but with me . . . he's nice.' She studies me. 'You think he did this? You think he killed Dom?'

I look questioningly. 'What do you think?'

She is biting her nails, chin cupped in her hand. Won't look at me now. There are tears budding in her eyes.

'I don't know,' she says, quietly.

Somewhere in the outer office a phone rings, the sound muted here in this quiet room with its lining of books. I feel like a child in the womb, sound filtered through my mother's stomach.

Fae glances over her shoulder. 'Excuse me. I have to get that.'

I look down at Dominic's formerly immaculate desk, at the papers I have left strewn, feel unaccountably guilty. I gather them up again, placing them back where I found them.

I push the drawer shut, allowing my fingers to slip downwards towards the lower drawer. Spare a moment to wonder where Beck Chambers is. Uniform are searching for him. Have been to his house, the few locales we know he frequents. And yet it seems that he has dropped off the face of the earth. This drawer is heavier, clinks when I open it. There at the bottom is a small bottle of gin, two-thirds full, a packet of Marlboro cigarettes. I grin. You keep your secrets out of view, hidden in a bottom drawer, so that you can look as you want the world to see you. I lift out the bottle, the cigarette packet. There is another sheaf of paper underneath and I pull it free.

It is a brochure, glossy, a picture of an eagle bold on its front. The Cole Group.

Going rogue

I can still smell the tip. It hangs about my clothes, stuffing the air in the car so that I can barely breathe. I took the statement, listening to the heavy tones of the man who found Dominic Newell's body slumped at the side of the road. Paying attention to every word and yet somehow not hearing what he had to say at all.

He shuffled in his seat, seemed like he couldn't keep still, the words spilling out, one after the other after the other. 'And I mean, I couldn't believe it. 'Cos you see it on the telly, and you think oh, right, bit far-fetched, like, but when it happens to you . . . Look at my hands.' He held out hands as big as spades. 'Still shaking.'

I take a left at the roundabout.

I made it into the office this morning in spite of all my brother's fears, arrived a little after 9.15, fuelled by the righteous virtue of a dawn start, a missing person now found.

'Leah . . .'

I winced, a schoolgirl caught sneaking into her room in the small hours, high heels in hand. Tried to arrange my features. Look confident. That's half the battle.

103

The DI leaned against the office door, eyebrow raised. 'Any explanation you'd care to give? You were supposed to be in at eight.'

'I was just closing down a case, sir. A missing person. We found her,' I add, as if this will in some way atone for my sin. As if I had actually done the finding.

He stared at me, eyes tinged yellow, skin pallid. 'I thought my instructions were clear? All cases were to be handed over?'

'Yes, sir, but . . .' My face began to burn, heads turning to watch the show. I opened my mouth, ready to point out that here in this room was eighty, let's call it eighty-five per cent of the force's investigative capacity. That there was no one left for me to hand over to, and that the missing woman was a mother, a single parent, whose children were waiting for her. But he stared at me, and under the useless force of his vapid gaze I backed down, snapped my mouth tight shut.

'Well you'd better turn back around. I need you to go out to the tip. Someone needs to interview the guy who found the body.'

I put my foot down, wind the window down so that the whipping air tears at the tip smell, pulling it away, tossing it into the passing trees. The traffic is easy now; most people have already arrived where they want to go. I pull past a Citroën Picasso, its driver twisted around in her seat so that she is almost facing backwards. The pitfalls of driving with children.

I think about Selena Cole in her hospital bed.

'Is that blood?'

She stared at me, her mouth opening, closing. Then, 'No. I'm not hurt. Well, just a few scrapes.' Held out her arms so that I could see the scratches, the fingermarks of branches. 'No, it's mud. From the bank, I think. I'm not sure, but I think I must have fallen.'

I stood by her bed, studying the dark stain, and then the light shifted again. No. Of course. It was mud, dark and oozing.

What had happened to her?

Was it the grief, the pressure of her loss? Did it become too much for her on that grey morning, and did she simply walk away, intending to give in to the urge for it all to end?

Of course, if that is what happened, then one thing is clear. Selena Cole is lying. So now the question is, is it a forgetting or a deception?

Twenty hours. She was gone for twenty hours. What the hell happened in that time?

I bite my lip, know that I am on thin ice, that the DI is already watching me from this morning's tardiness, that my timely return to the nick, to the murder, is critical. Then I indicate, pulling across two lanes of traffic, taking a hard right that I had no intention of taking. Heading straight for the Cole house.

When I knock, it is Orla who answers the door, her face a thundercloud. 'Oh.' She sees me, takes a step back, and I have a fleeting moment when I flinch, can picture her squaring up for a fight. 'Oh, I didn't think . . . Sorry. I . . . I thought you were moving on to something else, you said? A big case?'

'I did. I am.' I shift, wrong-footed. 'I just wanted to see . . . Is everyone all right?'

Orla frowns, and for the most absurd moment I want to tell her everything, explain why I am here, again, standing on Selena's doorstep, where I am absolutely positively not supposed to be. 'Okay,' she says, doubtful. 'Come in.'

She looks haggard, years older than she looked yesterday. I wonder if she has slept at all yet. I watch her as she closes the door behind me, slipping the chain across, and it occurs to me to question, is she trying to keep someone out or someone in? The house smells . . . efficient. Floor polish mingling with the crisp smell of burning wood.

I smile. 'How are they all?'

'Fine.' The word comes out hard, all sharp edges, defensive corners. She is watching me, a guard dog wondering if it will get petted or kicked.

I nod. 'And you? Are you okay?'

She stares some more, then I see her shoulders sink, the air let out of the balloon. 'I'm tired.' She smiles, shrugs. 'I'll be fine. Come on. Selena is in the kitchen.'

I hear the girls' voices first, the tone all wrong, off for two small girls. It is hesitant, seems staged for a church rather than a playroom. Orla pushes open the kitchen door, and I see an array of dolls, a cacophony in pink, scattered across the floor so that they almost hide the sheepskin rug beneath them. Heather sits, her legs crossed in front of her. She brushes her doll's hair with such ferocity that it seems inevitable that the head will come off in her hands, and her eyes flick from the doll to where her mother sits at the kitchen table, back again.

Selena sits on the blocky chair, long fingers curled around a red china mug. Her hair has been washed and dried, is neatly pulled back into a stubby ponytail. Her clothes are fresh. Her fingernails no longer bear the traces of mud on them. She looks up at me as I enter, and it seems that I can hear her heartbeat rise.

'You remember DC Mackay?' asks Orla. 'Or . . . it's Leah, isn't it?'

I nod, feeling Selena's searchlight gaze on me. 'How are you, Selena?'

She pushes herself up straighter. 'I'm fine now. Thank you. Is there a problem?'

She is frightened of me. The thought makes me take a step back. I have scared her by coming here like this. I feel a warmth rush through my face.

'No, no,' I stammer. 'I just, I had to rush away this morning. At the hospital,' I add redundantly. 'I was driving by and I thought I'd call in. Just to make sure that you were all doing okay. You know, after everything.' I clamp my lips together hard, attempt to force myself to stop talking.

'I'll make tea,' Orla says.

I try not to stare at Selena, although in truth it is all I want to do. It seems strange to me that she is sitting here beside me, the woman who vanished. Instead, I look around the kitchen. It is clean. Ridiculously clean. I think of mine, weighted down with stray toys, abandoned paperwork, those stains that simply will not come out, no matter how hard I try. I look around and feel a hunger. I want this kitchen. No. Not that. I want this life. I want to be this together, this composed in the face of chaos. I want to be Selena Cole. Apart, I remind myself, from the amnesia. I can live without that.

Orla sets a mug in front of me, pulls up a chair. She still doesn't relax, though. She sits, curled in it, as though at any moment she will need to pounce. I glance at the children. Tara is muttering quietly, talking to her dolls, but Heather watches me, her eyes tracking my every movement as if she is afraid that at any second I will scoop her mother up, slip her into my handbag and make a break for the door. There is a noise from above, the creaking of footsteps and I look around, suddenly uneasy.

'That's Seth,' Selena says.

I nod. Sip my tea. Burn my tongue. 'So, ah, they didn't keep you too long at the hospital, then?'

'No.' Selena smiles. 'They said I was fine. No sign of concussion.'

'That's good. And the girls?' I can see them, two small heads swivelling towards me, meerkats on a sandy dune.

Selena pales a little, her lips compressing into a tight line. Shrugs. Then she sees them watching her and breaks into a smile, the sun emerging from behind a cloud. 'They're great, aren't you, guys?' She glances at me, a moment of silent communication, down at her tea.

'So . . . have you . . .'

'Remembered?'

'Yes,' I say. 'I mean, I've heard that sometimes memories can come back, you know, given a bit of time.' I think that I sound like an idiot.

Selena shakes her head. 'I'm sorry. There's just nothing.'

Orla folds her arms. 'I think it was those tablets you were on.' She looks at me. 'The psychiatrist prescribed them for her, said they'd be fine. But the thing is, you just don't know, do you? I mean, cumulatively, these things could have an effect.'

I nod. The Cipramil. Think that I have absolutely no idea whether these things have an effect, cumulatively or not.

'I'm telling you,' says Orla, 'it was the antidepressants. You can't tell what that kind of medication will do to a person.'

Then the kitchen door opens.

I start, my body reacting to a list of threats my brain hasn't even considered.

'Leah,' says Selena, 'this is Seth Britten. He's heading up the Cole Group operations now. He served with Ed in Iraq.'

He nods at me. He is carrying a mobile phone in his hand that he taps repeatedly against his palm. Hair that was once blond shaved down to follow the contours of his scalp; tall, slender. The right side of his face is ridged, furrowed, a mass of scar tissue that runs from his hairline, down past his chin, along his neck and vanishes into the collar of the short-sleeved shirt that he wears in spite of the chill in the air. There is a stain on the collar, dark brown, that looks like aged blood, looks like he has cut himself shaving. My eye falls to his right arm, the skin that protrudes from beneath his shirt a twisted knot of scars that lace from his hand, up past his elbow.

'Roadside IED. Basra,' he offers, noticing my look. His accent is Scottish, the burr of it rounded down until it is only just there, barely noticeable beneath the English veneer. 'I was very lucky to survive. Many didn't.' He reaches out his hand to me. 'You are . . .'

'Detective Constable Leah Mackay.'

He nods, folding his arms across his chest. 'Good to meet you.'

'Seth has a book coming out. About his experiences in Iraq.' Selena looks at me, voice low. 'Well, his and Ed's.'

Seth shifts, his gaze fixed on me. 'So,' he says, 'is there a problem?'

'Leah was looking for me,' Selena says softly. 'She was kind enough to stop by to check on me.'

He is assessing me, untrusting. 'Good of you. Very good. Ah, Sel, I just got off the phone with Vince. He's heading out to Cuernavaca. Castle Electronics lost three men out there.'

'Again?' Selena sighs.

'This is the third time for them,' says Seth. 'They're on a roll.'

'They've been making cutbacks,' offers Orla. 'The company is in free fall. Pulling all the "unnecessaries". In their last quarter, they cancelled all crisis-management training. Trying to save money, I guess.'

'Well, that's the problem, right there. Their guys, they forget that it's a stupid idea to go out and get wasted in some Mexican town. They might as well have "Available for Kidnap" T-shirts made.' Seth bounces his phone against his hand, shrugs. 'I guess they're figuring it out the hard way. I told Vince to call in if he needs anything. Said you had experience with the place, Selena.'

Orla is looking at her husband, frowning. 'I don't think Selena should be thinking about business right now.'

Seth catches himself, glances from her to Selena. 'I'm . . . I didn't think. I mean, is that okay? I know, you know, things aren't great here, but I thought, because you and Ed worked there so much . . .'

Selena looks down at her lap, pulling in a breath. 'It's fine.'

'Do you good, anyway,' Seth says brusquely, suddenly confident again. 'Get you back into it.'

I sit at the table, unnoticed, unnecessary. I need to leave. I don't know why I came. 'I have to go. Look, if there's anything you need, or you remember anything . . .'

Selena studies me, smiles. 'I'll give you a call. Thank you, Leah. I appreciate your efforts.'

A fight to the death?

I flop into my chair. Stare at the blank screen of my computer, my attention caught by my reflection in the empty screen: reddened eyes, darkness of a two-day stubble. Dear God, I'm my father. Someone has taken my face, added thirty years on top.

I swallow some ice-cold coffee, left there from last night, instantly regretting it as it hits my palate. Leah still isn't back. I glance at her empty chair, then down at my phone. I could call her. Because the last time I tried that, it ended so well.

'So, anything new?' Willa's voice startles me from my deliberations.

'Huh? No. Why?'

She gives a laugh that is far too loud and far too bright for this day, settling herself on the desk in front of mine. She looks fresh. Downright perky, in fact. I wonder what time she finished last night. Decide that it must have been a damn sight earlier than me.

'You got the initial forensics back?' I ask.

She nods. 'He was killed with a single stab wound to

111

the neck. Wound is consistent with a small knife, kitchen knife, maybe. The amount of blood at the scene, no way the murder happened there, so looks like he was moved. Indications are that he was killed between six and ten p.m.'

'Any idea of angle of attack?' I'm trying to picture the scene. Was the killer standing over him? Did they surprise him?

'PM indicates a direct angle.' She demonstrates with her fingers. 'So, if you can imagine, knife goes in in a straight line.'

'Like whoever did it was the same height? Or similar?'

She shrugs. 'Could be. Alternatively, they could have been standing on a chair. Or hanging from the ceiling. Or—'

'Okay, I get it. Any DNA?'

'Interestingly, yes.' She grins. 'Always look to the lover first. Isaac Fletcher's DNA was found underneath Newell's fingernails.'

I think of Isaac, digging his fingers into his scalp like he wanted to tear out the news I had given him, that the love of his life wouldn't be coming home. 'Could be perfectly legitimate. They lived together. They were a couple.'

Willa shrugs. 'Could be. We also got a number of hairs, short, dark. No root, though, just the shaft, so only the mitochondrial DNA.'

'Right,' I say. Like I have a clue what the hell this means. She gives me a long look. Waiting.

'So . . .'

'So, nothing. Mitochondrial DNA isn't compatible with swabs or DNA records. I'm afraid you're going to have to do this the hard way.' She pushes herself to her feet. 'But I'm telling you, love can be murder.'

I watch her walk away, the distant sense that she knows this, that there is a consciousness in her sway.

Love can be murder.

Yeah.

I shake myself, turn the computer on, begin a search of arrest records. Maybe Willa is right. Maybe Isaac's tears were of the crocodile variety. It wouldn't be the first time that has happened. But I punch in the name Beck Chambers anyway.

Because the romantic in me doesn't want it to be Isaac.

I pull my chair closer, study the screen. Nothing, clean as a whistle, before about five years ago. Up until that point, Mr Chambers appears to have led a blameless life. Then, five years ago, something changed. The first arrest was for an assault. A night out with friends. Too much vodka. A word out of place. His 'friend' ends up with a broken nose, severe concussion.

I sit there. Thinking. Then raise my voice. 'Any sign of Beck Chambers yet? Anyone picked him up?'

Christa glances over at me. 'Still nothing. Everyone's looking.' She turns back to her computer, shaking her head. 'Wherever he is, he's gone dark.'

I look out the window, like I'll see him walking past. But no. Just the obligatory pigeon, staring back at me, gaze accusing.

'What's he done this time?'

For one deeply disturbing second, I think that the question comes from the pigeon. I start, looking around wildly.

'You all right, Sarge?' He is lean as a drainpipe, face scarred with the ghost of acne past. For the life of me I can't place him, for one beat, two. Then my brain comes back online, my memories shuffling sheepishly back from a talking pigeon.

'Greg.' I say it triumphantly and he glances around, expression one of confusion. 'Sorry. Yes. What?'

He stands to attention, God love him. He's twenty-three, so new to CID that his suit still has the price sticker on it. Is bubbling over with that barely suppressed thrill of having made it out of uniform alive. He looks at me like I'm a god. I move my chair backwards slightly.

'Sorry. I didn't mean . . . I just, I heard that uniform were on the lookout for Beck Chambers. And then I heard you asking about him. Chambers, I mean.' He waggles a thin finger at the computer screen, at Chambers' record. 'I just thought . . .'

'No, it's fine. It's fine.' I gesture at the screen. 'You know him?'

'Yes, Sarge. He was brought in on Sunday night. Assault. He'd been drinking in the Aubrey Arms, had a bit of a falling-out with one of the other drinkers. Hit him. Landlord called the police.'

'You dealt with him?'

'No, Sarge, not me. I was downstairs dealing with the Larson boys – burglary again. I saw them in custody on Monday morning.'

'Them?'

'Beck Chambers and his solicitor.'

'You mean Dominic Newell?'

'Yes, Sarge.'

'Dominic Newell, our murder victim?'

'Yes, Sarge.'

Jesus wept.

'And you didn't think . . .' I can feel my voice rising, my temper going with it.

Greg looks like a puppy about to be smacked with a newspaper, his fingers tangling themselves together.

Kids.

'Forget it. What happened? You saw them together, right? Anything stand out to you?'

He has pulled his head back into his shoulders like a turtle under threat. 'I . . . I don't know. I guess I thought they were friends.'

'What do you mean?'

'Just the way they were talking to each other. Didn't really seem like the way most solicitors and clients talk. They seemed . . . I don't know, comfortable, I guess.'

I nod slowly, drum my fingernails against the desktop. Then, in one quick movement, I push my chair backwards, come up to standing. 'What time was this?' I ask.

'Um, I don't know. Maybe ten? Ten fifteen?' He's still standing there like he's on a parade ground. He also looks like he's about to cry.

'Great. Good job.' I pat him gingerly on the arm. 'At ease, soldier.'

I hurry through the office, dimly aware of heads turning to follow me as I go, push open the door, down two flights of stairs, my footsteps echoing against the breeze-block walls. The CCTV room is quiet. Cameras cover the station, hitting it at more angles than you would think possible. It is, of course, like so much else here, a patchy system. Some of the cameras work. Others, not so much.

I find the one covering custody, say a brief, deeply hypo-critical prayer, then rewind it to Monday, 10 a.m.

I find Greg almost right away, standing patiently, awaiting

the custody sergeant's attention. I half expect to see him put his hand up. I see his gaze shift off camera. Then movement to the left. An elbow, a dark suit. Dominic Newell?

I lean in closer, like that way I will be able to see around corners.

Come on, you bugger.

The elbow vanishes, Greg's attention returning to the custody sergeant, his face arranging itself into a non-threatening smile.

I sigh heavily. Think for a moment. Then scan the bank of camera angles. There is a feed that covers the front door. Rewind it to 10 a.m. Watch as figures, solicitors, clients, come, go. Then I see the glass door slide open, see Dominic Newell step out into the liquid October sunshine.

Dominic doesn't walk. He stalks. You can see the anger in him, in the way he holds his shoulders, the way his hands ball into fists. I feel a strange sense of dislocation, like watching an actor playing comedy when you are used to seeing them in tragedy.

Another figure follows, bigger, broader. Beck Chambers.

My breath catches. He is a mountain, has danger written right across him.

But it's strange. The way he is walking, the way he holds himself, it seems off. His head is bowed, a child on his way to time-out. He is watching Dominic, expectant, fearful almost.

He waits. I wait.

Dominic marches away from the station, towards the limits of the camera's reach.

'No,' I mutter. 'Stay there!'

Then, like something has occurred to him, he spins, marching back towards Beck until they are toe to toe,

Dominic the smaller of the two, but swollen with an inarticulate fury. He waves his arms, hands flung up into the air, and you can feel the anger through the screen, the frustration.

I watch his lips. Wish to hell I could lip-read.

But all I can do is watch, mute, as Dominic Newell expels his anger.

I want to shout a warning. Because I can see the shift happening, the change in Beck's posture, his head coming up, shoulders moving back. And I think, this is it, this is where it happened, where Dominic placed himself within death's grasp.

Wait for it. Wait for it.

Then there is a movement, Beck Chambers' hands flying upwards, planting themselves on Dominic's shoulders, shoving him. Dominic stumbles back, and for a moment I think he will fall. But he saves himself, catching his balance at the last possible instant.

He looks shocked, like he had thought his client would simply stand there and take it, like he hadn't expected his own anger to come at a cost. But that cannot be true. Can it? Because Isaac said that Beck had been causing trouble. That he represented a danger. So what the hell would possess a solicitor, a man used to being around the worst of the worst, to act like that, to put himself squarely in the path of danger?

Beck stands there, his hands still high, like he is warding off attack. He isn't looking at Dominic; his head is down, like he is trying to pull the fury back together, keep things from tumbling further apart. Then he turns, spins on his heel and is gone.

I watch Dominic Newell, standing on the pavement outside the police station, scant hours from death. Watch him rub his hands across his face, like he is exhausted, has nothing left in him. His hands come up, a hopeless, helpless gesture, and his mouth forms a word.

I lean closer, stare at the screen.

I think what he says is 'Beck'.

Posted to service personnel forum

Corporal Beck Chambers
Pathfinder Platoon
16 Air Assault Brigade

I still see Musa Qala in my sleep. The sounds, the
constant snap, snap, snap, boom. I wake up covered
in sweat, and I think I'm still there, that I'm sweating
because I am in this piece-of-shit town in an Afghan
summer and that I'm about to die.

That's what I remember the most about Musa Qala,
the feeling that at any moment I would have to die,
that no other outcome made sense.

When I wake up like that, I can taste goat's milk.
Isn't that weird? I can't stand the stuff. But I was
glad enough of it once we had run out of food, water.
I taste it now whenever I get afraid. I drink to get
rid of the taste of it, prefer vodka to where goat's
milk takes me.

They sent us in for 'a couple of days'. Just hold it
until we get backup to you. We went in thinking we
were doing some good, setting up security, sorting out
the town's sanitation. But when the Taliban came, they
came with the thunder. They were determined, I'll give
them that. Pushed us and pushed us and pushed us,

119

until it seemed that every waking moment was full of the sound of gunfire, mortar attack. Their losses, they must have been devastating. Should have been devastating, but they just kept on coming.

They had the roads, knotted us up tight, so that the resupply missions couldn't get through, so we were pinned, alone in this northern Helmand town. A couple of days. Yeah, right. Fifty-two days. That's how long it took for us to battle our way back out.

Meanwhile, there's twenty-five of us trapped in this town. Waiting.

We ran out of food. We ran out of water. Counting every round we fired, because you had to make every single one count; who knew when more would come. We didn't sleep. Not for fifty-two days. We survived on catnaps, taken holding on to our weapons, broken by the sound of more goddam gunfire.

It was the end of the world.

It gets dark in a place like that. You get the feeling that death is standing next to you, biding his time. You know that rescue will come eventually, because you are aware that there are people just like you on the outside, fighting to get to you but being pushed back and pushed back. That there are deaths occurring amongst those who are attempting to back you up, even as you sit in your armoured bunker levelling your weapon at the sniper who has been taking potshots at you all day. You've got to have faith. You wouldn't survive a day in that without faith in your brothers, the ones who are coming for you.

But still, you get to the point where it seems like all that is left in the world is you, the guy standing next to you, the guy standing next to him, and a whole galaxy full of Taliban.

What happens then when you come home? When it's over and you're supposed to go back to being this normal guy, just slotting into life alongside everyone else like you didn't spend every hour of every day waiting to die?

I wake up, sometimes, shoot out of bed like my backside is on fire. Because I see one of them standing in the corner of my bedroom, an RPG aimed at me. I know it's not real. That Musa Qala is done, that I survived where others didn't. But in those moments when I wake and my heart is beating like a drum, it's hard to believe that's true.

That's when I have a drink. Because it makes the remembering a little easier, makes my guy with his RPG a little fuzzier round the edges.

I drink. I drink every day. For a little while there, I was just waiting for the drink to take me, figuring that cirrhosis, a sniper, it's all the same when you come right down to it. But the Coles, they saw it. They figured out just how low I had sunk. Ed took me in, gave me something new to live for, a career that wasn't just about waiting to die. Selena . . . the thing with Selena is that you don't even have to say it. She looks at you, and just by her looking at you, you know that she understands. That she knows men like me, our nightmares, the demons that sit right on our shoulders, the ones that we just can't seem to shake loose. Without Selena Cole, I would be dead. No doubt about it.

But death, he's a mean sonofabitch. You watch for

him, you wait, and then he comes at you from a direction you just weren't expecting. When I lost Ed, I lost everything all over again. You start to wonder what the hell it was you were fighting for. And after Ed, it all fell apart. Death took the Coles from me as surely as if he'd put them both in the grave.

Why don't I just give up? Get it the hell over and done with?

Because of Selena. Because of Ed. They fought for my life. Twice, actually. I figure the least I can do is try and hang on to the thing they fought so hard to save.

Survivors

The hallway is dim still, weak sunlight filtering in through the glassed front door. Seth closes the kitchen door firmly behind us, offers me an uncomfortable smile, his lip puckering into scar tissue. I'll see you out. His voice firm, an offer or an order, I am unsure. I saw Orla's gaze flick up to her husband, her mouth opening like she wanted to object, then closing again, her lips compressing into a thin, tight line. And Selena, sitting still at the kitchen table, composed, calm. A family pieced back together. Not by me, even though I would love to say that it was. But by some strange intercession of fate.

I hear the click as the kitchen door closes and take it for what it is, my goodbye to this case. I turn, begin to walk along the hallway, think that I should never have come here. I don't know why I did; what it was that I was seeking. Closure? For a case that has been with me for twenty-four hours? But we don't get closure. That's not part of what we do. We come into a tragedy, a murder, a vanishing, we play our part, we find the answers or we don't, and then we move on, leaving the main players behind to pick up the pieces.

Seth glances back at me, smiles. I can hear voices from behind that kitchen door, and think that they sound lighter now that I have left.

'You're Selena's business partner?' I ask, a useless question to fill in the silence.

Seth clears his throat, a strangled sound coming at the end of the breath, and I wonder if his throat too has been damaged, like his face, his arm. 'Took over as managing director after Ed's death. I do the day-to-day running of the company, make all the major decisions.' His gaze catches mine. 'Better for Selena that way, gives her more time here, with the girls.'

Or to vanish, I think. But I don't say it.

He clears his throat again, rolling the words across his tongue. 'Lot of travel, of course. But you expect that with a business like this. Got in from New York yesterday. Was in Caracas a couple of weeks ago. Venezuela,' he adds, helpfully. 'Couple of oil workers down there had been held for over eight months.' He pulls open the front door with his damaged hand. 'Tough job. Lots of moving parts. But we got it. Managed to work out a ransom that was acceptable to all parties. Hostages are probably eating bacon sandwiches with their families as we speak.'

A chill wind whips through the open door, tearing at the leaves that remain on the apple tree, and I step outside into the grey day.

'It must be a fascinating job.' The thing to say when there is really nothing to say at all. A shiver runs through me and I tuck my hands into my coat pockets.

His smile broadens, arms crossing over his concave chest as he leans against the frame of the door. 'I tell you, it never gets old. You just never know what will come next.

And the thing is, it's such a mystery to most people. Not the kind of thing that's talked about generally, you understand.' He lowers his voice. 'Insurance companies aren't keen to advertise the fact that they pay ransom demands.'

I pull my coat closer around me, turn my face into the wind. It scours me, making me gasp for breath. 'I can imagine,' I say. 'I have to admit, I struggle with the idea of paying criminals. But then,' I add, 'I'm police. Don't really fancy paying for the crime I'm supposed to be preventing.'

He compresses his lips, the scars joining together to form a perfect matching set, and for a moment I wonder if I have angered him. 'It's not an easy balance,' he says. 'Reality is, though, people are still getting kidnapped. In some areas of the world, travellers are more likely to get kidnapped than not. And whilst the principle is sound, it's not so easy to say you wouldn't pay when it's your child that's been kidnapped. Or your spouse.' He looks over at the apple tree, watches as the last remaining leaf gives up its fight to stay and is torn away by the wind, spiralling to our feet. 'Truth of the matter is, military rescues are dangerous. People die in them. Our best chance of getting a hostage back alive is to pay a minimal ransom.'

He looks back at me, smiles. That crinkle again, that unevenness on the edges as the scar tissue pulls at his lip. I feel myself staring, yank my gaze away, a heat rising through my cheeks.

'Not the prettiest, is it?'

He gestures at his face, his arm, and I feel my face flushing.

'No, I . . .'

'It's okay. It's just a part of me now. Scars, I find, make you who you are. Don't you think?'

I think about sitting on the cold kitchen floor, a bottle of wine between my knees. I nod.

'It's not just me. Not by a long chalk. Lots of boys I served with, they suffered worse. Plenty never came back.' He smiles an off-centre smile. 'You do what you can with it, you know?'

'This was before you joined the Cole Group?'

He grins. 'This was back in the old days, in Basra. Before the Cole Group was even a twinkle in Ed's eye. You been to Basra?' He looks at me like he expects an answer, then laughs. 'Kidding. It's a shit hole. Nah, we were just regular old boys back then, still all put together the way nature intended, without the cosmetic changes insisted upon by the Jam.'

'The Jam?'

'Jaish al-Mahdi. Insurgents. They didn't like us very much.' He glances down at his arm, laughs again. 'They didn't like us much at all. Understandable, I guess. Anyway, in my case, they expressed their disdain for me in the shape of a roadside IED. Damn thing took out our Warrior. Armoured vehicle, you know. Thought it had killed me. Did kill a couple of others.' He watches the barren branches of the tree, skeletal fingers waving and pointing. 'Flipped us right over. I managed to get out, although not without paying the piper, as you can see. Managed to find my way back in to get Fuzz . . . ah, Jason was his name, but we called him Fuzz. Dragged him out.'

'He's lucky you were there,' I offer.

Seth shrugs, still watching the tree. 'Not so lucky. RPG took him out, right after I rescued him.'

What do you say? What is there to say?

'I'm sorry.'

'You get on with it, don't you? We all have our crosses to bear. This one just happens to be mine.'

'And losing Ed, after everything.'

'Yes,' he says quietly. 'That's . . . yes.'

We stand there like that, the wind wrapping its way around us. I look out to the street. It is empty today, no cars, just crisp autumn leaves tumbling along the gutter.

'Can I ask you a question?' I say.

Seth looks at me, frowns. 'If you like.'

'What do you think happened? With Selena?'

'I don't know,' he says quietly. 'I really don't.'

'Your wife, she suggested that it could have been some medication. That maybe the antidepressants Selena was taking could have affected her recall . . .'

'I guess. I mean,' says Seth, 'I really don't know much about how those things work.' Then he laughs, an out-of-place sound against the whistling wind. 'If I didn't know better, I would say she was burundanguiado.'

'What?'

He laughs again, waves his hand. 'Nah, it's . . . it's nothing. It's this thing in South America. Look up "devil's breath". You'll get a kick out of it.'

Letter from Ed Cole to Selena Cole

What I remember most is the heat. Dense, chewy, the kind of heat that loads up your lungs with clay, so that the few breaths you manage to pull in are thin and useless. I remember the way it sat on top of my eyelids, forcing them downwards. Fifty degrees and change. Those temperatures, they're not meant for humans, they're really not. Or maybe it was just that they weren't meant for these humans, in our flak jackets, helmets that were now just a lid on a boiling pot. Our gear adding up until you could hit forty pounds in weight easy. In those temperatures? Yeah, double that, then you might have some idea how that feels.

I would say that it was a day like any other. But in Basra, there were no days like any other. They were leaden days. Days in which you knew you were about to die. Days in which the night-time that came whilst you were still breathing was a surprise, followed by the thought, well, maybe tomorrow. Basra airport. Home from home. Hell. Its soundtrack the permanent thud, thud, thud of missile strikes, the snap of bullets. We were all going to die. It was inevitable. It was just a matter of when.

Then would come the words. Resupply convoy.

And with that would come this twisted sense of

relief, that the day of our death had been marked now, that it would be over soon.

You have to understand how things were, the lie of the land. Basra airport was shit, no doubt. But if you compare it to Basra Palace, we were sitting pretty. The palace, God. I guess it could have been attractive, once. If you're into huge sandstone walls and pillars, an interior like Liberace's bedroom. But the way it sits. I mean, you can see why you'd do it, if you're a dictator and you want to stick two fingers up at your people. It's set apart from the city, fed into by three routes and three routes alone, a nice view across the Shatt Al-Arab river. That is, if you ignore the war that is carrying on all around you.

So, the guys who were sent there, who used it as their base, they start off thinking that life is going to be pretty sweet. After all, they're getting to live in a palace. Which is great, right up until you factor in the need to eat and drink and take a dump. Everything they had, we brought them. Everything they needed, they turned to us.

Hence the convoys.

You want to know how bad it was? The civilian drivers, the ones who would do anything for a couple of quid, they would get drunk before a run. Said it was better facing death through the blurry haze of alcohol.

Because there were only three routes in. And when we went, we went big. I mean, sometimes you're talking a hundred vehicles. That's one slow-moving beast, moving directly through Basra city centre. A place stuffed with many, many people who really, really did not like us. It was a good way to die.

That day, the day that it happened, we knew we were in trouble. We knew we were in trouble just because we were there. We were wedged into the back of a Warrior, seven men, more kit than you can shake a stick at. And the temperatures, they're just sky-rocketing. Seth, he's sitting right next to me, and you could tell he was nervous because he just would not shut the hell up. Ron says to him eventually, 'Give it a rest, Brit.' Only, once he did shut up, that was worse, because then all you can hear is the sound of tread on gravel, Seth's foot bouncing against the floor of the Warrior, and the pock, pock, pock of gunfire.

Jason – Fuzz to his friends – is just sitting there, looking around us like he's never seen us before, then he says, 'Well, it's a good day to die.'

That was when the IED blew.

I could try and describe the moment to you, but to be honest, I really don't want to. There was just sound, so much of it that you are convinced you'll never hear again. And after that . . . I don't know. All I remember is lying on the street, the remains of the tank tilted on its side beside me, over me. I remember tasting grit in my mouth. People moving, bam, bam, bam, gunfire way closer now. I remember seeing a leg. Nothing else. Just a leg. I remember wondering if it was mine.

Then a figure emerging from the wreckage of the vehicle. Fuzz, dragging Seth behind him. Seth was pretty beaten up, burns down half his body. He was in and out of consciousness through most of it, a blessing when you think of the pain he would have had. I remember feeling for my weapon, firing off some shots. Whether I hit anything or not, I couldn't tell you. The world was spinning around me and I'd have been surprised if I'd hit a barn door at five paces.

I remember knowing that we were going to die and not being scared. This, you have to remember, was before you. This was before our girls. If it were to happen to me today, I would be terrified. Now I have a lot more to live for.

So we're crouching there, me, Fuzz, Seth, using what is left of the Warrior for cover, knowing that it can't last long, knowing that we're about to die at any minute. An RPG whistles through, taking out the side of a building directly opposite us, Fuzz saying, 'Thank fuck these guys can't shoot for shit.' But we all knew that they only had to get lucky once and that the next missile or the one after that, one of them's going to have our name on it.

Then this surge of dust, the white horse replaced by a Bulldog, another Warrior, this one in fewer than a thousand pieces. Guys pouring out, bam, bam, bam. Somebody pulled me up. I never did find out who. Just throws me over his shoulder like I'm a side of beef. I remember arguing, saying I could walk, but them not listening.

I remember seeing the leg on the ground. Another guy scooping it up, cradling it. His eyes finding mine.

I remember Fuzz, half dragging, half carrying Seth. Another figure detaching himself, going to help, pulling Seth's arm up over his shoulder, shouting something. I never did find out what. Fuzz, released now, pulling up his weapon, and you could tell that he felt better, *that the ability to have hands on his gun had made him feel safer.*

I remember the RPG as it hit Fuzz square in the chest.

They said I passed out after that. That not remembering anything else was my brain's way of protecting itself. I told them that if it was that worried about protection, it would have wiped the whole damn thing away. I don't remember anything else until Germany. They told me I'd been out for days.

I don't remember knowing that I'd lost my leg. I don't ever remember that moment of realisation, that everything would be different from here on in because I was only sporting three good limbs instead of four. But I do remember lying in bed, not wanting to look down, because somehow I already knew that it was gone.

I remember allowing myself a day. To grieve. To know beyond all shadow of a doubt that my life was over, that I might as well have died in the Basra streets alongside Ron and Fuzz.

Then the next day, life began again.

They didn't kill me. They tried. But they failed. That had to count for something, right?

And then, six months later, there was you.

Ironic, really, that life handed me so much more to live for once I had so much less to live with.

I knew it the moment you walked in. I know you laugh when I say that, that the cynic in you doesn't believe in love at first sight. But, whatever, I knew. So you'll just have to deal with that. Okay?

We don't talk about this. I know that. I know that

you have tried and that I have said no, so that is entirely on me. But then I got to thinking. I owe it to you, to my girls, to explain how things were, to tell you what happened. I know you weren't there, but now it is as much your history as it is mine, because it has shaped what we have become. Ironically, in an incredible, amazing way. I'm writing this for you, so that when I am ready and when you are ready and when the girls are ready, you will know. I don't know when I'll show it to you. I have to be honest that I'm a little afraid that you will read it and that, just for a moment, you will look at me with something like pity, and I'm not sure that I can bear that. So, I'm stealing myself. In the meantime, Seth will take care of it for me. And if anything should ever happen, he will know what to do.

    All my love, always

    Ed

Finding Beck

I have the car keys in my hand. I do not know what I think I can do to find Beck Chambers that the rest of Hereford's finest can't, but whatever it is, I'm planning on doing it.

'Where are you going?' asks Oliver.

I swear beneath my breath. Arrange my face before looking at him. 'I'm going to see if I can unearth Beck Chambers.'

He gives me a long look. 'Course you are.'

My desk phone rings and we both look at it. I'm wondering how far my authority stretches. Can I get this prick to walk over here and answer my phone for me?

Probably not.

'DS Hale.'

'Vikki on the front desk here. I have someone to see you.'

I glance around, flailing wildly. 'Okay, well, ah, Oliver could . . .' I see Oliver look up at the mention of his name, his face warning of a protest to come. Ah, stuff it. There must be some perks to this sergeant lark.

'No.' Vikki cuts me off before I've had a chance to get into my stride. 'They want you. Sorry, Sarge.'

I sigh, loudly.

'Look,' she says, 'I understand that you're very important now, but still. Needs must.'

'Well are you going to tell me who it is, or should I guess?'

'Beck Chambers.'

For a second it is like I have heard an echo, that the name I have spent the last day thinking about has somehow escaped my head, bouncing back at me from the outside. 'I'll be right down.'

I hang up the phone. What the hell is he doing here? Why would he just wander in? My thinking splits, one half clinging to the idea that our main suspect may not be much of a suspect after all. Why would he come here? What could he have to gain?

Then there's the other half. That half says that this right here is a bluff. That I'm being played. I like this half far better.

'What was that?' asks Oliver, his face still dark, like he is waiting for a fight.

I glance at him, try not to look too smug. 'I found Beck Chambers.'

The reception area is quiet. A middle-aged man is half hidden behind the potted ficus, twisting a scarf around his hands, striped woollen handcuffs. A young woman sits five seats down from him, looks to be out of it, high on more than life with her painted-on jeans, a drowning knitted jumper that reaches to her knees.

And Beck Chambers.

He sits as if in front of a court martial, his hands neatly

folded in his lap, his knees steady, eyes hooked on a spot on the floor.

I find my gaze trapped on those hands, palms the size of dinner plates. Looking for cuts, scuffs, the telltale sign that they have recently been used to stab someone to death.

'Mr Chambers.' I try to sound pleasant, light. You get more results with honey than with . . . being an arsehole.

He looks up at me, gauging me. Then nods to himself, pushes himself up to his full height. He has lost weight since his last arrest photo, is leaner although still about twice as wide as I am. The once full cheeks now sink inwards to form crevices, and there are dark circles beneath his eyes.

I reach out, offer him my hand. 'DS Finn Hale.'

He looks at it like it is going to explode, then reaches out tentatively, an unenthusiastic shake. 'I heard you were looking for me. Fae, from Dom's office. She called me. Told me about . . . about what happened.'

'Fae called you?' I remind myself to thank her. Hell, I might deputise her at this point.

'She thought I should come and see you. That you'd have questions.' His tone is flat, voice low, although the words themselves are clear enough. I study him. What the hell is he doing here?

I smile, buying myself some more time. 'We really appreciate you doing that.'

Can I smell alcohol on him? Are his pupils dilated?

It's only in these moments that you realise how tough it is to check for these things without looking like a lunatic.

Beck is watching me, waiting.

'Why don't you come on through?'

He follows me, easy as a sheepdog. Waits as I unlock the interview room, turn on the lights. I watch him from the corner of my eye, looking for anything that will give me some kind of clue. Is he anxious? Fearful? But then I'd say this is a man who doesn't know fear, who has never known worry. He looks like a soldier about to undergo interrogation. I guess in a way he is.

He slides into the hard plastic chair. Folds his hands in front of him at the table. Waits.

'So.' I take the seat opposite him, feel his eyes resting heavily on me. 'Thanks for coming in. We've been looking for you for a while.'

Beck nods, the slightest movement of the head.

'Okay,' I say. I take a breath. Waiting for it all to go wrong. 'Beck, I'm placing you under arrest on suspicion of murder.'

After Vikki had called me, I sat at my desk, phone still in my hand, thinking. Beck Chambers was downstairs. Beck Chambers had had opportunity; he was the last person Dominic had headed out to see. He was on CCTV, his hands on our murder victim. He was downstairs.

I thought for a moment, then pushed my chair back, walked with quick strides into the SIO's office.

'Boss,' I said, pulling him away from an engrossing e-mail, 'we've got Beck Chambers. He's downstairs.'

'Excellent. Good work.' A pat on the back I'd done bugger all to earn. 'Right, get him arrested.'

'Sir?'

'He's our prime suspect. He's got form, nasty little temper to go with it. Arrest him on suspicion, let's get this all on record.'

It's a big deal, especially for a sergeant of eighty-three

days, to make the arrest of the prime suspect in a high-profile murder case, and my stomach flipped.

'Go on then, Sergeant,' said the SIO with a grin. 'Sort out the interview plan. Get it all on video. You lead.'

I'm waiting for Beck to blow. It seems that it is inevitable. But he just sits there, looking down at his hands, his breath coming in short, sharp bursts. Then he simply nods.

'Okay.'

I watch him, unsteady. 'Okay.'

Aware of the video running, I pull myself up straighter. 'I need to make sure that you are aware of your rights. Do you want a solicitor?'

Beck looks at me, gives me a smile that is not a smile. 'I don't have a solicitor any more, remember?'

It feels like someone has squeezed a wet sponge on the back of my neck, and now all I can see is Dominic Newell, dead on the side of the road.

'Well.' I feel like I'm floundering. 'Do you—'

'No.' His voice is as flat as his expression, so calm, and I have the sense of sitting right in the eye of the storm. 'I don't want a solicitor.'

I look at him, keep my own voice steady. 'You had a drink today, Beck?'

He gives a little laugh. 'Impressively, no.'

'When did you last have a drink?'

'It's been thirty-four hours.'

'Long time.'

'When you just found out your friend was murdered, yeah, it's a really long time.'

'You're ex-military, right?'

He nods slowly, gaze wary now. 'Yes. Why?'

I shrug. 'I served for a couple of years. Army. Fusiliers. Was out in Iraq for Op Telic.'

The words feel strange as they escape me. You never talk about it. You won't let me in. How many relationships have ended with that particular swan song? And here I am confiding in this towering hulk of a murder suspect.

He looks at me differently now, a visitor from a foreign land suddenly realising that we have the same native tongue.

'I know some boys who were out there for that. Tough times.'

It is hot in here now, like sitting inside a furnace. The sound of tread on gravel. The pock, pock, pock of gunfire.

'Yes,' I say. 'You were in Musa Qala?'

He fixes me with a look, and his expression answers any question I may have. See, the truth is, we never really leave there. Not really. The heat, the death, the fear. Once you have tasted them, they never go away, worming themselves into your life like they are a part of your DNA.

'So, why'd you come out?' he asks.

I'm pretty sure this wasn't a part of my interview plan.

I bite my lip. Consider not answering. But I tell myself that I am getting the suspect to open up, that by offering a little something of myself, I am encouraging him to do the same. I tell myself that. 'Love.' I grin. 'You know how it is.'

He raises an eyebrow, nods. Points at my left hand. 'You're not married.'

I look down too, like this is a surprise to me. Evie. That was her name. We had been together for seven years by the time I came home for good. It was time, we had agreed. We were going to settle down. Be together. Together together, not army together, when you see one another every six months if you're lucky. I would come home. It was the right thing to do.

I came home.

Three months later, she left me.

Turns out I was a far more attractive prospect half a world away, with the imminent threat of death hanging over me.

I shrug. 'Ah well. Life's a bitch.'

'Ain't that the truth.'

'You've had some troubles yourself.'

Beck nods. 'You mean I've brought some trouble on myself. Yes. Yes, I have.'

'I get it,' I say. 'Sometimes you just need to forget.'

'Trouble is,' says Beck, 'you get to a place where you've spent so much time trying to forget who you are that who you are becomes a completely different person.'

'You had any help with that? Rehab, anything like that?'

He looks at me, flat. 'Dominic. Dominic was my help.'

'I hear he's got a thing for that. Helping, I mean.'

He studies me. 'Fae told you?'

'About her history, you mean?' I ask. 'Bronwyn told me. Fae filled in the blanks.'

'Yeah,' says Beck. 'Dom, he cared. Probably more than he should. Most of us didn't deserve him to care that much.'

'Well,' I say, 'thirty-four hours. That's got to count for something, right?'

He doesn't answer, just looks down at his hands. Then, 'You know how many people have tried to put me right? How many people have given a shit when they frankly had no need to? And still I fall. And now this . . .' He looks up at me. 'You want to know where I was when Dom died.' It is a statement, not a question.

'Yes.'

He hefts his shoulders, deltoids heaving like a wave on to sand. 'I was out and about.'

'Where?'

He shrugs again. 'Nowhere special.' He gives me that look. 'And I was alone.'

It seems to me a challenge, that he is tumbling towards his upturned sword, daring me to stop him. I glance at my notes, try to find my feet, take back the reins.

'Look,' he says, leaning closer. 'Dom was a good man. He helped me. He cared. I let him down. But I didn't kill him.'

Tumbling back

DC Leah Mackay: Thursday, 1.53 a.m.

I push open my children's bedroom door, softly, softly, listening for the scrape where it hits the carpet, the soft squeal as the hinges whisper a protest. The room is a murky pale darkness, a low orange light bubbling from the unicorn night light. The rain crackles against the bedroom window, a questionable day tumbling into a full-blown storm, the wind clambering up, so that in the distance the garden gate slaps against its post, again and again and again. I stand in the doorway, listening to my babies' breathing, picking it out from in amongst the sounds of the rain, synchronised so that it sounds like distant singing; the soft whistle of Georgia's snores.

I breathe out.

It is almost 2 a.m. I no longer remember which day. I returned to the office far, far later than I should have done, a guilty husband returning from a late-night tryst, thinking that if anyone came too close, they would smell the Cole household on me, polish and firewood. I crept in, my shoulders tucked, as though that way I could ward off attack, and prayed. Don't ask me where I've been. Don't ask me where I've been.

I saw the DI, phone at his ear, looking up at me, a frown sitting on him so heavily that his entire face seemed to sink from it. Thought it was inevitable that he would pull me in, give me the bollocking I so richly deserved. But he is a man, and once he got over the initial disgust at my late entry, his attention returned to his call and he forgot about me.

I sat at my desk, played the good little girl.

I was at my desk for an hour, maybe more, before it dawned on me that Finn was missing.

'Where's . . .?'

Oliver grinned. 'He's in interview. Caught himself a big fish.' Gave me a wink that made me want to punch his lights out. 'Think your brother is under the impression that he's going to solve this case all on his own.'

I sat at my desk, did what I was supposed to be doing. Watched the clock ticking by. Ten. Ten thirty. Eleven.

Tess cups her moon-faced tiger in her rounded fingers, has it pressed up against her cheek so that they are nose to nose. She faces the wall, her knees drawn up to her chest, and I think that this is what she must have looked like in my womb. Without the tiger, of course. I pull her duvet up just a little bit higher, even though the room is warm enough and there really is no need. I hear her breathing change, responding to my touch.

Georgia sleeps in the adjacent bed, her arms flung wide, head tilted back, mouth open. I allow myself to rest my fingers gently on her cheek, pulling her duvet down a little lower. She doesn't like to get too warm, will sleep better if it is cool, if she is uncovered.

I should sleep too. The tiredness buffets me, so that it seems the ground is moving beneath my feet. I need to go to bed, lie down before I fall down. But instead I stand there listening to the waves of my children's breathing.

Finn came back into the office a little after midnight. The conquering hero. He headed straight for me, and I moved the mouse quickly, closing down the search screen. Although in truth it is unlikely that the words 'devil's breath' would have meant anything to him. But I closed it anyway, not stopping to question why, why I couldn't tell him, why it mattered so much to me to keep my thoughts a secret.

I rest a kiss on Georgia's head, feel the fragrant wisps of her hair brush my cheek.

I think of Selena, kissing her own girls goodnight. Of the fact that she is home, and that, whatever filled in those missing hours, at the end of them is a mother kissing her children. And so everything is well. Right?

'Hey.' Finn's smile was wide. 'What you doing?'

'Nothing.' The word came too fast, a child with her hand in a cookie jar.

Finn looked at me, eyebrow raised, and suddenly I expected him to turn, run to Mum, Leah's being naughty, Mummy.

'So,' I said, deflecting wildly, 'how's Beck?'

He sank to my desk, shrugged. 'Has no alibi. Says he didn't do it.'

'And did he?' I asked. 'Do it?'

My brother stared at his feet, a long way away in his mind. 'I don't know, Lee. I really don't know.'

We sat like that for a moment, two children in the tree in the back yard, just shooting the breeze.

'Hey,' said Finn, 'why are you still here?' He looked up

at the clock, shook his head. 'Go home, Lee. Give my nieces a kiss from me. See your husband.'

I look at my girls.

It is so precarious, this life of ours. You can be pushing your child on a swing one minute, and be gone the next. It can all change, just like that.

And then I think of that moment, the moment I do not allow myself to think about.

The lights are off in our bedroom. I pick my way through the heaped piles of laundry, the stacked-up toys that just need a quick sort-through, listening for Alex's breathing. I think he must already be asleep. Think? Or hope?

I will not think about it.

I cannot think about it.

Because it is like a portal, an opening in space and time, and through it creeps the darkness. So I will not think about the cold of the kitchen floor, the bottle of wine cradled in my fingers.

I climb into bed, pulling the covers up tight.

'Are we okay?' Alex's voice is soft, but still it makes me jump.

I turn, my eyes picking out his shape in the dark, and I wonder how he knew. Whether he could hear my thoughts, if they were as loud outside my head as they are in. 'What?' I am playing for time. I know exactly what my husband is asking me.

He goes quiet for a moment and I think it is over, but then he sighs softly. 'Will you ever forgive me?'

I don't want to talk about this. I don't want to think about it. Because if I do, then I will return there, to that kitchen floor, my hands shaking so that the bottle clinks against the ice-cold tiles, my world in pieces around me.

'It was a long time ago, Alex.'

I will him to stop. To just let me be. Even though that is cowardice, I am running.

'I know. But it just feels . . . I don't know, since the girls . . . I mean, we're so lucky, we really are, but it's just . . . It feels like we've . . . we don't get a chance to be us any more, just us. And it seems, you seem to be distant, and I know, I mean, it's not like I blame you. But I just keep wondering if we're okay.'

I close my eyes. Breathe in. Try to think about my children or a beach or a sunset. But it is too late. I am already there.

Standing at the kitchen counter. Stirring a pot. What was it? Pasta? I don't remember. I just remember the movement. Around and around and around. Hearing the car on the drive. The footsteps. Thinking that they were slower than normal. That he was probably texting, messing about with his phone. Smiling at the thought. God, I remember the smile, and how absurd it felt afterwards. Turning to him as he walked through the door, that same fucking smile plastered across my face. I remember how it froze. His expression one of horror, grief. But most of all guilt.

He never needed to say it. It was all there. Writ large across his face.

But of course, he did say it.

It was a mistake. It was only one time. It was at the works do last night. I didn't mean to do it. It just happened. I'm so sorry.

I remember the words flying at me like gnats, bouncing off me, so that all I was left with was a picture, my husband fucking some bit-of-fluff secretary.

It *was* pasta. That was what I was cooking. I remember

it now. I remember the sound it made as it hit the wall behind his head. I remember the snaking dance as it oozed its way down the tiles, puddling at his feet.

I remember waiting for the excuses, for him to say that it was because we had been arguing (we had), because the IVF was stripping us bare, taking from us anything that wasn't necessary for this oh so formal act of procreation (it was), because I had turned away from him, into myself, barely able to cope with making it through a day, let alone pumping life into a marriage (I had). I remember that he said none of that.

That he just stood there as I screamed, rounded globes of tears drifting down his cheeks.

I remember thinking that I had never seen him cry before. I remember telling him to get out. That we were done. Him standing there like he wanted to argue, wanted to beg, and part of me wanting him to, just so that I could unleash another round of fury on him, because there was so much inside me. So much anger that had nowhere to go. Then him lowering his head, turning, walking out the door.

Me sinking to the floor. The tiles so cold beneath me. Watching the pasta as it trickled down the wall. Waiting for the tears. Because surely there should be tears. But none came. Instead, sitting there for hours and hours and hours, a bottle of Rioja next to me, getting lighter and lighter.

I suck in a breath. Fix my vision on the spot of light on the bedroom ceiling, the street light breaking through a gap in the curtains. Tell myself that it is over. Tell myself that it is done. I feel a tear snake its way down my cheek, a surge of anger at him for doing this, for bringing me back here.

'It was a long time ago,' I repeat.

We lie there for a time in the unsteady darkness. The rain is coming harder now, the drumbeat a constant, dangerous thrumming, and it seems inevitable that at any moment the glass will break, will not be able to stand much more of this onslaught. But then, like with all things, there is a crescendo and then an ebbing, and what was once violent turns to an easy rhythm.

'You know I love you? Right?'

I nod. Then realise that he cannot see me. 'Yes.'

'And . . . you know that I would never—'

'I know.' I cut him off. The rain has eased now, and I fight the urge to stand, look out of the window. Because it seems absurd that something that has created so much tumult should simply vanish. 'We should get some sleep.'

He leans over. Kisses my cheek. Turns and settles on his side, his breathing gradually softening, lengthening.

I lie awake, staring into the darkness.

Case No. 38
Victim: Aria Theaks
Location: San Cristobal, Venezuela
Company: United Oil
2 February 2008

Initial event

At 5.30 p.m. on Tuesday 2 October, a young woman in a maid's uniform knocked on the door of Jessica and Connor Theaks. Mr Theaks is a UK national, employed by United Oil and based out of San Cristobal, Venezuela. He and his wife lived there in a home funded by United Oil, with their six-month-old daughter, Aria.

Mrs Theaks opened the door to the young woman. She does not remember anything after that. Mr Theaks claims to remember coming downstairs and seeing an unknown woman in a maid's uniform in the lobby of their home. He has no subsequent memories.

Examination of CCTV footage installed inside the downstairs lobby of the Theaks home allowed us to fill in the blanks. The footage shows Mrs Theaks opening the front door to a young Hispanic woman – approximately five feet five inches, shoulder-length black hair, slender, aged between twenty and twenty-five. It shows the woman blowing what appears to be a powder into Mrs Theaks's face. Mrs Theaks then recoils, and is guided back inside the house by the young woman. The footage further shows Mr Theaks coming down the main staircase of the house, looking to his wife. The young woman then blows powder into the face of Mr Theaks.

Subsequent testing confirmed that this powder was scopolamine (devil's breath).

CCTV footage then shows the Theakses standing passively in the lobby. The young woman appears to say something to Mr Theaks, who leaves, returning with a wad of money. He hands the money to the young woman and she places it inside her handbag.

Later examination showed that almost $5,000 in cash was removed from the house.

The young woman walks past the Theakses, out of camera view, returning holding their daughter, Aria Theaks. By all appearances, she is asleep, wrapped in a blanket. The young woman proceeds to walk calmly out of the house, leaving the Theakses standing in the lobby.

No attempt is made to stop her.

Upon regaining awareness, the Theakses realised that their daughter had been kidnapped and, as per their training and instruction, immediately placed a call to the headquarters of United Oil. A call was made to the Cole Group shortly thereafter.

Response
Initial contact with the operative of United Oil, and then with the Theakses, was made by Orla Britten, who served as a constant point of contact as the response team was assembled. The response team in

this case was made up of myself (Ed Cole), Selena Cole and Beck Chambers. This would be Beck Chambers' first case with the Cole Group, although he already had some considerable personal experience within the field of kidnap and ransom.

The team arrived in San Cristobal within twenty-four hours of the kidnap taking place. Upon arrival, we immediately attended the home of Mr and Mrs Theaks, who were, understandably, deeply distraught. They had independently viewed the CCTV footage, which had troubled them greatly.

The initial call from the kidnappers came in within minutes of our arrival at the home. The request was for £1 million in ransom.

The parents, whilst unable to raise such a considerable amount themselves, were very keen that the money be paid immediately, and a number of calls were made to the insurance company to this end. I explained to Mr and Mrs Theaks that any ransom paid would have to first be raised by themselves and only then refunded by the insurance provider, and advised them of the protocol in such cases, ergo the negotiation of the settlement in order to secure the release of their child.

The Theakses were somewhat sceptical of this policy.

I began negotiation with the kidnappers almost immediately, requesting an immediate proof of life before their demands would be considered. Selena Cole served as the interface with United Oil and with Rombok Insurance, United Oil's insurer. Beck Chambers took it upon himself to support the Theakses. He was very skilfully able to convey to them the importance of trusting the protocols we had in place and allowing us to do our job to secure the release of their daughter.

I believe that both Mr and Mrs Theaks were tremendously comforted by his presence and reassured by his calm and supportive manner.

After some hours, a proof of life was delivered in the form of a phone call. A baby could be heard gurgling in the background. Mrs Theaks immediately became hysterical, desperate to reclaim her child. Whilst Beck supported her, Mr Theaks was asked to confirm that the sounds heard were those of his daughter. He was unable to definitively do so.

I pressed for a more concrete proof of life but was unsuccessful in my efforts.

We continued with the negotiation, mindful that the proof of life was less than conclusive.

After three days of negotiations, a figure was reached that was acceptable to all parties. This figure was £15,000. The money was to be left in a dead drop, in a bin in a park in the centre of San Cristobal.

Beck Chambers volunteered himself for this role, extremely keen to bring this kidnap to a close and return Aria safely to her parents. It was noted that, due to the presence of scopolamine in the initial crime, the drop would be a high-risk approach and represented no small degree of danger to Mr Chambers himself.

The drop was successful.

Within an hour, a call had been received from the kidnappers informing us that Aria Theaks had been left at the rear of a local hospital. Myself and Mr Chambers attended the scene. We opted not to inform the Theakses of the drop and the exchange, as we were still extremely aware of the inadequacy of the proof of life and were unsure as to what condition the child would be in when we found her. Selena Cole remained with the couple in order to support them.

We attended the local hospital and found a cardboard box in the location described.

Mr Chambers immediately approached the box and, upon opening it, revealed Aria Theaks in the same blanket in which she had been kidnapped, sleeping peacefully.

Immediate medical advice was sought and the baby was given a clean bill of health.

Aria Theaks was then quickly reunited with her parents, much to their enormous relief and gratitude.

Selena Cole established a support system for the Theakses before our departure from San Cristobal. The family will be receiving post-trauma counselling via a colleague of Dr Cole's. Follow-ups to be undertaken by Dr Cole.

The breath of the devil

I walk slowly along the corridor. The major incident room sounds like the distant buzzing of bees, and I think of long hot summers on the Cornish coast, in my grandmother's garden, the brightly coloured flowers speckled with yellow and black forms, darting and dancing. It is a soporific sound, and yet I am tense, wired, so that I feel more awake now than I have felt in days.

I lay awake last night long after Alex's breathing had shifted into a soft, steady rhythm. I lay beside him, watching my fingers, my palm splayed flat on the mattress. He was so close to me, the tip of my little finger an inch, perhaps less, from the base of his spine. Yet I couldn't touch him. Incredible, really, how it works. I lay there and willed my fingers to move, to inch closer, make contact, but it seemed they were glued to the bed, that no will of mine was great enough to move them so that I could touch my husband.

He had left that night, the hot pasta still a wilting puddle on the kitchen floor. I had listened to his slow, defeated footsteps on the loose gravel drive. In my head, I knew where he had gone. He had gone to her, to this invisible

154

other who had blown our lives apart. In my head it was clean, this vivisection of our marriage, a straight choice, her, me. And why would he pick me? With my failing ovaries, and my arms sore with the pinpricks of IVF injections, and my ever-growing sadness? I had sat on the kitchen floor, had almost laughed. I would pick her over me too.

I found out later that he hadn't gone there, to his other woman. That he had gone to his mother's. That she had yelled at him long into the night, early into the morning. But still she let him stay. Perhaps she thought, as I did, that if she turned him away, he would have little choice but to return to the scene of the crime, and then it would be truly done.

I don't remember how long I sat there on that cold tiled floor. I remember that at some point I dragged myself into the living room and curled up in the armchair; it was too small to even consider sleeping in, but I needed its cold leather arms to cradle me as I cried myself to sleep. I remember calling in sick the next day, and the one after that.

It may have been days, or maybe it was weeks, I don't know. I don't like to think about it now. All I know is that he showed up at my door looking thinner, sadder, older. Can I take you to dinner? I always wondered, as the years passed and the wound began to knot over, criss-crossed by jagged weakened skin, if, when he stood at the door, behind him stood the spectre of his mother, hand raised to clout him should he fail. I do remember that she said to me, after, when it was all done and life had shifted again and I was swollen up with babies, 'You know that you are my child too, don't you?' She didn't look at me as she spoke, carried on briskly sorting Babygros into two piles, tiny baby, newborn. 'As much as Alex is my son, you are my daughter. Just remember that.'

I don't know why I said yes to that dinner. Maybe it was that I was lonely, maybe it was that I wanted to forget. And I still loved him, of course. But that's not always enough, is it? Not to explain, not to make a marriage survive.

But anyway, why seems irrelevant now. The fact is, I did say yes, and so we began anew, meeting each other as for the first time. And sometimes I would forget. We would be laughing and I would feel a flush of the old love, the ignorant love, and then it would hit me again, this recollection, and Alex would slip, sliding from his pedestal on to the cold hard ground. And I would see it in him, that he recognised it, knew what I was thinking. How hard it must be to be a fallen hero.

Then came the stomach that just wouldn't sit right, and two thin blue lines and the future that we were once so desperate for. I cried, we cried, happy, sad, who the hell knew? Because we were getting our castle, the one of our dreams. Only we both knew that the foundations were now built on shifting sand.

Alex moved back in. He had decorated the nursery inside of a month.

I pause at the door to the major incident room, listen to the flurry of voices, will them to wash my thoughts clean.

I push hard at the door.

No one looks up. We are in hour 18 of the custody clock. Beck Chambers has been held for eighteen hours. In another six, we will have to apply to magistrates for an extension. The work is frantic. You can see it in the tight expressions, the hard-edged voices. There is much to be done and limited time in which to do it.

I walk calmly towards my desk, try to look every inch the detective embroiled in a murder case.

But two words chase each other around my head. Devil's breath. Shimmy the mouse and pull up the Google page. Glance quickly over my shoulder. Type the words.

The world's most dangerous drug.

I purse my lips at the hyperbole, scroll down. Click on a link. It is scopolamine. It's used to treat motion sickness. It comes from the borrachero tree. South America.

It can be ground into a powder, is odourless, tasteless, and when it is blown into a victim's face, it will leave them lucid, coherent and yet entirely without free will.

My stomach flips.

I scroll down.

It produces a zombie-like state in which the victim is completely under the perpetrator's control. There are cases, many, many of them. People have been led into banks, have emptied out their life savings and handed them over to total strangers, all without any awareness of what they have done. Women have been drugged with it, gang-raped. Parents have had their children stolen out from beneath them.

There is a newspaper report. A chubby, smiling baby. My insides tighten further. Six-month-old Aria Theaks, kidnapped in San Cristobal, Venezuela, after her British parents were dosed with devil's breath.

I stare at the photo, her rounded cheeks, Cupid's bow lips.

Could this be it? Could this be what happened to Selena? Aria Theaks was rescued, eventually, a ransom negotiated.

Was found abandoned outside a hospital by a security operative, ex-military.

Why would someone do this to Selena? *Who* could do this to Selena? You'd have to have access to the drug for a start, experience of how it works.

And then the biggest question still remains. Even if this is it, even if Selena was drugged, dosed with devil's breath, what the hell happened to her during those missing hours?

I pick up the phone, dial quickly.

'Drug squad, Steve Linden.'

'Steve, it's Leah.'

'All right, Lee. How's it going? How're the kids?'

I like Steve, my tutor when I first joined. A large man with a large laugh, four children and a deeply twisted sense of humour. 'They're good. Trouble, but good. How's it going down there in Drugs R Us?'

'Ah, you know us, Lee. Keeping the world safe, one joint at a time.'

'Steve, I need to ask you about something. You heard of a drug called devil's breath?'

'Um . . . devil's breath. Yeah. Nasty stuff. Scopolamine base. Coming out of Colombia. You know,' he says, 'it's funny you should ask. One of our test purchasers came home with a couple of pills last week. Said the dealer was calling it El Diablo. Essentially a tidied-up version of devil's breath. It's been a thing in South America for a while now, but this is the first time we've seen it here. It'll catch on fast, though. Nothing junkies love more than a new high.'

'El Diablo? What can you tell me about it?'

'We've had a look at it. From what we're seeing, it's a manufactured drug, same basic components as devil's breath but they've ironed out some of the nastier side effects, made it a bit more fun for all the family. Causes some pretty intense hallucinations. Also has some of the depressant qualities you get with heroin, morphine, that kind of thing. The US authorities think it's coming from one of the drug groups in the Darién Gap in Colombia. Like I said, we haven't seen much of it as yet, but give it time. California, especially San Diego, is having a bit of a nightmare with it at the moment.'

'Okay. That's . . . thanks, Steve.'

'Any time. You kiss those babies of yours for me, okay?'

I grin, hang up the phone and stare at the screen. El Diablo. The devil.

'Hey, how's it going?' Oliver appears, as if from nowhere, before the phone even hits the cradle.

I quickly shrink the search engine on my screen. 'Oh, you know. Fine. Tired. You?'

'I'm good.' He's watching me intently, and I flush, thinking of a night, what, three years ago now, just barely pre-pregnancy, a Christmas night out in a fancy restaurant, the table slowly descending into alcoholic anarchy. Oliver leaning in, his voice almost vanishing into the sounds of drunken singing, the damp of his breath on my cheek. Why don't you get shot of that Alex? You know I'd treat you the way you deserve to be treated. The feel of his hand on my bare knee.

I blush, look away.

'Your brother still crowing over his big arrest?'

I glance up at him, feel my hackles begin to rise. 'Finn's doing his job. Perhaps you should try it some time.'

Oliver watches me, looks like he is about to say something and then thinks better of it. Good. I've heard enough.

I pull up Beck Chambers' record, trying to look busy, focus on the screen and wait as Oliver slinks away.

There is a photograph on his file. I study it. You could call him handsome: pronounced cheekbones, dark eyes. If this was anything other than very clearly a mugshot, you would say he was handsome. But the look in his eyes holds you back from that. It is fatigued, beaten, his chin sunk almost to his chest.

I scroll down through his criminal history. It is not insignificant. Assault, drunk and disorderly, driving under the influence, another assault. All alcohol-related. All the result of a quick temper, too-fast reflexes.

I study it for a moment, feeling something tickle at me.

Look back over the arrest record again.

It happens in pools. There are a handful of incidents, around five years ago. The first assault, a drunken brawl in a Hereford pub. Couple of minor irritants after that. Before that, however, there is nothing. Not even a parking ticket.

Then there is a hole, a gap of three years in which Beck Chambers either decided to walk the straight and narrow path, or got way better at not getting caught being windy and wide. Then the same again, arrests for drunk and disorderly, a DUI.

What the hell happened in this man's life five years ago? What changed? And what changed it back?

'Hey, Oliver? Do you know this guy?'

'Beck Chambers? Well, I've dealt with him a couple of times. I wouldn't say we're close personal friends.' Oliver pulls his chair closer to mine, peering over my shoulder at the screen. He smells of shampoo and cigarettes. 'Why?'

'I was just wondering – do you know what his background is? Where he came from?'

He shrugs, the motion of his shoulder jostling me. I nudge my chair slightly further away.

'He's ex-military, I think. I remember Dominic Newell saying something, mentioned Afghanistan. Chambers never told me so himself. The strong, silent type, if you know what I mean. I got the impression he might have been special forces, the way Dominic was talking.'

'Did he get dishonourably discharged?'

'Ah . . .' He frowns heavily. 'I don't think so . . . No, wait, I'm sure there was some talk of an injury. Did he get shot or something? I'm sure he spent time in Derriford.'

I think of what that would mean. A strong man, a soldier, an injury that takes him out of battle, brings him home where nobody quite understands, where no one really gets it. So he turns to drink, because it mutes the pain, dulls it, so that it becomes manageable.

I get it. I understand.

I think of the responses that he has been trained for, the violence he has been taught. How the alcohol will work, dulling the inhibitions as it dulls the pain, so that you are running on a hair trigger and all it will take is one word and then that violence that served you so well for so long is suddenly unleashed, unbridled and uncontrollable.

'So . . .' says Oliver, and I start. I had almost forgotten that he was there. 'How are things? With Alex?'

My heart thrums a little faster and it seems that I can once again feel his hand upon my knee. I force a bright smile. 'Good. The twins keep us busy, as you can imagine, but really good, thanks.' I try to pretend that this is all he is asking, that there is no undertone, nothing deeper than the words themselves.

'Well I'm glad, Leah. I'm really glad.'

I nod, moving my cursor across the screen and trying to focus on the arrow, blot out his voice. But it just will not stop coming.

'I mean, I'll be honest. I thought for a while there that you weren't going to make it.'

I pull up Google. Watch as balloons float across the screen. Wonder why they are there. Is there a balloon day? Maybe there is, because that would explain it. The girls like balloons.

'Anyway. I'll leave you to it.' He moves away, more slowly than he needs to, and it occurs to me that he is waiting for me to stop him, to confide all in him. But I won't do that.

I nod, smile although my jaw aches with the effort of it. Type in the words 'Beck Chambers', 'military'.

I do not know what I am expecting the search to bring. In truth, it was little more than a distraction device, a high-tech something shiny. But results flood my screen, news articles, reports, and I frown, thinking that the distraction device has actually worked.

I click on the first link.

British hostage freed

British hostage Beck Chambers has been freed from his prolonged captivity. Taken by a criminal group operating out of Mexico City while working as a security operative, ex-Pathfinder Platoon hero Chambers had been held for five months with little hope of release. It is believed that the criminals holding Chambers were part of a major operation running kidnap-for-ransom attacks throughout Mexico. Chambers was finally released earlier today after extensive negotiations with his captors. He is believed to be in reasonable physical health.

I stare at the screen. I do a swift mental calculation. Five years ago. This was what happened to Beck Chambers five years ago. This is why his entire life fell apart.

I am trying to concentrate, trying to focus my attention on Dominic Newell's murder, I really am. Because Dominic was a good man, and he deserved that, to have my full and undivided attention. But it is there, and I cannot ignore it. That in ten years in the police force I have never come across the world of kidnap for ransom, and yet here it is twice.

There is something there, something right in front of me that I'm not seeing. What is it?

I pull up the record of Beck's first arrest in the current batch, after his three years of good behaviour. Search the file.

And there it is.

Employer: the Cole Group.

The trouble with a closed case

DS Finn Hale: Thursday, 9.15 a.m.

I push open the door to the major incident room. Beck Chambers, it seems, passed a comfortable night in the cells without providing too much trouble for anyone. I looked in on him on my way in, found him lying on his bed, staring up at the ceiling. There's something about this man. Whenever I am around him, it is like I am back in the furious desert, a heartbeat from death. It is, I think, that thousand-yard stare of his. You see a lot of that when you are in a war. Men and women simply waiting for their number to be called, already resigned to their own death. I look at Beck and I see a battle. I wonder if he has ever left the war zone, in his head at least.

It is busy in the major incident room as the custody clock winds its way down. And at the end of it, that phone call, the CPS saying 'charge him'. And then a new battle will begin for Beck Chambers.

'All right, Sarge?' Christa grins at me. 'Heard the Chambers interview went well. Nice one.'

I shrug. 'Well,' I say, shooting for modesty, 'I mean, he didn't confess. But give me time.'

I try to push back the wave of guilt that is riding just

behind my success. Do I believe that he did it? Beck is a force of nature, there is no doubt about that. A walking bundle of anger. Dominic was on his way to see him, wasn't seen alive again. And yet . . .

Leah is at her desk, is staring at the screen, her top teeth worrying at her lower lip. Something is preying on her mind. She could never play poker.

'You okay?' I ask.

She looks up, a brief smile. 'Yeah.' Waves to the monitor. 'I'm just starting to plough through Dominic's e-mails. Although,' she flips back to the inbox, 'I may be here a while. Guy liked to mail.'

The teeth again, sawing into her lower lip, like they will hack it free.

'What?'

'What?'

'You're worrying about something.'

Leah looks up at me, snorts.

'Okay, you're worrying about something specific right at this moment.'

She turns away, focuses on the screen. 'It's nothing.'

'Seriously. Come on.'

'Are you sure?' she says.

'Yes,' I say. 'Tell me.'

'No. I mean, are you sure? That it was Beck Chambers?'

I wasn't expecting that. And yet I should have expected that. My sister has always had the uncanny ability to see right through the front I put up and get to the secrets behind it. I pull a chair up, sink into it. Sigh. 'I don't know, Lee. The SIO is pretty clear where he stands on it. And Chambers has got form, an alcohol problem . . . I don't know.' I study her. 'What's making you doubt it?'

She frowns a little, a glance at me, quick, assessing, then back to her monitor. 'I don't know. I've been doing some research on him. You know he's ex-military, right?' She pulls up a forum page dedicated to service personnel, points to a post. 'Pathfinder Platoon.'

I nod. 'I know. They're a reconnaissance unit in the British army. Not special forces, but their training is pretty much on a par with it. Beck served in Afghanistan. He was in Musa Qala, this huge battle against the Taliban. They . . . It was a tough op. Incredibly so.'

'It's weird,' she says. 'I just can't make it gel. The idea of this guy' – she gestures at the monitor – 'being the same guy who stabbed Dominic in the neck. It just . . . it doesn't seem to fit together.'

I know my sister. She's not done. I can see her arguing internally, and I sit, wait. It happens like this, as she rolls the thoughts over in her head, has all the arguments already so you don't have to. Then she says, 'Okay, and there's this.'

Moves the mouse. A new screen. An eagle crest.

The Cole Group.

'He worked for them.'

I study the screen, a dislocating sense of déjà vu. Struggle to place the name.

'Hey. Dom's work desk. He had a brochure from the Cole Group. I wondered why. This must be it. Because they were Chambers' employers.'

Leah nods, looking at me, eyebrow raised, waits for me to get it.

'What?'

'The Cole Group. It's run by Selena Cole. Or was run. Or was started by. I'm unclear at the moment.'

'Who?'

She gives me a long-suffering look. 'Selena Cole. The woman who vanished. My missing person case?'

I nod. Slowly. Have no idea what the hell I am supposed to make of this.

'So you think . . .?'

Leah sighs stormily. 'I have no idea what I think. What do *you* think?'

I shrug. 'Hell, I'm just happy I'm keeping up with this conversation.'

She rolls her eyes, clicks off the screen, back to e-mail, continues to scroll through. I watch her, her forehead furrowed.

'Bollocks.' She says it loud enough that it startles me.

'What?'

'Look at this!'

From: DNewell@HartleyNewell.co.uk
To: coyote@messagemail.net

Hey you,

Wow, this is weird. I don't know what to say to you.

I can't believe this. I can't believe that what happened happened. I'm sorry, does that sound bad? I don't mean it to, but I guess the thing is, I never thought of myself as the cheating type. I hate that word. Is that what I am now? A cheater?

I need to tell you, I've never done this before. I know that sounds clichéd, but it's true. I've never cheated, not once. Not on anyone. I never thought I could. I know that doesn't make what I've done any better, but somehow I'm using it to, I don't know, justify things.

Maybe it's because it's you. I mean, there's so much history with us. When we were together, it was so good. I know it didn't end well, but then what relationship does end well? You were so important to me. I don't think you realised quite how important. Not back then. Maybe that was my fault. Maybe I should have made it clearer how I felt about you when it could still have made a difference.

Getting over you nearly killed me. I don't mean to be dramatic, but it's true. It took me such a long time to get to a point where I could feel about someone the way I felt about you. I dated, obviously. But it was never the same. I just kept replaying how things went between us, over and over again. I don't know why. It's not like I could change any of it.

If I wasn't clear then, let me be clear now. You were everything to me. I loved you more than I can possibly say.

Sometimes I regret what I did. Ending it, I mean. It was all so complicated, so confused. I didn't handle it well, I know that now. But I wanted you to be happy. I needed you to be happy. And at the time, it seemed to me that you would be happier without me and all my baggage. I came to regret that decision.

But the truth is, that was all a very long time ago.

We have both moved on. We have both met other people, built lives of our own.

I know you're not going to want to hear this, and to be honest, I feel like a prick saying it after what I have done, but I love Isaac. He means the world to me. As much as you once did. We have built a life that works and we are happy.

I don't know what to do next.

I need some time. I need to figure out where I go from

here. I know that's not what you want to hear, but please, be patient with me.

I do love you.

D

I let my eye trail down the e-mail. 'Holy hell. Dominic was cheating.'

'Yes, he was,' says Leah distantly.

'Maybe,' I say, trying to push us back on track again, 'maybe he was seeing Chambers. Everyone said they seemed really close. Like, not client–solicitor close, but you know, close. It would certainly add another layer of motive.'

She frowns. 'Is Beck Chambers gay?'

'I don't know!' I whine. 'Crap!'

Leah taps her fingernails on the desk. 'Or . . .'

'What?'

'Or Isaac found out.'

'Finn?' The SIO's voice rings through the room, and I feel rather than see all heads swivel towards me. 'A word?'

I stand up, try to keep my shoulders back, but there's something about a summons to see the boss that makes you small, a schoolboy in trouble. His office is tucked away at the back of the major incident room, pretty modest, seriously impersonal. He waves me to a seat. Perches on the edge of the desk. He's a big man, must be six foot five if he's an inch, with a shock of steel-grey hair, a rough-cut beard. Essentially Tom Selleck on a bad day. He gives me a look. I'm pretty sure it's supposed to be sympathy.

'We're releasing Beck Chambers.'

I stare at him, at a loss for words.

He waves at the phone on his desk. 'I just got a call from the DI down on the surveillance team. Turns out they were running an op on Monday evening, surveilling a known dealer in the centre of Hereford.'

'Okay?'

'They picked up Chambers making a purchase. Seven o'clock.' He's watching me, lips compressed. 'They had eyes on him for most of the evening. Apparently he had a couple of drinks in a couple of bars. Crossed back and forth over their operational area. He's covered. Right up until about midnight. He's not our guy.'

A Hero, Then a Hostage

Oliver Lewis

(Originally published in *USA Today*)

It was gone eight, night falling fast across the glittering slums of Mexico City. A warm night, a storm approaching in clambering clouds that filled up the bowl of the valley, the volcanic peaks that ring the city vanishing into the ominous grey.

Beck Chambers was returning to his apartment, a perfunctory affair suited to a single man with a nomadic way of life. If you saw Beck, you would think that few people would be safer, even in a hotbed of violence like the Mexican capital. He was, after all, ex-military, a former member of the Pathfinder Platoon, 16 Air Assault Brigade, special forces in all but name. And he looked it, built like a slab of rock; looked like he could take care of himself, that he would be the last person you would cross.

But this was Mexico City, where the rules do not apply.

At 8.06 p.m., Beck returned to his apartment in the Alameda district, tired from a long day, bracing for another long day to come. As a security operative (a bodyguard, for those not in the know), he was at his client's constant command. This night, the night of 13 July, was an early one.

He was used to being kept far later. The irony of this would return to him many times in the months ahead.

He opened the front door of his apartment building and vanished inside.

Twenty-four hours later, Beck's client placed a call to Beck's employer. My bodyguard didn't show up to work today.

The violence and danger that lace countries like Mexico have become a gift for the security industry. Myriad companies operate throughout Latin America, protecting the wealthy from their lesser brethren. In 2010, Hector Security was just one of many; small, enjoying a limited success within its zones of operation. Started by a former US Army Ranger, Hector Security had a reputation for being cheaper than most, a no-nonsense approach. Sometimes, when you talk to people in the know, the words 'cowboy operation' will be used.

So that day, 14 July 2010, a phone call was received at the headquarters of Hector Security in Galveston, Texas. Your man didn't show. In a different operation, with different standards, this might have meant something. But Hector Security was used to this sort of thing, its operatives dropping in and out of employment. Sometimes there were psychological struggles – most of its employees were ex-military, most of them had seen action, most of them had scars. Sometimes it was alcohol or drugs. Whatever. The firm barely batted an eyelid. An apology, a quick scout around, and within two days a new security operative had taken over where Beck Chambers had left off.

And Beck remained simply gone.

It shouldn't be that easy to disappear. The human in us rails against that, that we should be able to just vanish without leaving as much as a ripple. And yet why not? Beck had no family. A nomadic lifestyle that left friendships as tenuous affairs.

It took two months for the repercussions of that night to hit full force. One lunchtime in September, a phone call was made to Hector Security HQ. We have your man. You're going to have to pay to get him back.

The first question they asked was 'Which man?'

Later examination of CCTV footage would reveal that on the night of 13 July, Beck Chambers had walked into his apartment building and was immediately attacked, incapacitated by a blow to the head, crumpling to the ground. If you watch the grainy footage, you then see a second attacker moving into camera shot, checking Beck, presumably to ensure that he is unconscious and not dead, then quickly making a call on a mobile phone.

There is no sound on the footage, but by that point, you really don't need it.

This is Mexico, one of the world's front-runners in the kidnap-for-ransom business. And they have just acquired a new commodity.

It takes a minute, a minute and a half at the most. Then the men look out of the front door, hurriedly drag Mr Chambers on to the street. It is small satisfaction that the task appears to be a struggle.

It turned out that as many as a dozen people saw Beck being loaded into the waiting van by masked men.

The Federales were not called.

No witness recorded the registration plates of the van or could describe the attackers.

There are procedures in a case like this. Kidnap and ransom is a steady-stream business, especially when you operate out of some of the world's most dangerous countries, and so firms take precautions. They insure themselves against kidnap, they ally themselves with K&R consultants, and, should the worst happen, they pull the trigger, bring in the big boys, the ones who know how to put right a bad situation.

Most firms.

Not Hector Security. It is unclear exactly why they didn't simply place a call to their insurers, get help, the backing that would ensure a smoother ride. Some speculate that they had let their insurance lapse, that these cowboys were riding bareback, risking the lives of their employees to save a few dollars.

Whatever the reason, the call was never placed and Hector Security decided to handle things themselves.

Negotiations did not go well.

An attempt was made to bring the purportedly high ransom demand down, but the negotiator for Hector Security only succeeded in infuriating the kidnappers. Instead of securing a proof of life, video footage was delivered of Beck Chambers apparently having his throat slit.

This was then followed by a month of silence.

The security industry is an incestuous one. Everyone knows everyone and there are few real secrets. When word of the situation trickled through to the Cole Group, a boutique K&R firm operating out of the UK, one of its founding members decided to intervene.

Call it a goodwill gesture. Call it an attempt to right the wrongs of a failing fellow company. Whatever the motivation was, Ed Cole, after much discussion in-house, flew to Mexico City.

At this point, Beck had been in captivity for two and a half months. His location was unknown, his condition was unknown, his captors were unknown. Ed Cole remained unfazed. He knew the area, knew the people, even knew the criminals who operated there. He got a message through to the kidnappers, informing them that there was a new sheriff in town.

Ten days after his arrival, contact was finally made. It was a rough road ahead. The previous failed negotiations had left a bad taste in their wake and the kidnappers were jumpy.

Kidnap for ransom happens all across Mexico, and its perpetrators are widespread and varied. But as luck would have it, the Coles had dealt with this group before. Unlike many of the groups operating in the region, they appeared to have made it a policy to target foreign victims, presumably in the hope of amassing a higher payment.

A request was immediately made for proof of life. No word had been heard from Beck in over a month. No one knew if he was dead or alive. Would there even be a hostage to negotiate for?

At 3 p.m. on 25 October, Ed Cole received a phone call. On the other end was an exhausted, hollowed-out Beck Chambers.

He had at that point been held captive for three months, one week and five days. As far as he knew, the world had forgotten about him.

He wept when he heard Ed Cole's voice.

I'm bringing you home, Ed told him. It's nearly over.

The new ransom requested was even higher than the one before, the kidnappers irritated by their dealings with Hector Security.

Ed Cole expressed to the kidnappers that there was no insurance in place and that any ransom would be a scrabbled-together affair made up of the generosity of friends.

What the final settlement was remains a mystery. You do not talk about the figures paid in the K&R industry. It's bad policy, giving other kidnappers a benchmark for future ransoms.

But after almost four months in captivity, Beck was released, handed over to the waiting Ed Cole.

You would think this would be an unusual affair. That things like this do not happen as a matter of course. The fact remains that throughout Latin America, and in fact the wider developing world, there are dozens, if not hundreds of innocents being held captive, waiting for their own Ed Cole to come and rescue them.

Would that they were all so lucky.

A question of what is important

DC Leah Mackay: Thursday, 9.25 a.m.

'Well that's that then.'

I don't look up at Oliver. I'm still reading about Beck Chambers, justifying it by telling myself he's the prime suspect in the murder of Dominic Newell, that it is nothing, nothing at all, to do with the fact that he was employed by the Cole Group. I keep my head down, in the hope that Oliver is talking to someone else, that if I do not look at him then he will slink away, back under the rock he crawled from.

I am, unfortunately, not that lucky.

'You heard, right?' He comes over to stand next to me, closer than I want him to. 'Surveillance team have Beck in Hereford at the time of the murder.'

I can hear the smile in his voice, although he is trying to fight it.

'Looks like Finn backed the wrong horse.'

I glance up at him, smile. 'Ol? Shut the hell up, okay?'

I grab my phone, push myself away from my desk. I should look for my brother. Check that he is okay. But, I tell myself, he's a big boy. He won't appreciate me attempting to mother him. And there's something else. Beck has been ruled out as the murderer. Surveillance has placed him in Hereford.

Hereford. Ten miles from the Cole home.

Because it's undeniable that there is a link between Beck Chambers and Selena Cole. They worked for the same firm. He worked in Mexico. If it was scopolamine, if that's what happened to Selena, Beck could have had knowledge of it, from his time there. He could have had access to it.

I walk with quick strides towards the door, slip into the empty hallway.

They are tied somehow, these two cases. A vanishing and a death. And Beck, somehow Beck is involved in it. Not the killing, perhaps. Maybe instead the vanishing.

I run down the stairs, feeling a strain in my quads. Think that I cannot remember the last time I trained, that I used to be fit. That I should do that. Should slip on my trainers, go for a run. I'd like that.

I push my way out on to the street. It is a grey day. Another grey day. Has there ever been another kind? I slip past the door of the police station, the bright lights of its lobby glowing in the dimness. Wish that I had thought to bring a coat. It is cold, the wind has teeth in it, and I shiver hard. Scroll through my contacts list.

Orla's number is still on my phone from an early-morning call, the one that woke me from a barely-there sleep, telling me that Selena Cole had been found.

My finger hovers over it as the cold nips at me.

I could just call Selena. She is, after all, found now. I could call her, ask her the questions that I have lined up for Orla. But I press Orla's number, tell myself that it is because we have a relationship, that we have built up a trust, that it will be easier. Yet that's not the truth, is it? The truth is that Selena Cole still seems barely real to me. The person she is, the things she has done. She feels like someone on a screen, in the pages of a book, not a person, not really. I listen to the ringtone. Am I afraid of Selena Cole? I shiver, push that thought away. No. I'm not afraid. Am I lying to myself? Maybe. Or is it that icons are harder to keep when they are up close, personal? That it is easier not to see the flaws when they are further away.

I listen to the ringtone, wait as it connects.

'Hello?'

'Orla? It's Leah. Leah Mackay.'

There is a hefty pause. 'Oh. I . . . Hi.'

'How are you all?'

'We're fine.' The words have edges. 'Everything's fine. Settling back down. Look,' she says, 'I appreciate you getting in touch. But really, it isn't necessary.'

I wonder if this is the same person, the one who was so grateful for my presence such a short time ago. The wind has changed, is blowing from a different direction now. I'm not the saviour any more. Now I am a nuisance. Or am I a threat?

'No,' I say, 'it's not that.'

'Oh?'

'Your husband, Seth . . .'

'What about him?' There is so much hardness in her voice; I am an invader attempting to batter down her defences. Why? There are secrets here, a treasure worth defending. But then what marriage does not have secrets buried at the heart of it?

'No, nothing, it's just that he mentioned something, about Selena. A drug. Something common in South America.'

179

She settles into a quietness, so that all I can hear is the sound of the traffic, the low thrum that tells me the phone is still alive, that she hasn't hung up on me. Not yet, anyway.

Then, 'Devil's breath.'

'Yes.' I wait for more. Know that I should hold my tongue. And yet . . . 'I mean, it would explain the memory loss.'

'Yes,' Orla says. 'It would.'

She subsides into silence again, and I think that she is done, that this is all she will say. But then she sighs.

'The Cole Group dealt with a case, in San Cristobal. A baby, kidnapped.'

'Aria Theaks.'

'Aria Theaks,' she agrees.

I line my words up, inspect them before allowing them out. 'If it was scopolamine, if that is what happened to Selena, then someone gave it to her. Someone did this.'

'Yes.'

'Orla, I've asked you this before. But I'm going to ask you again. Does Selena have any enemies?'

'No . . .'

'Orla.' I hear my own voice hardening up. 'If someone has done this, if someone took Selena, they could come back. We don't know what they wanted, we don't know if they got it. They may come back. And' – I feel a spurt of cold, hard genius – 'we need to think about the girls. If whoever did this cannot get Selena, it's reasonable to assume that they would consider her children to be viable targets.'

I hear her swallow, know that I have won.

'You don't think . . .' I can hear the fear now, thickening her voice. 'You think they could be in danger?'

Got you.

'We need answers, Orla. If we're going to keep them safe.' I turn my back to the wind, the traffic, feel oddly warmer now. 'I need to ask you about Beck Chambers.'

'Okay.' For a moment, I think she will give me trouble, but no. 'Beck used to work for us. For the Cole Group, that is.'

'And?'

Orla sighs weightily. 'He was one of Ed's. Hostage, no insurance, not much money. An excellent way of getting yourself killed in Mexico. Ed took pity on them, the family. He was like that, my brother. Got it all handled free of charge.' She gives a breath, a sigh or a snort, I'm not sure. 'He even threw in some of the ransom money, if you can believe that.'

I listen, straining out the growling of engines. There's something here, a back door into a secret.

'That must have been tough. On the firm, I mean. Quite a financial burden to carry.'

'It really was. I mean, obviously it's their firm, Ed and Selena's, so they can do what they see fit. But the thing is, Seth and I, we were invested too. Not financially, we didn't have the money for that, but it was our livelihood too. If the group had gone under, we'd have been stuffed. Seth especially. I mean, me, I could do accounts anywhere, but K&R is a tough business, it's secretive, competitive, and Seth, he's got no education, not to speak of. He came right out of foster care and into the military. He always jokes that it was the military or prison. The Cole Group, this job, it's everything to him. If it were to collapse . . . I just don't know what he'd do.'

I make a soft noise, agreeing. We are nowhere near where we're supposed to be. But that's the thing with investigating:

sometimes you just have to let people talk, even if it seems irrelevant, because you don't know what is going to matter until you get to the end of the story.

'So . . . What was I . . .' Orla is floundering, has realised that she is taking me on a walk in the woods. 'Beck, sorry. Yeah. He was one of our rescues. He fell apart afterwards. Drinking. Drugs. You know the drill.' It is a statement of fact, distaste clouding the words. 'Ed and Selena, they did their knight-in-shining-armour thing. The way they do. Selena sorted out rehab, got counselling for him. Once he was clean, Ed gave him a job.'

'You weren't happy about that?'

'To be honest, Seth and I thought he was a loose cannon. It just seemed . . . unwise. But, anyway, he was okay, did his job more or less. Until Ed . . .'

'What do you mean?'

'He was cut up about it, my brother's death. Like we weren't. And the thing is, he hadn't known him that long, so I don't know why . . . Anyway, he came into work drunk, and that was it.'

'You fired him?'

'Seth did.'

'How did he react?'

Another silence. 'He wasn't happy.'

'Go on.'

'He grabbed hold of Seth. He's a big guy. I thought he was going to kill him.'

'And?'

'And nothing. He just kind of shoved him, walked out. To be honest, I'm glad. We're better off without him.'

'What about Selena?'

'What about her?'

'Did Beck hold her responsible for his dismissal?'

Orla hesitates. 'I don't know.'

'You spoken to him lately? Has Selena?'

'No,' she says. 'Not for months. Not that I know of, anyway.'

I'm watching the lit-up lobby. I hadn't intended to do this. At least I hadn't thought I had. Then a figure moves across the glass and I realise that I had probably intended to do exactly this all along.

'Orla, I'm going to have to call you back.'

I pocket the phone, walk with quick strides. Beck Chambers is stepping through the sliding glass doors. He looks emptied out.

'Mr Chambers?'

The words are out of my mouth, bright against the dull day. He recoils, as if it was a gun retort.

'I'm DC Leah Mackay. I'm investigating the disappearance of Selena Cole.'

I lay it out at his feet, wait.

He is watching me, waiting for me to detonate, lowers his chin, and I suddenly realise how big he is, that he could snap me like a twig.

'She's been found, Selena,' he says. 'Right?'

I nod. Watching him. Waiting.

He is calm, looks at me levelly. 'Then there is no crime here.' He tucks his hands into his jacket pockets. 'I suggest you concentrate on the murder, Ms Mackay.' Then he is gone.

I stand there in the cold and the wind and watch him go. And I wonder how he knew that Selena had been found.

The cost of infidelity

DS Finn Hale: Thursday, 9.57 a.m.

I walk like I am on the deck of a ship. The evidence has led you one way, then comes a wave that tips you, destabilises your world, and now you're facing in an entirely different direction. Now what?

Oliver is watching me. I see him out of the corner of my eye. Want to tell him to piss off. But that would be childish. So instead I wait until I'm past him, then flip him off.

Leah grins.

'How old are you?' she mutters.

'Old enough to have arrested the wrong guy,' I say, a sullen teenager. I sit down next to her. Stare at my feet. I should polish my shoes occasionally.

I think of Beck, walking free. There is a bubble of something that it takes me a moment to identify. Is it relief? What's that about? That I do not want the killer to be just one more squaddie who's gone mental? Because if it can happen to him . . .

'So,' says Leah, swivelling her chair towards me. 'Where are we now?'

I shrug. 'Nowhere.'

'Bullshit, Finn.' She says it like she's kidding, but there is iron in her tone. 'Stop feeling sorry for yourself. What do we know?'

'We know it wasn't Beck Chambers who killed Dominic,' I mumble. Seriously, I'm starting to irritate myself now.

'Excellent. One crossed off the list. What else?'

'Dominic was having an affair.'

'Yes.' Leah looks away, her eyes resting back on her monitor. She goes quiet, a silence long enough that even I notice it. Then she shakes herself, looks back at me. 'So,' she says, 'that brings us to a bunch of questions. Who was he having an affair with? What was that relationship like? Did that person have a significant other who may have been put out by this turn of events? And . . .'

'Did Isaac know?'

'Did Isaac know?'

Leah pulls her chair closer to the computer, types quickly. 'Let me see . . . I've only just started looking at the e-mails, so maybe there's something . . .'

I watch her, her lips pursed.

'Okay . . . ah . . . yeah, Dominic and Isaac e-mailed a lot. God. Okay. Let's look at the last few days.' She clicks on one, swivels the monitor so that I can see it.

I pull my chair closer.

'This is, let's see, the Friday before.'

From: IsaacFletcher@kmail.net
To: DNewell@HartleyNewell.co.uk

Hiya,
    Don't forget to pick up milk on your way
    I x

Leah closes the e-mail, scrolls through the inbox. 'Okay, day of the murder. Ah . . . 9.15 a.m.'

From: IsaacFletcher@kmail.net
To: DNewell@HartleyNewell.co.uk

I booked the theatre. It's 10th. Second row. Put it in your diary!
　I x

'Awesome.' I sigh heavily. 'Love's young dream.'
'Finn?'
'What?'
Leah is staring at the screen. 'Look.'

From: IsaacFletcher@kmail.net
To: DNewell@HartleyNewell.co.uk

Why the fuck haven't you answered your calls? I've been trying to get hold of you all day. I know you've turned your phone off, and you've got that bitch of a receptionist on it. I keep calling the office and she won't put me through.
　Grow the hell up, Dom. You can't avoid me for ever.
　All right, you want to do it over e-mail because you're too chickenshit to look me in the eye? Fine. I know what you've been doing. I know you've been cheating on me. Don't even try to deny it. At least do me that courtesy. I can't believe you would do this to me, you fucking bastard.
　COME HOME!!!!!!!
　We are going to fucking talk about this. I'm serious, Dom. Come home now. This is not fair. Do you have any idea how crazy I'm going here? I thought you loved me. I

thought we were a family. That's what you said to me, remember?

I need to see you now. If you won't come home, I'm coming there.

WE NEED TO TALK!!!

Life beyond

'So,' I move into the outside lane, pass a Fiat doing twenty-eight, 'this is fun.'

Leah glances at me. 'What?'

I gesture to the radio, the clanking music loud. 'The wipers on the bus go swish, swish, swish . . .'

Leah grins, looks younger suddenly.

I had hurried back into the SIO's office. Or bounced, as Leah termed it. Whatever. The e-mails, the anger punching through them, it was something, a damn sight more than we'd had before. Boss, I think we need to go and interview Isaac again. He studied me, a look of long-stretched patience, opened his mouth, I'm pretty sure to suggest bringing Isaac into the station, his words vanishing under my enthusiasm. If you're okay with it, sir, I'd like to keep him in his home, play it softly-softly. I think he may be more willing to open up there. And with Leah. She's good at that. People like her.

Leah is watching the landscape, mounding mountain ranges beneath an iron-grey sky.

'You okay?' I ask.

She glances at me, a look of fear shooting across her face. 'Yes. Why?'

'I just . . . you've seemed, I don't know, quiet lately. Everything's okay, right? At home?'

I don't know what I'm doing. I don't know why I've gone all Oprah.

Leah looks away again, her voice distant. 'Yeah. You know. Marriage.'

'Yeah. So . . .' Shut up, Finn. Just stop talking. 'You and Alex . . . you're okay, right?'

I think she won't answer. Think, hope, I don't know.

'It's just . . . we feel a long way apart these days. I don't know if it's the kids or life or . . .' She drifts off, staring out of the passenger-side window. 'Things happen, you know, when you've been together a long time. And it's just, how do you get back to seeing that other person as the one you fell in love with?'

I want to make an inappropriate joke, a flippant comment, something a bit more within my milieu. But I restrain myself, shifting a little in my seat. 'Maybe you don't.'

Leah glances at me again, sharp, and I have the uneasy feeling that we are discussing more than generalisations.

I soften my voice. 'Maybe there is no way to go back to how things were. Maybe you have to just push through and build a new way of seeing each other.'

There is a long, weighty silence and then Leah makes a noise. For a horrifying second I think she has begun to cry. Then I realise she is laughing. 'Jesus, Finn. When did you get to be so sensitive?'

I grin. 'I'll have you know I'm maturing rapidly, thank you very much.'

I ease off the accelerator, a speed camera up ahead.

'So . . .' Leah says, not looking at me but studying the road in front. The lights turn to green and I pull away. 'Not Beck.'

'Not Beck,' I agree.

I open my mouth. Try something new. 'To be honest, I feel like a bit of a twat.'

'Why?'

I take a left, weaving through the roadworks that litter the road into the country's capital. 'I made the arrest. It was on me.'

'You followed the evidence. That's all. It led towards Beck Chambers for a while. Now that it doesn't any more, you're following it somewhere else.'

I nod, speed up to pass a bin lorry.

'So,' I say, shifting us on to safer ground. 'Isaac.'

'Yeah,' says Leah. 'Isaac.'

You cast people into roles. The hero, the villain. The victim. I did that with Isaac Fletcher. I watched his tears and, maybe because I am getting sensitive, I dismissed the thought that they might be of the crocodile variety. And so I cast him as the victim of the piece. Even though I know how often it happens, how many times the world has seen those closest to the victim weeping as though their hearts will break, only to later be revealed as the villain. Always look to the partner first.

I did.

And I dismissed him because he cried.

It takes Isaac Fletcher a long time to open the door, and when he does, I take a step back. The guy smells, a hanging stale scent of alcohol, old cigarette smoke. He looks like someone different, is wearing jogging bottoms, stained on the thigh, a T-shirt with a tear on the sleeve. His eyes are glazed, red, hair standing up on end, thick with grease.

'Isaac,' I say. 'DS Hale? You remember?' I feel like I am talking to one of my nieces, that I have slowed my voice down so he can keep up. His gaze weaves across me, unsteady. 'This is DC Leah Mackay.'

It's slow, but he gets there in the end, figures out just who I am. He takes a sharp step back into the hallway. I'm seeing him differently now, what with the old booze and the dead-man stare. Now I'm looking at the biceps that curve from underneath his sleeve, the long rope veins that clamber down his arm. I'm thinking of the e-mail, the fury in it. A row that goes too far. And Isaac, grabbing a knife.

He has shifted his weight, and for a moment I think he is about to slam the door in our faces, that life is about to get a whole lot more interesting.

But then Leah moves past me, smoothly rests her palm against the door. Her smile is wide but gentle, designed to disarm, and I don't need to look down to know that she has wedged her foot against the door. 'Isaac? Hi. How are you doing? I was so sorry to hear . . . Look, let's get you inside.'

She turns him, a lamb suddenly in her capable hands, steers him back along the hallway into the living room. I follow, pushing the door closed behind me, trying not to gag at the smell of smoke, gone-off food.

'Here, let me move some stuff so you can sit down. There. I was just . . . heartbroken when I heard. I worked with Dom a lot. Such a lovely guy. Mind,' Leah slots herself on to the sofa next to Isaac, 'he was a pain in the butt as a solicitor. Too damn good. But it was fun, you know. Almost like playing chess with him.'

Isaac is watching her, and you can see that he's losing his resolve, weakening in the face of her kindness.

'I just . . . I can't imagine what this must be like for you, Isaac. I really can't. To lose someone, that is hard enough. But to lose someone in these circumstances . . . I just, I can't tell you how very sorry I am that you have to bear this.'

A tear spills down Isaac's cheek. I sit on the boxy leather armchair. Am prepared to bet that he would hand Leah the pin number to his bank account right now.

'Dom used to talk about you all the time,' Leah says. 'Said you'd booked for . . .'

'Antigua,' offers Isaac, voice like cracked glass.

'Antigua, of course. He was so excited about that. Said he couldn't wait to spend some time, just the two of you, that he'd been so busy with work. He wanted to spoil you.' She watches Isaac, his head bowed so that his chin almost rests upon his chest. 'Mind,' it seems that something has occurred to her, 'it's never easy, is it? My husband and I, we can drive each other insane sometimes. Dom said, well, I got the impression that things had been . . . tough lately?' She waits, bait laid.

Isaac frowns, looking at her. 'Why? Why do you say that?' His accent is more noticeable now, the Welsh tint washed away in his grief, leaving behind pure Midwest American.

'No, just something Dom said. I mean, we all have our problems, don't we?'

He bristles, pulls back. 'Things were fine.'

Leah nods. I wait.

She leans closer, her voice honey. 'The thing is, Isaac, we've heard different things. People saying you guys had some issues. Now, like I said, it happens to all of us. I don't know a single couple who haven't had their share of arguments. But, the case being what it is . . .' She pauses, watching him. 'Isaac, I need you to tell me the truth. We want to make sure we investigate Dominic's murder properly. If you lie to us, we're going to end up chasing our tails figuring out that you're lying to us, and then we're going to have to start wondering *why* you would lie. And all that is time when we're not out looking for who killed Dom. So it is so important that you just be honest, and then we all know what we're dealing with.'

There is a taut stillness, and I feel my mouth open. I don't know why. I don't know what the hell I feel I need to insert. But Leah senses it, looks up at me, her eyes warning. I shut my mouth again.

Then Isaac begins to cry. 'I loved him. I loved him so much.'

We sit. We wait.

'Things were good. Things were so good,' he says. 'Then . . . they just weren't. They changed. You know when you just know that something is going on? Like, you have no proof but you can feel it in your gut? That was how it was. I could feel it. And then, of course, you start looking for things, and the signs, they were everywhere. He was working late, and I mean, all the time. He got really defensive if I asked questions, started locking his phone, taking it with him everywhere . . . I just knew.'

I see Leah nod from the periphery of my vision. Keep my eyes on Isaac.

'A couple of days before Dom's . . . before his death, he went in the shower and forgot to take his phone. So I looked. I'd been paying attention, I'd seen him unlock it, so I'd figured out the code. I didn't have long to look at it. I was afraid. I didn't want him to catch me. But that day, there had been all these calls to this number.' Isaac sucks in a deep breath. 'I wrote it down. Put the phone back. See, I wanted to be sure, before I said anything.'

'What happened?'

'I think . . . I think he guessed that I'd been on his phone. I don't think I put it back in the right place, and so he got really . . . antsy, argumentative. And I just, I lost it.'

I'm thinking I'm going to hear about the kitchen knife, the blood, the panic. I'm thinking that I need to call Willa, get a forensic search done on this apparently immaculate apartment.

'I hit him. I punched him in the face. I'd never done that before. Neither of us . . . that wasn't who we were.' Isaac isn't looking at us, his words spilling out in a low drone. 'I think it shocked us, both of us, that we had taken it that far. Dom said we needed to talk, that he was late for work, but that when he got home, we would talk properly, work things out.'

'What happened then?' asks Leah.

Isaac laughs sourly. 'He was late home. Again. I got tired of waiting. So I rang the number. If he wasn't going to tell me who he was sleeping with, I was going to find out on my own.' He shakes his head. 'You know what made it so much worse?'

'What?'

'It was a woman. He was cheating on me with a bloody woman.'

Held hostage

Isaac is crying. He sits on a tubular dining chair, pulled up close to the floor-to-ceiling windows, like he is enjoying the view. But his head is down, tears pouring down his cheeks in a steady stream. The search team is moving through the apartment, a flock of geese flying in formation. They work quietly, every now and again someone looking over their shoulder at Isaac and his tears. I suppress a shiver. I don't know if he is lying. I don't know if what I am seeing is grief or guilt. But then why not both? How many of us do not carry a weight of blame in our rela-tionships, even without resorting to murder?

Finn is standing beside me, drumming his fingers on his folded arms. Do you believe him? he asked me quietly as we stood to one side, allowing the search team to sweep past us. I looked up at him and shrugged. I just don't know.

They are searching for blood. They are searching for signs of a struggle. For anything that will place Dominic's death here, in this apartment overlooking the bay. I watch

Willa move from room to room, her perfectly made-up face a study in concentration.

Do I want her to find something?

No.

Yes.

I don't know.

I look away, out to the bowl harbour, the rain that has just begun to beat against the windows, then turn to watch Isaac. He has found a square of paper, from the colour of it a Post-it note, is shredding it into centimetre-square pieces. How must it have been for him when that knock on the door came? One minute you have a life, imperfect and yet whole. In the next moment it is gone, stolen away by the thrust of a knife. I watch him shred, his long fingers shaking. Or was he simply waiting? Had he been there, knowing that in a minute, an hour, the knock would come, his hand still throbbing from the force of the thrust as he stabbed Dominic in the neck?

My phone rings, a shuddering vibration against my leg, and I pull it free.

'DC Mackay.'

'Anything?' The DI sounds tired. Or drunk. I'm hoping it's the former.

'Not yet, sir. The search team are still working.'

He sighs noisily. 'Fine. Update me when you have more.' He hangs up without a goodbye, and I mutter under my breath, something about grumpy men.

One of the search team waves at us. A woman. I don't know her name. I detach myself from my position by the wall, move towards her.

'I don't know if this is relevant,' she says, 'but we found a bunch of paperwork in the bedside cabinet.'

She hands it to me, a sheaf of papers, and turns away. Anxious to get back, to get on. Maybe she has kids of her own to be getting home to.

I carry the paperwork back to Finn, the surface slip-sliding in my gloved hands. Spread it out across the kitchen counter. I spare a glance at Isaac, looking for some kind of reaction, some kind of sign. But there's nothing. Just the Post-it note squares, getting smaller and smaller.

Finn sorts through the printed pages, and I'm watching, half paying attention, half not. Then I see a flash of colour, an eagle that I have seen before, and my heart rate quickens. I lean across him, pull the slick pamphlet free.

A brochure for the Cole Group.

They are all there, their photographs neat against their names. Ed Cole. Seth Britten. Orla Britten. And Selena Cole. I stare at it, for a moment wonder if I am going crazy, if my fixation on the case is producing hallucinations so that I am seeing these people everywhere I turn. Selena looks younger, although perhaps the truth is that she simply looks less sad. The picture must be an old one, taken before her husband died. She is wearing more make-up, her face fuller, less weighted down by life. I pick up the leaflet.

'What's that?' asks Finn.

I pass it over to him.

He studies it, frowning. 'Okay.'

'Don't you think that's weird? I mean, seriously. Have you ever heard about the kidnap-and-ransom industry before? Why does Dominic have all this stuff about the Cole Group?'

Finn shrugs. 'I don't know. I guess because of Beck Chambers?'

'I guess.' Only I don't guess. It feels off to me. It feels like there's something here.

Finn is watching me.

'What else have we got?' I say, keeping my voice light. Nothing to see here.

He looks away, begins flipping again. But I can't. I can't stop staring at the eagle. At the Cole Group. There's something here. I know there is.

But I don't know there is at all, do I?

I look at Selena's picture. There are always cases that hook you. There are always cases that speak to you, pulling themselves out of the pile and grabbing hold of your consciousness. If there are children a similar age to your own, if the circumstances are the same as your own.

Maybe it's the children. Two little girls. Maybe that's why I cannot let go of Selena Cole and her disappearance. Why I need to know what took place in those missing hours, even though it feels now that I am the only one who gives a stuff.

Or maybe it's the other thing.

Selena Cole herself.

Because the thing is, I have a sneaking suspicion that I have a thing about putting people on pedestals, turning the ordinary into heroes.

I watch as Finn reads a printed page, his forehead creased into myriad lines. I am trying to fill in the gaps, supplement my own failings with the success of others. And then, when the successful fail . . . I look at Selena Cole, wonder why it is that I need this. Why I feel the need to look to others as I wish I could be. Why I simply cannot be enough on my own.

'There's more stuff here,' says Finn. 'Drug rehab stuff. Dealing with users, that kind of thing.'

I glance over my shoulder at Isaac. He's stopped with

the Post-it now. Is simply staring at the raindrops as they wind their way down the window. 'Is there any way Isaac could have a drug problem?' I ask, my voice low.

Finn shrugs. 'I guess. There's been no sign of it, though. Fae and Bronwyn both said that Dominic did a lot of work with people on drugs. That he was big into helping them get clean. I think he was trying to get Chambers into treatment.'

'I wonder how that was for Isaac? Dominic's attention so clearly caught up elsewhere. And with the affair . . .'

Finn looks at me, grins. 'Mysteries of marriage, eh?'

I've never forgiven Alex.

I look back at the Cole Group leaflet, my breath catching in my throat at the thought that I have kept at bay for all these years.

I've never forgiven Alex for that night.

I turn slightly, look out of the window into the bay. Whitecaps are whipping up now, speckling the grey water. Boats bounce rhythmically, engaged in a beat all their own. He shattered my faith. In him. In myself. Because how could I have been so wrong? How could I have trusted so blindly that he would never hurt me?

And then life moved on, and somehow, without me knowing it, I got whipped into pregnancy and babies and a family and home, and yet still I am held hostage, there on that cold kitchen floor, holding a bottle of Rioja, wanting to die.

Life moved on, leaving me behind.

'Bunch of stuff here on kidnappings. Newspaper article on Beck Chambers' kidnapping in Mexico. Looks like Dominic was doing some research.'

I pull in a breath, look away from the dancing sea, back

to Finn. I feel dizzy, as unsteady as the boats. Listening to him, yet not listening.

Because I need to get unstuck. I want to get unstuck. And right now, I just don't know what that means.

'Maybe,' says Finn, 'it would be a good idea to pay a visit to your Selena Cole. Dominic had an interest here, clearly. Maybe they'll be able to help.'

My stomach leaps. 'Yes,' I agree. 'I think that might be helpful.'

'Okay, ladies and gents.' Willa moves towards us, striding like she will take over the world. Spares a second to give my brother a conspiratorial grin. She glances at Isaac, then gestures out into the hall. 'You wanna come outside.'

She isn't talking to me. But I go anyway.

'Right then, I'm afraid to tell you, the place is clean. No blood. No evidence of a struggle. There's a knife block in the kitchen; the shape of the knives in that would roughly correspond with the wound, but to be honest, they're so generic as to mean pretty much nothing.'

'Any knives—' begins Finn.

'Nope. No knives missing.' Willa shrugs. 'Sorry, guys. Wherever Dominic was killed, it wasn't here.'

I drum my fingers against my arm. Think of something that I heard a lifetime ago. Or was it only a matter of days? I just don't know any more.

'Excuse me,' I mutter.

I let myself back into the apartment, walk straight towards Isaac. He has made a mountain of torn-up luminous Post-it pieces, is repeatedly sticking his thumb into it to form a valley, then scooping the pieces together again with his palms. The mountain reborn.

I sit down beside him. 'Isaac. I need you to tell me something.'

He looks at me with murky eyes, reminds me of someone on the wrong end of a bottle of Scotch.

'Why didn't you tell anyone? When Dominic didn't come home that night, why didn't you call the police? Or Bronwyn? Or . . . well, anyone?'

He looks down again, pushing his palm flat on to the mound of paper. Shrugs. 'You get where we were, right? The man I loved. He was cheating on me. He didn't come home. I assumed he was with someone else.'

I nod slowly, think that the logic is unassailably familiar. And yet . . .

'Isaac,' I say. 'Is there something you're not telling us?'

He picks up a single piece of paper, turns it around between his fingers. 'I've told you everything I know.'

A Start in Kidnap and Ransom
(continued)

Dr Selena Cole

It changed us, the rescue of my nephew Gabriel. Ed, of course, had seen so many things, had been in danger so many times. But my life was smaller, of the more sheltered variety. That the world was such that kidnap and ransom was a necessary role for someone, anyone, was vaguely shocking to me. And yet . . .

'You know,' said Ed, 'we could do this.'

We were lying in bed at the time; a relationship that had begun in need had turned into something different. We had returned from Poland, had not left one another's side since. Ed liked to joke that he had lost a leg, replaced it with me.

'Where would we even begin?' I asked.

Ed was a fighter, had spent his entire life pushing himself, taking himself places it seemed impossible for him to go. His leg, learning to live with a body that looked so different to the way it had before, that was simply another challenge to him. You would have thought it would be challenge enough.

'I know some guys in K and R. They go out to kidnap sites, liaise with the companies, the families, the insurance. Make sure everything runs as it should, that the hostages

202

get to go home. They do what you did with Gabriel. We could do this.'

Life for me was smaller then, more predictable. I had a good job, specialising in post trauma and rehabilitation for returning forces personnel. It would have been no great hardship to simply keep treading along the path I was on. Looking back now, I wonder why I agreed to it, to throwing in my lot with this seemingly insane venture, to go blundering into a world I knew little about. Then I remember that look in Ed's eye, that hunger, the need to push himself, the need to believe that he could be more than he was then. Just another wounded veteran. It was never a decision, never a choice. It was simply what must come next.

It shouldn't have been that easy, our start in kidnap and ransom. The community is a closed one, with high, impenetrable walls. And yet strangely, not for us. We both knew people. It is the nature of the beast, when one of you has been a warrior, the other has helped heal them. These men and women, they come home from war and yet still their blood bubbles, fizzing with the need to chase death, to walk beside danger. K&R is a fairly obvious place for them to head.

As it turned out, it was Ed who opened the first door for us. A retired major, Mike Lloyd, a softly spoken man, his voice belying the power hidden beneath. He had been in K&R for ten years, was approaching his seventies, had a wife who missed him, grandchildren who were sprouting up without him. It's time, he said. I need to be able to sit for a while without the fear of being shot. He looked us up and down, me more than Ed, because I was a young woman, an alien species, high risk in an already high-risk world. Made some private calculations, ones we were never privy to. Then, come with me. I have a job on, leaving tomorrow. Messy thing. Negotiation has been going tits-up for months. I'm going to go down, have a look at it, see if I can do anything to unpick the muddle they've made of it. He studied me, the way one would a particularly fascinating breed of butterfly. You might be able to offer something the rest of us can't.

We left early the next morning. Down, it transpired, was Mali. They had been taken from Bamako. Fourteen men, miners who had come to Mali to make a decent living from a dying industry. Or maybe they came for the adventure of it. Who knows. Fourteen men, from six different countries of origin, working for four different mining companies, all with different insurers.

A clusterfuck, said Mike. There is no other word.

It had been going on for eight months when we arrived. Eight long, exhausting months of captivity, of negotiations that built and built then collapsed. More K&R consultants in one place than you have ever seen, each working to a slightly different rule book, each with different priorities. Governments and insurers and families, all battling one another to ensure that their hostage was the one who walked away. It was breathtaking. In its complexity, in its otherworldliness.

For Ed, this was, instantly, the door to our future. He began reaching out, talking, learning everything he could, so that when it was our turn, when it was about us, we would have the tools we needed.

For me, though, it was something different. Base of operations had been established in the conference room of a local Radisson. After eight months, even the hotel had begun to tire of it. And walking into that room, you could smell it, the despair, the defeat, the knowledge that nothing was going right. It was almost like everyone knew that the hostages would live or die at the will of the kidnappers, our role reduced to mere spectators.

I confess that it made me angry.

I watched for two weeks. I held my tongue for two weeks.

Four different consultants, each asking for different things, each crippling the ability of the others to protect their hostages.

I watched for two weeks. Then I snapped.

I had come from nowhere, I was no one. I knew nothing. And yet fury propelled me. I spent days going back through the recordings, listened to every conversation with the kidnappers, until in the end it seemed that I knew them, that I could get some handle on their wants, on their weak points.

Nearly a month after we arrived, I marched into the control room, handed out printed sheets. This is our new strategy. This is what we are doing. What we are ALL doing. This is how we're going to get them home.

I remember Ed grinning. Mike nodding quietly to himself.

The hostages were released thirteen days later.

Everyone wants something. And often, what people say they want isn't what they want at all. You have to study people, allow them to teach you who they are. So that you can find those points at which they are soft, where the need truly lies. Because when you do that, then you get to understand why they do what they do.

And then you can bring your hostages home.

An unrequited love

'Did you know that Dominic was having an affair?'

'What?' Bronwyn whispers it, more of a breath than a word. Is staring at me with her over-made-up eyes. Tears spring to them.

I know that Leah is watching her, don't have to look to tell that. So we stand there, an unlikely trio, in the quiet office, empty but for us. The receptionist's desk is unmanned, Fae not in yet. Bronwyn clutches hold of the faux wood of its surface, fingernails painfully pink today, digging into the desktop like it is the edge of a cliff. We'd surprised her, were here when she arrived. Always the best way, I find.

The fact remains that Dominic Newell was having an affair, and that this woman, his business partner for many years, his ex-lover, is clearly still in love with him. Even I can see that. Which means, as Leah points out, it must be fairly obvious.

'He . . . Dom, he would never . . .' It is an empty protest-ation. Pointless, as it goes. Because it is clear that he did. Bronwyn shakes her head. 'I just don't understand it.'

She is wearing a skirt that is too tight for her, warping

itself into creases across her thick thighs. How long, I wonder, has she been in love with him? Maybe she never stopped. And yet he chose Isaac, he built a life with Isaac. That had to hurt. And maybe one day Bronwyn simply lashed out in a fit of rage.

I watch her, black tears spilling down chalky cheeks, and think that Bronwyn was also the last person who saw him alive.

'Who?' Bronwyn pleads. She looks from me to Leah. 'Who was it?'

We study her, both silent. There are voices, calls and laughter from the street outside, the world awake now, raring to go. We do not have long. I glance at the clock. In moments, this foyer will begin to fill. Fae will come in, sit at the desk at which we're standing, and everything will get a lot more fractured. Bronwyn looks back at us, open at first, then her face creasing into a heavy frown as the cards finish their shuffle, awareness dawning.

'You think it was me?' She says it bluntly, still looking from me to Leah, back.

'Was it?' I ask.

Bronwyn swipes her hand across her cheek, only succeeding in smearing the mascara further. 'As a matter of fact, it wasn't.' She folds her arms across her chest, forcing the grey silk blouse to gape at the buttons, showing a cream bra beneath. 'Look,' she says, 'let's get everything out on the table. Yes, I loved Dominic. I always have. Yes, I would have given anything for us to restart things again. And to be perfectly honest, I would have been quite happy to align myself against Isaac.' She stares at Leah like it is a challenge, daring her to protest.

Leah returns her gaze. 'Go on.'

'The fact is, Dom didn't want me.' Her voice breaks, another tear, thick, black, worms its way down her cheek. 'He knew how I felt. He always has. And last year . . .' She looks at her fingernails, picking flints of fuchsia and flicking them to the ground. 'Look, I'm not proud of this. I got drunk. At the Christmas party. I had too much. Dom said he'd take me home. He . . . he wanted to make sure I was safe. Take care of me. I tried it on.'

'By tried it on, you mean . . .'

Bronwyn shoots me a look, one designed to freeze lava. 'I tried to kiss him. Happy? Dom . . . he said . . .' She sucks in a deep breath, gaze now lost in the middle distance. 'He said that he'd always love me. As a friend. Fabulous, isn't it?'

'You must have been pretty upset by that,' says Leah, softly. 'I think I'd have been devastated.'

'Not enough to kill him, if that's where you're going.' Bronwyn leans behind her, pulling a desk diary from a tray. 'But seeing as you are doubtful, let me just reassure you. I last saw Dom at around six p.m. on Monday. He said goodbye as he was leaving the office. Fae can confirm that. She was here with me, worked late sorting out some paperwork on a case we were dealing with. I took a phone call from a client, which lasted forty-five minutes. I'll get you his details so you can check. Then at seven thirty, I had a dinner meeting in the bar just across the street. You can confirm that with the solicitor from Ashby and Frank, and with the bar. They know me there.' She sets it down. A challenge.

I nod, slowly.

'So . . .' she says. 'Who was it? Who was he sleeping with?'

'That's what we're trying to find out,' Leah says quietly.

'What can you tell us about Dom's relationship with Isaac?'

Bronwyn shrugs. 'Not much. As far as I was concerned, they were love's young dream.'

'Isaac has confessed to hitting Dom in the days leading up to his death,' I offer.

She seems to sway, grips the desk again with those terrible nails. 'I . . . I didn't know. I didn't know.' She looks away, more tears spilling.

It is, I suppose, another death to her. Not a physical one this time, but the death of who she had believed Dominic to be, what she had supposed their relationship was.

But then that's true of all of us, isn't it? We rarely know the people around us; only what they show us of themselves. And a thing like murder, it has the tendency to wipe all pretence away, show life in its ugly, gritty clarity.

'So what about Beck Chambers?' Bronwyn asks. 'Given up on him, have you?'

'Beck has an alibi,' says Leah, calmly. 'It wasn't him.'

'Are there any other clients? Anyone particularly unstable who has given you or Dominic cause for concern? Fae mentioned that Dominic was often involved in getting people into rehab, dealing with people with drug issues. Is there anyone you can think of who may have wanted to harm him?'

Bronwyn shakes her head. Then the sound of footsteps, the front door swinging inward. I glance at the clock: 8.59. Right on cue. Fae slips in, greets us with a small smile.

'Did you know about this?' Bronwyn demands.

'What?' Fae stops dead, shrinking under her boss's scrutiny.

'Isaac hit him.' There is no need to clarify who she is

talking about. I'm willing to bet that they have talked of little else in days.

Fae pales, a small, narrow hand flying to her mouth. 'Oh my God. I saw . . . He came in, Dominic, I mean. He seemed upset, but I didn't want to push him. Went straight into his office and closed the door. I . . . I took him coffee. He was looking in the mirror, at his eye. I . . . I teased him. I said he was getting vain. Oh my God.'

Leah is watching her, studying her. 'We need to ask you some questions, actually,' she says. 'About Dom. Did you know that he was having an affair?'

'What?' Fae looks like a child told that Santa is not real.

'You see,' says Leah, 'we need to find out who he was seeing. So that we can eliminate them, put our attention where it needs to be.' She is speaking softly, gently probing.

I look at her, am momentarily confused by where she is going with this. See the way she is looking at Fae, waiting, and it hits me. Leah suspects Fae of being the secret lover. I open my mouth to protest, close it again. Because it is ludicrous to me. She's a kid.

'Fae, were you and Dominic in a relationship?' asks Leah.

'No!' Fae recoils. 'No, I, we . . .'

Bronwyn is staring at her like she is seeing her for the first time. 'You spent a lot of time together.' Her voice is flat, the sea before a storm. 'Lots of private chats in his office.'

'No. We didn't, I never . . .' She is crying now. 'We were friends. That's all.'

She looks from me to Leah to Bronwyn, pleading.

'Honest. There's nothing more to it. He was just a nice man.'

'Okay,' I say. 'Let's all calm down. Fae, did you hear

anything, or see anything, that might have indicated who he was seeing? It's not a witch hunt, I promise you, but we need to find out who it was so we can eliminate them.'

She looks at me like I have saved her from drowning. 'I . . . I don't know. I didn't think he would ever do that. I . . .' Then she stops. Frowns. 'Wait, there was someone. On Monday. Someone called. A woman. She must have rung six times all told. Was desperate to speak to him. I kept saying he wasn't here, but she was having none of it.'

'Who?' demands Bronwyn.

'I don't remember her name. I . . . We get lots of hysterical people ringing. It didn't seem strange, not at the time. Wait a second.' She picks up the diary from where Bronwyn has left it, begins to leaf through. 'I would have written it down. I write everything down, so I'm sure . . . Yes, here it is. Six calls between nine a.m. and three p.m. Her name was Orla Britten.'

On the banks of the river

I drive steadily, watch the gaudy autumn trees as they flicker by. I breathe in, breathe out, and listen to the music with its joyful jangling rhythm – 'Dingle Dangle Scarecrow'. As I listen, it dawns on me that something is wrong, something I can't quite put my finger on, and then I realise that my children are not in the car.

Finn is sitting in the passenger seat, his fingers beating against the door in time to the painful rhythm. Perhaps it is the music. Or perhaps it is impatience, an urge to get to the Cole house. Orla Britten. Maybe it is nothing. Or maybe it is everything.

These cases, the disappearance of Selena Cole, the murder of Dominic Newell. Miles apart, and yet somehow inextricably linked.

The office had fallen quiet, hanging on our every word.

'Oliver,' the SIO said, 'you go over to the Cole house. I need you to interview this Orla Britten—'

'Sir,' Finn interrupted, bouncing on the balls of his feet. 'With respect, I think it should be me and Leah doing the interview. They know her, she's worked the case, and I think, the thing is . . .'

'All right, Sergeant,' said the SIO, an impatient edge to his voice. 'I'm assuming you're working on some kind of commission for your sister. Fine. You and Leah go. Go on then. Get on with it.'

We nodded, attempted to look like good little detectives, ignoring Oliver, his folded arms, flat expression.

I rotate the volume dial, allowing the music to slip into silence, and think of last night. Alex's breathing easy and soft, my own fractured, my heart seeming to race against the darkness. Bits of sleep that you dive into then climb out of, so fragmented that you wake certain you have not slept at all. Alex watching me as I dressed, as I gave the girls their breakfast, his voice too bright, too cheery. Shall I feed the girls? Why don't you go and have your shower? I can get them dressed. Do you want me to take them to crèche this morning? Wearing that damn shirt, its checks too bright, the one that he insists makes him look younger. I hate that shirt.

I wanted to scream.

'It's a nice day today,' Finn says.

'It is.' I nod.

I take a left, driving into the low autumn sun. The trees reach across the road, languid arms stretching for one another, dappling the tarmac with sunlight. The road sparkles, the diamond sheen of days of rain.

I ease my foot off the accelerator, am slowing now.

You're going to have to forgive me. If we're going to make this marriage work. He had flung that at me once, in the course of one of many, many arguments. And, of course, he was right. I would have to forgive him. But how do you forget? It changes who you are, this thing. It changes you as a couple, a person. It burrows under your skin like a splinter, seemingly harmless, and you assume that sooner or later it will work its way out and you will be left whole again. Unencumbered. But sooner has not come yet. It remains there, buried in a shallow grave. And every now and again it rears itself up, stinging me from the inside.

I can't do this any more. I can't do this any more.

Something has to change.

'So what do you think?' Finn's voice breaks into my thoughts, shocking me. I am not alone.

I shake my head. 'I don't know what to think.'

'You were clearly right. There is some link between your missing person and Dominic's murder. You said Selena Cole doesn't remember what happened to her?' Finn has that tone he gets, dripping cynicism from each syllable.

I shake my head. 'I know. It sounds . . . off, right? The brother-in-law suggested that she may have been drugged. There's this drug coming out of Colombia, devil's breath. It's not a big thing here yet, but the symptoms would fit.'

'So, what? Someone drugged her and took her and then . . . put her back?'

'I don't know, Finn.'

Finn nods, looking away and out of the window.

What do I think happened? To Selena. To Dominic. What is Orla's role in all this?

I have no idea.

'There's another option, you know.'

I know.

'Selena Cole could be lying,' says Finn.

I nod, slowly. 'Yes. Yes, she could.'

I watch the trees, orange and brown leaves dancing as the wind springs up. They flood the road, speckled flashes of colour. Then there is a break, a gulf that yawns between the sentinel trees, and I see a glimpse of grey. The river. I look around me, suddenly realising where I am. The river. I am at the spot where Selena Cole was found.

I slow, pulling the car into a lay-by.

'What are you doing?' asks Finn.

I flick the engine off, my eyes trailing the bank that lies level with the road. The river is high, water kissing the grass, and I think that much more rain and this road will flood.

'I just . . . I need to see something.'

I think about Selena Cole. There is a link. I don't know what it is, but it is there, just as the sun remains when you disappear into the shade of a tree. Something I do not yet understand ties her to the death of Dominic Newell. I taste the theory, test it.

What am I thinking? I don't know. I just . . . There are coincidences. They happen. But a woman vanishing, only to reappear hours later with no recollection of where she has been or what has happened to her, hours after a solicitor dies? A solicitor who apparently had an interest in collecting K&R information. Who was receiving desperate calls from Orla Britten.

I watch the river, the current pulling and tugging, bouncing over protruding rocks.

The link? Beck Chambers. A man with a nasty temper and a solid alibi for the murder of Dominic Newell. He worked for the Cole Group. Was represented by Dominic.

What the hell is going on here?

I push open the door.

'Leah? What are you doing?' Finn says again.

I look back at him. 'It's fine,' I say. 'I just have to look at something. Will you . . . can you trust me for a second? And wait?'

He stares, studying me like he is wondering if I have lost my mind.

Then, 'Okay. I . . .' He looks around the car, then, reaching for the dial, turns the volume back up. 'I'll listen to some music.' 'Old MacDonald' fills the car, and my brother grins at me. 'Take your time.'

I smile, push myself out, tugging my parka tight around me. With careful steps I climb up on to the riverbank. The grass is swampy, thick with the overnight rain. I study the path.

It is overgrown, unkempt. A new cycle track has been built on the opposite bank, its brightly wet tarmac glistening at me. If you were going to walk along the river, that is where you would go. Not here, to this padded-down facsimile of a path, the grass blades fighting back from their long oppression, springing up now that they have been freed from the weight of walkers. I look at the water, allow it to tug my gaze north. You can just about make out the town from here, Hereford's skyline, such as it is, peeking above the trees. You could technically walk from here all the way into town.

I glance back at the road, where the car sits waiting.

It would have been pretty isolated. Especially late at night, when Selena would have arrived here.

Arrived?

Yes. Had she been here throughout all those missing hours, someone would have seen her, surely. It's isolated, but there's a primary school a couple of hundred yards up on the opposite bank, its back gate letting out on to the cycle path. I watch the path; a mother, her raincoat hanging open in deference to the watery sunshine, walks slowly, pushing a pram. A dog-walker on the other bank, a driver passing along the adjacent road. Had Selena been here all that time, surely she would have been seen?

So then, let's say she arrived. Where did she come from? How did she get here?

If she was kidnapped, dosed with scopolamine and dumped . . . why? Why here? Why kidnap her at all if there would be no subsequent ransom, no apparent sexual motive, no physical injuries? What would be the point?

I look at the water again, Hereford beyond.

But you could walk here from town.

Selena says she regained awareness here. Sitting on the bank. Shivering from the cold.

I pull my feet from the sunken ground. Begin to walk towards the town, a leisurely afternoon stroll with no real objective to it at all.

I think about Selena at the hospital, her skin so pale it was almost white. Her hands, face streaked with mud. The stain on her top. As I walk, I am back in that hospital, staring at that stain, and in my memory it is mutating now, not mud.

Blood.

She had no wounds. No injuries.

If it was blood, where the hell did it come from?

I think of how Selena looked when I got there, like a kidnap victim. Like how in your head a kidnap victim would look, cold and dirty and damaged.

No coat.

I keep walking.

It is, what, three miles into town?

This spot is quiet. There is no reason to be here at three in the morning. The only explanation that would even vaguely make sense would be if you were a victim, if you were dumped here.

I keep walking.

The wind has a bite to it in spite of the sunshine, winter creeping ever closer, and I pull my hood up to protect my ears from its shriek. My trousers are damp now, a combination of dew and droplets from the river. My black shoes are brown. I glance back towards the car, where Finn still waits, to the spot where I figure Selena was found sitting. Orla mentioned that the taxi had stopped in a lay-by. There are no other lay-bys on this stretch of road. I can barely see it now. The trees have grown denser, are knitted together more tightly, so that even in the autumn you can no longer make out the road. I figure that I must have walked half a mile, maybe more.

Based on what Selena said, there is no reason why she should have been this far downriver. And yet . . .

What am I thinking?

You would be here if you had walked from town. You would be here if you were not dumped at all, but had walked, under your own steam, from the centre of Hereford.

My heart begins to beat a little faster.

I walk on, eyes down towards the river, let my eyes trail the edge of it, where the water meets the bank.

She looked just like a kidnap victim should look.

When I see it, it feels like déjà vu. As though I already knew it would be exactly where it is. I inch closer to the river, my unlikely shoe sliding sideways against the slick grass so that my knee lands in it, brown mud staining the grey fabric.

I reach into my pocket, pull free a pair of protective gloves, slip my fingers into them. And keep reaching.

It is well hidden. It has almost disappeared into the mud of the bank, the grey of the river. I hook the brown fabric between my thumb and forefinger, the wool heavy with the weight of the water that has leached into it. I pull, but it is stuck, trapped on something that hides beneath the water: a branch, a stone. I tug, feel it loosening in my grip, then sliding towards me.

I push myself up to standing, holding the coat in my hands.

It feels like a dream, my actions governed by something outside myself. I plunge my gloved hands into the ruined wool coat, my skin stinging with the cold of it. The first pocket is empty. But I can feel the weight in it, think it is more than simply the water. I find it in the second pocket. A small wallet, its outside decorated with flowers. I flip it open. A five-pound note, or what used to be a five-pound note, sits in the billfold, more like papier mâché than anything else now. There are some coins, small change, inside the zip.

Nothing else. Nothing that would identify it as belonging to anyone in particular.

I stand on the bank of the river, the coat heavy in my arms, and I stare at the almost empty wallet, willing it to give me something, anything concrete.

I turn it over in my hands, again, again.

And I see a small flap, an opening that would be so easy to miss.

I slide my fingers inside, no longer breathing.

The paper is waterlogged, comes apart in my hands. But the writing on it is broad, childish, and I can piece the words together.

To Mummy
Happy birthday
Heather

Case No. 41
Victim: Phoebe Hanson
Location: Madison, Wisconsin
Company: Private case, unaffiliated with any insurance
provider
13 September 2009

Initial event

At 5.30 a.m. on Wednesday 13 September, Mrs Phoebe
Hanson, a forty-eight-year-old stay-at-home mother,
left her family home on the outskirts of Madison,
Wisconsin, leaving her three children (aged sixteen,
twelve and ten) in the care of their father, Mr
Christopher Hanson. Mrs Hanson took her own car
and drove to Madison airport in order to catch a
7 a.m. flight to New York City. She had informed her
husband that she was due to meet college friends
there and would return no later than the following
Sunday.

At 7 a.m., Mr Hanson received a phone call from
an unknown caller, stating that his wife had been
kidnapped en route to the airport. A ransom of
$500,000 was demanded and the time period for this
ransom set at a mere twelve hours. Mr Hanson was
warned that should the ransom not be forthcoming,
his wife would be executed.

Mr Hanson immediately contacted the airline and

confirmed that his wife had not in fact boarded her flight.

Response

Mr Hanson is retired military and served with me (Ed Cole) in Iraq. At the time of this kidnapping, both Selena Cole and I were attending a series of meetings in Chicago. Mr Hanson, knowing that we were in the locale, immediately called on us for assistance.

We arrived at the Hanson home some three hours after the initial call. This left a response window of nine hours remaining.

Immediate assessment of the situation suggested to us that this kidnapping was problematic. Upon arrival at the Hanson home, Selena immediately gained access to the computer of Mrs Phoebe Hanson, in order to verify her travel plans and to track her recent communications. Mr Hanson revealed to us that his wife had planned to see friends in New York City and that the trip had been planned within the last week.

Upon accessing Mrs Hanson's e-mails, Selena was able to confirm our suspicions that the information given to Mr Hanson was inaccurate, that no plans had been made to travel to New York and there were no flight reservations to this effect. It became clear, after going through Mrs Hanson's internet history, that she had in fact been engaged in a lengthy correspondence with a man who claimed his name was Rick DeMarco. The correspondence was such that it could be reasonably concluded that an online affair was taking place. It was discovered that in the days leading up to Mrs Hanson's disappearance, she and 'Rick' had spent some considerable time discussing a trip that they would take together to Los Angeles. Further examination of Mrs Hanson's communications revealed a single coach-class ticket from Madison to LA.

Mr Hanson immediately contacted the carrier named on this ticket and was able to confirm that his wife had indeed boarded the flight to LA, and that the flight was currently airborne.

Closer examination of Mrs Hanson's communications with 'Rick' indicated that he had approached her in a chat room and had enthusiastically pursued her. An online investigation was unable to find the existence of anyone by that name who met the personal criteria supplied by 'Rick'.

Our conclusion was that this was a virtual kidnapping.

A colleague of the Cole Group who is based out of LA was able to go to LAX in order to meet Mrs Hanson's flight upon landing, thereby confirming her safety and our conclusions.

Despite an initial unwillingness to admit her duplicity to her husband and children, and a brief attempt to convince our LA colleague that she had in fact been taken by force and placed on the LAX flight against her will, Mrs Hanson was eventually persuaded to be candid. She had, it seems, left her home in the full and complete understanding that she was about to engage in a sexual affair with 'Rick', who, it must be noted, she had never met, nor had any video calls with. Mrs Hanson was then informed of her role as the victim in a virtual kidnapping. Our LA colleague noted in her report that Mrs Hanson seemed more distressed by the fictitious nature of her 'lover' than she was about the distress caused to her husband by the threats to her well-being.

Extensive conversations with the Madison Police Department and the FBI confirmed that 'Rick' was in fact a criminal gang operating out of northern Mexico who have been responsible for more than a dozen incidents in which unsuspecting people have been 'catfished' and their families subjected to hefty ransom demands. This virtual kidnap ring operates through the US and Canada and is, at the time of writing, a significant problem to law enforcement.

Mrs Hanson was returned to her home some thirty-six hours later, and, following a lengthy consultation with Selena Cole, referred for therapy in order to help her better deal with the issues that had made her vulnerable to this 'catfishing' incident. She and Mr Hanson have also been referred to a marriage counsellor.

A victim or a liar?

DC Leah Mackay: Friday, 10.35 a.m.

Selena Cole opens the door on the second knock. She looks surprised to see me standing there.

I smile brightly. 'Hi, Selena.' My voice comes out so chirpy that even I do not recognise it. 'This is DS Finn Hale. Finn, Selena Cole. We were wondering if we could come in for a moment?' I shiver, dramatically. It is, after all, a cold day. Of course we should come inside.

Selena studies me, and there's a look in her eyes, wariness or fear, I can't really tell. She looks from me to Finn, her expression warping to calm. She smiles, and it looks like it has taken no effort at all.

'Of course,' she says. 'Please, come in.'

I had stuck my head back into the car. 'Finn, give me an evidence bag.'

'Okay . . .' He reached into the glove compartment, pulling a large bag free.

I hoisted the coat inside, sealing it, passing it across to him. 'What the hell?'

Slipped the key into the ignition, started the engine. 'I found it. On the riverbank. It's Selena Cole's.'

I watched as Finn slid the evidence bag into the footwell, the chocolate wool drawing my eye through its plastic cover, over and over again, in the way that one's eye is drawn to a scar on a picture-perfect face. It was the piece out of place, the portion of the jigsaw that stood out proud. Something is wrong here, it screamed.

'So . . .' he said, aiming for casual.

'So,' I said, 'it wasn't where it was supposed to be.'

The tyres felt light on the still rain-slicked road. I thought about Selena's story, how ephemeral it seemed, that if you reached out, tried to take hold of it, it would evaporate before you. She vanished. She reappeared. She claimed that she had no recollection of the intervening hours.

'So . . . what are you thinking?' asked Finn.

I looked across at him. 'I'm thinking Selena is lying.'

I drove with half an eye on the coat. I should have assumed that she was lying. Right from the beginning, when I first heard the story, I should have assumed deception. Because when we get right down to it, isn't deception the most likely cause? And yet I didn't. Not didn't. Couldn't. Why? What was it about her that rendered me so incapable of seeing a lie? Or at least the possibility of a lie?

Finn looked at me, pursed his lips the way he does when there's something he wants to say. 'What makes you say that?' he asked eventually.

'The coat. It wasn't where she said she was. For it to have been where I found it, she'd have had to be a lot further down the riverbank, towards Hereford. Where I found it was a good half-mile away.'

'So . . .'

'So,' I said. 'The way I see it, there are two options.

Either she walked along the riverbank in a drug-induced haze, shedding the coat as she's walking.'

'Which means she was heading away from town.' Finn glanced back out of the rear window. 'You can't get to that part of the riverbank from the road. The only way to access it is to follow the path from Hereford.'

'Which means she was in Hereford during those missing hours.'

'Or at least some of them.'

'Or at least some of them,' I echoed. 'And the question then becomes, what was she doing there and how did she find her way there?'

'Okay,' said Finn. 'Let's call that option A. So option B is . . .'

'Option B is that she's lying to us,' I said. 'Option B is that she walked along the riverbank, that she shed her coat somewhere she wouldn't be seen from the road, so that she would look cold, vulnerable.'

'Like a victim.'

'Like a victim. And let's be honest,' I said. 'If anyone knows what a kidnap victim should look like, it's Selena Cole.'

I pressed the accelerator down harder, too fast for the slick road, the overhanging trees with the deposit of leaves they had left behind.

I didn't think Selena was lying. I didn't think she was lying because I didn't want to think that. I wanted a hero. I winced at the word, at the blissful naivety it implied. There was something about this woman, some kind of glamour. The fact that she had faced tragedy. That she had survived. That she had done something so far outside the common order of things, that she had done it well. That in amongst those things, she was raising two children – two girls – on her own. That she was succeeding in it. That her children loved her. That her children knew that their mother was a success.

It is obvious, when you come right down to it. I saw in this woman what I wanted to see in myself. It made me blind.

We step into the dim hallway, the smell of coffee, toast hanging heavy.

'Can I get you some tea? Coffee?' says Selena. Her smile is bright. As bright as my voice is.

I look at her. Really look at her.

She wears jeans, a slouch T-shirt, has her dark hair tucked up into a low bun. You can see her collarbone, the white skin standing proud against the deep navy of her top, the protrusion of it.

Her make-up is done, sparing, clean, and she screams efficiency, capability, calm.

She looks . . . normal.

Concentrate.

But there is a slight redness to her eyes, around the edges. Her voice has a thickness to it that would be oh so easy to miss. She has been crying. She steps back, waves a calm hand, ushering me in. It shakes, the tiniest of tremors. And it occurs to me that she is afraid of me.

There are voices in the house, low murmurs that drift along the tiled hallway. I strain to hear them. Selena looks at me, smiles.

'It's Orla and Seth. They're in the office. They've decided to run the business from here for a couple of days. Just to make sure we're all okay.'

I glance at Finn, a moment of silent communication.

'If you'll excuse me,' Finn says firmly, 'I need to have a quick chat with them.'

Selena stands, opens her mouth to ask why, then closes it firmly again, fixes a smile in place and indicates a closed door along the hallway. 'Help yourself.'

Finn and I share another look, then I too smile, thinking that it is a peculiar kind of madness where we are all pretending that life is light, acting like we are not here to discuss a murder and a vanishing. Selena and I turn in to the living room, allowing Finn to follow the rise and fall of the voices. There are logs burning in the fireplace, the fire spilling out heat into the generously sized room. It wants me to unravel, threatens to soothe me with its spit and crackle. I keep my shoulders pulled up tight. 'And are you?' I ask. 'Okay, that is?'

'Yes,' Selena says quietly. 'We'll be fine.'

'The girls?' I ask. 'Where are they today?'

'School. Well, nursery for Tara,' says Selena. 'We thought it was important that things started to get back to normal for them.' She waves me towards a large leather couch. 'Please. Have a seat.'

I sit carefully, watch as she crosses the room to a wing-back chair beside the window, watch as her hand swings out, her fingers grazing a photo in a thick wooden frame. Her husband. Dressed in military uniform. She touches his cheek as she passes, does it without looking. Is she even aware she has done it?

She sits, crossing her legs, and in a flash I am in the psychologist's office, the client. 'I'm sorry about the mess.'

There is, in truth, little mess. Just a few toys left heaped beneath the bay window.

'You have children?' Selena asks, her smile calm, professional.

I nod. Smile the way you do when you are a parent and someone asks if you have kids. 'Twin girls.'

'How old?'

'They just turned two.' I think of their hair, identical ponytails, Georgia's beginning to slip already, the band defeated by her exuberance, her energy.

'It's a crazy time.'

I can feel my mouth begin to open, the words waiting, desperate to be said. About how afraid I am, all the time, that they will trip or be pushed, that they will be sad or the cause of another's sadness, that I will not be enough, that I am split into too many parts to ever be whole to them, that I will fail. I can feel it, the promise of relief waiting just there over the horizon.

Breathe.

I sit up straighter in my chair. Nod towards the heavy-framed picture, the handsome man in his dress blues. Ask a question I already know the answer to. 'Your husband?'

Selena nods, a flicker of pain crossing her eyes, looks down. I feel the words in me begin to recede. A silence follows, heavy, and I fight the urge to slot words in, fill it up so that it is lighter.

'He passed away,' she says finally. 'Last year.' She speaks into her lap, looking smaller now, thinner still.

'I heard. I'm sorry.'

She nods again and the silence rolls back in.

'It was the attack in Brazil?' I say, quietly.

She winces, and I feel a stab of guilt, that I have wielded the words as a weapon, designed to destabilise her, throw her off balance so that I may regain mine.

I think she will change the subject. I am expecting her to talk about the weather.

'I had gone shopping,' she says. 'Isn't that frivolous?' She is looking out of the window, at the apple tree that over-hangs it. 'We had been in Brasilia for three days. We were due to come home the following day, and I wanted to get the girls presents. So I went shopping.' Her voice is steady, far away. 'Ed . . . he said he wouldn't come with me. That he was going to have a lie-in. Prepare for the meetings we had that afternoon. He said he wasn't planning on going to the seminar either. That he was all seminared out. So that's why at first . . .'

She takes a deep breath, lets it slowly out. 'I stopped at this little toy stall, in the Feira dos Importados. It's . . . it was beautiful. They had all these wooden toys, exquisitely made, and I remember thinking that I would get something like that, something special. I remember I was holding a wooden Noah's Ark and thinking of Tara. Then . . . it was like thunder. Only I knew it wasn't thunder. Right away I knew what it was. Like I'd been expecting it somehow.'

'Your husband? He was at the hotel when it happened?'

'He was at the hotel.' Selena looks back to the apple tree. 'He was supposed to be in bed. He was supposed to be relaxing. So for a while, I thought he was okay. They hit the seminar. It was the delegates they were after. Wiped out half of the K and R industry in one fell swoop. How they must have laughed at that. And of course it was chaos there for a while, and people were missing, and no one knew how many. So for a while there was hope.'

'Ed had gone to the seminar?'

Selena looks at me, then nods. 'He'd changed his mind. He was there when the attack began.'

'I'm sorry.'

'Me too.' Her fingers tie themselves around one another.

231

'It must be hard. With the kids, the business.' I am the therapist now, and I spare a minute to wonder exactly what it is I am doing, where these questions are going.

Selena leans her head against the chair back, her voice quiet, so soft that I can barely hear her. 'I keep thinking I've forgotten something. You know that feeling when you've not done something you should have done. And it's nagging at you, but you can't quite put your finger on it? It's like that, all the time. Just this feeling of wrongness. Like the world doesn't make sense any more without him in it.'

A tear rolls down her cheek.

I look away. Look at the fire. The flames dance, low.

'A friend of mine, a psychiatrist, Gianni, he says that I need to allow myself this. That I can't try and force my way through the grief and out the other side.'

I think of Vida Charles, her viper tongue – you know about the psychiatrist, don't you?

'Your friend, does he have an opinion on your . . . amnesia?'

Selena shakes her head. 'He stopped by, after I came home.' She looks at me, gives a brief smile. 'There are advantages to having friends in the mental-health community.' She shrugs. 'Gianni, he says trauma. We – Ed and I – have dealt with this kind of thing before: hostage is freed, doesn't remember what happened. Orla says I shouldn't worry about it. That it's over now. But . . .'

She wipes a neatly folded handkerchief across her cheek. This is my fault. I have cut her with memories so that I can regain control. I think of Alex, think of what it would be like if he were to simply vanish, and I feel my breath stop in my chest.

'I'm sorry,' I say again.

Selena smiles slightly. 'It is what it is. And you can't give up. You never give up. That's what Ed always said. No matter how tough life gets, you just keep moving. One foot in front of the other. And no matter how long you have to keep walking in the darkness, if you keep walking, sooner or later you will reach the sun.'

'Do you believe that?' I ask.

She looks at me, her gaze steady. 'What choice do I have? I'm sorry,' she says. 'You didn't come here to talk about this. What did you need to speak to me about?' She pushes herself upright, looks at me, waiting.

I feel the balance shift again.

'I need to ask you about Beck.' I do not need to ask her about Beck. There is nothing left I need to know. But it is a nudge, a move set to destabilise.

'Beck Chambers?'

I nod.

'Why?' Selena asks, leaning forward.

'His name has come up in an investigation. He worked for you. Is that right?'

'Yes. For a couple of years.'

'What was your impression of him?'

She is guarded now. 'He's a decent man.'

'And yet,' I say, keeping my voice flat, 'you let him go?'

Selena sinks back into the chair, sighs. 'Beck has had problems. After his kidnap, his release, he started drinking pretty heavily, started dabbling in drugs. Ed brought him in, helped him sort himself out. But then, after we . . . after Brazil . . . Look, the thing is, I wasn't there. At that time, it was just about me, the girls, surviving. Seth and Orla ran the business, made all the decisions. They said that

Beck was showing up smelling of alcohol. That he was no longer reliable. Seth felt he had no choice but to let him go.'

I nod, slowly. 'Are you afraid of him?'

'Who? Beck?' Selena looks at me like I am insane. 'No. Of course not.'

'So you've never had any concerns about him? Personally, I mean?'

'No. Why? What's this about?'

I glance out of the window, the apple tree swaying, its branches clawing against the glass. Think that I could tell her about my thoughts, about the idea of devil's breath. But I sit and watch the branches and keep my mouth shut. Because I no longer trust her.

'There was a murder the other night. You might have seen it mentioned on the news. In Cardiff. A solicitor. A lovely guy. I knew him pretty well. Dominic Newell?'

She is staring at me, watching my mouth, although I am almost certain that she can no longer hear the words. She has gone deathly white.

I watch her. 'Did you know him?'

Selena opens her mouth, closes it.

'No,' she says. 'No, I didn't know him.'

A Bombing in Brazil

Zachary Ellis

(Originally published in
The Security Journal, October 2014)

It wasn't the kind of day for a bombing. The Brasilia sky was too blue, the air too hot. It was day two of the conference – Inside Kidnap & Ransom – a gathering of people from the security and insurance industry. I'd been to these before and they're busy and quite frankly so-so, some good seminars, some not so good. But I was excited about this one. In particular I was excited about seeing Dr Selena Cole.

I was running late that day. I'll blame the heat. In truth, I had a hangover, the result of a heavy night catching up with colleagues I hadn't seen in a while. I walked slowly, movements weighed down by the breathless September heat. The Royal Palace, the conference hotel, is a baroque edifice, all white and sinuous. It stands proudly in the South Hotel Sector, its wide-slung front steps overlooking the expanse of the Monumental Axis. It is also expensive, more than my meagre reporting budget will cover. So every morning I had a walk: ten, fifteen minutes maybe. That morning it was more like twenty minutes. I think about that fact every day.

I have worked in the insurance industry for many years. I crunch the numbers. I try to keep my firm from going bankrupt. I specialise in kidnap-and-ransom insurance. It sounds pretty exciting. The truth is, I still work in insurance.

I remember looking at my watch. I remember that it was 9.05. I had missed the beginning of the first seminar, but that was okay. The one I really wanted to see, the one presented by Dr Selena Cole, wasn't on until after lunch. I had plenty of time. The seminar was titled 'Negotiating in a Psychological Way: A New Paradigm for Kidnap and Ransom'. People were saying that she was waking up the industry, changing the way things were done, tightening them up, helping operatives rescue kidnap victims more quickly and (importantly for the insurance companies) cheaply. No surprise then that the Cole Group had been making waves. Started in 2004 by Ed and Selena Cole, it had conducted almost a hundred successful negotiations, reuniting kidnap victims with their families. With their backgrounds in special forces and psychology respectively, it is hardly surprising that they would be able to contribute a thing or two to the world of hostage negotiation.

The kidnap-and-ransom industry is booming. According to some reports, approximately 75 per cent of Fortune 500 companies invest in K&R insurance. If an employee is taken hostage in some far-flung location, the insurance companies then turn to people like the Cole Group to remedy the situation, negotiating a ransom that is satisfactory to both sides. It is an industry in which we are familiar with bad people who do bad things. But not on a day like that, in the middle of September, in the heart of Brasilia.

I had turned in to the South Hotel Sector. The traffic was busy, cars whipping by faster than you would think they could. I remember the smog, the fumes catching in my throat. I remember the roar of motorbikes.

It's not an unusual sound in Brasilia. Not something that should have drawn my attention. But there was something about it that made the hairs on my neck stand on end. I slowed, scanning the road ahead, trying to make sense of what I was seeing. It was a motley collection of bikes. There were even a couple of mopeds. They rode two to a bike, driver and pillion passenger. I counted them, not really thinking what I was doing.

Six bikes. Twelve people.

They opened fire almost instantly.

Pop. Pop. Pop.

I would like to say that I rushed forward, that I took hold of the young woman with the jet-black hair as the bullet hit her in the chest, that I at least attempted to pull her out of harm's way. But the truth is, I did none of those things.

I froze.

Then I ducked behind a car. A Peugeot, I think.

They flooded from the bikes. People dropped in their path. They swarmed up the wide front steps, vanished inside. I didn't see what happened next, but I heard it. I heard the gunshots, the screams, and then, just when it seemed like there couldn't possibly be anyone left alive in there to kill, the explosion that ripped the front off the building.

I hid behind the Peugeot. It was red.

I hid there until my knees burned, as the police cars with their flashing lights, the ambulances whirred past me.

Thirty people were killed. More than two dozen injured.

Dr Selena Cole, the woman I was so keen to see, was one of the survivors. She had left the hotel early that morning and hadn't yet returned. Her husband wasn't so lucky. Ed Cole was killed in the detonation of the IED.

The culprits were not difficult to identify. A neo-paramilitary group, based in the Colombian portion of the Darién Gap, took to the internet to proudly proclaim their success, crow about the blow they had struck to the world of kidnap and ransom. Escorpion Rojo – the Red Scorpion – had been around for the last decade or so, making a small but solid name for themselves in the production and distribution of drugs, kidnapping unwitting travellers as a nice little sideline to help keep the coffers full.

Yet things had grown lean for the group, as Colombia's newly introduced anti-narcotics policies began to bite. Escorpion Rojo let their displeasure be known, with IEDs left at police stations in Medellín and Bogotá. A small-arms attack that crossed the border into Venezuela.

And then Brasilia, the brightest and best of the world's K&R industry gathered together in one place.

It was an awesome attack, one that shifted the paradigm that had for so many years been applied to Colombian paramilitaries. It showed that borders meant little, that it wasn't simply about territory, power within their own small domain. Not any more.

I still dream about that day. Night after night I wake, sweat pooling across my chest, and I hear the screams, smell the burning flesh. I survived. And yet I did not escape. I think there are few who did. I wake, day after day, in my own bed. But still I have never left Brasilia and the day that the K&R industry was brought to its knees.

THE MISSING HOURS

Author's note: I attempted to contact Dr Selena Cole whilst writing this article. The Cole Group is still in operation, still successfully negotiating the release of hostages, but Selena Cole, its founder and owner, is no longer involved in its day-to-day running. Management has now been handed over to the Coles' managing director, Seth Britten. Selena was unavailable for interview.

The compromise of marriage

DS Finn Hale: Friday, 10.41 a.m.

There are voices on the other side of the door. I stop, listen. No, one voice. It has lowered now, as though whoever it is does not want to be overheard. I stand there trying to pull words out of the hushed rhythm, but it is futile.

So instead, I just march right in.

A woman sits at one of a pair of desks, receiver tucked into her shoulder, her head in her hands, long copper hair hanging loose down her back. She looks up at me, her mouth dropping open, eyes flaming. I smile, flash my warrant card. She stares at it like it has frozen her to the spot, and it seems that I can hear her heart rate increase.

Interesting.

'No. No, of course. I understand. Yes. I'll look into it. I'll get straight back to you.' Her accent is northern, unadulterated and clear. She spins the chair away from me slightly as she talks, so she is facing the patio doors that let out on to the bright green garden beyond. There's a fish pond.

I pull out the chair that is tucked beneath the adjacent

desk, sit down without being asked. She glances at me, a quick flare of the nostrils, and I know I've got to her.

'Okay. Yeah. Well, thanks for letting me know.'

Orla Britten hangs up the phone with a thump, turning her chair so that she is facing me dead on. 'Can I help you with something?' She doesn't smile, isn't going to do the whole playing-to-the-police-officer thing. Which is fine. Because quite frankly I've had a titful of this.

'Detective Sergeant Hale.'

'Okay.' She looks at me like she's about to slap me. But she is shifting in her chair, blinking rapidly, more nervous than she wants me to know.

'We need a chat, Mrs Britten.'

She stares at me. 'Sure,' she says flatly.

'Your husband around?'

She glances back at the closed patio doors, and it is then that I notice a tall figure at the bottom of the garden. He is walking back and forth across my line of sight, phone clutched tight to his ear.

'He had to make a call.'

I look pointedly at the phone on the adjacent desk. 'Cold out today,' I offer.

'What did you say you wanted?' she asks. 'You know that Selena is back now? That everything is absolutely fine? To be honest, I really don't understand why you lot keep coming here.'

In my defence, this is my first visit.

I shake my head. 'It's not about Selena.'

'Okay.'

I'm waiting for something. For tears, for a flourish of guilt to erupt from her. She simply stares at me.

'I'm here about Dominic Newell.'

There it is. A fury of reactions races across her face. She leans back in her chair like she is trying to get away from me, like that will help.

'I assume you know? About his murder?' I ask.

She looks from me out into the garden to where her husband is standing. Then closes her eyes briefly and nods. 'I saw it on the news. At first I thought it couldn't be him. You know? You never think that someone you know will end up being murdered.'

'You knew him well?'

She shrugs, a quick glance up at me, then away. 'Not well. We've had a couple of overlapping areas of interest.'

'Beck Chambers?'

'Yes. We – Dominic and I – communicated about Beck's various legal issues.'

'What was your relationship like with him?'

Orla looks out into the garden. A robin has hopped up on to the path that leads to the patio doors, is staring in at us. I roll my eyes at it.

'I didn't have a relationship with him. Not really.'

'And yet,' I say, 'you called him six times on the day he died.'

She looks back at me, and I can see fear in her.

'Fae, Dominic's receptionist, said that you seemed pretty upset. That you were desperate to speak to him.'

Orla takes a breath. Readies herself to lie to me. 'I don't remember.'

I don't respond to that. Just look at her. The robin has given up, is hopping away. I don't blame him.

'See, what's interesting to me, Mrs Britten, is that Dominic's partner Isaac has confirmed that in the days leading up to his death, he discovered that Dominic was having an affair. With a woman. Isaac actually called her. Spoke to her.'

She's keeping my gaze, but only just. Has the look of a deer about to take flight. There are tears building in her eyes.

'You were having an affair with him, weren't you?' I soften my voice right up, a priest now, ready to take confession.

The tears are overfilling, spilling down her cheeks. She shakes her head, a little exhalation, and I think that this is it, that the confession is coming.

Then she looks directly at me, her expression sad. 'I wish that was the way of it.'

I watch her. Am wondering what the hell she is about to say next when the patio doors swing open. I didn't see the husband hang up the phone, didn't see him approach along the long path. I'm getting sloppy in my old age.

He hasn't noticed me, is bouncing his mobile phone in his hand, looks like he is carrying the weight of the world on his shoulders. He is a little shorter than me, although his slenderness gives the impression of height. He's wearing a shirt and tie, and I wonder if he has had meetings, or if he always dresses that way, even though the office is set within the Cole home. My eyes fall to the scars that crease his face, and I snatch my gaze away, guilty suddenly.

'Everything okay?' He looks from me to his wife.

'DS Hale, Mr Britten.'

He nods. 'Hi. Seth. What's all this?' He's asking his wife, or me, whichever one of us feels like answering. But Orla has turned her chair now, so that she is facing the wall. I can just about make out the tears trickling down her cheeks.

Guess that leaves me, then.

'Seth,' I say, 'I'm here investigating the murder of Dominic Newell.'

I don't know what response I was expecting. I don't know what it was I thought he would say. Whatever it was, I don't get it. The mobile phone hits the floor with a clatter, a tinkle that suggests the screen has smashed against the hard tiles. I stare at it for a moment, trying to piece it all together, then look back at Seth. He is staring at me, his mouth moving even though not a sound escapes him. He has paled, his skin taking on an almost grey sheen.

I look at him. Look at Orla.

She has turned her chair around now, is watching her husband. She has stopped crying.

'He's . . . Dom . . . he's . . . he's dead?'

He doesn't wait for me to confirm it. It is both a statement and a curse. Then his knees buckle beneath him and he slides to the floor. His hands cover his face and a noise breaks from him, a coarse keening.

I feel the pieces shift before me. The wife staring. The husband bereft. I see all of my expectations crumbling away and the magnitude of my error becoming clear. Isaac was wrong. Dominic was having an affair. But it wasn't the wife. It was the husband.

A Start in Kidnap and Ransom
(continued)

Dr Selena Cole

She was an elegant woman, tall, slender, the type for whom the word willowy seemed to have been invented. A suede coat, faux-fur collar standing up tall, her hair pulled back into a neat bun. Every now and then you would see some tourist or other pause in their picture-taking, leaving off from the London Eye or the Thames with its perennial river cruises, just to watch her pass. She drew attention.

Kate walked like she had all the time in the world, paid little attention to the man following her. But then few people did. He was grey, unremarkable in the best possible sense, seeming to vanish even as you stared at him.

Then came a roar of engines, a car pulling up on to the Embankment kerb, its rear door flung open.

She stopped, her hands flying to her mouth, the sudden realisation that she had made a mistake.

But it was too late.

The grey man was already on her, pushing her into the waiting car.

And then they were gone, like they had never been there, leaving behind only a knot of confused tourists.

'You drew attention,' I said.

She stared at me, an alien life form. 'Well, yes,' she allowed.

'When you are in a kidnap hotspot, the last thing you want to do is draw attention. Your clothing, your car, your jewellery, all of it screams out that you would make a valuable commodity.'

The group nodded, transfixed.

It was day five. An intensive training course designed to prepare the employees of Lexix Oil to survive in Nigeria. In fairness to Kate, she had handled her kidnapping with restraint, the fear showing in only the dancing of her fingers.

'It's known as stress inoculation. We expose you to stressful circumstances, in a controlled environment, so that if the worst were to happen, you will already have the responses in place to deal with it.'

Kate nodded fiercely, pen moving rapidly across paper. It happens this way: employees coming in, expecting that what we do here will be a cakewalk. Then they experience it, the reality, or the facsimile at least, of a kidnapping, and suddenly life becomes far more serious.

'Situational awareness,' barked Seth. He strutted across the classroom, each step a bounce. 'When you are out there, you are always watching. A stroll isn't a stroll any more. It is a chance to detect threats.'

Ed looked at me, grinned.

Seth had been with us for a few months at that point, four, five at the most. Was still a child playing Cowboys and Indians. Maybe it was us, the burgeoning Cole Group, that thrilled him. Or maybe it was simply being back in the world again, no longer held prisoner by his still livid scars. Here they gave him an extra dimension, a kudos that he would not have had without them.

'He's had a tough life,' Ed had said, a package of persuasion designed to induce me to bring Seth into a company that was not yet big enough to feed another mouth. 'Bad childhood, bounced around foster homes; there was abuse, I think. Left school without any qualifications. Then what happened in Basra. He needs us, Mogs.'

I stood, my gaze hooked on the participants, their gaze hooked on Seth. The room fizzing with energy now, the sudden realisation that this was not a game after all, that the next time they saw us would be when we were trying to save their lives. You do what you can. You give them what they are able to receive. You hope it's enough.

Blood

We sit still, the spindly branches of the apple tree tapping against the window like a minor character from a Poe story. We are now in the realm of polite conversation. Selena is desperate for me to go. You can see it in the way she leans forward in her chair, her eye contact becoming more desultory, there, then gone again. She is on the run, uncomfortable in her own home, her fingers tapping against the rough denim of her jeans, gaze leaping from me to the photograph of her dead husband and back again.

I know that I have her on the ropes. I should feel good about this, I suppose. I should feel that I am doing my job again, that I have washed the glamour from my eyes. But I don't. I feel like crap.

I shift on the sofa, and Selena's gaze flies back towards me, her expression lifting. I know that she is hoping that this is it, that I am finally about to leave.

I smile. 'Could I possibly use your bathroom?'

Her face falls, is gathered up just as quickly, and she nods. 'Of course. It's out through this door, take a left towards the kitchen and it's the last but one door on your right.'

I stand slowly, stretching it out. My heart is beating faster now, and I pray that she cannot hear it. I very carefully pull the living-room door closed behind me on my way out.

The hallway is cold after the heat of the living room, the Victorian tiles seem to be made of ice, and I suppress a shiver.

She lied to me.

I saw it, before she remembered herself, looking at me steadily as she told me she did not know Dominic Newell. I saw the alarm that flashed across her eyes, the slight tremble to her fingers, the contraction of her forehead. She lied.

I walk quickly along the tiled floor, straight past the bathroom to the closed door beyond it. Place my hand upon the wood and feel a thrum, thrum, thrum from beyond. The laundry room. Once I saw that, once I saw the lie, it was like someone had lifted a shade. I could see it all then in glorious Technicolor. The flimsiness of her story, her coat abandoned on the riverbank.

The sweater, the stain that I took to be mud.

I push open the laundry-room door. It is small, neatly organised. The machine gurgles, spinning the clothes in a dizzying rhythm. I sat there watching Selena Cole in her high-backed wing chair, looking every inch the professional, looking unsuspectable, and yet seeing her somewhere else. On a hospital bed, her hands folded into her lap, her skin pale, fingernails muddy. The white jumper with its dark stain.

Blood.

I slip inside, close the door tight behind me.

I am too late. My heart dances. The machine is on, spinning, gurgling. I am too late. She has washed it already, washing away the evidence of . . . what? Her involvement in a murder?

My breath catches at the thought, spiking where it settles. Can it really be that?

I stop for a moment, gather myself. There is a basket in the corner, laundry waiting for the wash. I send up a prayer to a God I'm not sure I believe in, pull a pair of protective gloves on, and plunge my hands into the folds of fabric. Please let it be here.

My gloved fingers run through cotton, some kind of viscose, then, finally, at the bottom they hit wool. Soft. Cashmere. I pull it free, the clothes that top it avalanching towards me with the movement. And there it is. A white cashmere sweater. Across its front a dark stain, almost black in the light from the small square window.

I stand, breathe out.

Why the hell hasn't she washed it? I take a moment to be offended by this. That this woman who so blinded me with her capabilities, her success, should fail at something so basic, so obvious. At the very least she should have shown some evidence of criminal mastermindedness. Some greater guile. Did she too believe herself to be unsuspectable? Beyond reproach?

I breathe in the smell of fresh laundry, that ineffable cleanness, and study the jumper in my hands, the dark patch now, at a near distance, unmistakably blood.

The washing machine is spinning, faster, faster, and then it begins to slow, dwindling into silence. I feel dizzy from the loss of the sound, reach out a hand to the counter to steady myself.

I can hear the oversized clock that hangs on the laundry-room wall ticking now. And something else. Voices.

I pull an evidence bag from my trouser pocket, put there for this very purpose, slide the sweater inside. Move towards the door, pull it open. I assume that the voices have been there the entire time, masked only by the roar of the washing machine. I slip into the hallway, walking with soft steps past the bathroom door until I reach the one beyond it. It is closed tight, but the voices cannot be contained by mere wood. They slither underneath, low, urgent.

'Where were you?'

'What do you mean, where was I?'

A weighty silence, the calm before the storm. I listen for Finn's voice, for his breathing, but there is nothing, just Orla and Seth locked in a marital war. I know how that feels.

'You're not seriously asking me this?'

'You knew? About me and Dom?'

'Of course I bloody well knew. I always know. You're not as cunning as you think you are. I always know when you've got a new conquest. What? Did you think I was that stupid? Really?'

Another silence, the sound of someone crying. In my gut, I know that it's Seth.

'You loved this one?'

I strain, craving the answer, but there is nothing, just the creak of a chair, a heavy sigh. Did he nod, I wonder, or shake his head? Which is worse? That you have been betrayed for love? Or that you weren't even given that courtesy?

Where is Finn? I lean into the hallway, can just about see an indistinct shape through the glass diamond cut into the front door. Think that I recognise my brother's silhouette. Maybe it would have been better if my husband had loved her, the secretary. Then again, maybe not.

'The bank called.'

You can hear that Orla is working to keep her voice flat, that it is taking all her resources. Is she always so capable? I wonder. Or did those resources crumble when faced with her husband's lover? Then what role Selena?

'They said we're overdrawn on the business account, that we've reached our overdraft limit.'

Another scrape of a chair. 'How the hell could that be?'

'I don't know, Seth.' A pause. 'I had them check back through the transactions. There was a fifty-thousand-pound withdrawal.'

A sound that my imagination twists into an intake of breath. 'What? Who the . . .'

'I don't know, Seth,' Orla repeats. 'All I know is that there are very few people authorised to make that kind of withdrawal. And I know I didn't do it.'

'So you think I did?'

'You think I'm a murderer.'

'It must have been . . .'

'Yes.'

'But why?'

'I don't know.'

'You know this means we can't cover wages? Insurance. Expenses. You know this means we're done?' Seth's voice has climbed, a tinge of the hysterical. There is the ruffling of papers. Then, 'Fifty thousand pounds. What the hell are we going to do?'

'Are you . . . I mean, the police . . .'

'No.'

Silence.

'But . . .'

'No, Orla. We are not getting them involved.'

I hear footsteps, someone twisting the handle of the living-room door. I spring back just in time, so that I could have been coming out of the bathroom, so that it isn't blindingly obvious that I was eavesdropping.

I smile brightly at Selena. 'Well, I'd better be on my way.'

She looks dazed, as if she has been startled awake by something, looks up and down the hallway. 'I . . . I thought I heard voices.' Her gaze moves to the closed office door, locks on it.

'Oh,' I say. 'I didn't notice.'

I move towards her, and it is then that she looks down, realises what is in my hands. I lift the evidence bag up. 'I'm going to need to take this.'

The suspect

I stand in the weak sunlight, look to the sky.

'Seth says they've been together for six months, on and off. That they dated, years ago. They were one another's first relationship. Gay relationship, I mean. Apparently, once Beck Chambers came to work for the Cole Group, Seth got wind of the fact that Dominic represented him. I don't know, must have brought back fond memories or something. Anyway, he reached out and they reconnected.'

'Bloody Facebook.' The DI's voice is tinny down the phone line.

'Indeed.'

'He have an alibi?'

I kick at some moss growing through the cracks in the pavement. 'He was on a plane. Overnight flight from Newark to Gatwick, landed at 7.20 the morning after the murder. Pretty good as alibis go.' I watch as a neighbour, an elderly woman with a frizzy knot of battleship curls, struggles with her shopping, her bag for life dragging against the ground. It occurs to me that I should offer to help, but I'm on the phone with my DI, so of course I don't. Then, as if she senses me watching, her gaze swings up towards me and the Cole house. 'It'll have to be checked, of course, but if it's real, then . . .'

'Then he's out.'

'Sir.'

She stares at me, shifts her shopping from one hand to the other, then turns to begin her slow progress into a sad-looking semi.

'I'll get Christa to take a look. What about the wife? Opal?'

'Orla, sir. The wife isn't doing as well. She admits that she knew about the affair, says that it was by no means her husband's first and that she, and I quote, had "learned to live with it". She does admit that she tried to contact Dominic repeatedly that day and that he never returned her calls. Says that she didn't speak to him, didn't see him, and that she spent her evening polishing off a nice bottle of Merlot in the comfort of her own home.'

'Witnesses?'

'A cat, apparently.'

The DI sniffs. 'Fabulous.'

I shift from foot to foot. Watch a kestrel riding high above me, plunging down towards the mountain slopes that surround us, then climbing again.

'So,' says the DI. 'The wife, eh?'

'Sir.'

Did she do it? Did she get frustrated with Dominic's refusal to acknowledge her, make the drive into Cardiff and wait for him coming out of the office? Did she talk, get close to him; did he, feeling guilty, feeling sorry for her, the wronged spouse, let his guard down? And then, when he had decided that he was safe, did she plunge a knife into his neck?

I watch the kestrel. Think that I just don't know.

'Well, best bring her along.'

'I'm sorry?' The kestrel is plummeting downwards now, a flash of darkness against the hillside.

'You'd better arrest the wife. Get everything on record. We'll assemble a team, have them do a house search. You never know. Maybe they'll find Newell's car in the downstairs toilet.'

'Yes, sir. Sir, best do the Cole house too.' I look up at its fascia, catch a glimpse of a figure moving across the living-room window. 'Both Mr and Mrs Britten work from the office here.'

I am looking at the door when it swings open. Feel myself tense. But it is merely Leah, a plastic evidence bag gripped in her hands, jaw set in that way that means trouble for someone.

I mutter a swift prayer to the gods that it's not me.

'All right. I'll get the ball rolling here. Keep me updated.'

I open my mouth to reply, but he has already gone, leaving me clutching my phone uselessly to my ear. I look at Leah, shake my head.

'Okay?' she asks.

'DI,' I say, gesturing with the phone. 'Orla is coming with us.'

She nods, her face getting grimmer by the second. 'I had a feeling she might be.' She crosses her arms across her blouse, barely controlling a shiver, and looks back to the house. 'Something is going on in there.'

'Like what?'

'No idea. But I'm pretty sure we're being lied to.'

I study her. 'By whom?'

Leah shrugs, glances at me. 'By everybody.'

'Awesome.'

'Look,' she says, 'there's somewhere I need to go.' She is assessing me, waiting for me to interrupt, object, so I keep my mouth sealed shut. 'I have a hunch. There's money missing from the Cole Group account.'

'Okay?'

'So I want to chase it down. Now. I've called the SIO and arranged a production order for the bank.' She is preparing for a fight, lining up her defensive moves before I can begin. 'I know this isn't strictly speaking related to the murder, but I just can't shake this feeling that if I can fill in those hours of Selena's, it will also lead us to what happened to Dominic.'

I open my mouth, see her brace herself. 'Drop me back at the station with Orla,' I say, 'then take the car.'

Leah nods. 'Cheers, Finn.' Gestures back to the house. 'What do you think?'

I sigh. 'Buggered if I know.'

But she isn't looking at me now, is looking beyond me, at a house across the street. I turn, squint at the bay window, the sun reflecting off it.

'What?'

'Will you wait for me?'

'What, again?'

She grins. 'Cool your jets, hotshot. Your big sister has a potential witness to interview.'

She walks off, not waiting for my reply.

'Okay,' I say, 'but if Orla Britten decides to go loco and stab me too, it's on you.'

'I'm okay with those odds.' Her voice drifts over her shoulder.

The watcher

DC Leah Mackay: Friday, 11.11 a.m.

The neighbour sits in the window, the thickly stuffed armchair pulled up unapologetically close so that his knees must touch the glass. He sees me coming, as I knew he would, pushes himself to his feet so fast that he nearly tumbles. Has yanked the door open long before I have the opportunity to knock.

'I was wondering when you'd come.'

'I'm sorry?'

'Well, I heard. You know. About Mrs Fancy Pants over yonder. That you were asking around. Only I wasn't here, see. My daughter, she'd driven up to get me. Cotswolds she lives. Pretty, if you like that sort of thing.' A sniff suggests he doesn't. 'Mind, expensive. Scandalous what they charge for them houses.'

He looks eighty if he's a day, the kind of short that suggests he was once much taller, but that life has worked him down into the miniature package before me. He leans on a walking stick, has a shock of white hair that rings his head in a halo.

'Can I . . .?'

'Yes, come in. Come in. About time we saw the police doing something, all that taxpayers' money, and on what? Never see them around here. Not ever.'

I nod, patient, fight back the urge to remind him that this quiet hamlet in the countryside is hardly South Central LA. Follow his awkward progress down the narrow hall. The living room is small and breathtakingly full. Ornaments, papers, things adorn every surface. A smell of damp hangs in the air.

'Sit down, then.'

He waves me to a two-seater sofa, its cushions bowed and warped, and returns to his armchair, his gaze settling back on the street beyond.

'I'm Detective Constable Leah Mackay.' I am talking to the back of his head, watch it bob up and down in response. 'I did call to see you, on Tuesday, but there was no answer. You said you'd heard about the disappearance of Dr Cole?'

'Doctor, is she? Well, I don't know about that. Never spoken to the woman. See her taking those girls of hers out, but that's all. Aye, Tuesday, well, I was away with my daughter. Like I said.'

I let my gaze track over his head, the street beyond laid out like a television screen, the Cole house front and centre. 'You have quite the view here.'

'Aye, well, nothing on the box these days. All sex and blood. Who wants to see that, eh? So I sit here. Mind, not that much happens, but still, it's something to do.'

I look beyond him to the leafy street, the clambering mountains behind. 'I'm sorry,' I say. 'I didn't get your name?'

'Ernest Thomas. Mister. Lived here for forty years now. Me, the missus. Of course, she died, ten years ago now. Still, they never really leave, do they?' He waves at a sepia photograph in a heavy gold frame. 'There she is on our wedding day. Not much to look at, mind, but still . . . we made do.'

'Of course. Um . . .' I am thrown. 'So you said you were away with your daughter on the day Dr Cole went missing . . .'

'That's right,' he agrees, affably. 'Lower Slaughter with our Beth.'

'Right,' I say. 'So if you weren't here . . .'

'Oh, well,' he says, shifting in his chair so he's looking at me. 'I didn't go till that morning, did I? Beth was late. She usually is. And, thing is, I get up early, about four normally, so there's lots of time to kill. And it was there, even then.'

'Sorry, what was there?' I ask.

'The car.'

It feels like trying to grip the tail of a tiger. 'What car?'

'Well, I get up, like I always do, at four or thereabouts, put the kettle on, and get two Rich Tea biscuits. I come in here, and there's this car parked right in front of my house.' He looks indignant. 'I mean, that's just wrong, isn't it? Parking in front of someone's house like that?'

'Do you drive?'

'No, but that's not the point. Where was Beth supposed to park? Anyway, I thought, oh no, Ernie, leave it, wait and see. They'll probably move soon. But I thought, well, you know, I'd keep an eye to make sure, and if they didn't, then I'd go and see if I could get them to shift. But the funny thing was, he was in there.'

'Who was in there?'

'The man. Sitting in the driver's seat as bold as you like. At four thirty in the morning. I mean, who does that?' He shakes his head. 'I'm telling you, I nearly went out then and there to tell him to sling his hook. Only the thing is, once I had a better look at him, I thought maybe best not. Big lad, see. Looked like one of those squaddies you get hereabouts. Always drifting over from Stirling Lines. Said to myself, now, Ernie, Beth will be properly angry if you get into a physical with one of those boys.'

I nod, keeping my face flat, trying to bat away the image of eighty-year-old Ernest Thomas taking on the might of the SAS.

'Can you describe him?'

'Big.'

'Okay. Anything else you remember? Hair? Skin colour?'

'Oh, he wasn't one of those immigrants like you get nowadays.'

I bite my lip and make a show of writing on my pad.

'Dark hair, short, you know the way them squaddies have it.'

'And what about the car? Can you describe that at all?'

'I can do you one better than that.' He pushes himself up effortfully and, leaning heavily on his stick, makes his way to the mantelpiece. 'I took his licence plate. Thought, well, you never know. Course, if I'd been here when you came round, I'd have given it to you then. Then I heard she was back, that Mrs Cole or whatever her name is, so I figured, well, you wouldn't need it. But anyway, there it is.'

He hands me a sliver of paper, the licence number written in spidery ink.

CV02 HTY.

'Was it blue?' I ask, thinking of Beck's file, the information it contained and straining to hear my voice over my heart beating.

Ernest watches me intently, nodding furiously. 'Ford Fiesta. Closer to navy, I'd say. Know it, do you?'

I smile. Do not answer.

Yes.

Beck Chambers.

Chasing the money

I stand in line, waiting for the bank teller to finish with the middle-aged couple before me. The teller sits patiently as they squabble amongst themselves, which account it should be, who's in charge of it, who forget to close the fridge door so that the food inside spoiled.

Am I wrong? Am I seeing monsters where there are none?

And yet . . .

Few people would have unrestricted access to the business account of the Cole Group, such that the withdrawal of fifty thousand pounds could happen without some very serious questions needing to be answered. Seth didn't know about it. Orla didn't seem to either. And so honestly, unless they have been subject to fraud on a prodigious scale, that only leaves Selena Cole.

'I told you to bring the chequebook. Didn't I tell you to bring the chequebook?' The woman's voice has clambered up an octave, has become querulous and shrill. The man turns to the bank teller, rolls his eyes in exaggerated toddler style.

Could it really be a coincidence? Selena Cole vanishing

263

at the same time as fifty thousand pounds? So what is it? What does that mean? She's stealing from her own business?

Why was Beck Chambers parked outside her house on the morning of her disappearance?

And what about Dominic's murder? Where does that fit in? Does it fit in at all?

I had returned to the Cole house, was the one who arrested Orla. In spite of the questioning, in spite of what we had said, I don't think she was expecting it. She looked at me, her gaze pinned to my lips as if she was deaf and the only way she could translate what I was saying was by their movement. I had expected a fight, some kind of token protest at the very least. But instead, she merely nodded, allowed me to lead her by the hand, a small child in my grasp. Looked at me like I had betrayed her.

They are arguing about parking now. I can see the teller, her face sliding into a flat irritation loosely covered in an ineffectual smile.

I had dropped Finn at the station, watched him leading Orla inside and felt a splurge of guilt. For abandoning my duty yet again, or for arresting someone who had grown to trust me, I'm not sure. I watched them go. Did I think she was a murderer?

I don't know.

They are moving finally, the woman painfully slow, tucking a wad of notes into her handbag, the man striding away, a loud huff of impatience following in his wake. I wait for her to clear the desk.

I no longer know what the hell to think. Instead I am just following where the evidence leads. What I should have been doing all along.

I lay my warrant card down before the teller, take a breath and say it. Hold my breath.

'Yes, we have the Cole Group business account here.'

It feels strangely unsteadying.

'I understand that rather a large withdrawal was made from that account recently,' I say.

She types, frowns. Then, an eyebrow raised, says, 'Yes, a total of fifty thousand pounds.'

'When was this?'

'Ah . . .' More typing. 'The first withdrawal was Tuesday at 5.26 p.m.' She bites her lip. 'Ten thousand pounds. That seems high . . . oh, here it is . . . the Cole Group have a long-standing arrangement with us that allows for large withdrawals. Still, that is a lot.'

And it is during the missing hours.

'The first withdrawal?'

She nods. 'A request was put in on that day for a withdrawal of an additional forty thousand pounds. We need time to accumulate that amount of cash, so the balance wasn't released until yesterday afternoon.'

'And can you tell me who made the withdrawals?'

'Just a . . . Dr Selena Cole.'

I am not sure if I have heard the words or if I have willed them into being. All the same, there they are.

The deck is reshuffling, fast. What does this make it? A kidnapping? A classic case of burundanguiado? Drugging, emptying the bank account? So then, the next question is, who? It comes back to Beck Chambers. Beck Chambers who has been watching the house, who has a history in South America, who would have access to the drug. Did he drug her, take her, empty her bank account . . . and then what? Go home? Sit on his couch and watch *Jeremy Kyle*?

Or is it Selena herself, stealing from her own company for her own gain?

I think I'm getting a headache.

'Could I possibly see your CCTV footage?'

The CCTV room is quiet, a blessed relief. I rest my head back, breathe. Think that the end is in sight and that when I reach that end, I can return home, to my babies.

The footage shows a dwindling day in the bank, crowds dissipating as the clock drags closer to 5.30. At 5.25, Selena Cole walks into the bank. She is wearing the wool coat, has her back to the camera so I can't see her face. She heads straight to the desk. I pause it, study the room. Because if she is the victim of a drugged kidnap, wouldn't the kidnapper want to be there, to keep an eye on his prize? There is a young woman, bent forward over a buggy, a recalcitrant toddler caught mid-scream. Two slightly older children hang off her from either side, look like their even distribution of pull is all that is preventing her from toppling over. A middle-aged man stands behind Selena. He is clutching a sheaf of paper, his glance caught over his shoulder, at the mother, her young children. The curl of his lip suggests they are irritating him.

I switch to a different camera, this one positioned directly behind the teller's head. In this shot, I can see Selena's face. What am I looking for? What would make someone obvious as burundanguiado? Would there be a dazed look to them, the suggestion of one who is sleepwalking through life? Would they look afraid or lost? Selena looks none of those things. Her glance flicks up to the camera, once, twice. She has been crying. I pause on that.

She stares at me.

It occurs to me that if I was the teller, I wouldn't know

she'd been crying, but that I have begun to understand Selena Cole, that I have made her a matter of close study. I can see the slight downturn at the corners of her mouth, the very subtle puffiness that edges her eyes. I have learned to see behind Selena's show.

I unpause it. Watch as the teller leads her away, into a side room. Switch to another camera, a different room now, small and sparse. Watch as Selena sits in a solitary chair, waits, picking at a thread on her coat. Then the door opening, a woman, a different one, entering – a manager? She smiles brightly, her mouth moving in silent conversation. Selena leaning forward, her gaze hooked on the money tray before her. And then the money. A pile of notes, stacked like a row of terraced houses, then slipped into a large envelope.

Selena picks it up, cradling the envelope that contains ten thousand pounds. Spares some thin words to the woman who holds open the door for her, and vanishes into the waiting foyer beyond.

I flip back to the original camera, watch the foyer. Wait for someone I haven't noticed before, beyond the lip of the camera's angle maybe, to peel away, follow Selena with her ten thousand pounds.

But there is nothing.

Okay.

I turn to the outside camera.

They have to be here. Surely. If it is a kidnapping for ransom, they will be waiting to collect, if not inside, then right outside the doors.

There are people moving, the crowd thinned out by the weather. I curse. Umbrellas are up, and so from my angle I can see little but a series of circular shapes moving through

Hereford city centre. Even if Beck is here, I may not recognise him.

There she is.

Selena comes out. Pauses.

Is she afraid? Is she considering running? Or is she too drugged to know where she is?

Or is none of that the case?

She looks up to the sky, blinks as the rain hits her face, and tucks her collar up, a fairly useless concession to the weather. Holds the envelope tight to her.

Is she waiting for a handler to come and get her and their money? Is she waiting for Beck? Has she been told to come out of the bank, to wait, and is following her instructions helplessly?

But then she begins to walk.

There is no meandering, no dawdling, no ducking under a shelter to escape from the rain. She walks with a purpose. She knows where she's going even if I have no clue.

I shift to a different camera as she walks out of shot.

This one is set to a wider angle, encompasses the length of the pedestrianised zone. I can see the train-station from here.

I watch as Selena cuts through the umbrellas, a line straight and true into the open train-station doors.

She vanishes from view.

I sit back, my heart thumping.

That, then, is it. I have filled in some scant minutes in those missing hours. She went to the bank, withdrew ten thousand pounds, then caught a train. Where? Where the hell was she going? I gather my belongings, think that the train station is my own next destination. She must have got a return, come back late at night, walked the river from Hereford to where she was found, confused and coatless.

I . . .

I pull my own coat on.

I have no idea what the hell is going on.

The footage is still running, albeit unintentionally. And a movement at the train-station door stays me. I can't see her face; the station is far too far away for me to be sure who I am seeing. But, like I said, I have made a study of Selena Cole. So I recognise her figure, the way she walks.

I sit back down.

She re-emerges from the train station. She's still wearing the coat, her hand pulling from the inside of it. Has she tucked the envelope inside, protecting it from the rain? She walks confidently back towards the camera. I scan her surroundings. From what I can see, she is alone. Then she walks past the limits of the camera range and is gone. I race the footage forward, to see if she comes back, but there is nothing.

I sit. Stare at the rapidly darkening screen.

Why did she go into the station? What did she do there?

Case No. 55
Victim: Tom Villier
Location: São Paulo, Brazil
Company: Private case
18 May 2010

Initial event

Tom Villier, aged twenty-three, was travelling around
Latin America as part of a gap-year programme. On
Friday 18 May, Mr Villier was enjoying his second
week in São Paulo, Brazil, staying at the Ascension
Youth Hostel in the city. He was travelling independently but had made a number of friends, largely
other young people residing in the same hostel. On
the evening of the 18th, he went to a local bar with
a small group of them.

Mr Villier reports that he was drinking heavily and
that sometime during the course of the night he became
separated from his group. At approximately 2 a.m.,
he left the bar, intending to walk the short distance
back to the hostel. According to Mr Villier, upon exiting
the bar he noticed a taxi idling at the kerb, its driver
talking to another young man. The driver then offered
him a shared ride, as his passenger was heading in
the same direction.

Due to Mr Villier's excessive levels of inebriation,
he failed to wonder how the taxi driver knew where

he was going, and both young men climbed into the rear of the taxi.

After travelling less than a hundred metres, Mr Villier's fellow passenger pulled a handgun on him and ordered him to remove his watch (Breitling), his sunglasses (Ray-Ban) and his trainers (Air Jordan). His wallet was taken from him and all cash removed.

Mr Villier was then informed that he would be taken to the nearest ATM, where he would withdraw $500. After handing over the cash to his kidnappers, he would then be released.

Mr Villier, in the hope of bringing the incident to a close, followed the kidnappers' instructions and withdrew $500 – the ATM daily limit in Brazil at this time. However, immediately after handing the money over, he was forced into the boot of the car.

He reports that he was driven around for some indeterminate period of time, but that when the kidnappers stopped at a second ATM (presumably in the hopes of utilising one of the other four credit cards in Mr Villier's wallet) and attempted to remove him from the boot, he fought back.

This is the end of Mr Villier's recollection.

After a period of approximately thirty-six hours, Mr Villiers was discovered, bruised and seemingly disoriented, sitting on the kerb outside the bar from which he had originally been kidnapped.

Response

After being informed of this incident by his son, Mr Leighton Villier – the victim's father – contacted the Cole Group directly. He informed us that $4,000 had been taken from his son's various cards over that thirty-six-hour period, and that his son had been unable to impress the gravity of the situation upon local police. He requested my – Ed Cole's – immediate attendance at the scene.

Although Mr Leighton Villier was advised that my contribution to events at this point was likely to be negligible, he was insistent that he wanted me to attend, and was more than happy to cover the cost of my services.

Upon arrival in São Paulo, I immediately sought out Mr Tom Villier. I located him back at his hostel, ostensibly none the worse for his experience. It was, however, difficult to obtain a full and complete accounting from the victim, as at the time of my arrival, he was severely intoxicated.

Initial attempts were made to secure Mr Villier, in terms of both his personal safety and his possessions, which were, upon my arrival, strewn across his room in easy access of anyone within the hostel. After this, I immediately proceeded to the local police station in order to ascertain the level of progress that had been made on this case. I was quickly informed that they had no leads and were, frankly, unlikely to get any. However, the officer on duty did express to me that leads might be more forthcoming were I to make him a gift of some modest amount of money. I declined.

After a lengthy conversation with the victim, I reached the conclusion that, after attempting to put up a fight, he was dosed with scopolamine – a drug in common usage in kidnap-for-ransom cases throughout Latin America, and known by the street name of devil's breath. This would account for his lack of memory for the intervening thirty-six hours, and for the apparent ease with which his kidnappers then went on to access his bank accounts.

Upon liaising with Mr Leighton Villier's insurer, I was informed that as the victim was highly intoxicated and had failed to make even the most basic efforts to ensure his own safety, the policy would not pay out to reimburse the money lost.

Mr Leighton Villier expressed to me his frustration at this. He then informed me that his priority at this point was the safety of his son. Two airline tickets were purchased, one for myself, one for Mr Tom Villier, and it was requested that I collect the victim from his accommodation and ensure his return to the UK. Mr Leighton Villier advised me that he had spoken with his son, and that he was happy to accept my escort out of São Paulo.

I had at this point been in São Paulo for less than twenty-four hours.

Upon returning to the hostel to collect the victim for transport to the airport, I discovered his room empty and his belongings gone. My initial response was to begin initialising kidnap protocols, believing that his original abductors had identified him as a lucrative target and that we were now likely to see a more protracted, and considerably more expensive, kidnap event.

I was then approached, however, by a friend of Mr Tom Villier, who informed me that he had decided to decline his father's invitation for a speedy return home and had instead left São Paulo, with the plan of heading to Lima, Peru. I am unclear as to how he believed he was going to do this, as at that time he was without money, transport or, importantly, shoes.

Nonetheless, given that he had reached the age of majority, I felt that Mr Tom Villier was well within his rights to continue his travels if he so wished.

I subsequently returned to the UK.

Note

Approximately two years after these events, Mr Villier was once again a victim of kidnap for ransom. This time in Bogotá, where he was holidaying with friends. Unfortunately for the Villier family, this kidnap event would prove to be far more costly and time-consuming. His release was secured after eleven months in captivity (see case no. 83).

A deal with the devil

DS Finn Hale: Friday, 2.49 p.m.

'I didn't kill him.'

'You can understand how we might wonder.'

'Yes. But I didn't kill him.'

'Were you angry with him?' I ask.

'With who? My husband or the man he was sleeping with?'

'Either. Both.'

'Yes. And yes. But I didn't kill him.'

'How did you find out?'

Orla shakes her head, a tired smile. 'Seth isn't as good a liar as he thinks he is. Besides, this isn't the first time.'

'There have been other men?'

'Yes. And I didn't kill any of them either.'

'Did you never think of leaving?' I am intrigued, I confess. They talk about the mysteries of marriage, and I get that. The idea that you will never know what goes on within a relationship. But this . . . this apparent acceptance of . . . betrayal, is there another word for it? This willingness to allow your spouse to do the same thing over and over again. Surely at some point it must become too much.

Surely at some point you would snap. And then what? A knife stabbed into the lover's neck?

Orla looks at me, appears to be considering. Then, 'I always knew that I loved him more than he loved me. When I first met him, when Ed introduced us, I fell for him, I mean, head over heels. And I knew that he was . . . calmer, more measured. But, I mean, whatever, it worked for us. The first time, when I realised what was happening, I was horrified. Heartbroken. And yet, in a strange way, it made me feel better. That the reason he wasn't as crazy about me as I was about him was that he just couldn't be, because there was this whole other side of him that he kept hidden.'

'So you stayed.'

She shrugs. 'I loved him. I love him.'

'And Dominic?'

'What about Dominic?'

'Was it different with him? From the others?'

'Maybe. You'd have to ask my husband.' Orla leans forward. 'Look, I'm going to make myself as clear as I can. No, of course I wasn't happy with my husband's seemingly endless need for affairs. Of course I wasn't. But it was a deal I had made with my own private devil. I wanted to keep my marriage together. Seth, in spite of everything, he wants to keep us together. So I deal with it. Sometimes I cry over it, but then I pick myself up and move on. It's a compromise that I am willing to make. I did not kill Dominic.'

'Why were you trying to contact Dominic?'

Orla sighs, looks away. 'I . . . I didn't know, about this one. Not until Isaac called me. It was our home phone. I assume Seth had been calling Dominic from it. I think Isaac thought that it was me. That Dominic and I were . . . you know. And I'll be entirely honest with you, I was angry, once I realised what was going on. It had been a while since the last time Seth had done something like this. And I thought . . . I thought we'd turned a corner, you know?'

'So you were planning on confronting Dominic?'

'I was planning on venting. I was planning on yelling at him and then going home and drinking myself into a stupor so I could try and forget. I didn't manage to achieve part one. I'm pretty sure he knew what I was about to say. I managed part two, though. I left Selena's at about five o'clock. Went home and drank two bottles of wine. Fell asleep, passed out, whatever you want to call it, on the sofa and woke up at about five the next morning with a cat sleeping on my head.' She gives me a level look. 'I understand it isn't the best of alibis.'

'No. Not really.'

'Are you going to let me go?'

'Not right now.'

She sighs heavily. 'Then I'm sorry, but I think I'm done here. I'd like to see my solicitor, if you don't mind.'

I nod slowly, acknowledging the inevitable. 'I'll get the ball rolling,' I say, standing.

She looks up at me. 'I didn't kill him.'

I walk slowly up the stairs. Did she kill him? I don't know.

The major incident room has settled into its rhythm, that segment of an investigation where everyone knows where they should be, what they should be doing. Busy but steady, unlike the first frantic hours and days. I look for Leah and then remember where she is, that I am lying for her should the need arise.

I pull up a chair. Did she see the signs, right back in the beginning? Did Leah catch what I had missed, the interconnectedness of these two cases? Because it is becoming apparent that they *are* connected. I shimmy my mouse, bringing my computer screen to life, feel a quick spasm of guilt. I doubted her, thought she had lost her edge, that her interest in the disappearance of Selena Cole was more about her own struggles than about the case itself.

'You okay, Finn?' Christa asks.

I am staring into space, I realise. 'Yeah, fine. What's up?'

'Oh, nothing. Just doing the call logs.'

'For Dominic Newell's mobile?' I pull my chair closer to hers.

'Yeah. Done the office. God, that took for ever. Nearly finished with the mobile.'

'Anything interesting?'

'Ah . . .' Christa scans her notes. 'Bunch of calls throughout Monday. Isaac was apparently quite keen to talk to him. We have about eight missed calls from his mobile to Dominic's, a couple from their home phone as well.'

'No answer?'

'Nope. We also have Orla Britten, calls him . . . one, two . . . four times on his mobile. Again, all go unanswered.'

'Maybe he wasn't feeling chatty.'

'Well I guess that would depend who you were. He took a number of calls. Three of them we traced to clients. He spent about fifteen, twenty minutes apiece talking with them. Then we have two, one lasting ten minutes, another thirty, from a mobile number that we have linked back to Seth Britten.'

'What time was that?'

'What? Those calls? Um . . . one was at 4.02 p.m., the other at 4.30.'

'So Seth was calling from New York?'

Christa looks up at me, shrugs. 'I guess. Then we have a final outgoing call made from the phone at 6.02 p.m.'

'Must have been right after he left the office.'

'Just before his murder, based on our timeline. Lasts about fifteen minutes.'

'Who did he call?'

'A landline in Endleby.'

I stare at her. 'Selena Cole's house?'

'Um . . . number is registered to an Ed Cole. So, yeah.'

Bugger.

I turn away, without explanation, pull out my mobile, press speed-dial one.

'Hey.'

'Hey, it's me. She lied.'

'Who?' Leah's voice is echoing, sounds like she is in a concert hall. Then there is a tinny voice, a tannoy announcement.

'Are you at the train station?'

'Yes. Who lied?'

'Selena. You said she told you she didn't know Dominic. Well, we have him placing a call to her home phone – private number, not the business line – at 6.02 p.m. Orla says she left at five. Seth was in New York. Dominic and Selena talked for fifteen minutes.'

Leah has stopped walking. I can hear it in the rhythm of her breath. 'I'm going back,' she says. 'You need to get the search teams up there. Now.'

'On it.'

I turn to Christa and do what my rank tells me to do.

Delegate. We need the search team to head out to the Cole house. As soon as. Then I pick up the desk phone, punch in the number from memory.

It takes five rings before it is answered, long enough that I have begun to question whether it will be.

'Hello, Hartley and Newell. Fae speaking. How may I help you?' She sounds like someone jolted from a deep sleep, answering the phone in a dream.

'Fae, it's DS Finn Hale. You okay?'

It takes her a moment to place my name. I am strangely insulted by this.

'Finn. Yes. Sorry. I didn't . . . I'm fine. I didn't sleep last night, what with everything.' A shift and her tone changes, as if she has sat up straighter. 'What can I do for you?'

'Ah, is Bronwyn there?'

'Sure. Let me just connect you.'

A minute. Two. I watch Christa as she organises the search teams. Give her a patronising thumbs-up when she glances over. She grins. Returns the gesture, only with two fingers. Okay, then . . .

'Finn. To what do I owe the pleasure?' Bronwyn sounds husky and hoarse. She also sounds as if this is anything but a pleasure.

'I need to ask you something.'

'Okay.'

'We have a call on Dominic's phone log that we're trying to make sense of. At 6.02 p.m., he called a Dr Selena Cole. Name ring any bells with you?'

'No.' The single word is thrown at me. 'But then it wouldn't, would it? Because apparently I had little real idea as to what was going on in Dom's life.'

'Ah, right.' I look at the phone and try to roll back time

so that I never picked it up in the first place. It doesn't work. 'So you don't have any idea . . .'

'No, Finn. I have no idea who that is.' A long pause and I think she is done, then, 'Perhaps he was shagging her.'

The line goes dead in my hand.

I sit there, thinking.

Perhaps he was.

Lies

It has come full circle.

I stand on the pavement, close the car door softly behind me and watch Selena Cole as she stands in the playground on the brow of the hill. Tara is in the swing, just where she was on the fateful day. But this time, the older girl, Heather, stands beside her mother, so close that there is no air between them. She too has been here before.

Selena bends down, says something to her daughter, her words tugged away by the wind, and then I see her catch sight of me, her body reacting like an electrical current has been sent through it. She stands up straight, turns to face me.

I don't bother attempting a smile this time.

'Heather,' she says as I draw nearer, 'will you take your sister on the slide for me?'

The little girl looks from me to her mother, opens her mouth to protest.

'It's okay. I promise. You'll be able to see me the entire time.' Selena rests her hand against her daughter's cheek. 'It's okay.'

'I only need a quick chat with your mum, honey,' I say. 'We'll stand right here.'

Heather stares at me, and for perhaps the first time in my life I feel that I have been warned off by a seven-year-old. Be nice to my mother or else. I'll try, I think. But my God, is your mother making it difficult.

Selena lifts the smaller girl out of the swing, plants a swift kiss on her forehead and then places her hand within her sister's. 'Go on, Tar. Go with Heather. She'll take you sliding.'

Tara's face balls up, chubby arms reaching for her mother, and I know that she too is afraid that the vanishing act will be repeated.

'Come on, Tar,' says Heather. 'We can slide together.'

It appeases her, her sister's willingness to leave the stronghold undefended, and Tara complies, allowing Heather to lead her away. But she glances backwards every few feet, just in case.

Selena looks at me, waiting.

'Was Orla here on Monday night?' I am done with preamble, with politeness and pretext. I have my own kids I want to go home to.

'I wish I could say she was. But no. She left about five o'clock.' She is square on to me, challenging almost. 'She didn't kill him, you know.'

'Who? The guy you claimed not to know?'

Selena looks away.

'You've been lying to me, Selena.' It is a statement of fact, and yet I am dimly aware of a faint flicker of hope buried within it, that she will deny it, that she will clarify. Do I still somehow hope that she will turn out to be who I thought she was? Why? So that I may feel vindicated? Somehow less foolish?

I went to the train station, marched in, so confident that it would all unspool before me, that they would have CCTV, that the cameras would be pointing just the way I needed them to point, that then I would understand and all that had been opaque would become clear. So sorry. Our internal system is down. We're waiting on engineers. Budget cuts. Everything takes forever now. Sorry about that.

Selena looks back at me and I am surprised by how calm she is, how cool in spite of my accusation. 'It is not always as simple as lying or telling the truth. Sometimes it is merely a matter of perspective.'

'From my perspective, Selena, when someone lies to me, particularly in the midst of a murder investigation, I am forced to question why they would feel the need to do that. What bad thing they have done that they are afraid I will find out about. So,' I say, 'just to clarify – you do know Dominic Newell, don't you?'

She lets go a breath, and I think of resignation, perhaps relief. 'I didn't know him well. But yes, to a certain extent, I did know Dominic.'

'Why did you lie to me?'

She opens her mouth, closes it again, watches her girls as they careen down the slide, the smaller in the lap of the bigger.

'Okay,' I say, making little effort to hide my irritation, 'let's try this. A call was placed to your house at 6.02 p.m. on Monday. Who was that?'

I can see her weighing up, making the decision whether to tell me the truth or to try another lie.

'Selena,' I say, 'my patience has run out. Let's not worry about perspectives. Let's just stick to facts. A call was made to your home phone at 6.02 p.m. on Monday. Who called you?'

'Dominic.' She says it quietly.

'Excellent. Who received that call?'

'I did.'

'How long did you talk for?'

'About fifteen minutes.'

'What did he want?'

She waves her hands. 'Some legal stuff. Wasn't really my thing. I told him Orla handles all that.'

It is strange how I have come to know this woman, how the lies she tells now seem to be highlighted in a painful, vicious yellow.

'And that,' I say, 'took fifteen minutes?'

She glances at me. 'Well, there were pleasantries, chit-chat, you know.'

I could confront her with the money, tell her that I know what she has done. But I don't. I hold it, for now.

'Tell me some more about Beck.'

She blinks at me, seems genuinely surprised by my detour. 'Beck Chambers? What else do you want to know?'

'What is your relationship with him?'

'I . . . I don't really have one.'

'No? You know he's been watching you, right?'

'Watching me?' It is the first time that I have seen her truly wrong-footed. 'What do you mean, watching me?'

I suddenly feel unsteady again, the solid ground uncertain beneath my feet. Perhaps it *was* a kidnapping, perhaps he took her and she genuinely does not remember.

'He was parked outside your house. On the day you vanished. I was just wondering how long that had been going on.'

'I genuinely had no idea. I . . . I don't know.'

She is telling the truth.

'Have the two of you ever had a relationship?'

Selena pulls herself up, a flash of anger distorting her features. 'You're asking me if I cheated on my husband with him? No. No, I did not.'

'Then or since?'

Selena lowers her voice, leaning into me, and I fight the urge to take a step back. 'My husband has been gone for a year.' There is a tremor in her voice. 'And every day has felt like the first day. Do you genuinely think that I have had any thoughts, any whatsoever, of sleeping with Beck Chambers? Or anyone else, for that matter? He was Ed's protégé. He was Ed's friend. That is as far as it goes. As to what he's doing parked outside my house, you'll have to ask him that.'

'Could he be in love with you?' She opens her mouth and I hold up my hands. 'I'm not saying that it is reciprocated. But I am asking if there is any possibility that he has feelings you haven't been aware of?'

'I suppose.' Selena watches her girls. 'No. Look, I can't know the answer to that. How could I? But I truly do not believe that is the case.'

'Which then returns us to the question, why was he watching you?'

She doesn't answer, doesn't look at me, and I realise that there is something there, that the blankness in her expression is a forced one and that she is thinking of something that she will not tell me.

There is the sound of an engine, two engines, the police cars pulling up before the Cole house. I watch Selena as she turns, catches sight of them, watch her as she begins to process the implications of this.

'Oh,' I say, 'we have a warrant to search the house. You know, because of Orla. You don't mind, do you?'

That blankness again. What is she calculating?

'No. Of course. That's fine.'

We stand together, looking down the hill towards the search team as they begin to tumble out on to the quiet street.

'Selena,' I say quietly.

She looks at me, braced.

'What happened to you? When you disappeared? Where did you go?'

She studies me. Then, 'I'm sorry. I still don't remember.'

It's funny, when you get to know somebody, just how obvious their lies become.

The car

I put my foot down, speed along twisting country roads, going way too fast. They found the car. The DI came marching into the office. 'Uniform found Dominic Newell's car. Lay-by on a B road, couple of miles from Hay-on-Wye. Finn, get your backside there now.' I take a hairpin bend fast enough that I end up on the wrong side of the road. Ease my foot off the gas.

Killing myself isn't going to make Dominic any less dead.

My headlights catch a plastic bag trapped in the hedging, and for a fleeting moment I think it is a face and feel my breath catch in my chest. I need to sleep more. Eat more. Everything more. Apart from work. That I do plenty of.

I reach the crest of the hill, feel the car picking up speed as it swoops into the valley below. Then I see it. A pool of light in a sea of darkness. The car. Dominic Newell's car. It looks like a star in a puddle of spotlights, the focus of everyone's gaze. The white light is tinted by the flash of blue from the uniformed car, shadowy figures breaking the beam as they surround the vehicle.

288

I slow, slow, slot in behind the patrol car with the dizzying flashing lights, turn the engine off. I cannot see the car from here, but the hum of activity tells me it's there. Can see white-suited CSI, uniform behind the cordon. I slide out of the driver's seat, begin to pull on my white forensic suit, my movements so rapid that they are destined to fail, fingers becoming thumbs.

Inside the cordon, Willa withdraws her head from inside the Audi A6. Her face is flat, less made up than usual, like even she has finally buckled under the pressure. Her lips are pursed as she makes quick notes, throwing choppy instructions at her colleague, a girlish-framed man I have never seen before.

'How is it?' I ask, as much to announce myself as anything else.

Willa looks up at me, and I can tell that I have pulled her back from miles away. Frowns as if she's trying to place me. Then she shrugs. 'Awesome.' Her voice is throaty, like she too needs sleep. 'Inside is a complete nightmare.'

'How do you mean?'

She gives me a long look. 'See for yourself.'

I want to. And yet I don't. The car. The damn car. It has come to promise answers, has developed its own mythology, that once it appears, all things will become clear. I walk around Willa towards the open passenger door. It should be parked outside a nice restaurant, the valet having just dropped it off. I duck my head, keeping a good distance. Then I reel back.

I was expecting it. But still the amount of blood staggers me, literally knocking me backwards so that for a moment I feel unsteady. It coats the cream leather seat, a red winter shawl dumped there by some cavalier passenger. It covers the centre console, has turned the dark panelling darker still. The driver's side, that's taken a hit too, albeit a lesser one. But the passenger seat . . .

'That's where he died.'

Willa shrugs again, doesn't answer.

But I can see it, can see Dominic Newell curled in on himself, desperately trying to hold together the gaping hole in his neck, breath coming shorter, briefer. Was he conscious? Was he begging for help, for a hospital, for his mother? I can see him, his hands over his neck, slumping lower and lower into the seat as the life runs out of him.

I step back, look out over the fields, breathe in the country air.

The wound, it was on the left side of his neck. So . . . either he was sitting in the passenger seat and someone reached in from the outside . . . but why would he be in the passenger seat of his own car? Or . . .

I lean, look in through the passenger door towards the driver's seat, the line of blood smudged and uneven on the left side of the seat. Or he was sitting in the driver's side when he was stabbed? By someone sitting in the passenger seat. Then . . . what? I look at the blood again, the driver's side; it looks less defined, like someone has pressed a cloth to it. So someone, his passenger, stabs him, gets him over into the passenger seat – did they pull him, did they get out, go round to the driver's side, push him from there? – and then climbs in and drives off while Dominic sits beside him or her, bleeding to death.

I stand up again, lean backwards, trying to make the move look casual. Willa isn't looking at me. I glance at her, features tight, expression pinched, and I think that it has got to her too, finally. The reality of murder when it is, if not one of your own, then almost one of your own.

'You, ah, you okay?' I say it not looking at her, my gaze still on the blood. Such simple words, but they seem to open up so much. I'm not this guy. I'm not the one you want to spill your troubles to. Unless what you are looking for is asinine repartee. Then I'm your guy.

Willa stares at me, seems that she's thinking the same thing. 'Yeah.' It is defensive. Said in the same way she would tell me to piss off. Then she sags, air out of a tyre. 'I'm tired. I haven't slept in . . . I don't know how long. And this . . .' She waves to the car.

'I know,' I say. See? I got this. 'It's a really hard thing to deal with.'

She looks at me, snorts. 'Not the blood, you wanker. What do you think I am? New?' She jabs her gloved hand back at the car. 'Do you have any idea how long this shit is going to take?' She leans in closer, scowling fiercely. 'I want to go to bloody sleep. I want to eat something. Anything. I'm not picky.' She makes an irritated noise in the back of her throat.

Okay. Maybe I don't have this.

On the plus side, I'm starting to like this woman.

'So,' I say, desperate to change the subject, 'we have our murder scene?'

'I'd say,' she agrees.

'Fingerprints?'

Willa nods. 'Car is full of them. We'll have to eliminate Dominic, of course, but frankly, it doesn't look like his killer made any attempt to clean up after themselves.'

'Panic?'

'Maybe.'

I stare at the car, the star of the show in its spotlight. Watch as the other CSI does whatever the hell it is they do in the back seat. What a bloody mess.

Literally.

Sorry.

'We'll run these prints, hopefully get a hit,' says Willa. 'One thing we can be damn sure of, this was no professional assassin.'

'Yeah,' I say. 'You aren't kidding.' I kick at the grass beneath my feet, a ring of mud lapping at the toe of my shoe. 'Well, look, I'll let you get back to it.' Suck in a breath. 'And, ah, maybe when we're all wrapped up on this case, I can take you out for an Indian. You know, as a thank-you for all your hard work.'

Willa stares at me, apparently as surprised by this as I am. Then she smiles, the lines on her forehead vanishing so quickly that I think I must have imagined them. 'That would be good.'

'Got something.' The CSI's voice is muffled, strangulated by his awkward position, body half in, half out of the rear of the car.

Willa hurries over to him as he emerges, panting like he's run a marathon. He looks pale. Must be new.

I cannot see what he is holding, but I see Willa frown. Hear her say, 'Well, isn't that interesting?'

'What's that?'

For a moment I think she is going to ignore me, but then she beckons me closer, holding something up to the light. I frown, squint at it, can just make out flashes of red beneath the plastic. But then, I think, maybe I'm not seeing red at all, maybe it's just that my eyes have become so accustomed to the blood that the red is habit for them now.

Then I come closer and I realise what it is that I am seeing.

A penknife, its handle slick with blood.

Addendum to Cole Group case files (CONFIDENTIAL)
Ref: Case No. 68
THIS SPECIAL NOTE IS RESTRICTED ACCESS. THIS
NOTE IS ONLY TO BE REFERENCED BY ED OR SELENA
COLE.

The victim in this case is Harold Bayliss, CEO of
Whalley Oil, and the location of kidnapping is Caquetá,
Colombia.

Whalley Oil is a small British firm that has proven
moderately successful with its oil operations within
Latin America, particularly Colombia. They have established a highly profitable operation within the district
of Caquetá. However, as is typical within this area,
they have experienced a number of security concerns,
primarily stemming from FARC rebels and a number
of offshoot groups.

In September 2013, a bus carrying employees to
Whalley's base of operations within the region was
attacked by more than a dozen gunmen. Five employees
were killed, three others seriously injured. Later examination of the circumstances surrounding the attack
suggested that the attackers – believed to be a neo-
paramilitary group operating out of the Darién Gap
– had been provided with information about the movement of the employees into the base.

Whalley Oil has been a customer of the Cole Group

for a number of years and, as such, is in receipt of both security training for its personnel and an annual audit of its security practices. Such an audit was carried out in early October 2013 in the aftermath of the attack on Whalley personnel. Our findings were that, whilst good practice procedures were in place in principle, there were a number of indications that there had been leaks in information from Whalley Oil to the rebels. Despite a shifting timetable and route for bus transports to and from headquarters, the rebels were in position waiting to attack. In the months leading up to this attack, one employee – Carol Amis, a researcher with Whalley Oil – was shot and killed exiting her home address. Meanwhile, another – Jensen Frank – was kidnapped from his home and a ransom leveraged for his safe return (see case no. 56, 2007, for further details). Following on from these events, the conclusion was drawn that someone within the Whalley Oil operation was providing information to the rebels.

A number of recommendations were put forward by the Cole Group, including a cessation of operations within the Caquetá region until such a time as the safety of such operations could be assured.

Whalley Oil refused to act on these recommendations.

On 5 November 2013, the CEO of Whalley Oil, Harold Bayliss, aged sixty-one, travelled to Colombia in order to visit the scene of the attack and perform an inspection on the company premises. The Cole Group, upon learning of this plan, strongly advised against it. Whalley Oil had brought in a greater number of security personnel and shifted their operational schedules to make procedures less predictable. However, there was still the very great concern of information being provided to the rebels from within the company. Mr Bayliss, however, remained determined to attend the scene, citing staff morale as his primary motivation.

Mr Bayliss arrived at the company's base of operations at 10.25 a.m. As per his wishes, he met with survivors of the attack and was able to tour the facility. He was scheduled to depart for a lunch appointment at 12.05 p.m.

At 12.04 p.m., as Mr Bayliss was being escorted to his waiting vehicle, an open-bed truck carrying armed men and four motorbikes, each with a rider and armed pillion passenger, arrived at the scene. Two of Mr Bayliss's bodyguards were shot, one fatally. Mr Bayliss was ushered into the truck, and after a number of rounds were fired into the engine and tyres of his vehicle in order to avoid pursuit, the kidnappers left the scene with Mr Bayliss as their hostage.

Response

At 12.15 p.m., a call was placed to the Cole Group. Beck Chambers and I (Ed Cole) were attending a conference in San Francisco at the time. However, due to the high-risk nature of Mr Bayliss's visit to Caquetá, plans had been put in place to transport us immediately to Colombia should such an incident occur. We were on the scene within fifteen hours of the kidnapping. Seth Britten joined us at the scene twelve hours later.

Upon our arrival, it was established that an operations manager within Whalley Oil had already begun the negotiation process with the kidnappers. Given the security concerns previously cited, it was decided that Mr Chambers would take over this negotiation process in order to establish a ring of secrecy around our operations.

It was rapidly determined that the kidnappers were the same group that Seth Britten had dealt with on the Jensen Frank case (see above), a neo-paramilitary group locally known as Escorpion Rojo who have, over recent years, begun to expand their kidnap-for-ransom portfolio in order to fund their illegal drug operations. This group has also identified itself as the culprits behind an IED attack on a police station in Medellín.

Having dealt with these particular kidnappers before, and knowing that they were experienced in kidnap for ransom, we had every reason to believe that Mr Bayliss would be treated relatively well and that, as long as the negotiation was seen to be moving forward in a timely manner, there was excellent reason to hope for a positive outcome. However, it also gave us fair warning that the ransom would be unlikely to be settled cheaply. In this group's history of kidnapping, they have made a name for themselves with their demands for high ransoms and their determined unwillingness to shift from this position. In 2011, they were responsible for the kidnapping of Tamara Chase, a US citizen. Her family's inability to pay the hefty ransom demanded led to her swift execution.

Ultimately a ransom of £200,000 was settled on.

Mr Bayliss was released after three weeks in

captivity. Whilst in purported good health, he was unfortunately reporting chest pains and as such was transported immediately to the local hospital, where it was determined that he had suffered a fairly major heart attack whilst in captivity. After an initial treatment period, he was then flown back to the UK, where he underwent open-heart surgery. Despite a lengthy hospital stay, he is expected to make a full recovery.

Special considerations

In the aftermath of this case, Mr Chambers reported to me that during the course of his negotiation, a suggestion was made that he might like to operate for the cartel as a drugs mule. Evidently, Escorpion Rojo are looking to expand their operations from Latin America into Europe, the UK specifically. The suggestion that was put to Mr Chambers was that he would serve as an excellent vehicle to transport their product – a scopolamine-based manufactured drug known throughout Latin America as El Diablo – into mainland Britain, and that he would be very generously reimbursed for his troubles. In ten years in the kidnap-and-ransom industry, and having dealt with many drug cartels, I have never been propositioned in such a manner. Neither has Seth Britten, in spite of the fact that he has had previous dealings with this group. This raises a number of questions for me. Mr Chambers has experienced difficulties in the past with substance abuse; has he made himself vulnerable to exploitation by using this information as a means of building trust during his negotiation? When this issue was raised with him, Mr Chambers steadfastly denied that he had provided too much information about himself and his background to the kidnappers. However, it should be noted that this was only his third time leading a negotiation. My concern is that his inexperience has led to an error in judgement that has opened him up to danger. Until this issue is resolved to my satisfaction, all further negotiations conducted by Mr Chambers will be closely supervised.

Selena Cole has been informed of these developments, and will henceforth be responsible for monitoring Mr Chambers' progress within the company until such a time as we can be confident that substance abuse or the accompanying criminal offshoots of such are no longer an issue. Until then, Mr Chambers will be unable to handle negotiations independently. The decision has also been made to avoid involving Mr Chambers in cases where drugs are likely to be a factor.

Becoming unstuck

DC Leah Mackay: Friday, 11.01 p.m.

The leftover frozen pizza is congealing beside me, the strings of mozzarella forming icicle shards. I push at it with my fingers, watch as a layer of oil weeps on to the plate, swamping a lonely olive in a slick of sunshine. I should wash up or – I glance at the clock – go to bed. But I don't do either. Instead I sit, prodding at the long-dead pizza with the nub of an overbitten nail. My kitchen has transformed. Has morphed into my office. There are papers strewn across the table, confetti at a wedding. The Cole Group case files.

I stayed later than I needed to. The DI released me at seven, told me to go home, spend some time with my kids. But it was seven. My kids were already in bed, settled there by my long-suffering mother-in-law, and he wasn't thinking about my family life but about his overtime budget, the man-hour numbers ratcheting ever upwards. I made a show of smiling, looking appreciative, then went back into the office, printed off every single one of the Cole Group's case files.

Alex texted a little while ago, said that he was on his

300

way. A business in Worcester, its entire IT system crashing at the worst possible time. But then, he had laughed, isn't it always the worst time? He's been there since early, trying to repair the damage that I can't even begin to understand.

I look at the littered papers. I should probably gather them up, but I don't. I just sit there.

I pick up a printed sheet, my fingers turning the white paper transparent. Case number 38. Aria Theaks.

Was this it? Was this what happened to Selena? A drugging? A disappearance.

Shuffle further back.

Case number 8. The Arthurs children. Dubai. That hovering question mark, the residual uncertainty between who was taken and who did the taking.

Case number 25. The Venezuelan housekeeper. There is the post-traumatic amnesia. So it is possible. But then Selena Cole would know that better than I would. And so, if she wanted to lie . . .

Then the kidnapping that was not a kidnapping, case number 41. The victim not a victim. Not really. Proven a liar. Am I closer with this one?

But I think of the CCTV footage, Selena withdrawing all that her company has in the bank and walking away. And I pull free case number 55, the Villier case. The express kidnapping in São Paulo, Brazil. Was this it? Was this what filled those missing hours?

I don't know. I sit, rest my head in my hands. The answer is here, somewhere before me. What happened is hidden in these files. I know it. I just can't find it. Can no longer see the forest for the trees. This whole thing, this vanishing, this disappearance, the world of kidnap and ransom constantly intruding where it has no place. And Dominic, lying dead.

What the hell am I missing?

We stood together, in the playground, watched as the search teams climbed out of the police cars, moving in steady concert towards her house. I looked at her, trying to read her face, but she had already vanished, locking herself away behind a stoic wall. Watching the children playing, their air distracted, their attention hooked on the police cars parked outside their house.

I reach out, begin to gather together the case files, stacking them in order. There are ninety-one. Ninety-one different stories. Ninety-one tales of tragedy, loss, sometimes redemption.

What do I take from them, now that I have them all gathered here together? That I cannot even begin to imagine the life and mind of Selena Cole. That what she does, what her husband did, extends so far beyond my realm of experience that I simply cannot fathom what it is to be her.

I take a sip of wine, a rich red Merlot.

Concentrate.

The answer is here somewhere.

I pull my pile apart again, reshuffling it now so that I have grouped all the cases involving Beck Chambers to one side. Now I lay them out, one beside another, a poor man's jigsaw. There was a lot of work in Latin America, in many of the cases drugs a common theme. That must have been tough for him. He had a history, had already had problems with substance abuse when Ed took him on. I study the addendum to case number 68 again. The kidnapping of Harold Bayliss.

What about this? Was that what happened? Did the proximity to drugs simply become too much, the promise to make big money fast too alluring for Beck?

I make a note on an A4 pad. I need to check on Beck's travel history. Has he been flying into and out of Latin America, perhaps making up for his lost wages by ferrying drugs into the UK?

And then what?

Think.

Did Dom find out? Did Beck lose his temper? Stab him? No. Beck wasn't in Cardiff at the time of Dominic's murder, was he? He was in Hereford.

So . . .

Okay, he's in the clear for one case. But what about the other? In Hereford, he was right on hand for Selena's vanishing. He had easy access to scopolamine, the means of drugging her quickly, quietly. She knew him; he could get right up close to her without her raising the alarm. And fifty thousand pounds . . . that would be handy for a guy out of work.

I think of Selena in the playground, putting her best smile on for her children as they screech down the slide, their gazes flicking back, again and again, to their house, to what is going on inside.

She was lying to me.

I sip the wine, know this fact like I know my own name. Selena Cole is lying. The only problem is, I have no idea what she is lying about. Does she know something about Orla, is she trying to protect her? But if she was going to lie for her, surely she would give her an alibi?

Orla.

I wonder how she is coping alone in the police cell. I try to imagine her sticking a knife into Dominic's neck, but I come up short.

But then murderers are rarely who you imagine them to be. And I understand betrayal, the fury it brings with it.

I turn, look at the kitchen wall, fancy I can still see the mark of the pasta as it slid inexorably downwards, my husband standing before it awaiting his sentence.

And now I'm there again.

I put the wine glass down with a thump, the Merlot lapping at the rim. 'No. I can't do this any more.'

As if on cue, the front door opens, closes, Alex's footsteps soft on the hall carpet. He looks tired, his dark hair standing on end, eyes heavy. I rub my hands across my face, try to wipe away the recollection, arrange my features so that he will not see. Attempt a smile.

But he walks into the kitchen and instantly I see fear, and I know that my poker face is nowhere near as good as Selena Cole's.

'What's wrong?'

'Nothing.' I don't think before I say it. I don't need to. It is, after all, what I always say. I say 'nothing' and he accepts it, and then the conversation drifts on to the children or food or the weather, and what is wrong gets buried beneath a mountain of life. And then one day you realise the foundations are all eaten through, cracked by the weight of what you did not say.

I look at Alex. I open my mouth to tell him that his dinner is in the oven, that there is wine on the counter, and instead I say, 'I don't know that I am ever going to get over it.'

I don't need to define 'it'.

He rocks on his feet, like I have delivered a blow. Then, nodding slowly, he slides into the seat next to me, so that we are not looking at one another but instead looking outwards in the same direction.

'I'm sorry,' he says.

I shake my head. He has said this before. Once, twice, a thousand times. There is nothing that this sorry will fix that the last one could not.

'What can I do?' he asks.

'I don't know.'

'Do you want me to go?'

I don't answer right away, because the future has split before me and I think of a lifetime of this, of silence where there should be words, of an etched memory of a betrayal that you never, ever thought you could survive, of missed communications and scars. And then I think of the other lifetime. Myself alone at the kitchen table, a vacuum where once he was.

'No.' I am surprised at the quality of my voice, the sturdiness of it. Am equally surprised to realise that I am telling the truth. I do not want him to go.

'So . . .'

'So . . .' I say. 'I want to be different. I want us to be different. I can't stay here, stuck like I have been. I need things to move on.'

Alex nods, his expression one of relief and fear combined. His hands are resting on the table, pressed tight together, and I reach out, take one in mine. He stares at it for a moment, then at me, and again I am back there, the pasta sliding down the wall, the guilt standing stark on his face, and I want to stand up, to walk away. Instead I lean in, kiss him.

I don't remember the taste of my husband. Isn't that strange? I don't remember the way that his lips slot against mine, even though they must have done it hundreds of thousands of times before.

After moments, hours, I release him, and he looks at me, his eyes damp.

'Are we . . .'

'Yes,' I say. 'We're okay. But Alex?'

'Yes?'

'I hate that damn shirt.'

Square one

DS Finn Hale: Saturday, 8.36 a.m.

No one says a word. I lean against the desk, look out across the major incident room, think that I have never seen it so full and so quiet. Leah sits at her desk, her arms folded, her gaze locked on Willa's. The others, well, they're just waiting to know if we're nearly done here, if we've got what we need to lock down a murderer and if, finally, life can begin its slow return to normal.

'Willa,' says the DI. 'You want to brief the team on what you found in the victim's car?'

Dominic. In Dominic's car.

Willa stands up. She's wearing little make-up, has her hair pulled back into a high bun. She looks tired still, but she smiles at me as she passes.

'Thanks, boss. Okay. Car was a mess. We're pretty sure it's the murder scene. It didn't hurt that we had this.' She holds up a photograph of the penknife, its blade black with blood. 'Matches the wound and we're confident in saying that this is our murder weapon. We're in the middle of processing fibres as we speak, but as to fingerprints, we got a high number. Mostly Dominic, as you would expect, some from Isaac. Again, not a surprise. And then a fairly large number of third-party prints. We compared those to the suspect we have in custody . . .'

There is an audible intake of breath. This is what they have been waiting for. To hear that Orla is the murderer, that we have the evidence, that the mania of a murder hunt can begin to slow, that we can move on to building a case and, perhaps, you know, sleep.

'I'm sorry to tell you that none of the prints in the car was a match to Orla Britten.'

You can feel it, the sinking that follows the pronouncement. That not only are we not over, we are back to square one.

Willa looks a little like she is going to cry. 'The prints on the handle of the murder weapon are clear, but they also are not a match to the suspect.'

The DI looks grim. 'Willa brought this information to me first thing this morning. In the light of this, Mrs Britten was released half an hour ago.'

There is an outbreak of mutters.

'What about the boyfriend?' asks Oliver, a hint of desperation in his voice that almost makes me smile. 'Isaac Fletcher. His DNA was on Dominic, prints in the car. Shouldn't we . . .'

'We did a search on the apartment,' I say, trying not to sound smug. 'We got nothing. As things stand, we have nothing on him.' I think of Isaac, head in his hands, tears flowing, and finally relax into it, the thought that he is a victim. 'At this point, I think we have no reason to think he is anything other than a grieving family member.'

'So,' says Oliver, 'why the hell didn't he report Dominic missing? Wouldn't you? If your partner didn't come home one night?'

'They were having issues,' offers Leah. 'Perhaps he thought Dominic had simply left him.'

'Did he say that?' asks Oliver.

Leah gives him a level look. 'Perhaps you should go chat with him. Give those excellent interpersonal skills of yours a leg stretch.'

'Look,' says the DI. 'I know. We're all tired. We've all been working hard. Take five minutes. Have a break, have a bitch, and then let's get back to it. We may not have the suspect yet, but we have eliminated a number of people from our enquiries. We are getting there.' He looks at us, willing someone, anyone to believe him. 'All right, everyone back to your assigned roles. Thank you.'

We sit, trying to look obedient long enough for him to return to his office.

'Dammit,' says Christa.

'Yeah,' agrees Leah.

'Are they done processing the evidence from the Cole house search?' I ask. I am, admittedly, grasping at straws.

'Just came through,' says Christa. 'As you might expect, nothing tying Orla to Dominic's murder except what we already knew about. Although interesting to see how families work, isn't it?'

'What do you mean?' asks Leah.

'That Selena, she really doesn't trust her brother-in-law, does she?'

'Her brother . . . you mean Seth?' Leah frowns. 'Why? What did they find?'

'Apparently she's been e-mailing people, checking up on him. Wanting to make sure he was where he said he was going to be.'

'Perhaps she had an idea he was having an affair?' I

offer. 'Maybe she was doing some detective work of her own before she took it to Orla?'

'Yeah,' says Leah. 'Maybe. Hey, what time did you say those calls to Dominic's mobile came in from Seth? You know? The ones on the day of the murder.'

Christa looks at her computer screen. 'Ah, 4.02 and 4.30.'

'And we're sure they were from New York?' asks Leah.

I frown. 'What are you thinking?'

Leah looks at me. 'I'm thinking that if Selena suspected Seth was a liar, why are we so confident he's told us the truth?'

I nod. Pick up the phone. 'You make an excellent point. Who did he say he was flying with?'

'Atlantic Air.'

I pull their website up on the screen, find the number, dial quickly. I often think it would be far easier to book holidays if I could simply tell the operator it was part of a police investigation. I look at Leah, roll my eyes, as I am quickly transferred through three ranks of airline staff before finally landing at a supervisor. Leah grins.

'You were looking at passenger manifests for Tuesday the twentieth?'

'I was. I'm interested in the Newark to Gatwick flight, lands 7.20 a.m.'

'No.'

'Sorry?'

'No, we don't have one at that time. It lands at 9.05 a.m.'

Okay, two hours, give or take. Easy mistake for Seth to have made, I guess.

'Okay, no problem. Can you just confirm that you have a passenger by the name of Seth Britten on board that flight.'

'No.'

'Sorry?'

'No, there was no passenger by the name of Britten on that flight.'

I am momentarily floored. I sit with the phone to my ear and try to think of the next words that should be coming from my mouth. Leah is watching me, frowning.

'There was a Mr Seth Britten on an earlier flight.'

'How much earlier?'

'That flight . . . Newark to Gatwick, landed at 10.36 a.m. on Monday the nineteenth.'

He lied. The sonofabitch lied. He was in the country. He had almost eight hours to make it to Dominic's workplace in time to pick him up coming out. He could have killed him.

'That was a connecting flight.'

'Sorry? What was?'

The woman on the phone sighs noisily. 'The passenger, Mr Britten, he connected through Newark on to that flight.'

'So . . . he wasn't in New York.'

'No. The origin of that first flight was Bogotá. Colombia.'

Case No. 79
Victim: Gerald Breen
Location: Prague, Czech Republic
Company: EuroTech
3 October 2013

Initial event

Mr Gerald Breen, an employee of EuroTech and a UK national, left his home in the Vinohrady quarter of Prague 2 at 7.36 on the morning of Thursday 3 October. He said goodbye to his wife and informed her that he was heading straight in to EuroTech's offices, located in the Nove Mesto quarter of Prague 1.

At 8.31 a.m., Mrs Cynthia Breen placed a call to EuroTech asking to speak to her husband, and was greatly alarmed to discover that he had not yet arrived. His supervisor was, at this point, however, unconcerned, and expressed to Mrs Breen that it was not unknown for her husband to be late.

Mrs Breen, unconvinced, began a search of the surrounding area in the hope of locating her husband. She also contacted EuroTech's head office (based in Madrid) and informed them that her husband had been receiving threats for a number of weeks, and that over the previous days he had expressed to her a concern that he was being followed.

Upon returning to their apartment, Mrs Breen found

a letter waiting for her confirming that her husband had in fact been kidnapped and requesting a ransom of £500,000 for his safe return.

Response

Immediately upon notification of the disappearance of Mr Gerald Breen, the head office of EuroTech placed a call to their insurance provider (Triumph Global). The Cole Group were immediately asked to respond to the scene. The response group consisted of myself (Ed Cole) and Mr Seth Britten. We were on site within twelve hours of Mr Breen's disappearance.

We immediately attended the residence of Mr and Mrs Breen, where the local police had already assumed control of the case. Mrs Breen handed over the ransom note, and also provided a full and graphic account of the threats that had been levelled at her husband in the preceding weeks.

I served as liaison with EuroTech and the local authorities, whilst Mr Britten acted as liaison for Triumph Global.

It should be noted that this case prompted no small degree of speculation. Whilst kidnap for ransom is not unheard of in the Czech Republic, it is not considered to be a high-risk area. In fact, this was the Cole Group's first case within the Czech Republic. Human trafficking must always be considered a possibility in this region. However, given Mr Breen's age – fifty-three – and his fairly obvious health issues (he is both medically obese and has cartilage damage in both knees, and so is physically quite compromised), he seems to be an unlikely candidate.

The ransom note itself was typed and gave no signifiers indicating its point of origin, or any clues as to the identity of its author.

After seventy-two hours, no further contact had been received from the kidnapper, thus making it impossible to establish proof of life or begin any kind of negotiation process.

Mrs Breen was, by this point, tremendously distressed and began, despite our efforts to restrain her, to repeatedly contact Triumph Global herself in the hope that she could convince them to pay the ransom in full. Myself and Mr Britten (and eventually also an operative from Triumph Global) explained to Mrs Breen that this would not be policy in such cases, and that she would first have to raise the £500,000, which would then be refunded to her by the insurer.

Mrs Breen appeared to lose her enthusiasm for a quick payment after learning this.

Investigations into Mr Breen's background also caused us no small measure of concern. It was revealed by his supervisor at EuroTech that Mr Breen had been due to attend a disciplinary procedure on the day of his disappearance. His work record, performance and levels of non-attendance were such that he would have been fired at that meeting. Moreover, the seriousness of his situation had been made abundantly clear to him.

After ninety-six hours during which the kidnappers had remained resolutely silent, the local police began an examination of the Breens' home computer. There they discovered the original ransom note, plus an extensive history of researching kidnap-for-ransom cases. They also discovered a booking in the name of Mr M. Jones for a room in the Hotel Merkur in Prague's historical district.

Mr Breen was later located in said hotel.

Both he and Mrs Breen were immediately arrested for attempted insurance fraud.

Note

This is by no means the only case of faked kidnapping that the Cole Group has dealt with (see case nos. 12, 47, 60). In each of these cases, the insured individual has vanished without explanation, only for a ransom demand to come in to a family member or employer some time later. In the vast majority of these cases, the fraud is recognised as such and the plan foiled. However, there are cases on record (most notably the Swain kidnapping, 2005 – dealt with by Empire Security) in which the perpetrator has successfully managed to create the impression of a kidnapping, to the extent that the insurer pays the 'ransom'. In the Swain case, the deception was only identified some four years later, when an eagle-eyed associate noticed that the Swain family had suddenly become far wealthier in the aftermath of Mr Swain's 'ordeal'.

Whilst the industry has good safeguards against such criminality, the system is not foolproof and it remains an ever-growing problem. As the general public's awareness of K&R insurance grows, it is likely that these issues will only become more pressing.

What comes next

Orla sat, her head resting on her sister-in-law's outstretched hand, the hard wood of the kitchen table cold against her cheek. She was crying. Could she even remember the last time she had cried? In truth, it felt like a relief, that the tears might have some shot at washing clean all that had become so corrupted.

'Let me get you something to eat.' Selena's voice was soft, her hand stroking back the hair that had fallen into Orla's eyes.

It felt like being at home again, in the old days, when it was her and Ed, before Mum's cancer, Dad's stroke. That was what she wanted now, when it came right down to it. She wanted to be a child again, to be taken care of and to know that there was a clear run ahead, that her life hadn't already been destroyed by myriad bad decisions.

'They fed me.'

She missed Ed, missed him with a fierceness that seemed to eat through her insides. She had never known a world without him, not until that Brazilian day. Her big brother,

316

a knight at arms, he would protect her, he would make everything well. He always had.

'Some tea, then?'

What would he say, that brother of hers, if he could see where they were now? A husband with a parade of gay lovers. An arrest for murder. He wouldn't know them.

Orla pushed herself up, her head swaying with exhaustion, the suddenness of the movement. 'Yes,' she heard herself say. 'Tea. Tea would be good.'

She watched as Selena stood, her hand gripping Orla's own, one tight squeeze and then gone. How fast it happens, she thought. There and then gone again. Like Ed. And now Seth.

'Have you heard from him?' Selena asked, her voice quiet.

No need to ask who she was talking about. 'Not since my . . .' Orla stopped, felt tears catch at her throat. If she said it, then it would become so. She would become the kind of person who could possibly be arrested for murder. 'I thought he would be here when I came out. I thought he would have come for me.'

Selena made a small noise in the back of her throat, dropped a tea bag into the teapot, rattling the china lid more than she needed to.

'I think he believes I did it.' Orla hadn't known she thought that. Not until she said it. But now that the words were out, she was sure. Her husband thought her a murderer.

The kettle thundered to a boil, a click, the silence afterwards deafening. 'Then he's an idiot,' said Selena shortly. She poured the water into the pot. 'Why don't you stay here with us? Just for a little while? Until you figure out your next move.'

Her next move. What would that be? What could it possibly look like? Where could you move to when you had so neatly boxed yourself into a corner that seemed to have more sharp edges than could ever be feasible?

'Have *you* heard from him?' It irritated Orla how plaintive her own voice sounded, how needy. That in spite of everything that had gone before, she could still cling to this man, her husband in the thinnest of all senses.

Selena shook her head. Or was she simply trying to pull back from the steam escaping from the kettle? 'No,' she said, killing all hope. 'I'm sorry.'

It should be over. That would be what her mother would have said. That would be what her brother would have said. And Orla herself? What would she say?

That she was thirty-six years old, that relationships before Seth had been pale, uninspiring affairs, that it had seemed inevitable that she would remain alone, towed along in the shadow of her brother's family, a tug behind a cruise liner. She wanted children. She had always wanted children. It had been one of the constants of her life. And marriage would allow her that, wouldn't it? That was, after all, what it was for. And yet . . . I don't want kids, Seth had said. It's just not me. I'm not the fatherly kind. She had cried, not in front of him, but privately, had watched as her future landscape shifted, an earthquake of staggering proportions. In the end, she had taken it. Had traded one future for another. A husband for children. She was a grown-up; it was all about compromise.

Without him, what did that future look like?

'I'm out of sugar.'

'What?'

'Sugar. I don't have any.'

'That's okay. I can do without.'

'It's okay. I forgot the shopping bag. It's just in the car.'

'Honestly . . .'

Selena turned towards her, smiled. Planted a kiss on her forehead. 'I'll just be a sec. The girls are upstairs. They're playing. You . . . you'll keep an eye on them, won't you?'

Orla nodded. Wiped a tear from her cheek. Perhaps Seth had returned to London. He always preferred it there, said he needed to be around people, to feel part of things, was never entirely comfortable down here in the sticks, with just the mountains and the quiet for company. He said it was his background, that the military got you used to constant company, made silence seem suffocating. He would have gone to the flat in London. For some breathing space.

She picked up her phone, pressed the home button, the screen lighting up, screen saver of her, Seth, the girls. Of course he hadn't called. She would have heard it. And if she hadn't heard it, she would still have known, instinctively.

Dimly, somewhere on the edge of her awareness, Orla heard a car engine.

She studied the picture. The girls. Daughters to replace the ones she would never have. And yet they weren't, were they? They were her brother's, they were Selena's, but they were not hers.

She tapped the phone with her finger's fleshy pad. She could call Seth. He was her husband after all. Surely that was the very least privilege that such a relationship should allow.

She stared as the screen gradually darkened, it too tired of waiting.

Dr Minieri, he said that he was comfortable that Selena was well. They were communicating regularly; he had no real concerns at this point. Would he say the same about Orla herself if he could see her now?

Her stomach had begun to flip, inelegant somersaults that brought with them a sharp sting of pain. What was that? She breathed out slowly, an effort to re-establish control. Something had frightened her, something had set her nerves on edge. What was it?

Then she remembered the sound, the dim throaty rumble of a car engine, and her stomach stabbed at her, a throb of pain that lanced to her hip bones.

Was it him? Was it Seth?

She sat at the kitchen table, barely able to breathe, let alone move, and listened, straining to hear above her own heartbeat. The girls were playing upstairs, childish voices raised into faux adulthood. She listened for a car door, for footsteps on the path. But there was nothing, just the children.

It took another moment, longer perhaps than it should have. It began as a vague unsteadiness, a creeping sense of wrongness.

Where was Selena?

She had only gone out to the car. The car was parked just outside. It shouldn't take this long, should it?

Orla looked at the clock, studying it fiercely, trying to remember where the big hand had sat when Selena had walked out of the door. The pain in her stomach was fierce now, an air-raid siren, take cover, danger coming.

She strained, listening for Selena's footsteps, for the sound of her voice, perhaps caught on the phone, perhaps talking to a neighbour. But no, her phone had been on the kitchen counter, hadn't it? Orla cast about, the vague recollection of a vibration against the granite counter. When was that?

She hadn't been paying attention, had been too busy drowning in her own misery to really notice. But, yes, it was just before Selena had left, wasn't it?

So that was it, then.

She would be outside, on the phone.

Everything was fine.

Orla sat there, her eyes fixed on the clock, watching. One minute. Two minutes. Three minutes. She couldn't move. She shouldn't move. Because when she did, it would be real. It would have happened again.

But stillness could not be bought, and the silence that came with the absence of an expected sound was no real silence at all. Orla pushed herself to her feet, hurried down the hall.

It would be nothing.

It would be fine.

Hadn't Selena's coat been on the peg when she first came in? Hadn't her handbag been slung over the banister?

Her head was light now, and for a brief, unsteady moment, Orla wondered if she was asleep, if this was a nightmare and she would wake up alone, in a police cell. She pulled open the front door, stepped out on to the porch.

It had begun to rain again, a steady plock, plock, plock on the drive. She ventured out into it, wincing as cold drizzle snaked its way between her shoulder blades. And stood, her feet welded to the ground. The car was gone.

She looked wildly, left to right. It had to be . . . She'd been wrong. It must have been parked . . . She ran down the path, yanking open the small gate so that she was standing out in the street.

The rain washed over her.

There was no car. Selena had gone.

Full circle

'Why would he lie?'

'Because he's a murderer?'

I look at Finn, pull a face. 'Well, okay, but why lie about being in New York? The Cole Group work out of Colombia, it wouldn't be weird. Why not just say he was there?'

'Maybe he wasn't there for work,' suggests Finn. He leans forward in his office chair, getting into the swing of things now, just a boy, my little brother, playing at detectives. 'Maybe the lie wasn't for our benefit, but for Selena's or Orla's. They would both know where he was supposed to be, what cases they've got running.'

'Okay.' I turn, stare out of the window at the fog of rain. Think of Seth, a lover. Spurned, maybe? Or perhaps simply afraid that Dominic will not be discreet enough, that his secret will escape with this one miscalculation. And maybe he gets afraid, maybe he loses it, stabs him in a spurt of anger.

'So why the hell is he carrying round a knife?'

Finn shrugs. 'People have penknives. It's not that weird. He's ex-military.' He blows out a breath. 'I don't know,

322

Lee, maybe he was a boy scout and thought he'd need to make a fire. Or . . .' he gives me a long look. 'Maybe it wasn't as spontaneous as we thought?'

It feels as if the answer is before me, that if I concentrate hard enough, I can line my thoughts up, get them to make sense. 'He goes to meet Dom, armed, knowing he's going to kill him, then, after doing it, he just dumps the car, dumps the knife, legs it, leaving all the evidence there for us?'

Finn shrugs, biting his nails. 'We need to get his prints. It should have been done by now. We need DNA, fibres. We could have closed this down by now.'

I push myself up. 'Come on,' I say. 'Let's head up there. Get Seth's prints. Have a little chat with him.'

Finn is out of his chair before the sentence has time to grow cold. 'Yes. I'll drive.'

I smile, am grabbing for my phone when it begins to ring. I don't recognise the number.

'Hello, DC Mackay.'

There is a patch of silence. Then a hefty sigh. 'It's Orla. Orla Britten.'

I sink back down, pull my chair closer to my desk, gesture to Finn. 'Orla. Hi.'

I haven't spoken to her, not since I arrested her, and the weight of that sits between us. My insides have turned soft at the sound of her voice, as if somehow they know it will bring something with it that I have not accounted for.

'I didn't know who else to call.'

'Okay.'

'She's gone.'

'Who's gone?'

'Selena. Selena is gone. Again.'

I stare at Finn, trying to find my balance, the déjà vu shifting my foundations. 'She's . . .'

'I know.'

'Well, what . . .?'

'She went to her car.' Orla sounds like she has been crying, her voice thick, tired. 'She said she was only going to grab the shopping. That she would be right back. But the car, it's gone. She's gone.'

It is like I expected this all along, that somewhere deep down I always knew that we would go in a full circle, ending up right back here, where we began.

'Seth . . .' I begin.

'I don't know where he is either. He had left by the time I got back from the station. I assume London, but I really don't know. It's just me now. Me and the girls.'

'Okay.' Possible futures shift before me, the cards shuffling fast. 'I'm on my way. We'll find them. I'll be there soon.'

Finn is watching me as I hang up the phone, is still standing, his keys in his hand. 'What?'

'Selena is gone again.'

'She's . . .'

'There's something else going on here,' I say. 'She's connected. Somehow, whatever has happened. She's involved. Seth isn't at the house. We need to put a wanted marker out on both of them.'

Finn already has the phone in his hand, is dialling. 'So you think Selena . . .'

'I don't know. I don't know what I think.'

'The prints in the car weren't a match for Selena's. They didn't find anything in the search of her home.'

'I know.' And yet it remains, the knowledge of being lied to.

I wait as Finn gets through to the SIO, briefs him, aware that it is now me who cannot stay still, that I am bouncing in place. She has gone again. It is turning into a farce. Has she walked? Was she kidnapped? The same questions, just a different day. Then I think of Beck Chambers outside the Cole house on the morning of her disappearance. Her first disappearance.

I hurry over to my computer, pull up Chambers' file. Find the number. Dial.

I am expecting it to ring out. Do not think for a moment that he will answer.

'Yeah.'

I stand there, stunned into silence. Then, 'Beck?'

'Yeah? Who's this?'

I suck in a breath, aware that Finn is watching me. 'Beck, this is DC Leah Mackay. Where are you?'

A long, stagnant silence. 'What do you need, DC Mackay?'

I roll the dice. 'I need to know where you are, Beck. And I need to know where Selena Cole is.'

I can hear him thinking, and for a foolish, optimistic moment, I think that he is going to talk, that the end is at hand.

'This is none of your concern, Leah. You need to leave it.'

A click and he is gone.

I stand in the office, the phone limp in my hand, feel seasick.

'What?' asks Finn. 'What did he say?'

'Call the SIO back,' I say. 'He needs to put out an additional wanted marker on Beck. He's with her.'

Everything changes

DS Finn Hale: Saturday, 10.20 a.m.

I take the corner way too fast, the rim of the tyre bumping up over the kerb, back down the other side.

'Whoa, cowboy,' mutters Leah.

'Sorry.'

I bust through lights as they are flicking to red, put my foot down. Heading out of Hereford, away from the crowds, the low-slung buildings, out into the countryside. Towards the Cole house. We head here because we have nowhere else to head to, and the thought of just sitting in the office and waiting is unbearable.

'Maybe there'll be something there – at the Cole house, I mean. Something that'll give us a lead as to where she went.'

'Yeah.' Leah is staring ahead of us, her hands wrapped tight around the seat. 'Maybe.' She gives a little laugh that is covered in edges. 'I'm pretty sure I've done this before, you know.'

The Hereford traffic gives way to country calm. We are heading along a country lane now, bare branches scraping overhead. It occurs to me where we are, that the river, the place at which Selena Cole was found, is right there, its water a grey sheen glimpsed through the autumn remnants of trees.

'It feels like a lifetime ago, doesn't it? That first day?'

'Yes.' Leah's lips are sewn up tight, her pallor has sunk towards grey. She always was a terrible passenger, bringing the threat of sickness on any childhood journey we took. I ease my foot off the accelerator, take the next bend a little slower. Look down and can see her grip has loosened, just slightly.

'I was a prick.'

She looks at me. 'You weren't a prick. What do you mean?'

I glance across. 'I thought you were overidentifying. With Selena Cole. I thought it was, you know, a mother thing.'

'A mother thing?'

'You know, she has two girls, you have two girls.'

She gives me a look that I try studiously to avoid. 'You know that Selena Cole and I are not the only people in the world ever to have kids, right?'

I snort. 'Look, do you want me to apologise or not?'

'Sure. Go for it.'

'I'm sorry for not trusting you.'

Leah looks away out of the window, then back at me. 'You know what? You *were* a prick. But I forgive you.'

'Thanks.' I grin. Then I sigh. 'I didn't think they were connected.' My God, it's like a confessional in here.

Leah smiles. 'Neither did I. I just . . . I had to know. What happened in those missing hours.'

Strange how I now cannot disentangle these two cases, how they have come to form one in my mind.

'Still,' I say, resolutely determined to throw myself on

327

my sword, 'I should have listened to you.'

Leah doesn't answer for a moment, is watching the river as it flashes by. Then she reaches over, pats my shoulder. 'Ah well. You'll know better next time.'

The airwave set beeps, sending a jolt of electricity through me. Leah grabs for it.

'Leah Mackay.'

'Yeah, we've had a result on your wanted marker. Mobile ANPR unit picked up Selena Cole's Range Rover passing by Llanthony, heading into the Brecon Beacons National Park.'

I yank the car over to the side of the road, pulling it into an unrealistically tight turn, Leah's hand flying up to grab the passenger-side handle, and head back the way we came, my foot flat now.

'Got it. We're en route.'

We are flying now, whipping by the trees so fast that even I feel sick. There are so many questions rising up. Unfortunately neither of us knows the answers. I turn in to another country lane, narrower now, the speed feeling painful. We have begun to climb, the landscape rearing up towards the sky.

Where the hell is Selena Cole going?

Music. For a dislocating moment I think we have stumbled on a countryside rave. But it is just Leah's phone.

She answers without looking at it, hand still clutching the overhead handle.

'Hello? Yes. Hi, Willa. No. No, I'm not. Okay. So, did you . . . Okay.'

I strain to listen, trying to find Willa's voice against the sound of the engine, the whoomp, whoomp, whoomp of tyres on the uneven road.

'You're kidding.'

I look at Leah. Mouth 'What?' but she is ignoring me, is looking straight ahead.

'So there's no way . . . Okay, you're sure? Yeah, well, you understand why I ask? I know. Right.'

I can't sit on it any longer. 'What? What is it?'

Leah waves me away. 'I know. Okay, thanks, Willa. Yeah. That . . . that changes everything.' She glances over at me, away again.

'What?'

'Yeah, thanks. Bye.'

We have burst through the trees, out on to an open mountain road, a precipitous drop one side, vertiginous climb the other. I really should be concentrating.

'What is it?'

Leah releases her death grip on the handle, stares straight ahead. 'I . . .'

'Oh, sweet Jesus, if you don't tell me right now, I'm calling Mum!'

In spite of herself, Leah laughs. 'Um . . . right . . . The sweater. Selena Cole's sweater. The results are in.'

'Okay?'

'It was blood.'

'Dominic's?'

Leah shakes her head slowly. 'No, Finn. It wasn't Dominic's.'

Into the mountains

DC Leah Mackay: Saturday, 10.39 a.m.

There is a wildness here. The mountains etched green with scrub, climbing, their tips vanishing into the cloud that lies flat over them. Finn has slowed now, is driving carefully on the snaking road.

'You got anything?'

I glance down at my phone, signal non-existent. 'Nothing.' Pick up the airwave set and fiddle with the buttons. 'Airwave is down too.'

'Awesome.' Finn sighs.

'Yes.'

I don't know how long we've been driving, but it cannot be as long as it feels, because had it been, we would have pushed straight through the Beacons, right out the other side. But we have seen no cars, no lights, nothing to tell us that this is anything other than a wild-goose chase, Selena Cole at the centre of it. Again. The rain has begun to drive hard now, is bouncing off the windscreen, seems inevitable that it will eventually break through.

'It's getting worse,' I offer.

Finn flips the wipers, the arms increasing their speed so

that the water swashes across the surface of the screen. We are starting to drop down now, the road winding its way out from the clouds, into the valley below.

'We're nearly out of the Beacons,' mutters Finn. 'This road connects back to the main road.'

I look out the window, squint like that will help. 'Where the hell is she?'

'Is it possible she turns into a bat or some other small mammal?' Finn asks through gritted teeth.

I look back, trying to make out shapes through the cloud. 'We must have missed her.'

'How? It's us and four thousand sheep. Wouldn't we have noticed a Range Rover in amongst them?'

I look at the road behind, turn, look ahead, then glance at Finn.

'No.'

'We've missed her.'

'No, we haven't.'

I give him a moment to pull himself together, feel the car creaking to a painful vertiginous stop. 'Remember you said you'd listen to me next time? Welcome to the next time. We need to go back.'

Finn doesn't look at me. I'm pretty sure he's counting to a high number. Then, grinding his teeth, he steers the car carefully into a lay-by.

'If we die doing this ninety-eight-point turn, I'm blaming you.'

'Yeah, well,' I mutter. 'Maybe try not to drive us off the edge of the mountain.'

He is sweating by the time he is done, the car now facing uphill, into the cloud, the driving rain. He looks at me, smiles brightly. 'Let's try that one again, shall we?'

We inch forward, slower now. I kid myself that it is because we are searching, but in truth I know that any speed and we will drive right off the precipitous mountain road into the crevasse below. The world is opaque, cloud thick enough that the mountain beyond has vanished.

'There.'

Finn slams on the brakes, sending us ricocheting against our seat belts. 'What? Where?'

'There's a road.'

In truth, it is little like a road. More a track, uneven and winding, that dips down the mountainside, vanishing into a clump of trees.

'You are shitting me.'

'Finn.'

'Leah, we don't know where that leads. If we can't turn round down there, we are stuck. With no signal. No radio.'

I lean forward, peer through the rain. 'There are tyre tracks. There in the mud. Someone has gone down there.'

'God, now she's Poirot.'

'Finn!'

'Fine. Fine. I'm going. But if we die, I'm not just blaming you, I'm suing you.'

I grin.

The track is narrow, rough enough that I begin to doubt my own assertions. It judders us through a copse of trees, snaking round and out the other side.

'There's a house down there,' I say.

It is, of course, a house in theory only. A stone-built cottage, so small that it would be a wonder if it has ever housed anyone. I open the window in spite of the rain, and catch a glimpse of metal. 'There's a car too.'

'Marvellous,' grumbles Finn.

We inch closer, the cottage vanishing behind a rise, only to reappear again minutes later. 'Surely no one lives there?' I say.

'We may have to live there,' mutters Finn. 'I think the back axle just went.'

Further down the slope, a glint of metal again. 'There's the Range Rover,' says Finn, voice grim. 'At the side of the house.'

'She's here,' I say, redundantly.

It feels strangely redemptive, this sense of having found her. That at last I have solved a mystery rather than having it handed to me.

'There's someone else . . .' I lean forward, try to understand what I'm seeing. 'There's another car. Just behind hers.' I glance at Finn.

He steers the car to a stop, pulling it to the side of the cottage, easing the engine off. Checks the airwave for signal, shakes his head. 'Nothing.'

'Got your ASP?' I ask.

He nods, jaw set. 'Let's go.'

The rain hits us as we push open the doors, drowning all other sound. I duck pointlessly as it beats against my head, resist the urge to run to the half-open door of the cottage. Because I cannot fool myself that safety lies behind it. I am coming to realise that I have no idea what is waiting for me. I push my hair back from my eyes. Share a glance with Finn, rack my ASP. Begin to walk quietly towards the open door, holding the metal baton to my thigh.

We step softly into the narrow hallway, the smell of damp almost overwhelming. The rain is softer now, muffled by the aged roof, the thick stone. Now another sound creeps in, separating itself out from that of the rain. A woman crying.

I freeze. It is a sound of anguish, of someone being ripped apart. I feel Finn's hand on my arm, counselling caution. Breathe. Nod. Soft steps, steady, ASP ready.

The hallway gives on to a living room, small and dark. A sixties tiled fireplace, a bowed sofa. And Selena Cole slumped to the floor, weeping. A figure holds her, and in the dim light I cannot see if it is an embrace or an attack. But as my eyes adjust, I realise that she is weeping against him, her head resting on his chest, his hand stroking her hair. They have not heard us, are wrapped up in this moment of theirs.

Then I hear the scrape of metal against stone behind me, Finn brushing awkwardly against the cottage wall. I see the man jump up, shoving Selena behind him.

Then I know him.

I hold my hands up, school my face to neutral. 'Beck. It's Leah Mackay. It's okay.'

I want to look to Selena, but something about Beck holds my attention. His size maybe, but something else too, the excruciating awareness that he has sensed danger, and that that in turn has made him dangerous. I watch him look from me to Finn, back. Then it is like he folds in on himself, growing smaller before us. He glances back at Selena, where she sits on the floor, her knees tucked up before her.

'It's okay, Beck,' she says.

He nods briefly, then turns his back on us, hunkering down before her. 'It's all going to be all right.'

Selena shakes her head, burying it in her knees. 'No.' Her voice bursts, a cloud that carries endless rain. 'I was too late.'

'No. We'll fix this. I promise you, Selena. We'll fix it.'

I fold my ASP up, slip it into a pocket, and move past Beck, sinking to the floor in front of Selena. She stares at me, what was hidden clear now, waits for me to speak.

'Your husband, Ed. He's alive, isn't he?'

The disappearance of Selena Cole

Dr Selena Cole: Tuesday, 7.45 a.m.

I can't breathe. No, that can't be right. Because my chest is climbing and sinking, climbing and sinking, just like it always has. But still, it feels like there is no air left on the earth. I watch Tara, her baby face creased into laughter, the swing sailing up into the blackening sky. I reach out, but I cannot touch her, even when my fingers are right there on her pudgy thighs.

What have I done?

She is talking to me, garbled words that make sense to no one but her mother. And I stare at her, at a loss. She looks at me, expectant, waiting for a reply. But I have nothing. So I smile, a cheap facsimile of a smile, and although she is not utterly convinced, it seems that will be enough. She giggles. 'Higher.' I push the swing so that it sails backwards, her stunted ponytail touching the sky.

I should have known. I should have seen this. How could I have not?

The ground is unsafe beneath me, the quaking movement brought about by lack of sleep. Or maybe by the sudden awareness that the world I stand in is not the world I thought it was at all.

The phone rang at 6.02. Who was I at 6.01? A mother, a grieving widow, no space in my loss for me to be anything but these fundamentals. I was a woman placing one foot in front of the other, because life demanded it of me. Then came 6.02 p.m.

I almost didn't answer.

I watch Tara flying backwards in the swing, my hands outstretched to catch her, to fling her away again, and my heart stops beating at the thought of that. I almost didn't answer.

The children were winding down, exhausted after a day of school and playing and whatever else used to fill up our days before the phone rang at 6.02 p.m. I was folding laundry, standing beneath the oversize clock that hangs in the utility room, marking the passage of my days from one useless moment to another. I could hear the girls, Heather shouting at her sister for yet another catastrophic misdemeanour, Tara beginning to cry. The blouse I was holding was once vibrant yellow, now dulled with age, a grease stain on its upper sleeve. I stared at the stain, listened to the tumult in the living room and felt the tears coming, darkness creeping in. Brushed them away. Because it was only 6.02 p.m. In fifty-eight minutes, both girls would be in bed. In fifty-eight minutes, I could flip on the shower, let the water run over me, and my heart could break again, just like it did every night at 7 p.m. precisely. But not now. Not at 6.02.

Then the phone began to ring.

I stood in the laundry room, let the irreparably damaged blouse drop to the basket on the floor, raised my eyes to the ceiling. Who? What? Why?

I wouldn't answer.

I had the girls to get ready for bed, the laundry to finish, the darkness beckoning.

I wouldn't answer.

But my feet moved anyway. I don't know why. Maybe they knew what I did not.

I turn, a gust of chill wind hitting me full in the face, look for Heather. She is angry with me. Some little fury about shoes that I was too tired to fight. But it isn't about shoes, is it? It never is. She is angry with me that her father never came home. I get that. I'm angry with me too. She is trudging around the limits of the playground, kicking at the gravelled surface with the shoes she shouldn't be wearing, every now and again glancing over to me, a test: what will I do? I turn away. I am too tired for this particular battle.

'Dr Cole?' The voice on the phone was entirely unknown.

'Yes?'

'My name is Dominic Newell. I'm, ah, I'm Beck Chambers' solicitor.'

I closed my eyes, suppressed a sigh. Why had I picked up the phone? Why hadn't I just let it ring out? It is always this way, the world carrying on as it always has, expecting me to carry right along with it, like anything matters any more. I forced my face into a smile. 'Of course. What can I do for you, Mr Newell?' It is this way. It is always this way. You force your heart to keep beating, your lungs to keep taking in air, even though all you want to do is die.

'Dr Cole, Selena . . .' He was walking. I heard it in the unevenness of his breath, the sounds of the traffic that filled the spaces where the words should be. 'There's something I need to tell you . . .'

I pull my wool coat tighter around myself, the creak of the swing breathtakingly loud, and watch Heather. She has turned her back on me now, resolute, unforgiving. Is clambering up the incline that leads to a bank, down to a stream. She is not allowed to go beyond the limits of my sight. She knows this. She stops halfway up the incline, stands up tall, and for a moment I think she will turn, concede defeat, that we will be able to settle once more into a tremulous detente. But then her hands fly to her hips and she carries on, a difficult walk in a defiant stance.

I watch her go.

I should call her back.

But there is something in those shoulders, those triangles of her hands on her hips, that makes me peculiarly proud. She is both of us. She is me. She is Ed. She is tough and defiant and often a giant pain in the arse. And yet she keeps moving onwards. I let her go. Those traits may one day prove critical to her.

I don't know how I got the children into bed. It was done, though, because one moment they were there, the next they were tucked under their various duvets, doors closed with a quarter-inch gap as prescribed. But I have no recollection of doing it. Because of Dominic Newell and that phone call and who I was vanishing, who I was to become still struggling to be born.

It was horror and grief and elation and fear.

I spent the night in the office, pulling up files, opening e-mails that were not mine to open. It was right there, right under my nose. How had I not seen? What had I done?

At 1.53 a.m., I sent an e-mail of my own.

Then I waited.

You would think that I would have dozed, at some point during that painfully long night, but no. I sat before the computer and I waited.

I look up to the sky. The rain is coming. I can feel it hanging in the air. I close my eyes briefly, feel myself sway. Wish that the storm would simply break. Better always to be in the storm than to be anticipating it.

There was no reply.

I finger the mobile phone in my pocket, imagining the ting of an incoming email. But there is nothing, just the creak of the swing. I feel tears building again and I pull in a breath. No. You will not cry. But the thoughts circle me, so that I am trapped by them: you were too late.

Then I hear something.

I open my eyes, turn so that my back is to the park, so I am looking down the shallow incline to the road below.

As soon as I see her, I know.

She stands beside a car, an equivocal silver Mondeo. Watching me.

I turn, look for Heather, but she has vanished over the bank, is likely sticking her new shoes in the narrow stream beyond, in overt defiance of my rules. I take a breath, pray, kiss Tara on the forehead. 'You stay here, okay? Mummy will be right back.'

I want to run. I want to grab hold of her, this woman who has stolen my life, and shake her and demand that she give it back, but I don't. I force myself to walk, calm. This is a negotiation. Appearances count. It is, after all, all about perception, what they think you are, rather than what you are.

She studies me as I cross the road towards her.

'Mrs Cole.'

'Yes.'

'You want to do a deal?' She is my age, maybe a little younger, would be attractive in any circumstances but these. The accent is soft but there. I don't bother to ask how she found me. I don't bother to ask why she did. All that matters is that she is here and I am here and my future is in flux.

I force myself to breathe. It is a dance, this. Calm.

'I will need proof of life.' I wonder how many times I have said those words before, how little they have meant until now.

'Get in.'

I open my mouth, am momentarily wrong-footed.

'There has been enough delay. Let's do this deal, yes? Get in.'

I look up the bank to the park, to where my girls play, alone. 'I . . .'

'Mrs Cole, our patience has been sorely tested. What has come so far has been less than satisfactory, and frankly, we have other deals that need to be handled. If you are unable to work with us, then we must move on.' She holds open the passenger door. 'It is, of course, your choice.'

I look up at the park. I cannot see them. I cannot make them safe.

Is this how it will be? How it will all end, after so much?

Then I hear a door, look down the road to where my neighbour, an elderly woman with whom I have barely exchanged more than a dozen words, is coming out of her house. She pulls the door tight shut behind her and then, head down, begins to trudge towards us. Towards the park. Towards my girls. I see her gaze meander across the mountains and then fall, down to the playground, to where my children are. I see her face crease into a smile, a hand raise in a wave.

I close my eyes. I pray.

'Let's go.'

A placing of pieces

DC Leah Mackay: Saturday, 10.51 a.m.

Selena is staring at me, still unsure if she can trust me, whether the risk is too great. She glances at Beck and I sense Finn stiffen behind me, as I wonder if here is where it will all go so very wrong.

'Ed,' I say again. 'He's alive, isn't he?'

Selena looks back at me. 'Yes.'

The pieces slowly begin to slide into place, Selena shifting from a grieving widow to a desperate wife in the blink of an eye.

'He's . . .' I glance about, at where we are, the loneliness, the isolation. 'He's being held?' I hazard. 'He's a hostage?'

I no longer know where I am, what my focus is. A murder? A disappearance? A kidnapping? But I watch Selena, am prepared to go with it for a little while. The floor is cold through the knees of my trousers, a rising damp that creeps into my bones. The rain has settled into a steady thrumming, and the distant thought occurs to me that much more and we will be washed away.

I look to Finn, see him folding away his ASP, although

343

his gaze never leaves Beck, his hulking frame stuffing the tiny cottage.

'Can you tell me what happened?' I ask.

Selena laughs, although it seems just as likely that it will become a sob. 'I wish I could. I was a widow until five days ago. Then Dominic Newell called. And everything changed.'

'Dominic . . .' Finn is focused on Selena now, has stepped closer, his attention momentarily swayed from Beck.

'He called me on Monday evening. He had found an e-mail. He pieced it together.'

6.02 p.m.

Dr Selena Cole: Monday, 6.02 p.m.

'There's something I need to tell you . . .'

'Okay.'

'Ed . . . he's alive.'

There are no words for a moment like this. Nothing that comes, freshly prepared, no obvious first response. Because my husband, my love, was dead. Had been dead for almost a year. I had lived almost 365 days without him. Or rather, I had not lived. I had existed. For 365 days.

What do you feel when someone tells you something like this?

What should you feel?

One imagines elation. Euphoria.

I felt anger.

'What the fuck are you talking about?' My words scalded, me as much as him. But you cannot do that, hang the promise of life over a home in which there is death. It is too much, too excruciatingly painful to even entertain the possibility of hope.

'I know this doesn't make much sense.' Dominic sounded afraid, like he had gone for a stroll on a wafer-thin ledge, was only now coming to appreciate the depth of the drop below. 'Please, just let me explain. Seth . . . He didn't mean it to be like this, I know he didn't. But he's weak. And with his family background, where he came from, the Cole Group, its reputation, his reputation, it means everything to him.'

'Mr Newell,' I said, straining to keep my voice even, 'I'd appreciate it if you'd get to the point.'

He sighed heavily. A car horn beeped in the background. 'I found an e-mail, on his computer.'

'What were you doing on Seth's computer?' I am fighting now, struggling to hold on to the tail of a bucking horse.

'We were . . . we are . . . Look, it doesn't matter. Please, I just need you to listen to me. I found this e-mail. And then, I mean, I had to know, so I confronted him . . . we argued. It was . . . it was pretty bad. Ed . . . he's being held. He's been taken hostage.'

'I . . .' My brain froze in place. My husband, my dead husband, here in conversation, in the present tense. It made no sense to me, and yet the need I had for it to be true was breathtaking. I sank to the floor, sitting on the cold Victorian hallway tiles.

'Look, I don't know much else. All I know is that he's being held, that Seth . . . his negotiations, they haven't gone well. And the kidnappers, I don't know how much time you have left.'

I gasped for air, trying to form words, or if not words then thoughts.

'Look, there's someone here. I have to go. You . . . you'll take care of this, right? You'll deal with it? Quickly?'

I heard him, but from far away, a ghost whispering in a crowded room. 'Yes,' I said. 'I'll take care of it.'

'Okay. Okay, good. Look.' He must have turned from the phone, his voice dropping, words I could not make out directed at someone that wasn't me. 'I have to go. But . . . good luck.'

I nodded, forgetting for a moment that he couldn't see me. Then, 'Dominic? Thank you.'

A click, and he was gone.

A primer in K&R

'Do you know who?' asked Leah. 'Who has your husband?'

I have my mouth open, an entirely different question ready and waiting. I close it again. I can wait a few more minutes.

'It's the group that orchestrated the hit in Brasilia.' Selena still has her knees pulled up in front of her, her mouth buried in the denim of her jeans. Her voice is steady now, calmer. 'Escorpion Rojo. Primarily they're into drug development, but they run a healthy sideline in kidnap for ransom. There were a couple of incidents before Brazil. Attacks on police stations, that kind of thing, but nothing like what we saw in Brasilia. That was just completely out of left field. And now . . . now I think that was what it was about all along. After it happened, everyone said that it was a hit against the K and R industry, that they were trying to destroy us. But it was more than that. They were trying to show us that despite what we thought, they were still the ones running the show.'

Beck stands in the doorway, blocking out what little light there is, not to mention, I can't help but notice, the exit. I scan him, looking for signs of weapons, and he catches my gaze, returns it in kind. Honestly. The guy doesn't need weapons. He could kill me with his big toe.

He clears his throat, sounds like a landslide of rubble down a mountain. 'Things had begun to shift in Latin America, Colombia especially. FARC's position was changing, they were scaling back their kidnap operations. And people were getting wise. Pretty much all of the foreign companies setting up there had insurance, which meant they had access to people like us, and lots of the K and R companies were providing value-added stuff – situational awareness training, security audits. The operations throughout Colombia were getting smarter, safer. Over the last couple of years we saw a whole bunch of failed kidnap attempts, mainly due to what the K and R industry had put in place. And the drug groups, they were getting squeezed by Colombia's new anti-narcotic strategies. They were hurting.'

'We think Brasilia was an attempt to strike back, to hit us where we least expected to be hit,' says Selena. 'And I don't think Ed is the only hostage. The woman, the one who collected me, who brought me here' – she looks about the struggling cottage, her face a battle – 'she talked about other deals they needed to be working on. I think there were others taken that day.'

'Of the ones supposedly killed in the attack,' offers Beck, 'there were four whose remains were never found. We're guessing they have them.'

I shift. My glance pulls back again and again to the doorway, the looming mass of Beck. 'Why so long, though? Wouldn't they want to get the money as soon as possible.'

'You have to remember,' says Beck, 'it's a business to them. Lengthy kidnappings aren't uncommon, especially in

Colombia. They weaken the hostage, the will of the family, their ability to deal with a lengthy negotiation.'

'Doesn't that only work if the family know the hostage is alive?' asks Leah.

Beck turns, makes a noise deep in his throat. Adrenalin spurts through me, my hand drifting to my ASP.

'What?' says Leah.

'Seth knew. He hid it. If Dominic hadn't found out . . .'

I look to Leah. Dominic had found out, had uncovered something that Seth was working to keep secret. How angry must that have made Seth?

'You have to understand,' says Selena. 'I was struggling to cope with getting out of bed, let alone doing anything else, so Seth stepped up, took over everything. When the e-mail came in, he was the first one to see it.'

'Bastard isolated it,' growled Beck. 'Made sure that he was the only one who knew, that they only contacted him.'

Leah looks from Beck to Selena. 'Was he trying to protect you?'

They exchange a look. Beck's shoulders stiffen, anger radiating from him. 'He was trying to protect himself. All he cares about is the company, his precious role in it. He wanted to make sure it remained nicely solvent.'

'I went through all his e-mails,' says Selena dully, 'the night that Dominic called to warn me. They contacted Seth five months ago.' Her voice breaks on this. 'He ran it like a negotiation. Like any other negotiation. Right up until the end. He got the ransom down to a level where we could have paid it. Where the company could have paid it.'

'Fifty thousand?'

Selena nods. 'Fifty thousand. We could have covered that. Our insurance could have covered that.'

'So why . . .'

'He wanted to keep it a secret. He wanted to make sure that Ed being a kidnap victim didn't compromise the reputation of the Cole Group, weaken our negotiating position in other cases, our ability to get new work. So he didn't disclose it to the insurers. He carried on a protracted negotiation without informing them, which instantly invalidates our policy. Then, when he got it down to a level we as a company could have paid . . .'

'He put himself above Ed's survival. He was more worried that the company survived than that Ed did.'

Selena closes her eyes, covers her face with her hands. 'We could have handled it. If he'd told me, we could have made it work. The company, we built it from nothing, we could have done it again. But to do this . . .'

'Selena,' says Leah, 'the blood, on your sweater. That blood was your husband's. His DNA, it's on file.'

Selena looks up at her, and you can tell that she's trying to piece things together. Then her expression clears. Piecing done. 'It was the arrest. Must have been . . . what, ten years ago? He got picked up for affray, Seth drinking too much, shooting his mouth off. They dropped the charges after letting them spend a night in the cells. His DNA . . . I didn't think.'

Leah studies her. 'You saw him, didn't you?'

The value of money

'Fifty thousand?' She says it like she doesn't quite believe it, looks at me like I am some kind of lunatic. Or a multi-millionaire. She cannot be sure, so her disdain walks a fine line.

'Yes,' I say, quietly. 'Fifty thousand. I'll take ten today. I'm going to need to order the remaining balance to collect as soon as possible.'

There is a camera in my face and I glance up at it, and then away. I am a bank robber, stealing from myself.

'This . . . Okay, sure.' She is hovering, stands up, sits down, looks up at me, smiles. Multimillionaire, then. 'It will just take a couple of minutes.'

I nod, no longer trust my voice.

I see his face. In this bank, amongst these people, the few stragglers left at the end of a long day, his face is all I see. My Ed.

I paid attention when the woman drove me. I didn't bother asking her name, because what would be the point? I simply sat quietly in the passenger seat of the car, wondering distantly if I had handed myself over, walked

352

quietly into my own kidnapping. Wouldn't that be the ultimate irony?

I paid attention to the roads, trying to remember the maps I had seen, trying to imprint the turns, so that I could find my way back here. Or out of here. Whichever it would turn out to be.

As the trees whipped by, I sat, neither in one world nor another. I had abandoned my children, had left my babies to fend for themselves, whilst I ran off after the distant dream of finding their father alive. What kind of mother was I?

What kind of fool?

I looked at the woman, small, lithe, shaped muscles beneath her thin jacket, and knew that there would be no point in trying to run, that she had contained in her small frame far more power than I could muster. Could dimly make out the hard shape of my mobile phone pushing her pocket into a bulge. Let's just turn this off, shall we? She'd taken it from my unresisting fingers. Don't want any interruptions.

The neighbour would look after the girls. I clung to the thought as surely as if I had seen it happen. They would be safe. They would tell her to call Auntie Orla. They would be safe.

And I?

It had begun to rise in me, unchecked by the presence of my children. The grief that had been circling me since that Brazilian day. I stared out of the window at the climbing mountains and allowed myself to sink. I didn't care. A terrible thing for a mother to admit, isn't it? But I didn't. I wanted to plunge down into the gloom, to give up.

We took a turn, down a narrow unmade path hanging precipitously from the mountainside.

It wasn't possible that Ed could be alive. Too much had happened since, too much of life had passed.

And yet I, who knew better, had simply allowed myself to be taken.

I wouldn't fight. I knew that. I was too damned tired to fight.

The girls would be safe. Orla loved them. She would care for them. And Seth . . . perhaps, with the girls to call her own, she would be able to cast him aside as she should have done so long ago.

The woman stopped the car before a tumbledown cottage, gestured for me to get out. I waited for a moment before obeying, my final act of rebellion.

The cottage was blackness, a cell in everything but name. The air was chilled, colder inside than out, and I dimly felt myself shiver, thinking that I should be noticing this more, that my own discomfort should register with me, at least a little.

Then my eyes adjusted.

He was sitting in an armchair, a king without a throne. Had lost weight, so much so that it seemed he had begun to disappear into himself, that one sudden movement and one of those sharp, angular bones would snap. But he was looking at me, smiling, tears rolling down his cheeks.

I could not breathe.

'Hey, Mogs.'

'Would you like to follow me?'

I pull in a breath, realise that the bank teller is staring at me, that her internal barometer is shifting back towards crazy again. 'Of course,' I manage.

Can only see Ed's face.

'We have wasted enough time on this,' the woman had

said shortly. 'We need to be moving on. We will give you four days to get the payment in place. On the fourth day, we will contact you with a location and a time. I'd encourage you to be there, with the money ready.'

'I'll go now,' I said, not looking at her, only at him.

I wanted to run to him, to put my head in his lap, to have him stroke my hair, to prove to myself that it was real. But there was to be no touching. This was proof of life, after all. Only that.

'Four days. We will tell you when and where.'

I looked past her, at Ed.

There should be something to say at a moment like this, something that made sense. But there was nothing, only disbelief, and a hope that I had forgotten, and so much fear that it seemed like my entire body would be insufficient to contain it.

'He's bleeding.'

It was a small wound, a thin laceration that wrapped its way around his knuckles.

She shrugged. 'It's nothing.'

'I need to check.' Inspecting the product for damage, wanting to make sure that you get what you pay for. The absurdity of it clambered across my chest, choking me.

I wanted to touch him, to feel his skin against mine. Otherwise, how would I know that this was not all some unlikely dream?

The woman had made a small noise, a *tcchh* in the back of her throat. Yet still had gestured me forward.

Ed's eyes never left mine, his lips curled into the tiniest of smiles.

His hand had slotted into mine. Had felt like it had never left. Had grazed the cashmere of my jumper.

My knees threatening to buckle beneath me.

'It's so good to see you, Mogs.'

'You've seen. You've touched. That's enough. You have four days.' She sounded bored. But then that was it, wasn't it? Just another day at the office for her.

I simply looked at my husband, and looked and looked. 'Four days,' I said. To her. To him. 'It's time to come home.'

The small room in the bank is closing in on me, the woman stacking notes like she is playing with Lego. She hands me the envelope, the notes forcing it to bulge at the joints. 'Is there anything else I can help you with?'

I shake my head, attempt to muster a smile. 'This is all I need.'

I am afraid. I am so afraid. I thought there was nothing left to fear, but now that is no longer true. My heart thrums in my chest, a beat that it cannot possibly sustain, and I walk like I know where I'm going.

I will go home. Check on my girls.

Our girls.

But then I feel the thickness of the money in my pocket and know that I cannot. Seth lied to me. Seth attempted to stop me from doing this. If he were to find out . . .

I walk confidently through the sliding glass door of the bank.

I cannot take this money home. I cannot tell anyone what I know.

It has begun to rain, a light splutter. The main street is a carousel of umbrellas. I walk through them, not caring that the dampness is beginning to leach through my coat, into my trousers. I head to the train station.

I need to hide the money, somewhere Seth will not know to look.

I walk steadily into the station, take a left at the main desk, spare a second to nod to a security guard and wonder if it is written across my face, the way in which my world has flipped inside out. A bank of lockers lines the far right wall. I put some coins in, slide the envelope inside, secure the door shut.

And pray.

I want to go home. I want to go home so badly that it feels that my skin will slough right off if I do not.

And yet . . .

Where have I been? What have I done? What the hell am I going to say?

I begin walking, with no real destination in mind. I walk thinking of Ed, of his face, so thin, so unlike himself. His eyes, utterly unchanged.

I'm bringing him home. No matter what I have to do, I am bringing him home.

I think of kidnapping, of the taking of Aria Theaks, of Venezuela and Alexa Elizondo. Of all of the victims I have known.

I begin walking towards the river. Because sometimes you have to lie. No. Not lie. Simply be aware of how you present yourself, in order to serve a greater good.

The only way

DC Leah Mackay: Saturday, 11.13 a.m.

The rain has eased, cascade softening to a thrum. The cold
is biting at me, my legs cramping on the chill cottage floor.
I study Selena, wonder if she has come to the same conclusion that I have.

She looks up at me, our gazes locking.

'They're not coming back, are they?'

I shake my head slowly. 'I don't think so. It wouldn't
make sense to return to a place that you have seen.'

'But the money . . . the exchange. They texted me, like
they said they would. Said I had to come here, now. That
Ed . . .' She begins to cry again. 'Ed.'

'It's okay, Selena.' Beck's voice rolls like thunder. 'These
things happen. You know that. We make it work. We always
make it work.' He hunkers down next to her. 'Come on.
It's pointless you staying here. We'll get you home, to your
girls. We'll make contact with the kidnappers, set up a new
exchange.' He smiles, something that until now I hadn't
thought he could do. 'We've got this. Ed'll be home before
you know it.'

I do not think she will move. I think she will sit there,

waiting, until time rots away the little that remains of this once-was home. But she takes a breath, straightens her shoulders, nods briefly. I allow myself a moment to be impressed by her, now a widow, now not, taking hit after hit after hit, and each time pulling herself back to her feet.

'Let's do it then,' she says quietly.

Finn and I separate at the door, an agreement reached without words. I climb into the car beside Selena. Is it that I do not trust her not to make a bolt for it again? I'm not sure.

She drives carefully, taking the mountain road with the care of a woman who has children to return to, a husband to bring home.

I sit in silence. So much I want to ask, and yet I say none of it. Could I have survived this? Could I have done what she has done?

The cloud is beginning to lift, the day dull still but the road now visible, the threat of a fiery vehicular death diminished with the increase in light.

I think of my children, waiting at home for me. I think of what I would do to keep my family intact, what I have done. Yes. Yes, I would do what she has done, and more.

'It's going to be okay,' I say quietly.

Selena glances across at me, surprised seemingly by the words, or perhaps by the mere fact that I am there. She nods. 'Yes. Yes it will.'

We speak little on the return journey, a silence that feels calming, soporific almost. Then, as Selena steers the car into her street, I see her expression change, a steel bar shooting through it.

'What?'

She nods at the roadway ahead.

I do not see it at first. Just a pointless sports car, its boot open, driver hidden by the height of it. Then the driver moves, and I understand.

Seth.

Selena brakes hard, the door open almost before the car has come to a stop, is out, gone before I am able to react. But still, she is slower than Beck. He darts past her, his car left abandoned in the road behind us, is on Seth in an instant, large hands shoving him up against his expensive car, raising him so that his feet are barely touching the ground.

I sigh heavily. I really don't want to work another murder. I push open the car door, cover the intervening distance, feeling Finn's breath on my back.

'Beck,' I say. 'Put him down.'

Seth is panicking, fighting against Beck's grip, his feet slip-sliding on the wet tarmac. 'Get off. Get him off me. What the hell?'

'You sonofabitch,' Beck growls. 'You left Ed to die.'

Finn stops beside me, is watching the scene with interest. I nod to him, a silent message – we should do something – and he shrugs expressively, giving me a quick grin.

Men.

'I didn't.' Seth's voice is clambering up the octaves, panic in full flow now. 'I swear to God, I didn't. I was trying to help him. The entire time, I was trying to get him out.'

'How?' Selena steps forward, is looking up at Seth, radiating fury. 'How the hell were you trying to help him?'

'I . . .' Seth's mouth flaps and he glances at me, at Finn, anything to avoid Selena's fury.

'You went to Colombia?' I offer. 'When you were supposed to be in New York? You went to Colombia instead.'

'I thought . . . if I went there, a show of goodwill, that sort of thing . . . Can he put me down?' He is speaking to me, to Finn, but his eyes are locked on Beck, afraid that at any moment he will snap him in two.

'I'm not sure he can,' shrugs Finn. 'You were saying?'

'I went to Colombia. To try and make contact with them. But they weren't there, they'd left. I did everything I could. I'm telling you. All I've thought about for these last five months has been getting Ed home safe.'

'You utter arsehole,' Selena growls. 'We had insurance. We had the money in our bank account. We could have handed it over, had my husband back, my children's father, and instead you chose to let me think he was dead. How could you do that? I—'

'I know, I know . . .' He looks at Beck, tries to shrink away from his hands. 'I did it to protect you. I wasn't sure. I wanted to be sure first. And then . . . you were such a wreck, Selena. I thought you'd just compromise the negotiation. So I decided to keep it to myself. Handle it and then tell you when it was done. When I'd rescued him.'

'So why the hell didn't you?' demands Beck. 'Why didn't you do your job? Notify the insurance firm, pay the damn ransom.'

'I . . . the company . . .'

'Fuck the company.' Selena is shouting now, has stepped forward until her nose almost touches Seth's. 'This is my family. This is Ed's life. How dare you gamble with that?'

I think it is all about to erupt, that Selena is about to streak from suspect to victim to perpetrator, and that Finn and I will be standing here simply watching it unfold, too stunned to prevent it.

Then there is a sound. A door opening.

Selena's head snaps around.

A blonde head is just visible above the line of the hedge. We all turn, watch it bobbing closer to the gate, and then it is through, and Heather stands on the pavement, watching.

Selena's face lightens, breaking into a smile, and she turns her back on Seth as if he no longer exists. Walks towards her daughter and scoops her up into her arms.

'Mummy,' I hear Heather say. 'Where were you? Auntie Orla said you'd gone shopping, but I was worried.'

'I'm sorry, my love. I'm back now.'

They vanish inside the house, leaving us, our little tableau, frozen in time.

'Beck,' says Finn. 'If you wouldn't mind putting Mr Britten down now, I'd like to have a quick word with him. There's the small matter of lying to the police and a dead solicitor to wrap up.'

Seth's mouth drops open.

Beck looks at us, seems to be pondering whether we can be trusted with the weight of this task, and then steps aside. 'Keep him. I have a negotiation to conduct.'

The Kidnapping of Ed Cole

Ed Cole

I had planned to sleep. Selena had laughed. Who comes to Brazil to sleep in? She said that I was getting old. Privately I agreed with her. I lay in bed, watching her get ready to go shopping.

Now, looking back on it, I wish that I could say I was thinking something profound – that I had looked at my wife and thought that she was the most beautiful woman on the planet (which she is), that I was the luckiest man alive (which I am). In all honesty, I watched Mogs getting ready and wished that she would hurry, spent those long minutes mentally calculating the time I had left to sleep, wishing her away.

You have no idea how much those wishes would come back to haunt me in the months that followed.

I waited, impatient for my wife, my love, my best friend to get the hell out of our hotel room and let me sleep. Then, once she had gone, finally, I lay there staring at the ceiling.

We were almost done in Brasilia. Our time was almost over. And there remained so much left to do. So many meetings, so much advertising. Because that's what it is at these things. A bunch of people who all do something that few other people do, moving around one another, being seen. Because if you're seen in amongst them, somehow you become one of them.

We were doing well, in all aspects. Selena and I. The company. The kids. It was all working as it should.

And the most profound thing I can find to say to you now is that all of that, you only see it once it is gone and you are locked in a dark, damp cell, wondering if you will ever see the sunlight again.

I gave up trying to sleep in the end. Got up, took a shower.

It's strange, the things that come to matter. In the months that followed, I was always grateful that I took that last hot shower in a surgically clean hotel room, with good soap, warm towels. I just wish I'd had breakfast.

The attack itself. That started before it started, if you know what I mean.

I had dressed, was just pulling on my shoes when there was a knock on the door. Afterwards, there would be anger that I didn't react better, that my situational awareness didn't warn me that something was wrong, that life was about to go deeply wonky for a while. But I'm going to be honest with you here, it didn't.

I looked through the peephole, saw a woman in a maid's uniform with a cart of supplies alongside her.

And so I opened the door.

I don't remember being Tasered. In the months that followed, myself, the three others who were taken, we would come to piece together what that day must have looked like to anyone who wasn't having fifty thousand volts shoved into them.

And the best we could come to was this – they came for

us separately, a number of different teams hitting us, as best we could figure, simultaneously. Each of us was Tasered and, we think, loaded into the cleaning carts that weren't cleaning carts at all, taken down the service elevator, out to a waiting truck and away.

They took our belongings, our wallets, watches, the lanyards bearing our conference ID. They distributed them throughout the ballroom.

Then the attack proper began.

The first few days were hazy, for all of us. My assumption is that I was drugged, that some kind of scopolamine-based substance was given to us to keep us quiet, compliant. I don't know how long it was before I came to and developed an understanding of my situation.

I know that I was alone, in what can best be described as someone's basement. A deep-set room subdivided into cells for the purpose. I know that it was weeks and weeks before I again saw sunlight.

I'm going to be honest with you. My first reaction, when I realised where I was, what had happened, was to laugh.

I've always been a big fan of irony.

In fairness, the laughter was pretty short-lived.

I don't know how long I was in that first cell, alone with the darkness, my thoughts, three fairly insubstantial meals a day. I know that life becomes a whole lot more focused when you are alone in the dark, that everything that matters becomes sharper in your mind, that the rest of the stuff simply falls away.

I also knew that I wouldn't die there. That I was going home.

We talked about this, once we were moved from the dungeon to new, damper but slightly less oubliette-like surroundings. It's the way of things, with a protracted kidnapping, you get moved about, always harder for the authorities to hit a moving target. My leg caused some trouble. I'm pretty sure it's the first time these guys had ever lifted someone with a false leg. But we worked it out.

That's the thing with kidnappings. You get to understand the routine, how your abductors work. And if you're lucky, they get to understand you, begin to relax just a little. They let us out, first one at a time, then, once they'd realised we weren't going to run, two at a time, and finally all four of us together.

They let us have our conversations, play some cards, keep each other from going crazy.

They couldn't stop Mick from dying, though.

In their defence, it was the heart condition that did for him in the end. Well, that piled on top of the cold, the imprisonment and the all but inedible food. One day he was there, quiet, troubled, but there. The next he was gone.

Life got darker after that.

With Mick's death, it seemed that life was telling us not to be too cocky, that all our talk about going home, it could all just be empty wishes. We took it hard.

Then one day they came for me, sat me on a chair, handed me a copy of that day's newspaper, told me to smile for the camera, and I knew that I was going home.

It took a damn sight longer than I thought it would.

They separated the three of us after that, placing us with our own individual teams. And day after day after day, I waited.

I never tried to escape.

When I talk to people now, they look at me like I'm crazy. Say things like, with your background, why didn't you just make a run for it?

Well, couple of reasons. First, I had no idea what country I was in, what landscape I was in, if I could speak the language, where the nearest city was. Second, false leg, so, you know, terrain-dependent in terms of mobility. Third and most importantly, I had a wife and two little girls to go home to. I was getting out of there alive. And my best chance of doing that was with a negotiation, a settlement.

I say that, and then it occurs to me that all those reasons amounted to nothing in my head.

I didn't attempt to run because of Selena. Because I knew she would get me out.

Hurrying to wait

'What now?' I ask.

Beck pushes the chair back from the computer, glances up at me. 'Now, we wait.'

I can hear Selena, her voice lighter than you would think it could be, the girls' voices chiming in with hers. She is putting on a show for the children, a pretence that their future does not hang in the balance. Such is parenting. One soothing lie following another in the service of a greater truth.

I nod, a knot of anxiety wrapping my stomach. 'They'll get back in touch?'

I can see the battle in Beck's face, the shot of fear, quickly hidden. 'Yes. They want their money. This is a business to them, don't forget.'

Finn has taken Seth back to the station, buoyed up like a small child on Christmas Day. Whilst I am here, in the Cole house, where it seems I have been since the investigation first began. Even now, here at the end, I cannot keep my focus, cannot give Dominic's death the attention it deserves. I feel a spurt of guilt, tempered by resignation. I will see this through here. That, it seems, has been inevitable from the start.

Beck is leaning back in the chair, threatening to snap it before too much longer. He stares at the computer screen, waiting. For a reply, for relief. There is nothing we can do now but wait. I study him while he is distracted. I cannot see what I have seen before in him, the junkie, the alcoholic. He is calm, clean-shaven and neat. He still looks like he could take down a wall by walking through it, and yet it seems that things have shifted for him.

'Can I ask you something?' I say.

Beck looks at me from under lowered lids. 'Sure.'

'Are you in love with Selena?'

I am expecting anger. I am expecting an explosion and to find myself shoved up against a wall as Seth was. Instead, he laughs.

'Believe me,' he says, 'I've got enough trouble without going looking for more. The thing you've got to under-stand is, where I come from, in the military, we're family. We take care of one another. Ed saved my life. Twice, actually. He got me out when I was kidnapped, he got me clean when I was spiralling. I owe that man everything I have.'

'Is that why you've been watching his wife?' I ask.

Beck shrugs. 'Yes,' he says simply. 'I . . . I've not been in a good place, the last year, losing Ed, then my job. I've been . . . it's been rough. I couldn't do anything to help Selena and the girls. I was a train wreck. So I did that. I sat outside. I watched.'

'And you saw her being taken?'

He nods. 'I was in a mess. Shouldn't have been driving.' He looks at me shrewdly. 'If you're going to arrest me for drunk driving, do me a favour and let me sort out this negotiation first.'

I nod, suppress a smile. 'We'll see.'

'I was kind of dozing. I'd been having issues with the drink, had a run-in with Dom . . .' His voice wavers on the name and he coughs, an attempt to pretend that the shake isn't there. 'He was mad at me. The drinking . . . It was rough. I came up here because, well, it was just kind of what I did. A habit, you know? And then I see Selena coming down the bank, talking to the woman. When she got in the car, leaving her kids in the park alone, I knew we had a problem.'

'You followed?'

He laughs. 'Well, yeah, but it was a pretty shit follow and I lost them twice. Picked them up coming out of the Brecon Beacons and then lost them in traffic. I had no idea that it was, well, what it was. But I was . . . concerned. Stepped up my game a bit. Stopped drinking and . . . everything else. Decided to sit it out, see if it happened again.'

'What did you think was going on?'

Beck shrugs. 'I don't know. But I'll tell you this much. I thought Seth was a little weasel. Under his influence, anything could happen.'

'And today?'

'Today I was clean. I can pull off a much better tail when I'm clean.'

I nod, look around the office.

'You might as well pull up a chair,' says Beck. 'If you're planning on waiting this one out, you're going to be here for a while.'

I should go back.

Instead I sink into a chair, lean back on it, stare at the ceiling. 'You think Orla knew?'

She was waiting for us when we returned, her expression fear tumbled with confusion.

Selena had touched her arm. 'It's going to be okay.' Had forestalled the question that parted her lips with a nod towards the children. 'I will explain. Once they're in bed.'

'What? That her brother was alive?' Beck snorts. 'Orla adores her brother. When she finds out what Seth has done, there isn't an ocean wide enough that she won't cross to kill him.'

'Maybe,' I say. But I don't believe it. I'm thinking of their marriage, of all that she has allowed to slip by her, un-remarked on, unnoticed seemingly.

'Don't be fooled,' Beck says. 'You're thinking that since Seth is a cheating, lying scumbag and Orla lets that slide, then maybe she'll let this slide too.' He grins when he sees my expression. 'I'm not just a pretty face. I'm telling you, Orla had no clue.' He shakes his head, seems to deflate before me. 'I should have known. I should have seen what was happening earlier. If I'd been sober . . .'

'How could you have known?' I ask. 'How could anyone?'

Beck stares off into the middle distance, forehead creased. 'The drugs. I should have known because of the drugs.'

'The drugs . . .'

He sighs, looks back at me. 'They say confession is good for the soul, right? I . . . sometimes the drink, it's not always enough, you know, to get my head to quieten down. Sometimes I dabble . . . pills, that kind of thing.'

I think of the surveillance team who identified him as being in Hereford on the night of Dom's murder. Purse my lips. 'Okay.'

'Lately, I don't know, I've been doing more than I should. Anyway, it was one day last week. Friday, I think. I go to my guy to get some stuff, and he says he's got something new. Just arrived in the UK but that it's setting Colombia on fire.'

I think of what drug-squad Steve told me. 'El Diablo.'

'El Diablo,' he agrees. 'I knew as soon as I saw it what it was going to be about. Colombia, Panama, Ecuador, they're all being hit pretty hard by it. It's a nasty little pill and its creators, Escorpion Rojo, they've been making some big waves in the K and R world.'

'Bombing Brazilian hotels?'

'The very same. They even offered me a job once, operating as a mule for them. I don't know, I must have the look of the junkie about me.' He gives a wry grin. 'So, my dealer tells me that they're here. That they're trying to break into the UK market with El Diablo. He even gave me a pill to take away. A freebie.'

'Did you take it?' I ask, curious.

Beck shakes his head. 'Nah. Been there before. I made the mistake of popping El Diablo one time out in Medellín. Not long after we lost Ed. Had wrapped my case, got my hostage safely home, so decided to reward myself with a little treat. I woke up three days later. I'd ripped my hotel room apart, busted my hand, missed my flight. It left me with nightmares for months after.' He shakes his head. 'I'm not doing that again. But, see, if I hadn't been so out of it on the booze when Selena was taken, maybe I'd have pieced it together. The thing is, El Diablo. Once I saw it, I knew there was something wrong. I just didn't know what.' He leans his head back against his chair, looks older now, sadder.

'If it helps, I don't think you could have known. I don't think anyone could have known,' I offer.

He isn't who I thought he was.

'I'm sorry that things have been so rough for you.'

Beck nods, turns in his chair so that he is facing the computer again. 'Well, it is what it is. Lots of people have done a lot of things to help me. I couldn't help Dom in return. Maybe I can help Ed.'

'It seems to me that Dom really cared about you.'

He isn't looking at me. A set, rigid not-looking that from another man I would assume meant emotion swelling. 'He really cared about lots of us. Never stopped trying to get us better, get the drink, the drugs to release their hold. I guess you could say it was his calling in life.'

I nod, think back to something Finn told me, what seemed like a lifetime ago. 'That's what Fae said too.'

'Well, she would know,' agreed Beck. He shakes his head. 'It's . . . it's such a tough thing. And she's so young. But these drugs, once they have you, they don't let go. I wish . . . I wish I could have been a better man. More like Dom. Protected her from herself.'

I frown. 'What do you mean?'

He turns, his gaze dropping. 'The El Diablo. I . . . I gave it to Fae.'

None so blind

DS Finn Hale: Saturday, 6.00 p.m.

She is at home. A tiny box of a home, one among thousands on a modern estate. I knock on the door, my heart thundering, and wait.

Footsteps, one, two, three.

She has been crying. Is wearing leggings, an oversized T-shirt. Looks smaller still in the fading light.

'Fae,' I say.

She stares at me, and it seems that her mind is spinning, trying to place me, here where I don't belong. I feel a grim kind of satisfaction at that.

I look at her. Really look at her. She is elfin thin, gaunt, really. Her hair looks . . . not styled as I first thought, rather greasy, roughened from sleep. There are bags under her eyes. Her hands are shaking.

'A word, if you don't mind?'

I gesture for her to step back, follow her inside, Leah quiet behind me. She can feel it, the balled-up rage that is rolling from me. I can tell by the lock of her shoulders, the way she is holding her lips.

'Is there a . . .' Fae attempts, then, seeing my face, drops into silence. It is over and she knows it.

'I'd like to talk to you about the night Dominic Newell was killed.'

'Okay.'

She is shaking now, her T-shirt balled up uselessly in her hands. And I wonder how I missed it, what made me so blind that I did not see.

'You were in his car?' I say.

'No.'

I don't respond. Just study her. 'You were in his car,' I repeat.

Fae looks from me to Leah and begins to cry.

A good man

Fae stared at the tablet. Small. Red. It would look so inno-
cent if not for the grinning face of the devil embossed upon
it. She shouldn't. She had come so far. And yet . . .

They tell you that you never stop. Once an addict, always
an addict; that the curse you bear will live on inside you
for always and that every day will be a battle to keep it
from taking control.

She had lost so many battles lately.

It had been three years. A sobriety that had stretched
itself out for one thousand and ninety-five days. And to
celebrate, she had worked until a little after nine, acqui-
escing to every single damned whim that should happen
to cross Bronwyn's mind. Had smiled a bright and happy
smile, even though rolling through her mind was the fact
that it had been three years. And that at the end of the
three years and one remarkably long day, she would go
home to an empty house and eat a celebratory dinner that
would consist of a Pot Noodle and maybe a Mars bar.

She had done her job, the way she had always done her
job. Impeccably, exactingly. And then she had gone home,

stretched thin with exhaustion, and had stopped in the supermarket on her way. Telling herself that she was out of bread, out of milk, pretending the whole way that she wasn't going to pick up a bottle of vodka.

It had been just the one drink.

A single shot as an attagirl.

But there is no such thing as a single shot. Not really.

There had been no doubting the trajectory, not once the seal was cracked, the clear liquid poured into the perfectly moulded glass.

But she still had her job. She still remained the model employee. Timely, efficient, collected. And as long as she had that, Fae knew that she could survive. That this was just one more slip in a lifetime of trips and falls. That she could pick herself up, dust herself off, and move on.

It could still be okay.

A sound broke in through her contemplations, and it seemed to her that it had been there for ever. What was that? The phone. It was the phone. Her hand shot out for it, grasping and awkward, but she was too late. The caller had rung off.

Fae stared at it. Things were beginning to unravel. She could pretend as much as she wanted, but she was starting to fall apart.

And then what? Back to where she began? In some filthy bedsit with a skinny, drug-addicted boyfriend with loose fists?

She slipped the single red pill into her pocket.

Beck hadn't wanted to give it to her. You don't want this, Fae, he had said. It's nasty stuff. The things you see . . . you won't know yourself when you're on it. She had laughed and said that not knowing herself seemed like a remarkably

good idea indeed. No, said Beck. I'm serious, I'm not . . .
But the door had opened, Bronwyn coming in, shaking her
umbrella free of the remnants of yet another autumn storm.
And Fae, quick as a snake, had reached out, tugging the
solitary pill from Beck's unwitting hand, vanishing it away.
Had refused to look at him, even though he stared at her
open-mouthed; had instead formed her face into a Bronwyn-
worthy smile. Wet out there?

Maybe Beck had been right. Maybe she didn't want this.
She stared at the lines of text on her computer screen, the
letters shimmying, dancing before her eyes. It was getting
away from her. That much was clear.

She looked up, at Dom's door.

Maybe . . .

But if she asked him for help, then he would know. And
he would be so disappointed in her. And he had done so
much already.

But if she didn't . . .

Every day will be a battle. And sometimes you have to
call in reinforcements.

She pushed herself up, legs unsteady, and walked softly
to Dom's office door. He would understand. It was Dom.
He always understood.

'Come in.' His voice didn't sound right, had an edge to
it, one Fae was not used to hearing.

'Dom, I . . .' I've fallen. I can't get myself back up. Help
me.

'Fae, where the hell is the paperwork on the Wright
case?' Dom was leafing through a folder, his back stiff, face
a storm. 'I asked you to have it all together. Why isn't it
here?'

'I . . .'

'This isn't the first time this has happened. If you can't handle this job, just say so, and we'll find someone who can.'

Fae stood in the open doorway, her mouth flapping uselessly. A strange stray thought that maybe she had taken the pill, that she had done it without meaning to, that this was why nothing was as it should be, why Dom, so kind, so considerate, was barking at her with barely contained fury. Then a distant recollection, of him coming back from the police station, slamming the front door. Hearing him rage to Bronwyn in tones she'd never heard before that he was sick of Beck Chambers, that the man needed to take control of his own life, that he'd had enough of having to save everyone from themselves.

She closed her mouth, dipped her head. 'I'm sorry. I must have forgotten. I'll get on it right away.'

She turned, crept out of the room, her heart thrumming. He was right. It wasn't up to him to save her, to save Beck. They were worthless, the pair of them. A burden on humanity. She had no right to expect anything from anyone, not when she had fallen again.

Her hand went to her pocket, closed around the tablet. There seemed little reason to abstain.

She swallowed it quickly, without water, feeling the sides of it catch on her throat. It hurt. That was good.

In two minutes she could leave. In two minutes she could walk out of the door and let El Diablo sweep away all that lay so heavy on her.

'For God's sake, I've told them they need to get everything to me by this afternoon at the latest, and now look, nearly six o'clock and I'm still chasing.' Bronwyn swept in in the way Bronwyn always did, so certain that the world would rearrange itself around her. 'I'm going to be here for hours now. Fae, I need you to dig out the Collins file, it should be in the back office. You don't mind staying on a bit, do you? No? Great. It really irritates me when they do this. And . . . oh, are you going?'

Was she talking to Fae? Fae opened her mouth, even though her tongue had already become thick and unwieldy, to offer up some lie, to say she wasn't feeling well, anything so that she could escape.

Bronwyn wasn't looking at her, though, but at Dom. He was standing in his office doorway, eyes flitting from Bronwyn to Fae. Resting there.

Did he know? The way he was looking at her, searching. He knew, didn't he?

He moved past Fae, said something to Bronwyn in low tones that she couldn't catch. But she heard the words Beck Chambers.

He knew. He knew about the pill that she had taken from Beck. He knew and she would be fired and then there would be nothing to stop the slide.

Fae opened her mouth. But she couldn't think. Couldn't get the words to line up so that they would leave.

'I'll see you in the morning.' Then Dom was gone, with just the briefest of backward glances at her.

Was it a warning? Was that what it was?

The room had begun to shimmy and shift, the walls disintegrating, re-forming, disintegrating again.

'Fae, I need you to sort those papers out for me.' Bronwyn threw the words over her shoulder as she headed back to her office. 'Quick as you can.'

Fae nodded, turned towards the back office, her body moving, her brain left behind. Then she heard Bronwyn's door shut, and just like that, her body reversed itself. What are you doing? Don't worry, I've got it handled.

She hurried down the front steps, easing the door back on the catch so that Bronwyn wouldn't hear, out into the cool Cardiff evening air. The cars danced unevenly. Where was she going? She wasn't sure. But another voice, one that didn't feel like hers, said, it's fine. We'll go talk to Dom. Make him understand.

She didn't know how long she wandered, up side street, down side street. She just knew that she had to find him. Because he knew. And if she talked to him, it would all be okay.

Then, in one of a thousand identical streets, she stopped. Someone was standing there. The devil? No.

Someone else . . . Dominic.

'Dom . . .'

He was holding his phone, had turned, was looking at her with an expression of weary disappointment. 'Look, there's someone here. I have to go . . .'

Fae felt the pavement move beneath her, a roaring, clambering wave that bucked and threatened to throw her to the ground. She reached out, grabbed for a railing.

When she looked back, he was watching her.

'You're using again, aren't you?' He looked so sad. Why was he so sad when it was her life that was the tragedy?

She didn't answer. But that was mainly because the air had turned to lava, was rushing into her mouth, filling up her throat, drowning her.

'Get in.' Dom held open the car door for her, gripping her arm, too tight, too tight, helping her, no, pushing her inside.

'No, I . . .'

He slammed the door, locking her in a tomb. She would suffocate. There was no air. She scrabbled, pulling at her clothes, loosening them so that her skin could breathe, her hand brushing against her pocket, something hard. What was that?

But whatever it was, it was too late. Dom was in now, driving. Taking her away. Where was he taking her?

'Why, Fae?'

She started to laugh. 'Because I celebrated my anniversary with a Pot Noodle, that's why.'

He didn't laugh. Just kept driving. Faster. Faster.

'I need . . .' A dim recollection of something she was supposed to be doing. 'Work. I have to . . . the Collins file.'

'There's no more work, Fae. Not for a while.'

'You . . .' They were moving so fast. They were about to crash, surely. 'You're firing me?'

A long, heavy silence, a weighty sigh. 'I'm telling you to go and get help. When you're clean, we'll discuss your options.'

So that was it then, it was over.

Fae peered out into the plunging darkness. They were at the bottom of the sea, sinking deeper and deeper. Had been driving for so long, for ever, it seemed.

Where was he taking her? Where were they? Where were all the lights? The people?

She could feel the panic rising in her throat. 'Need to get out.'

'Fae, we're in the middle of nowhere. Just wait. I'm taking you home.'

She would die here. He would kill her.

She watched him. Only it wasn't him. His face shimmied. Now Dom. Now the devil.

She felt the sharpness digging into her side and remembered what it was. A pocket knife. Because you just never knew. And it was better to be safe than sorry.

'Stop!' she roared, a sound like she had never made before. Felt the car swerve, brakes squeal.

'Jesus, Fae!' Dom reached out, hand on her shoulder, gripping tight, so tight, moving towards her neck.

The devil. He was going to kill her.

She pulled out the knife.

The arrest

Fae sits crying. Her head is in her hands.

How did I not see this? How did I miss it?

I look at Leah, helpless. She looks at me, shakes her head.

You couldn't have known.

Could I?

'It was just . . . it was that pill. It just twisted everything until I didn't know who I was or where I was. And I was so scared. I thought . . . I know you won't believe me, but I thought he was going to kill me.' She looks up at us, tears spilling again. 'I didn't mean to kill him. You have to believe me, I never, ever meant to hurt him. And afterwards, I just couldn't believe I'd done it. I thought it must have been a dream or a hallucination.' She reaches out towards us, fingers steepled as if in prayer. 'I can't have done it. Please tell me it isn't really true.' She dissolves, weeping as though her heart will break. 'I didn't mean to hurt him. He was such a good man.'

To her. He was such a good man to her. To his partner, he was a cheat. To his lover . . . what? A betrayer? To Orla, a threat. And yet, in the end, the person who brought his life to a close was the one he was trying to help. And why? Because of a drug. A drug funded by the ransoms that ensured the release of other good men.

It was a never-ending circle. A snake chewing on its own tail.

'Fae Lewis,' I say, quietly, 'I'm arresting you for the murder of Dominic Newell.'

Homecoming

Dr Selena Cole: Tuesday, 4 p.m.

It has been three days. Three days that have stretched themselves out so that they form an eternity in my mind. I have not eaten. I have slept in the barest of fits and starts. And yet still those three days have inched their way by and we are here.

The mountains leer over me. The forecasters are talking about an early snow, and you can feel it, the threat of it that hangs in the air.

I shiver.

And I wait.

Beck wanted to come with me. It was too dangerous, he said, for me to come alone. Leah begged, pleaded that I allow her to come. That I allow someone to come. After all, she said, your girls need you alive.

They do, I agreed.

And they need their father too.

I stand beneath the mountains, and I wait alone.

This time I will take no chances. This time there will be no deviations from the plan. This time I am bringing my husband home.

I stand on the single-track road and at first I think that I have begun to hallucinate, that the mountain air is creating a vision, a movement of light. But then I look closer, and no, it is real. It is a car, winding its way beneath the steep overhangs to where I stand.

They are coming.

I am bringing Ed home.

ACKNOWLEDGEMENTS

This book has been a work of many contrasts for me. There have been times at which the complexities and demands of it have driven me to utter distraction. At others, it has been a complete joy. Yet, as with any book, this is not a journey I have undertaken alone. *The Missing Hours* has become what it is thanks to the assistance of many wonderful people.

Firstly, inevitably, the ever-supportive Camilla Wray, agent extraordinaire. She has cheered with me, comforted me, and, on more than one occasion, told me to step away from the computer and eat some cake. I could not do what I do without her as my trusty sidekick. To the rest of the wonderful Darley Anderson Agency, thank you for all that you do. I'm so proud to be able to call myself one of your authors.

Jenny Geras, publishing director of Arrow, your incisive editorial mind and your passionate support for my work have truly made this the career of my dreams. Francesca Pathak, thank you for your insightful editorial work and for just generally being an utterly lovely person. Philippa Cotton, wonderful publicist and friend – I still think fondly of our extensive tromp around London bookstores. Millie

Seaward, thank you for taking over where Philly left off, attacking the role of publicist with zeal. Matthew Ruddle, for all your marketing brilliance and for rescuing me from the horror of building a Facebook page.

To my many, many crime-writer friends – you know who you are. You keep me sane when I'm beginning to unravel (haha, just kidding!) and support me in tough times. Thank you. And to the many bloggers and reviewers who have supported me unfailingly throughout my career. You guys rock!

Kidnap and ransom is a murky world. It keeps many secrets, and so attempting to research this book was challenging to say the least. I am incredibly lucky that I have had so many wonderful people willing to help me. Martin Medcalf, after years treading the NATO boards together, it is an utter delight to be back arguing rugby scores with you. As always, thank you. (PS Wales won, which means lunch is on you.) Chris Williams, who went far above and beyond the call of duty in finding me the information I needed. You are a star. And to my friend in Hereford – thank you for introducing me to the sometimes dark, always fascinating world of K&R, and for answering my many, many questions whenever they should happen to occur to me. It has been an absolute honour and a privilege to talk with you.

To Zoe Cadwell, my old friend and constant source of forensic information. You are brilliant and I am very sorry that I made you miss your train stop!

Finally, and most importantly, to my nearest and dearest.

Matthew, my greatest and most unswerving supporter. Thank you. To my boys, Daniel and Joseph, for just being your wonderful, brilliant selves. To Mum and Dad, you

ACKNOWLEDGEMENTS

always have been a fantastic cheerleading team. To Ma and Pops – life has thrown much at you, and yet you have come through it all with humour and a positive spirit. You are incredible! Deb, Dai, Ffi and Beth – mwah!!! Donna and Sarah, my sisters in arms, thank you for all the tea.

AUTHOR'S NOTE

I am a passionate advocate of research and accuracy in writing. And yet the world of kidnap and ransom is one that is awash with secrets. And for good reason. If the level of ransoms paid becomes common knowledge, then the next kidnapper will ask for more, and so on and so on. The terms of insurance policies are closely guarded secrets, and consultants within this field operate under a cloak of secrecy. And so the problem – how do I tell a story set in the K&R industry without giving away more than I should? The events contained within *The Missing Hours*, including the case studies, are all fictional and are entirely unrelated to real-world cases. All of the workings of the K&R industry reflected here are from open source material. There are people who do what Ed and Selena do. They operate in an incredibly dangerous world, putting their own lives on the line in order to ensure the safety of their clients. In the interests of protecting these individuals, I have occasionally fictionalised certain procedural elements within *The Missing Hours*.

The book also contains references to a number of military operations – most notably the events at Musa Qala in Afghanistan and the road to the presidential palace in

Basra. Again, although these events did take place within the real world, what is included here are the accounts of fictionalised characters. Many servicemen and women carry the wounds, both physical and psychological, from battles such as those depicted in this book. If you would like to help support them as they continue the fight on their road to recovery, please consider donating to Help for Heroes at helpforheroes.org.uk.

One final point – although I have done my utmost to ensure accuracy in police procedure, there is one area in which I have strayed from reality. The police force depicted here is entirely fictional and has responsibility for an area that would in reality be covered by a number of different forces.

Thank you for reading.